D0017944

Police

Police

JO NESBØ

Translated from the Norwegian by Don Bartlett

RANDOM HOUSE
LARGE PRINT

Translation copyright © 2013 by Don Bartlett

All rights reserved.
Published in the United States of America by
Random House Large Print in association with
Alfred A. Knopf, New York.
Distributed by Random House, LLC, New York,
a Penguin Random House Company.

Originally published in Norway as **Politi** by
H. Aschehoug & Co. (W. Nygaard), Oslo, 2013.
Copyright © 2013 by Jo Nesbø.
This translation was originally published in
Great Britain by Havrill Secker, an imprint of the
Random House Group Ltd., London, in 2013.

Cover design by Peter Mendelsund

The Library of Congress has established a Cataloging-in-Publication record for this title.

ISBN: 978-0-8041-9446-4

www.randomhouse.com/largeprint

FIRST LARGE PRINT EDITION

Printed in the United States of America

10 9 8 7 6 5 4 3 2

This Large Print edition published in accord with
the standards of the N.A.V.H.

To Knut Nesbø,
football player, guitarist, pal, brother

Police

Prologue

It was asleep in there, behind the door.

The inside of the corner cupboard smelt of old wood, powder residue and gun oil. When the sun shone through the window into the room, a strip of light shaped like an hourglass travelled from the keyhole into the cupboard and, if the sun was at precisely the right angle, there would be a matt gleam to the gun lying on the middle of the shelf.

It was a Russian Odessa, a copy of the better-known Stechkin.

The ugly automatic pistol had had a peripatetic existence, travelling with the Cossacks in Lithuania to Siberia, moving between the various Urka headquarters in southern Siberia, becoming the property of an ataman, a Cossack leader, who had been killed, Odessa in hand, by the police, before ending up in the Nizhny Tagil home of an arms-collecting prison director. Finally, the weapon was brought to Norway by Rudolf Asayev, alias Dubai, who, before he disappeared, had monopolised the narcotics market in Oslo with the heroin-like opioid violin. Oslo, the very town where the gun now found itself, in Holmenkollveien, to be precise, in Rakel Fauke's house. The

Odessa had a magazine that could hold twenty rounds of Makarov, 9x18mm calibre, and could fire single shots and salvos. There were twelve bullets left in the magazine.

Three of them had been fired at Kosovo Albanians, rival dope pushers. Only one of the bullets had bitten into flesh.

The next two had killed Gusto Hanssen, a young thief and drug dealer who had pocketed Asayev's money and dope.

The gun still smelt of the last three shots, which had hit the head and chest of the ex-police officer Harry Hole during his investigation into the above-mentioned murder of Gusto Hanssen. And the crime scene had been the same: Hausmanns gate 92.

The police still hadn't solved the Hanssen case, and the eighteen-year-old boy who had initially been arrested had been released. Mostly because they hadn't been able to find, or link him to, any murder weapon. The boy's name was Oleg Fauke and he woke every night staring into the darkness and hearing the shots. Not those that had killed Gusto, but the others. The ones he had fired at the policeman who had been a father to him when he was growing up. Who he had once dreamt would marry his mother, Rakel. Harry Hole. Oleg's eyes burned into the night, and he thought of the gun in the distant corner cupboard, hoping that he would never see it again. That no one would see it again. That it would sleep until eternity.

• • •

He was asleep in there, behind the door.

The guarded hospital room smelt of medicine and paint. The monitor beside him registered his heartbeats.

Isabelle Skøyen, the Councillor for Social Affairs at Oslo City Hall, and Mikael Bellman, the newly appointed Chief of Police, hoped they would never see him again.

That no one would see him again.

That he would sleep until eternity.

Part One

1

It had been a long, warm September day. The light transformed Oslo Fjord into molten silver and made the low mountain ridges, which already bore the first tinges of autumn, glow. It was one of those days that make Oslo natives swear they will never, ever move. The sun was sinking behind Ullern Ridge and the last rays swept across the countryside, across the squat, sober blocks of flats, a testimony to Oslo's modest origins, across lavish penthouses with terraces that spoke of the oil adventure that had made the country one of the richest in the world, across the junkies at the top of Stensparken and into the well-organised little town where there were more overdoses than in European cities eight times larger. Across gardens where trampolines were surrounded by netting and no more than three children jumped at a time, as recommended by national guidelines. And across the ridges and the forest circling half of what is known as the Oslo Cauldron. The sun did not want to relinquish the town; it stretched out its fingers, like a prolonged farewell through a train window.

The day had begun with cold, clear air and sharp beams of light, like lamps in an operating theatre.

Later the temperature had risen, the sky had gone a deeper blue and the air possessed that pleasant physical feel which made September the most wonderful month in the year. And as dusk came, tentative and gentle, the air in the residential quarter on the hills towards Lake Maridal smelt of apples and warm spruce trees.

Erlend Vennesla was approaching the top of the final hill. He could feel the lactic acid now but concentrated on getting the correct vertical thrust on the click-in pedals, with his knees pointing slightly inwards. Because it was important to have the right technique. Especially when you were tired and your brain was telling you to change position so that the onus was on less tired, though less effective, muscles. He could feel how the rigid cycle frame absorbed and used every watt he pedalled into it, how he accelerated when he switched down a gear and stood up, trying to keep the same rhythm, about ninety revolutions a minute. He checked his heart rate monitor. One hundred and sixty-eight. He pointed his headlamp at the satnav he had attached to the handlebars. It had a detailed map of Oslo and its surrounds. The bike and the accessories had cost him more than, strictly speaking, a recently retired detective should spend. But it was important to stay in shape now that life offered different challenges.

Fewer challenges, if he was honest.

The lactic acid was burning in his thighs and calves now. Painful but also a wonderful promise of what was to come. An endorphin fest. Tender muscles.

Good conscience. A beer with his wife on their balcony if the temperature didn't plummet after sunset.

And suddenly he was up. The road levelled out, and Lake Maridal was in front of him. He slowed down. He was out of the town. It was absurd, in fact, that after fifteen minutes' hard cycling from the centre of a European capital city you were surrounded by farms, fields and dense forest with paths disappearing into the dusk. The sweat was making his scalp itch beneath the charcoal-grey Bell helmet—which alone had cost the same as the bike he had bought as a sixth-birthday present for his granddaughter, Line Marie. But he kept the helmet on. Most deaths among cyclists were caused by head injuries.

He looked at his monitor. A hundred and seventy-five. A hundred and seventy-two. A welcome little gust of wind carried the sound of distant cheering up from the town. It must have been from Ullevål Stadium—there was an important international match this evening. Slovakia or Slovenia. Erlend Vennesla imagined for a few seconds that they had been applauding for him. It was a while since anyone had done that. The last time would have been the farewell ceremony at Kripos up at Bryn. Layer cake, speech by the boss, Mikael Bellman, who since then had continued his steady rise to take the top police job. And Erlend had received the applause, met their eyes, thanked them and even felt his throat constrict as he was about to deliver his simple, brief speech. Simple, sticking to the facts, as was now the tradition at Kripos. He'd had his ups and downs as a detective, but he had avoided major blunders. At least as far as he knew. Of course you were never a hundred per cent sure you had the right answer. With the rapid advances made in DNA technology and a signal from the upper echelons that they would use it to examine isolated cold cases, there was a risk of precisely that. Answers. New answers. Conclusions. As long as they concentrated on unsolved cases, that was fine, but Erlend didn't understand why they would waste resources on investigations which had long been filed away.

The darkness had deepened and even in the light from the street lamps he almost cycled past the wooden sign pointing into the forest. But there it was. Exactly as he remembered. He turned off and rode on to the soft forest floor. He slowly followed the path without losing his balance. The cone of light from his headlamp shone ahead, and was halted by the thick wall of spruce trees on either side when he turned his head. Shadows flitted in front of him, startled and hurried, changed shape and dived under cover. It was how he had imagined it when he had put himself in her shoes. Running, fleeing with a torch in her hand, after being locked up and raped over three days.

And when Erlend Vennesla saw a light suddenly come on in front of him, for a moment he thought it was her torch, and that she was running again, and he was on the motorbike that had gone after her and caught her up. The light ahead of Erlend flickered before it was flashed straight at him. He stopped and dismounted. Shone his headlamp on his heart rate monitor. Already below a hundred. Not bad.

He loosened the chin strap, took off his helmet and scratched his scalp. God, that was good. He switched off his headlamp, hung the helmet from the handlebars and pushed the bike towards the light. Felt the helmet banging against the frame.

He stopped by the torchlight. The powerful beam hurt his eyes. And, dazzled, he thought he could hear himself still breathing heavily. It was strange his pulse was so low. He detected a movement, something being lifted behind the large, quivering circle of light, heard a hushed whistle through the air and at that moment a thought struck him. He shouldn't have done that. He shouldn't have removed his helmet. Most deaths among cyclists . . .

It was as if the thought stammered, like a displacement in time, like an image being disconnected for a moment.

Erlend Vennesla stared ahead in astonishment and felt a hot bead of sweat run down his forehead. He spoke, but the words were incoherent, as though there were a fault in the connection between brain and mouth. Again he heard a soft whistle. Then sound went. All sound, he couldn't even hear his own breathing. And he discovered that he was on his knees and his bike was slowly tipping over into a ditch. Before him danced a yellow light, but it disappeared when the bead of sweat reached the ridge of his nose, ran into his eyes and blinded him.

The third blow felt like an icicle being driven into his head, neck and body. Everything froze.

I don't want to die, he thought, trying to raise a

defensive arm above his head, but, unable to move a single limb, he knew he had been paralysed.

He didn't register the fourth blow, although from the aroma of wet earth he concluded he was now lying on the ground. He blinked several times and sight returned to one eye. By his face he saw a pair of large, dirty boots in the mud. The heels were raised and then the boots took off from the ground. They landed. The same was repeated: the heels were raised and the boots took off. As if the assailant were jumping. Jumping to get even more power behind the blows. And the last thought to go through his brain was that he had to remember what her name was, he mustn't forget her name.

2

Officer Anton Mittet took the half-full plastic cup from the small, red Nespresso D290 machine, bent down and placed it on the floor. There was no furniture to put it on. Then he took out another coffee capsule, automatically checked that the aluminium foil lid wasn't perforated, that it was in fact unused, before inserting it in the coffee machine. Set an empty plastic cup under the spout and pressed one of the illuminated buttons.

He checked his watch while the machine began to sputter and groan. Soon be midnight. Shift change. She was waiting for him at home, but he thought he should teach the new girl the ropes first; after all she was only a police trainee. Silje, was that her name? Anton Mittet stared at the spout. Would he have offered to get coffee if it had been a male colleague? He wasn't sure, and it made no difference anyway, he had given up answering that kind of question. It was suddenly so quiet he could hear the final, almost transparent, drops dripping into the cup. There was no more colour or taste to be had from the capsule, but it was vital to catch every last droplet; it was going to be a long night shift for the young woman.

Without any company, without any action, without
anything to do, other than to stare at the inside of the
Rikshospital's unpainted, bare concrete walls. Then
he decided he would have a coffee with her before
leaving. He took both cups with him and returned.
His footsteps resounded against the walls. He passed
closed, locked doors. Knowing there was nothing or
no one behind them, only more bare walls. For once
Norway had built for the future with the Rikshospital, realising that Norwegians were becoming more
numerous, aged, infirm and needy. They had taken a
long-term approach, the way the Germans had with
their autobahns and the Swedes with their airports.
But had it felt like that for them, the few motorists
crossing the German countryside in isolated majesty
on the concrete leviathans in the thirties or the Swedish passengers hurrying through the oversized lounges
in Arlanda during the sixties? Had they sensed that
there were ghosts? That despite it being brand new
and unspoilt, and despite no one having died in a car
accident or a plane crash yet, there were ghosts. That
at any moment car headlamps could pick out a family
standing on the curb, staring blankly into the light,
bleeding, ashen, the father impaled, the mother's head
the wrong way round, a child with limbs on one side
only. That charred bodies could come through the
plastic curtain on the baggage carousel in the arrivals
hall at Arlanda, still glowing, burning the rubber,
silent screams issuing from their open mouths, smoke
coiling upwards. None of the doctors had been able
to tell him what this wing would be used for eventu-

ally; all that was certain was that people would die behind these doors. It was already in the air; invisible bodies with restless souls had already been admitted.

Anton rounded a corner, and another corridor extended before him, sparsely lit, equally bare and so symmetrical that it created a curious **trompe l'oeil:** the uniformed woman sitting on the chair at the far end of the corridor looked like a little picture on a flat wall in front of him.

"I've got a cup of coffee for you," he said, standing by her. Twenty? Bit more. Maybe twenty-two.

"Thanks, but I brought some with me," she said, lifting a Thermos from the little rucksack she had placed beside her chair. There was a barely perceptible lilt to her intonation, the residue of a northern dialect perhaps.

"This is better," he said, with his hand still outstretched.

She hesitated. Then took it.

"And it's free," Anton said, discreetly putting his hand behind his back and rubbing the burnt fingertips on the cold material of his jacket. "We've got a whole machine all to ourselves in fact. It's in the corridor down by—"

"I saw it when I came," she said. "But the regulations are that we mustn't at any time move away from the patient's door, so I brought some coffee from home."

Anton Mittet took a sip from his cup. "Good thinking, but there's only one corridor leading to this room. We're on the third floor and all the other doors are locked between here and the coffee machine. It's impossible to get past us even if we're helping ourselves to coffee."

"That sounds reassuring, but I think I'll stick to the rules." She sent him a fleeting smile. And then, perhaps as a counterbalance to the implicit reproof, she took a sip from the cup.

Anton felt a stab of irritation and was about to say something about the independent thinking that would come with experience, but he hadn't managed to formulate it before his attention was caught by something further down the corridor. A white figure appeared to be floating towards them. He heard Silje get up. The figure took on firmer features. And became a plump blonde nurse in a loose hospital uniform. He knew she was on the night shift. And that tomorrow night she was free.

"Evening," the nurse said with a mischievous smile, holding up two syringes in one hand, walking towards the door and placing the other on the handle.

"Just a moment," Silje said, stepping up. "I'm afraid I have to examine your ID. Also, have you got today's password?"

The nurse sent Anton a surprised look.

"Unless my colleague here can vouch for you," Silje said.

Anton nodded. "Just go in, Mona."

The nurse opened the door and Anton watched her enter. In the darkened room he could make out the machinery around the bed and toes sticking out from under the duvet. The patient was so tall they'd had to requisition a longer bed. The door closed.

"Good," Anton said with a smile to Silje, and could see she didn't like it. Could see she regarded him as a male chauvinist who had just assessed and graded a younger female colleague. But she was a student for Christ's sake, she was supposed to learn from experienced officers during her training year. He stood rocking back on his heels, unsure how to tackle the situation. She spoke up first.

"As I said, I've read the rules and regulations. And I suppose you have a family waiting for you."

He lifted his coffee to his mouth. What did she know about his civil status? Was she insinuating something, about him and Mona, for example? That he had driven her home a couple of times after her shift and it hadn't stopped there?

"The teddy bear sticker on your bag," she smiled.

He took a long swig from his cup. And cleared his throat. "I've got time. As it's your first shift perhaps you ought to use the opportunity to ask any questions you may have. Not everything's in the rules and regulations, you know." He shifted feet. Hoping she could hear and understand the subtext.

"As you wish," she said with the irritating self-confidence you have to be under twenty-five to be so presumptuous as to possess. "The patient in there, who is he?"

"I don't know. That's also in the rules. He's anonymous and has to stay that way."

"But you know something."

"Do I?"

"Mona. You can't be on first-name terms with people without having chatted first. What did she tell you?"

Anton Mittet weighed her up. She was attractive, that was true enough, but there was no warmth or charm about her. Bit too slim for his taste. Untidy hair and a top lip that looked as if it was held in place by an over-taut tendon, causing two uneven front teeth to appear. But youth was on her side. Firm and fit underneath the black uniform, he would bet on it. So if he told her what he knew, would it be because he was subconsciously calculating that his obliging attitude would increase his chances of bedding her by 0.01 per cent? Or because girls like Silje would be inspectors or detectives within five years? They would be his bosses, while he would remain on the beat, an officer on the bottom rung of the ladder, because the Drammen case would always be there, a wall, a stain that could not be removed.

"Case of attempted murder," Anton said. "Lost a lot of blood. They reckon he barely had a pulse when he came here. Been in a coma the whole time."

"Why the guard?"

Anton shrugged. "Potential witness. If he survives."

"What does he know?"

"Drugs stuff. High level. If he wakes up he probably has the goods to bring down some important heroin dealers in Oslo. Plus he can tell us who was trying to kill him."

"So they think the murderer will return and finish off the job?"

"If they find out he's alive and where he is, yes. That's why we're here."

She nodded. "And is he going to survive?"

Anton shook his head. "They reckon they can keep him alive for a few more months, but the odds of him pulling out of the coma are slim. Nevertheless . . ." Anton shifted feet again; her probing stare was becoming uncomfortable. "Until then we have to keep an eye on him."

Anton Mittet left her, feeling crushed, went down the stairs from reception and stepped into the autumn night. It was only when he was sitting in his parked car that he noticed his mobile was ringing.

The call came from the Ops Room.

"Maridalen, murder," 01 said. "I know you've finished for the day, but they need help to secure the crime scene. And as you're already in uniform . . ."

"How long for?"

"You'll be relieved after three hours, max."

Anton was astonished. These days they did whatever they could to prevent people from working overtime. The combination of rigid rules and budgets didn't even allow deviations for reasons of practicality. He had an intuition there was something special about this murder. He hoped it wasn't a child.

"OK," Anton Mittet said.

"I'll send you the coordinates." This was new: sat-nav, a detailed map of Oslo and district and an active transmitter for Ops to track you down. That must have been why they rang him. He was closest.

"OK," Anton Mittet said. "Three hours."

Laura would be in bed, but she liked knowing when he would be home from work, so he texted her before putting the car into gear and heading for Lake Maridal.

Anton didn't need to look at the satnav. At the entrance to Ullevålseterveien there were four patrol cars, and a bit further away orange-and-white tape showed the way.

Anton took the torch from the glove compartment and walked over to the officer outside the cordon. Through the trees he saw lights flashing, but also the forensics team's lamps, which always reminded him of film sets. Not so daft actually; nowadays they didn't just take stills, they used HD video cameras as well, which not only captured the victims but the whole crime scene so that at a later date they could go back, freeze and zoom in on details they hadn't appreciated were relevant at first.

"What's going on?" he asked the officer with crossed arms, who was shivering by the tape.

"Murder." The officer's voice was thick, his eyes red-rimmed in an unnaturally pale face.

"So I heard. Who's the boss here?"

"Forensics. Lønn."

Anton heard the buzz of voices from inside the

trees. There were lots of them. "No one from Kripos or Crime Squad yet?"

"There'll be even more officers here soon. The body has just been found. Are you taking over from me?"

Even more. And yet they had given him overtime. Anton examined the officer closer. He was wearing a thick coat, but the shivering had got worse. And it wasn't that cold.

"Were you the first on the scene?"

The officer nodded without speaking, looked down. Stamped his feet hard on the ground.

Bloody hell, thought Anton. A child. He swallowed.

"Well, Anton, did 01 send you?"

Anton looked up. He hadn't heard the two of them coming, although they emerged from dense thickets. He had seen it before, how forensics officers moved at crime scenes, like somewhat ungainly dancers, bending and twisting, positioning their feet, as though they were astronauts on the moon. Or perhaps it was the white overalls drawing that association.

"Yes, I had to take over from someone," Anton said to the woman. He knew who she was, everyone did. Beate Lønn, the head of Krimteknisk, who had a reputation as a kind of Rain Woman because of her ability to recognise faces, which was often employed to identify bank robbers on grainy disjointed CCTV footage. They said she could recognise even well-disguised robbers if they were ex-cons and she had a database of several thousand mugshots stored in her fair-haired little head. So this murder had to be special, otherwise they wouldn't send out bosses in the middle of the night.

Beside the petite woman's pale, almost transparent face her colleague's appeared to be flushed. His freckled cheeks were adorned with two bright red mutton-chop sideburns. His eyes bulged slightly, as though there was too much pressure inside, which lent him a somewhat gawping expression. But what attracted most attention was the hat which appeared when he removed his white hood: a big Rasta hat in Jamaican colours, green, yellow and black.

Beate Lønn patted the shoulder of the trembling officer. "Off you go then, Simon. Don't tell anyone I said this, but I suggest a strong drink and then bed."

The officer nodded, and three seconds later he was swallowed up by the darkness.

"Is it gruesome?" Anton asked.

"No coffee?" Rasta Hat asked, opening a Thermos. These two words told Anton he wasn't from Oslo. From the provinces, that was clear, but like most Norwegians from Østland Anton had no idea about, and no particular interest in, dialects.

"No," Anton said.

"It's always a good idea to take your own coffee to a crime scene," Rasta Hat said. "You never know how long you'll have to stay."

"Come on, Bjørn. He's worked on murder investigations before," said Beate Lønn. "Drammen, wasn't it?"

"Right," Anton said, rocking on his heels. **Used to** work on murder investigations, more accurately. And unfortunately he had a suspicion as to why Beate

Lønn could remember him. He breathed in. "Who found the body?"

"He did," said Beate Lønn, nodding in the direction of the police officer's car. They could hear the engine revving.

"I mean who tipped us off?"

"The wife rang when he didn't come back from a bike ride," Rasta Hat said. "Should have been away for an hour, and she was worried about his heart. He was using his satnav, which has a transmitter, so they found him quickly."

Anton nodded slowly, picturing it all. Two policemen ringing the doorbell, a man and a woman. The officers coughing, looking at the wife with that grave expression which is meant to tell her what they will soon repeat in words, impossible words. The wife's face, resistant, not wanting to hear, but then it seems to turn inside out, shows her inner emotions, shows everything.

The image of Laura, his wife, appeared.

An ambulance drew up, without a siren or a blue light.

It slowly dawned on Anton. The fast reaction to a missing-person message. The rapidly traced satnav signal. The big turnout. Overtime. The colleague who was so shaken he had to be sent home.

"It's a policeman," he whispered.

"I'd guess the temperature here is one and a half degrees lower than in town," Beate Lønn said, pulling up a number on her mobile phone.

"Agreed," Rasta Hat said, swigging a mouthful

from the Thermos cup. "No skin discoloration yet. So somewhere between eight and ten?"

"A policeman," Anton repeated. "That's why they're all here, isn't it?"

"Katrine?" Beate said. "Can you check something for me? It's about the Sandra Tveten case. Right."

"Goddamn!" Rasta Hat exclaimed. "I asked them to wait until the body bags had come."

Anton turned and saw two men struggling through the forest with a stretcher between them. A pair of cycling shoes poked out from under the blanket.

"He knew him," Anton said. "That was why he was shaking like that, wasn't it?"

"He said they worked together in Økern before Vennesla started in Kripos," Rasta Hat said.

"Have you got the date to hand?" Lønn said on the phone.

There was a scream.

"What the . . . ?" Rasta Hat said.

Anton turned. One of the stretcher-bearers had slipped into the ditch beside the path. The beam from his torch swept over the stretcher. Over the blanket that had fallen off. Over . . . over what? Anton stared. Was that a head? The thing on top of what was indubitably the human body, had it really been a head? In the years Anton had worked at Crime Squad, before the Great Mistake, he had seen a great many bodies, but nothing like this. The hourglass-shaped substance reminded Anton of the family's Sunday breakfast, of Laura's lightly boiled egg with the remains of the shell still hanging from it, cracked with the yellow yolk running out and drying on the outside of the stiff but still soft egg white. Could that really be a . . . **head**?

Anton stood blinking in the darkness as he watched the rear lights of the ambulance disappearing. And he realised that these were replays, he had seen all this before. The white figures, the Thermos, the feet protruding from under the blanket, he had just seen this at the Rikshospital. As though they all had been portents. The head . . .

"Thanks, Katrine," Beate said.

"What was that about?" Rasta Hat asked.

"I worked with Erlend on this very spot," Beate said.

"Here?" Rasta Hat queried.

"Right here. He was in charge of the investigation. Must have been ten years ago. Sandra Tveten. Raped and killed. Just a child."

Anton swallowed. Child. Replays.

"I remember that case," Rasta Hat said. "Fate's a funny thing, dying at your own crime scene. Imagine. Wasn't the Sandra Tveten case also in the autumn?"

Beate nodded slowly.

Anton blinked, and kept blinking. He **had** seen a body like it.

"Goddamn!" Rasta Hat cursed under his breath. "You don't mean to say that . . . ?"

Beate Lønn took the cup of coffee from him. Took a sip. Passed it back. Nodded.

"Oh shit," Rasta Hat said under his breath.

3

"Déjà vu," Ståle Aune said, looking at the packed snowdrift across Sporveisgata where the December-morning gloom was receding to allow a short day. Then he turned back to the man in the chair on the opposite side of the desk. "Déjà vu is the feeling we've seen something before. We don't know what it is."

By "we" he meant psychologists in general, not only therapists.

"Some psychologists believe that when we're tired, information sent to the conscious part of the brain is delayed, so that when it surfaces it's already been in the subconscious for a while. And that's why we experience it as recognition. The tiredness explains why déjà vu usually occurs at the end of a working week. But that's about all research has to contribute. Friday is déjà vu day."

Ståle Aune had perhaps been hoping for a smile. Not because smiling meant anything at all in his professional efforts to get people to repair themselves, but because the room required it.

"I don't mean déjà vu in that sense," the patient said. The client. The customer. The person who in roughly twenty minutes would be paying in reception and helping to cover the overheads of the five psychologists who each had their own practice in the featureless, yet old-fashioned four-storey building in Sporveisgata which ran through Oslo's medium-elegant West End district. Ståle Aune sneaked a glimpse of the clock on the wall behind the man's head. Eighteen minutes.

"It's more like a dream I have again and again."

"**Like** a dream?" Ståle Aune's eyes scanned the newspaper he had lying open in a desk drawer so that it couldn't be seen by the patient. Most therapists nowadays sat on a chair opposite the patient, and when the massive desk had been manoeuvred into Ståle's office, grinning colleagues had confronted him with the modern therapy theory that it was best to have as few barriers as possible between themselves and the patient. Ståle's retort had been swift: "Best for the patient maybe."

"It's a dream. I dream."

"It's common," Aune said, passing his hand over his mouth to conceal a yawn. He reflected longingly on the dear old sofa that had been carried out of his office and now stood in the reception area, where with the weight racks alongside and a barbell above, it functioned as a psychotherapist's in-joke. Patients on the sofa had made the uninhibited reading of news-papers even easier.

"But it's a dream I don't want." Thin, self-conscious smile. Thin, well-groomed hair.

Enter the dream exorcist, Aune thought, trying to respond with an equally thin smile. The patient was wearing a pinstriped suit, a red-and-grey tie, and black, polished shoes. Aune had a tweed jacket on, a cheery bow tie under his double chins and brown shoes that hadn't seen a brush for quite a while. "Perhaps you might tell me what the dream was about?"

"That's what I've just done."

"Exactly. But perhaps you could give me some more detail?"

"It starts, as I said, where **Dark Side of the Moon** finishes. 'Eclipse' fades out with David Gilmour singing about everything being in tune . . ."

"And this is what you dream?"

"No! Yes. I mean, the record stops like that in reality too. Optimistic. After three-quarters of an hour about death and madness. So you think everything will end well. Everything is back in harmony. But then as the album fades out, you can just hear a voice in the background mumbling something about it all being dark. Do you understand?"

"No," Aune said. According to the manual he should have asked "Is it important for you that I understand?" or something like that. But he couldn't be bothered.

"Evil doesn't exist because everything is evil. Cosmic space is dark. We are born evil. Evil is the starting point, natural. Then, sometimes, there is a speck of light. But it is only temporary, because we have to go back to the darkness. And that's what happens in the dream."

"Continue," Aune said, swinging round on the chair and gazing out of the window with a pensive air. The air was to hide the fact that he only wanted to gaze upon something that was not the man's facial expression, which was a combination of self-pity and self-satisfaction. He obviously considered himself unique, a case a psychologist could really get his teeth into. The man had undoubtedly been in therapy before. Aune watched a car-park attendant with bow legs swaggering down the street like a sheriff and wondered what other professions he might be cut out for. And drew a speedy conclusion. None. Besides, he loved psychology, loved navigating the area between what we knew and what we didn't, combining his heavy ballast of factual knowledge with intuition and curiosity. At least, that was what he told himself every morning. So why was he sitting here wishing this individual would shut his mouth and get out of his office, out of his life? Was it the person or his job as a therapist? It was Ingrid's undisguised, clear ultimatum that he should work less and be more present for her and for their daughter Aurora which had enforced the changes. He had dropped the time-consuming research, the consultancy work for Crime Squad and the lectures at PHS, the police training college. He had become a full-time therapist with fixed working hours. The new priorities had seemed like a great decision. For of the things he gave up what did he actually miss? Did he miss profiling sick souls who killed people with such gruesome acts of brutality that he was deprived of sleep at night? Only to be woken up by Inspector Harry Hole demanding quick answers to impossible questions if he did finally fall asleep? Did he miss Hole turning him into the inspector's image, a starved, exhausted, monomaniacal hunter? Snapping at everyone who disturbed his work on the one thing he thought had any significance, slowly but surely alienating colleagues, family and friends?

Did he hell. He missed the **importance** of it.

He missed the feeling that he was saving lives. Not the life of a rationally thinking suicidal soul who could on occasion make him ask the question: if life is such a painful experience and we can't change that, why can't this person just be allowed to die? He missed being active, being the one to intervene, the one to save the innocent party from the guilty, doing what no one else could do because he—Ståle Aune— was the best. It was as simple as that. Yes, he missed Harry Hole. He missed having the tall, grumpy alcoholic with the big heart on the phone asking—or to be more precise, commanding—Ståle Aune to do his social duty, demanding him to sacrifice his family life and sleep to catch one of society's poor wretches. But there was no longer an inspector at Crime Squad by the name of Harry Hole, and no one else had rung him either. His eye ran over the pages of the newspaper again. There had been a press conference. It was almost three months since the murder of the police officer in Maridalen, and the police still didn't have a lead or any suspects. This was the kind of problem they would have rung him about in times gone by. The murder had occurred at the same scene and on the same date as an old, unsolved investigation.

The victim was a policeman who had worked on the original case.

But that was then. Now the problem was the sleeplessness of an overworked businessman he didn't like. Soon Aune would begin to ask questions that would presumably eliminate post-traumatic stress disorders. The man in front of him wasn't incapacitated by his nightmares; he was only concerned about getting his productivity back to its previous heights. Aune would then give him a copy of the article "Imagery Rehearsal Therapy" by Krakow and . . . he couldn't remember the other names. Ask him to write down his nightmares and bring it along for next time. Then, together, they would create an alternative, a happy ending to the nightmare, which they would rehearse mentally so that the dream either became easier to cope with or just disappeared.

Aune heard the regular, soporific drone of the patient's voice and reflected that the Maridalen murder had been in a rut from day one. Even when the striking similarities with the Sandra Tveten case— the date, the place—and the connection between the victims had come out, neither Kripos nor Crime Squad had managed to make any headway. And now they were urging people to rack their brains and come forward, however seemingly irrelevant their information might be. That was what the previous day's press conference had been about. Aune suspected it was the police playing to the gallery, showing they were doing something, that they weren't paralysed.

Even though that was exactly what they were: help-less senior management under attack, desperately turning to the public and asking "let's see if you can do any better."

He looked at the picture of the press conference. He recognised Beate Lønn. Gunnar Hagen, head of Crime Squad, resembling a monk more and more with the rich abundance of hair like a laurel wreath around his blank, shiny pate. Even Mikael Bellman, the new Chief of Police, had been there; after all, it had been the murder of one of their own. Taut-faced. Thinner than Aune remembered him. The media-friendly curls that had been on the verge of being too long had obviously been shed somewhere along the line between being the head of Kripos and Orgkrim and the sheriff's office. Aune thought about Bell-man's almost girlish good looks, emphasised by the long eyelashes and the tanned skin with its charac-teristic, white patches. None of which were visible in the photo. The unsolved murder of an officer was of course the worst possible start for a Chief of Police who had based his meteoric rise on success. He had cleared up the drug wars in Oslo, but that would be forgotten quickly. It was true the retired Erlend Ven-nesla hadn't been killed on active service in a formal sense, but most people knew that in some way or other it was tied up with the Sandra Tveten case. So Bellman had mobilised every available officer and all the external manpower there was. Except him, Ståle Aune. He had been crossed off their lists. Naturally enough—he himself had asked them to.

And now winter had arrived early and with it a sense that snow was settling on the tracks. Cold tracks. No tracks. That was what Beate Lønn had said at the conference, an almost conspicuous lack of forensic evidence. It went without saying that they had checked the evidence in the Sandra Tveten investigation. Suspects, relatives, friends, even colleagues of Vennesla who had worked on the case. All without success.

The room had gone quiet, and Ståle Aune saw from the patient's expression that he had just asked a question and was waiting for the psychologist's answer.

"Hm," Aune said, resting his chin on his clenched fist and meeting the other man's gaze. "What do **you** think about it?"

There was bewilderment in the man's eyes and for a moment Aune feared he had asked for a glass of water or something like that.

"What do I think about her smiling? Or the beam of light?"

"Both."

"Sometimes I think she's smiling because she likes me. Then I think she's smiling because she wants me to do something. But when she stops smiling the beam of light in her eyes dies and it's too late to find out, she won't talk to me any more. So I think perhaps it's the amp. Or something."

"Erm . . . the amp?"

"Yes." Pause. "The one I told you about. The one Dad used to switch off when he came into my room, when he said I'd been playing that record so long it was bordering on insanity. And then I said you could see the little red light beside the off switch fade and disappear. Like an eye. Or a sunset. And then I thought I was losing her. That's why she says nothing at the end of the dream. She's the amp that goes quiet when Dad switches it off. And then I can't talk to her."

"Did you play records and think about her?"

"Yes. All the time. Until I was sixteen. And not records. The record."

"Dark Side of the Moon?"

"Yes."

"But she didn't want you?"

"I don't know. Probably not. Not then."

"Hm. Our time's up. I'll give you something to read for next time. And then I want us to make a new ending for the story in the dream. She has to speak. She has to say something to you. Something you wished she would say. That she likes you perhaps. Can you give that a bit of thought for next time?"

"Fine."

The patient stood up, took his coat from the stand and walked towards the door. Aune sat at his desk and looked at the calendar shining at him from the computer screen. It already looked depressingly full. And he realised it had happened again: he had completely forgotten the name of the patient. He found it on the calendar. Paul Stavnes.

"Same time next week OK, Paul?"

"Yes."

Ståle entered it. When he looked up, Stavnes had already gone.

He got up, grabbed the newspaper and went to the window. Where the hell was the global warming they had been promised? He looked at the newspaper, but suddenly couldn't be bothered, threw it down, weeks and months of grinding his way through the papers were enough. Beaten to death. Terrible force. Fatal blows to the head. Erlend Vennesla leaves behind a wife, children and grandchildren. Friends and colleagues in shock. "A warm, kind person." "Impossible to dislike." "Good-natured, honest and tolerant, absolutely no enemies." Ståle Aune took a deep breath.

He gazed at the phone. They had his number. But the phone was mute. Just like the girl in the dream.

4

The head of Crime Squad, Gunnar Hagen, ran his hand across his forehead and then further up, through the entrance to the lagoon. The sweat collecting on his palm was caught by the thick atoll of hair at the back of his head. In front of him sat the investigative team. For a standard murder there would typically be twelve officers. But the murder of a colleague was not typical and K2 was full, down to the last chair, just shy of fifty people. Including those on the sick list, the group consisted of fifty-three members. And soon more of them would be on the sick list, as they felt the full force of the media. The best that could be said about this case was that it had brought the two big murder investigation units in Norway—Crime Squad and Kripos—closer together. All the rivalry had been cast aside, and for once they were collaborating with no other agenda than to find the person who had killed their colleague. In the first weeks with an intensity and passion that convinced Hagen the case would soon be solved, despite the lack of forensic evidence, witnesses, possible motives, possible suspects and possible or impossible leads. Simply because the collective will was so formidable, the net spread was so tight, the resources they had at their disposal boundless. And yet.

The tired, grey faces stared at him with an apathy that had become more and more visible over the last few weeks. And yesterday's press conference—which had been like an ugly capitulation, his plea for help, wherever it might come from—had not raised fighting spirits. Today there were two further absentees, and they weren't exactly throwing in the towel over a sniffly nose. In addition to the Vennesla case there was the Gusto Hanssen murder which had gone from solved to unsolved after Oleg Fauke had been released and Chris "Adidas" Reddy had withdrawn his confession. Ah, there was one positive side to the Vennesla case: the murder of the policeman overshadowed that of the young beautiful drug dealer called Gusto Hanssen so completely that the press hadn't written a word about the resumption of this investigation.

Hagen glanced down at the sheet of paper on the lectern. There were two lines. That was all. Two lines for a morning meeting.

Gunnar Hagen cleared his throat. "Morning, folks. As most of you are aware, we have received some calls after yesterday's conference. Eighty-nine in all, of which several are being followed up now."

He didn't need to say what everyone knew, that after close on three months they were now scraping the bottom; ninety-five per cent of all calls were a waste of time: the usual nutters who always rang in, drunks, people wanting to cast suspicion on someone who had run off with their other half, a neighbour shirking their cleaning duties, practical jokes or just people who wanted some attention, someone to talk to. By "several" he meant four. Four tip-offs. And when he said they were being "followed up" it was a lie, they had finished following them up. And they had led where they were now: nowhere.

"We've got an illustrious visitor today," Hagen said, and immediately heard that this could be construed as sarcasm. "The Chief of Police would like to join us and say a few words. Mikael . . ."

Hagen closed his folder, raised it and placed it on the table as though it contained a pile of new, interesting documents instead of the one sheet of paper, hoping he had smoothed over the "illustrious" by using Bellman's Christian name and nodding to the man standing by the door at the back of the room.

The young Chief of Police was leaning against the wall with his arms crossed, waiting for the brief moment when everyone turned round to look at him, then in one sleek, powerful movement he pulled himself away from the wall and strode to the rostrum. He was half smiling as though he was thinking about something amusing, and when he turned to the lectern with a casual swing of his heel, rested his forearms on it, leaned forward and looked straight at them as if to emphasise that he had no typed speech ready, it struck Hagen that Bellman had better deliver now what his entrance promised.

"Some of you may know that I'm a climber," Mikael said. "And when I wake up in the morning on days like today, look out of the window and there's zero visibility and more snow and gusting winds are forecast, I think about a mountain I once had plans to conquer."

Bellman paused, and Hagen could see the unexpected introduction was working; Bellman had caught their attention. For the moment. But Hagen knew that the overworked unit's bullshit tolerance was at an all-time low, and they wouldn't go out of their way to hide it. Bellman was too young, had taken up his post too recently and had arrived there with too much haste for them to allow him to test their patience.

"Coincidentally, the mountain has the same name as this room. Which is the same name some of you have given the Vennesla case. K2. It's a good name. The world's second-highest mountain. The Savage Mountain. The hardest mountain in the world to conquer. One in four climbers dies. We'd planned to tackle the southern ascent, also known as the Magic Line. It's only been done twice before and is considered by many to be ritual suicide. A slight change in weather and wind, and you and the mountain are enveloped in snow and temperatures none of us is made to survive, not with less oxygen per cubic metre than you have underwater. And, as this is the Himalayas, everyone knows there **will** be a change in the weather and wind."

Pause.

"So why should I climb this mountain of all mountains?"

Another pause. Longer, as though waiting for someone to answer. Still with the half-smile. The pause dragged on. Too long, Hagen thought. The police are not fans of theatrical effects.

"Because . . ." Bellman tapped a forefinger on the table beneath the lectern. ". . . **because** it's the hardest in the world. Physically and mentally. There's not a moment's pleasure in the ascent, only anxiety, toil, fear, acrophobia, lack of oxygen, degrees of dangerous panic and even more dangerous apathy. And when you're on top, it's not about relishing the moment of triumph, just creating evidence that you have actually been there, a photo or two, not deluding yourself into thinking the worst is over, not letting yourself slip into an agreeable doze, but keeping your concentration, doing the chores, systematically like a robot, while continuing to monitor the situation. Monitoring the situation **all** the time. What's the weather doing? What signals are you getting from your body? Where are we? How long have we been here? How are the others in the team coping?"

He took a step back from the lectern.

"K2 is an uphill climb in all senses. Even when going downhill. And that was **why** we wanted to have a go."

The room was silent. Utterly silent. No demonstrative yawning or shuffling of feet under chairs. My God, Hagen thought, he's got them.

"Two words," Bellman said. 'Stamina' and 'solidarity.' I had considered including 'ambition,' but the word isn't important enough, not big enough in comparison with the other two. So you may ask what's the point of stamina and solidarity if there's no goal, no ambition. Fighting for fighting's sake? Honour without reward? Yes, I say, fighting for fighting's sake. Honour without reward. When the Vennesla case is still being talked about years from now it's because it was an uphill climb. Because it looked impossible. The mountain was too high, the weather too treacherous, the air too thin. Everything went wrong. And it's the story of the uphill climb which will turn the case into mythology, which will make it one of the tales around the campfire that will survive. Just as most climbers in the world have never got as far as the foothills of K2, you can work all your life without ever being on a case like this one. If this case had been cracked in the first weeks it would soon have been forgotten. For what is it that all legendary criminal cases in history have in common?"

Bellman waited. Nodded as if they had given him the answer.

"They took **time.** They were **an uphill climb.**"

A voice beside Hagen whispered: "Churchill, eat your heart out."

He turned and saw Beate Lønn standing beside him with a mischievous smile on her face.

He nodded and watched the assembled officers. Old tricks maybe, but they still worked. Where, a few minutes ago, he had seen only a dead, blackened fire, Bellman had managed to blow life into the embers. But Hagen knew it wouldn't burn for long if results were not forthcoming.

Three minutes later Bellman had finished the pep talk and left the podium with a broad grin and to great applause. Hagen clapped along dutifully, dreading his return to the lectern. For the certain showstopper, telling them the unit would be cut to thirty-five. Bellman's orders, but which they had agreed he would not have to pass on. Hagen stepped forward, put down his folder, coughed, pretended to flick through it. Looked up. Coughed again and said with a wry smile: "Ladies and gentlemen, Elvis has left the building."

Silence, no laughter.

"Well, we have a few matters to deal with. Some of you are going to be transferred to other duties."

Stone dead. Fire extinguished.

As Mikael Bellman left the lift in the atrium at Police HQ he caught a glimpse of a figure disappearing into the adjacent lift. Was it Truls? Hardly likely, he was still suspended after the Asayev business. Bellman walked out of the building and struggled through the snow to the waiting car. When he took over the Chief of Police post he had been told that in theory he had the services of a chauffeur, but his three predecessors had all refrained from using them because they thought it would send the wrong signals, as they were the ones who had to deliver all the cuts in other areas. Bellman had reversed this practice and said in no uncertain terms that he wouldn't let that kind of social-democratic pettiness threaten his productivity, and it was more important to signal to those further down the food chain that hard work and promotion brought certain benefits. The head of PR had subsequently taken him aside and suggested that if the press were to ask him he should limit his answer to productivity and lose the bit about benefits.

"City Hall," Bellman said as he settled in the back seat.

The car glided away from the curb, rounded Grøn-land Church and headed towards the Plaza Hotel and the Post Office building, which despite the excavations around the Opera House still dominated Oslo's small skyline. But today there was no skyline, only snow, and Bellman thought three mutually independent thoughts. Bloody December. Bloody Vennesla case. And bloody Truls Berntsen.

Mikael had neither seen nor spoken to Truls since he had been forced to suspend his childhood friend and subordinate last October. Although he thought he'd glimpsed him outside the Grand Hotel last week in a parked car. It was the large injections of cash into Truls's account that had led to his suspension. As he couldn't—or didn't want to—explain them, Mikael, as his boss, had had no choice. Of course Mikael knew where the money had come from: burner jobs— sabotaging evidence—which Truls had done for Rudolf Asayev's drug cartel. Money the idiot had put straight into his account. The sole consolation was that neither the money nor Truls could point a finger at Mikael. There were only two people in the world who could expose Mikael's cooperation with Asayev.

One was the Councillor for Social Affairs and she was an accomplice, and the other lay in a coma in a closed wing of the Rikshospital.

They drove through Kvadraturen. Bellman stared with fascination at the contrast between the prostitutes' black skin and the white snow in their hair and on their shoulders. He also saw that new layers of dope dealers had moved into the vacuum left by Asayev.

Truls Berntsen. He had followed Mikael through his childhood in Manglerud the way sucker fish follow sharks. Mikael with the brain, the leadership qualities, the eloquence, the appearance. Truls "Beavis" Berntsen with the fearlessness, the fists and the almost childlike loyalty. Mikael, who made friends wherever he turned. Truls, who was so difficult to like that everyone actively avoided him. Yet it was precisely these two who hung out together, Bellman and Berntsen. Their names were called out one after the other in class and later at Police College, Bellman first, Berntsen tagging along afterwards. Mikael had got together with Ulla, but Truls was still there, two steps behind. As the years passed Truls had lagged further behind; he had none of Mikael's natural buoyancy in his private life and career. As a rule Truls was an easy man to lead and to predict—when Mikael said jump, he jumped. But he could also get that blackness in his eyes, and then he seemed to become someone Mikael didn't know. Like the time with the young guy they arrested, whom Truls blinded with his truncheon. Or the guy at Kripos who tried it on with Mikael. Colleagues had seen, so Mikael had to do something to avoid the impression he would let such matters go. He had tricked the guy into meeting in the Kripos boiler room, and there Truls had attacked the man with his baton. First of all, in a controlled way, then more and more savagely as the blackness in his eyes seemed to spread, until he appeared to be possessed, his eyes wide and dark, and Mikael had to stop him so that he didn't kill the guy. Yes, Truls was loyal, but he was also a loose cannon, and that in particular worried Mikael Bellman. When Mikael had told him the Appointments Board had decided he was suspended until they were satisfied they knew where the money in Truls's account came from, Truls had just shrugged as though it was of no significance and left. As if Truls "Beavis" Berntsen had anything to go to, a life outside work. And Mikael had seen the blackness in his eyes. It had been like lighting a fuse, watching it burn in a mine gallery and then nothing happens. But you don't know if the fuse is just long or if it has gone out, so you wait, on tenterhooks, because something tells you the longer it takes, the worse the explosion is going to be.

The car parked behind City Hall. Mikael got out and walked up the steps to the entrance. Some claimed this was the real main entrance, the way the architects Arneberg and Poulsson had designed it in the 1920s, and that the drawing had been turned round by mistake. And when the error was discovered in the late 1940s the building was so far along that they hushed the matter up and went on as if nothing was wrong, hoping that people sailing up Oslo Fjord to Norway's capital city wouldn't realise the sight that met them was the kitchen entrance.

Mikael Bellman's Italian leather soles gently caressed the stone floor as he marched over to reception, where the woman behind the counter flashed him a dazzling smile.

"Good morning, sir. You are expected. Ninth floor, end of the corridor on the left." Bellman studied himself in the lift mirror on his way up. And reflected that was exactly what he was: on his way up. Despite this murder case. He straightened the silk tie Ulla had bought him in Barcelona. Double Windsor knot. He had taught Truls how to tie a knot at school. But only the thin, easy one. The door at the end of the corridor was ajar. Mikael pushed it open.

The office was bare. The desk cleared, the shelves empty and the wallpaper had light patches where pictures had hung. She was sitting on a windowsill. Her face had the conventional good looks that women often call "nice," but it had no sweetness or charm despite the blonde doll's hair arranged in comic ringlets. She was tall and athletic with broad shoulders and broad hips which had been negotiated into a tight leather skirt for the occasion. Her thighs were crossed. The masculinity in her face—emphasised by an aquiline nose and a pair of cold, blue lupine eyes—combined with a self-confident, provocative, playful gaze had caused Bellman to make a couple of quick assumptions the first time he saw her. Isabelle Skøyen was an initiative-taker and a risk-loving cougar.

"Lock," she said.

He hadn't been mistaken.

Mikael closed the door behind him and turned the key. Walked over to one of the other windows. City Hall towered above Oslo's modest development of four- and five-storey buildings. Overlooking Rådhus- plassen, the City Hall square, was the 700-year-old Akershus Fortress, on high ramparts with ancient, war-damaged cannons pointing at the fjord, which seemed to have goose pimples as it trembled in the freezing gusts of wind. It had stopped snowing, and under the leaden grey sky the town was bathed in a bluish-white light. Like the colour of a dead body, Bellman thought. Isabelle's voice echoed off the bare walls. "Well, my dear, what do you think of the view?"

"Impressive. If I remember rightly the previous councillor had an office that was both smaller and lower down."

"Not that view," she said. "This one."

He turned to her. Oslo's latest Councillor for Social Affairs had spread her legs. Her panties were on the windowsill beside her. Isabelle had repeatedly said she didn't understand the attractions of a shaven pussy, but Mikael reckoned there had to be a halfway house as he stared into the thick bush and mumbled a repeat of his comment about the view. Truly impressive.

Her heels hit the parquet floor hard and she walked over to him. Brushed an invisible speck of dust off his lapel. Even without stilettos she would have been a centimetre taller than him, but now she towered over him. He didn't find this intimidating. On the contrary, her physical size and domineering personality were an interesting challenge. It required more of him as a man than Ulla's slender figure and gentle compliance. "I think it's only right and proper that you're the person to inaugurate my office. Without your . . . willing cooperation I wouldn't have got this job."

"Ditto," Mikael Bellman said. He breathed in the fragrance of her perfume. It was familiar. It was . . . Ulla's. The Tom Ford perfume—what was it called? Black Orchid. Which he'd bought for her when he was in Paris or London because it was impossible to get hold of in Norway. The coincidence seemed highly improbable.

He saw the laughter in her eyes as she saw the astonishment in his. She interlaced her fingers behind his neck and leaned back laughing. "Sorry, I couldn't stop myself."

What the hell. After the house-warming Ulla had complained that the bottle of perfume had disappeared and that one of the celeb guests he'd invited must have stolen it. He'd been pretty sure it had been one of the local Mangleruders, namely Truls Berntsen. He wasn't exactly unaware that Truls had been head over heels in love with Ulla ever since their boyhood days. Which of course he had never mentioned to her or Truls. Nor the business with the bottle of perfume. After all, it was better that Truls pinched Ulla's perfume than her panties.

"Have you ever wondered if that might be your problem?" Mikael said. "Stopping yourself?"

She laughed softly. Closed her eyes. Her long, broad fingers opened behind his neck, moved down his back and stole inside his belt. She looked at him with mild disappointment in her gaze.

"What's up, my stallion?"

"The doctors say he's not going to die," Mikael said. "And recently he's been showing signs of coming out of the coma."

"In what way? Is he moving?"

"No, but they can see changes in his EEG, so they've started doing neurophysiological examinations."

"So what?" Her lips were close to his. "Are you frightened of him?"

"I'm not frightened of **him** but of what he could say. About us."

"Why would he do anything so stupid? He's alone and he has nothing to gain by it."

"Let me put it this way, my love," Mikael said, shoving her hand away. "The thought that there's someone out there who can testify that you and I have been working with a dope dealer to further our careers—"

"Listen," Isabelle said. "All we did was make a careful intervention to prevent market forces ruling. It's good, tried and tested Socialist Party politics, my dear. We let Asayev have a monopoly on dope, and we arrested all the other drug barons because Asayev's goods caused fewer ODs. Anything else would have been an unsatisfactory drugs policy."

That made Mikael smile. "I can hear you've been honing your rhetoric on the debating course."

"Shall we change the topic, darling?" She slipped her hand around his tie.

"You know how it will be interpreted in a court of law, don't you? I got the Chief of Police number and you the Councillor job because it looked as if we'd personally cleaned up Oslo's streets and brought down the death rate. While in reality we let Asayev destroy the evidence, remove his rivals and sell a type of drug that was four times as potent and addictive as heroin."

"Mmm, you make me so hot when you talk like that . . ." She pulled him close. Her tongue was in his mouth, and he could hear the crackle of her stockings as she rubbed her thigh against his. She towed him after her as she backed unsteadily to the desk.

"If he wakes up in the hospital and starts blabbing—"

"Stop it. I didn't get you here for a chit-chat." Her fingers were working on his belt.

"We've got a problem we have to solve, Isabelle."

"I know, but now you're Chief of Police you're in the prioritisation business, my love. And right now your City Hall prioritises **this.**"

Mikael parried her hand.

She sighed. "Fine. Let me hear. What have you got planned?"

"He has to feel threatened. In a credible way."

"Why **threaten** him? Why not just kill him now?"

Mikael laughed. Right up to the moment he realised she was serious.

"Because . . ." Mikael held her eyes, his voice firm. Trying to be the same masterful Mikael Bellman who, half an hour ago, had stood in front of the assembled detectives. Trying to come up with an answer. But she was quicker on her feet.

"Because you don't dare. Shall we see if we can find someone under 'Active Euthanasia' in the Yellow Pages? You remove the police guard, misuse of resources blah blah blah, and afterwards the patient receives an unexpected visit from the Yellow Pages. Unexpected as far as he's concerned, that is. Or, no, as a matter of fact, you could send your shadow. Beavis. Truls Berntsen. He'll do anything for money, won't he?"

Mikael shook his head in disbelief. "First of all, it was the head of Crime Squad, Gunnar Hagen, who ordered the twenty-four-hour police supervision. If the patient was killed after I'd overruled Hagen, that would make me look bad, if I can put it like that. Secondly, we're not going to murder anyone."

"Listen, darling, no politician is better than her adviser. That's why the basic premise for getting to the top is you always surround yourself with people who are smarter than you are. And I'm beginning to doubt that you're smarter than me, Mikael. First off, you can't even catch this police killer. And now you don't know how to solve a simple problem of a man in a coma. So when you don't want to fuck me either, I have to ask myself: 'What am I going to do with him?' Answer me that, please."

"Isabelle . . ."

"I'll take that as a no. So, listen to me. This is how we're going to play it . . ."

He had to admire her. Her controlled, cool professionalism, yet her risk-embracing unpredictability, which made her colleagues sit a little further back on their chairs. Some saw her as a ticking bomb, but they hadn't realised that creating uncertainty was a feature of Isabelle Skøyen's game. She was the type to soar farther and higher than anyone else, and in a shorter time. And—if she fell—to plummet to a nasty end. It wasn't that Mikael Bellman didn't recognise himself in Isabelle Skøyen, he did, but she was an extreme version of himself. And the strange thing was that instead of dragging him along, she made him more cautious.

"The patient hasn't come out of the coma yet, so for the time being we do nothing," Isabelle said. "I know an anaesthetist from Enebakk. Very shady type. He supplies me with pills that as a politician I can't get on the street. He—like Beavis—does most things for money. And anything at all for sex. Apropos of which . . ."

She had perched herself on the edge of the table, raised and spread her legs and unbuttoned his flies in one go. Mikael grabbed her wrists. "Let's wait until Wednesday at the Grand."

"Let's **not** wait until Wednesday at the Grand."

"Well, actually, I vote that we do."

"Oh yes?" she said, freeing her hands and opening his trousers. She looked down. Her voice was throaty. "The noes have it by one, darling."

5

Darkness and the temperature had fallen, and a pale moon was shining in through the window of Stian Barelli's room when he heard his mother's voice from the living room downstairs.

"It's for you, Stian!"

He had heard their landline ringing and hoped it wasn't for him. He put down the Wii controller. He was twelve under par with three holes left to play and thus very well on the way to qualifying for the Masters. He was playing Rick Fowler, as he was the only golfer in the Tiger Woods Masters who was cool and anywhere close to his own age, twenty-one. And they both liked Eminem and Rise Against and wearing orange. Of course Rick Fowler could afford his own flat whereas Stian still lived at home. But it was only temporary, until he got a scholarship to go to university in Alaska. All semi-decent downhill skiers went there if they got good results in the Nordic Junior Ski Championship and so on. Of course, no one became a better skier from going there, but so what? Women, wine and skis. What could be better. Perhaps the odd exam if there was time. The qualification could lead to an OK job. Money for his own flat. A life that was better than this, sleeping in the slightly too short bed under posters of Bode Miller and Aksel Lund Svindal, eating Mum's rissoles and obeying Dad's rules, training mouthy brats who according to their snow-blind parents had the talent to be a Kjetil André Aamodt or a Lasse Kjus. Operating the ski lifts in Tryvannskleiva for a wage they wouldn't bloody dare give child workers in India. And that was how Stian knew it was the chairman of the Ski Club on the phone now. He was the only person Stian knew who avoided ringing people on their mobiles because it was **a bit** more expensive, and who preferred to force them to run downstairs in prehistoric houses that still had landlines.

Stian took the receiver his mother held out for him. "Yes?"

"Hi, Stian, Bakken here." Bakken meant slope, and it really was his name. "I've been told the Kleiva lift's running."

"Now?" Stian said, looking at his watch. 11:15 at night. Closing time was at nine.

"Could you nip up and see what's going on?"

"Now?"

"Unless you're extremely busy, of course."

Stian ignored the sarcasm in the chairman's intonation. He knew he'd had two disappointing seasons and that the chairman didn't think it was down to lack of talent but to the large amounts of time Stian did his best to fill with general idleness.

"I haven't got a car," Stian said.

"You can use mine," his mother chipped in. She

hadn't gone away; she was standing next to him with her arms crossed.

"Sorry, Stian, but I heard that," the chairman commented laconically. "The Heming skateboarders must have broken in. I suppose they think it's funny."

It took Stian ten minutes to drive the winding road up to Tryvann Tower. The TV mast was a 118-metre-long javelin drilled into the ground at the top of Oslo's north-western mountains.

He came to a halt in the snow-covered car park and noted that the only other vehicle there was a red Golf. He took his skis from the roof box, put them on and skated past the main building and up to where the main chairlift, Tryvann Ekspress, marked the top of the skiing facilities. From there he could see down to the lake and the smaller Kleiva lift with T-bars. Even though there was light from the moon it was too dark to check whether the bars were moving, but he could hear it. The hum of the machinery down below.

And as he set off, skiing in long, lazy curves, it struck him how strangely still it was up here at night. It was as if the first hour after they closed was still filled with the echoes of screams of pleasure, girls' exaggerated whines of terror, boys' testosterone-filled cries for attention, steel edges cutting into hard-packed snow and ice. Even when they switched off the floodlights the light seemed to hang in the air for a while. But then, gradually, it became quieter. And darker.

And even quieter. Until the silence filled all the hollows in the terrain, and the darkness crept out from the forest. And it was as though Tryvann became a different place, a place which even for Stian, who knew it like the back of his hand, was so unfamiliar it might as well have been another planet. A cold, dark and uninhabited planet.

The lack of light meant he had to ski by feeling and try to predict how the snow and the ground would roll and pitch beneath the skis. But that was his special talent, which meant he always did best when there was bad visibility, heavy snow, mist, flat light: he could feel what he couldn't see, he had that kind of clairvoyance some skiers just have and others—most of them—don't. He caressed the snow, moving slowly to prolong the enjoyment. Then he was down and pulled up in front of the ski-lift hut.

The door had been smashed in.

There were splinters in the snow, and the door gaped wide open. It was only then that Stian realised he was alone. That it was the middle of the night, that at this moment he was in a deserted area where a crime had just been committed. Probably only a prank, but nevertheless. He could not be entirely sure. Sure it **was** only a prank. Sure he **was** on his own.

"Hello!" Stian shouted above the hum of the engine and rattle of the T-bars coming and going on the buzzing wire above him. And regretted it at once. The echo returned from the mountainside with the sound of his own fear. He was afraid. Because the brain had not stopped churning at "alone" and "crime," it had carried on. Back to the old story. It wasn't something he thought about during the day, but now and then when he was on the evening shift and there was hardly anyone on the slopes occasionally the story did creep out of the forest with the darkness. It had been late one night, a mild snowless December. The girl must have been drugged somewhere in the city centre and been driven up here. Handcuffs and hood. She had been transported from the car park to where the door had been smashed in and she was raped inside. Stian had heard that the fifteen-year-old girl was so small and slim that if she had been unconscious the rapist or rapists could easily have carried her from the car park. You could only hope she had been unconscious throughout. But Stian had also heard that the girl had been attached to the wall by two big nails, one under each collarbone, so that he or they could rape her standing up with minimal physical contact with the walls, floor or girl. That was why the police hadn't found any DNA, fingerprints or clothing fibres. But perhaps that wasn't true. What he knew was true was that they had found the girl in three places. At the bottom of Lake Tryvann they had found the torso and head. In the forest down from the Wyller slalom course half of her lower body. On the banks of Lake Aurtjern the other half. And it was because the two last parts were found so far apart and so far from where she had been raped that the police had speculated that there might have been two rapists. But that was all they had, speculation. The men—if they were men; there was no sperm to prove it—were never found. But the chairman and other jokers liked to tell younger club members doing their first evening shift that on still nights people said they had heard sounds from the hut. Screams. Nails being hammered into the wall.

Stian released his boots from the bindings and walked to the door. Bent his knees and tensed his calves, trying to ignore his racing pulse.

Jesus, what was he expecting to see? Blood and guts? Ghosts?

He reached inside the door, found the switch with his hand and twisted.

Stared into the lit room.

On the unpainted pine wall, hanging from a nail, was a girl. She was almost naked, only a yellow bikini covering the so-called strategic parts of her suntanned body. The month was December, and the calendar was last year's. One very quiet evening, a few weeks before, in fact, Stian had masturbated in front of that picture. She was sexy enough, but what had excited him most was the girls passing outside the window. Him sitting there, stiffy in hand, only a metre from them. Especially the girls who took the T-bar on their own, who with an experienced hand placed the erect pole between their thighs and squeezed them together. The T-bar lifting their buttocks. Their backs arched as the extended spring attached to the pole and the wire contracted and jerked them away from him, out of sight, along the aerial tramway.

Stian entered the cabin. There was no doubt someone had been there. The power control was broken.

The plastic knob lay in two sections on the floor, leaving the metal spindle sticking up from the console. He held the cold spindle between thumb and forefinger and tried to turn it, but it just slipped between his fingers. He walked over to the little fuse cupboard in the corner. The metal door was locked, and the key that used to hang from the string on the adjacent wall was gone. Strange. He went back to the console. Tried to pull the plastic covers off the controls for the floodlights and the music so he could swap one over, but realised he would destroy them as well; they were either glued or moulded. He needed something he could tighten round the spindle, a monkey wrench or something similar. As Stian pulled out a drawer from the table in front of the window he had a premonition. The same one he had when he was skiing blind. He could **feel** what he couldn't see. Someone was standing outside in the darkness watching him.

He looked up.

And into a face staring at him with large, wide-open eyes.

His own face, his own terrified eyes in the reflection in the windowpane, a double exposure.

Stian breathed out with relief. Shit, he was so easily frightened.

But then, as his heart began to beat again and he shifted his attention back to the drawer, it was as if his eye caught a movement outside, a face detaching itself from the reflection and vanishing to the right and out of sight. He looked up quickly again. There was still a reflection of himself. A double exposure as before. Or was it?

He'd always had an overactive imagination. That was what Marius and Kjella had told him when he said thinking about the raped girl turned him on. Not her being raped and killed of course. Or rather, yes, the rape was . . . something he thought about, he had added. But mostly, that she was very nice, nice and pretty, kind of. And that she had been in the cabin, naked, with a dick in her slit, that . . . yes, that was a thought that could turn him on. Marius had said he was sick and Kjella, the bastard, had of course blabbed, and when Stian heard the story again Stian was supposed to have said he would have liked to have joined in the rape. That's pals for you, Stian thought, rummaging through the drawer. Lift passes, stamp, stamp pad, pens, tape, scissors, sheath knife, invoice pad, screws, nuts. Bloody hell! He went on to the next drawer. No wrench, no keys. And then he realised he could just look for the emergency stop pole they usually kept rammed in the snow outside the cabin so that anyone could stop the lift by hitting the red button on top of the pole if something happened. And something was always happening: children banging their heads on the T-bar and beginners falling off backwards as the lift jerked into action, hanging on and being dragged up onto the cable. Or idiots who wanted to show off and wrapped a knee round the bar while leaning over the side to piss into the edge of the forest as they went past.

He ransacked the cupboards. The pole should be easy enough to find, about a metre long, made of metal and shaped like a crowbar with a pointed end so that it could stick into packed snow and ice. Stian pushed aside forgotten mittens, hats and goggles. Next cupboard, firefighting equipment. A bucket and cloths. First-aid kit. A torch. But no pole.

Of course they might have forgotten it when they locked up for the night.

He grabbed the torch and went outside, did a circuit round the cabin.

No pole there, either. Christ, had they **stolen** it or what? And left the lift passes? Stian thought he heard something and turned to the forest. Shone the torch on the trees.

A bird? A squirrel? Elk did sometimes come down here, but they didn't make much of an effort to hide. If he could only switch off the bloody lift, he would be able to **hear** better.

Stian went back into the cabin and noticed that he felt more at ease inside. Picked up the two pieces of the plastic knob from the floor, tried placing them around the spindle and turning, but it was no use.

He looked at his watch. Soon be midnight. He wanted to finish the round of golf in Augusta before going to bed. Wondered whether to phone the chairman. All he had to do was give this spindle a half-turn!

His head shot up instinctively and his heart stopped beating.

It had happened so quickly he was unsure whether he had seen it or not. Whatever it was, it was **not** an elk. Stian keyed in the name of the chairman, but his fingers were trembling so much he made several mistakes before getting it right.

"Yes?"

"The emergency pole's gone. I can't turn the lift off."

"The fuse cupboard . . ."

"Locked and the key's gone."

He heard the chairman cursing under his breath. Then a sigh of resignation. "Stay there. I'm on my way."

"Bring a wrench or something."

"Wrench or something," the chairman repeated, making no attempt to conceal his contempt.

Stian had long known the chairman's respect was measured in terms of your ranking in skiing championships. He put his mobile in his pocket. Stared out into the darkness. And it struck him that everyone could see him with the light on and he couldn't see anyone. He got up, closed what was left of the door and switched off the light. Waited. The empty T-bars coming down from the slopes above his head seemed to accelerate as they swung round the end of the lift before starting the ascent again.

Stian blinked.

Why hadn't he thought of that before?

He turned all the knobs on the console. And as the floodlights came on over the slope Jay-Z's "Empire State of Mind" rang out from the loudspeakers and filled the valley. That's the way, now it was a bit more homely.

He drummed his fingers and looked at the spindle

again. There was a hole at the top. He got up, grabbed the string from beside the fuse cupboard, doubled it and threaded it through the hole. Wrapped it round the spindle once and pulled carefully. This could actually work. He pulled a little harder. The string was holding. Even harder. The spindle moved. He yanked it.

The sound of the lift machinery died with a long-drawn-out groan culminating in a squeal.

"Take that, you motherfucker!" Stian shouted.

He leaned over the phone to ring the chairman and inform him the job was done. Remembered the chairman would hardly approve of rap being played at full blast over the speakers at night and switched it off.

Listened to the phone ringing. That was all he could hear now; suddenly it was very quiet. Come on, answer! And then there it was again. The feeling. The feeling that someone was there. Someone was watching him.

Stian Barelli slowly raised his head.

And felt the chill spread from an area at the back of his head, as though he were turning to stone, as though it were Medusa's face he was staring at. But it wasn't hers. It was a man dressed in a long, black leather coat. He had a lunatic's staring eyes and a vampire's open mouth with blood dripping from both corners. And he seemed to be floating above the ground.

"Yes? Hello? Stian? Are you there? Stian?"

But Stian didn't answer. He had stood up, knocked the chair over, edged backwards and clung to the wall, tearing Miss December off the nail and sending her to the floor.

He had found the emergency stop pole. It was protruding from the mouth of the man attached to one of the T-bars.

"Then he was sent round and round on the ski lift?" Gunnar Hagen asked, angling his head and studying the body hanging in front of them. There was something wrong about the shape, like a wax figure melting and being stretched out towards the ground.

"That's what the young man told us," said Beate Lønn, stamping her feet on the snow and looking up the illuminated tramway where her white-clad colleague had almost merged with the snow.

"Found anything?" Hagen asked in a tone that suggested he already knew the answer.

"Loads," Beate said. "The trail of blood carries on four hundred metres to the top of the lift and four hundred metres back again."

"I meant anything apart from the obvious."

"Footprints in the snow from the car park, down the short cut and straight here," Beate said. "The pattern matches the victim's shoes."

"He came here in **shoes**?"

"Yes. And he came alone. There were no prints

other than his. There's a red Golf in the car park. We're checking now to find the owner."

"No signs of the perpetrator?"

"What do you reckon, Bjørn?" Beate asked, turning to Holm, who at that moment was walking towards them with a roll of police tape in his hand.

"Not so far," he panted. "No other footprints. But loads of ski tracks, of course. No visible fingerprints, hair or fabric so far. Perhaps we'll find some on the toothpick." Bjørn Holm nodded towards the pole sticking out of the dead man's mouth. "Otherwise all we can do is hope Pathology might find something."

Gunnar Hagen shivered in his coat. "You make it sound as if you already know you won't find much."

"Well," Beate Lønn said, a "well" Hagen recognised; it was the word Harry Hole used to introduce bad news. "There was no DNA. There weren't any fingerprints to be found at the other crime scene either."

Hagen wondered whether it was the temperature, the fact that he had come straight from his bed or what his Krimteknisk leader had said that made him shiver.

"What do you mean?" he asked, steeling himself.

"I mean I know who it is," Beate said.

"I thought you said you didn't find any ID on him."

"That's correct. And it took me a while to recognise him."

"You? I thought you never forgot a face?"

"The fusiform gyrus gets confused when both cheeks have been smashed in. But that's Bertil Nilsen."

"Who's that?"

"That's why I rang you. He's . . ." Beate Lønn took a deep breath. Don't say it, Hagen thought.

"A policeman," Bjørn Holm said.

"Worked at the police station in Nedre Eiker," Beate said. "We had a murder just before you came to Crime Squad. Nilsen contacted Kripos thinking the case bore similarities to a rape case he'd worked on in Krokstadelva, and offered to come to Oslo to give a hand."

"And?"

"Dead duck. He came, but basically just delayed the proceedings. The man or men were never caught."

Hagen nodded. "Where . . . ?"

"Here," Beate said. "Raped in the ski-lift hut and carved up. Part of the body was found in the lake here, another a kilometre south and a third seven kilometres in the opposite direction, by Lake Aurtjern. That was the reason it was thought there was more than one person involved."

"And the date . . . ?"

". . . is the same, to the day."

"How long . . . ?"

"Nine years ago."

A walkie-talkie crackled. Hagen watched Bjørn Holm lift it to his ear and speak softly. Put it back down. "The Golf in the car park is registered in the name of a Mira Nilsen. Same address as Bertil Nilsen. Must be his wife."

Hagen released his breath with a groan, and it

hung out of his mouth like a white flag. "I'll have to report this to the Chief," he said. "Don't mention the murdered girl for now."

"The press'll find out."

"I know. But I'm going to advise the Chief to let the press speculate for the time being."

"Wise move," Beate said.

Hagen sent her a quick smile, as thanks for very much needed encouragement. Glanced up the mountainside to the car park and the march ahead of him. Looked up at the body. Shivered again. "Do you know who I think of when I see a tall, thin man like that?"

"Yes," Beate Lønn said.

"I wish he was here now."

"He wasn't tall and thin," said Bjørn Holm.

The two others turned to him. "Harry wasn't . . . ?"

"I mean this guy," Holm said, nodding towards the body on the wire. "Nilsen. He got tall overnight. If you feel his body it's like jelly. I've seen the same happen to people who've fallen a long way and crushed all the bones in their body. With the skeleton broken the body hasn't got a frame, and the flesh says follow gravity until rigor mortis sets in. Funny, isn't it?"

They regarded the body in silence. Until Hagen turned on his heel and left.

"Too much information?" Bjørn Holm asked.

"A trifle superfluous perhaps," Beate said. "And I also wish he was here."

"Do you think he'll ever come back?" Bjørn Holm asked.

Beate shook her head. Bjørn Holm didn't know if it was in response to his question or the whole situation. He turned and his eye caught a spruce branch swaying on the edge of the forest. A chilling bird cry filled the silence.

Part Two

6

The bell over the door rang furiously as Truls Berntsen stepped in from the freezing cold street and into
the damp warmth. There was a smell of rotten hair
and hair lotion.

"Trim?" said the young man with the glistening black hairstyle Truls was fairly confident he had
acquired in a different salon.

"Two hundred?" Truls asked, brushing snow off
his shoulders. March, the month of broken promises.
He jerked his thumb over his shoulder to make sure
the board outside was still accurate. Gentlemen 200.
Children 85. Pensioners 75. Truls had seen people
bring their dogs in here.

"Same as always, pal," the hairdresser said in a
Pakistani accent, ushering him into one of the salon's
two free chairs. In the third sat a man Truls immediately categorised as an Arab. Dark terrorist eyes
beneath a fringe plastered to his forehead. Eyes that
darted away in fear after meeting Truls's in the mirror. Perhaps the man could smell bacon, or recognised
the police look. In which case perhaps he was one
of those selling drugs down by Brugata. Just hash.
The Arabs were cautious with harder drugs. Maybe

the Koran equated speed and heroin with a pork chop? Pimp maybe—the gold chain suggested as much. Small-time one, if so. Truls knew the faces of all the big-timers.

On with the babies' bib.

"Hair's got long, pal."

Truls didn't like being called "pal" by Pakis, especially not Paki poofs and extra-especially not Paki poofs who would soon be touching you. But the advantage of these powder-puffs was that at least they didn't rest their hips against your shoulder, tilt their heads, run a hand through your hair, look into your eyes in the mirror and ask whether you want it like this or like that. They just got down to it. They didn't ask if you wanted your greasy hair washed, they just sprayed it with water, ignored any instructions you might have and went for it with scissors and comb as if it were the Australian sheep-shearing championships.

Truls looked at the front page of the newspaper lying on the shelf below the mirror. It was the same refrain: what was the so-called cop killer's motive? Most of the speculation centred on a crazy police-hater or an extreme anarchist. Some mentioned foreign terrorism, but terrorists usually claimed the honour of a successful action, and no one had come forward. No one doubted that the two murders were connected—the dates and the crime scenes saw to that—and for a while the police had searched for a criminal both Vennesla and Nilsen had arrested, questioned or offended in some way. But no such connection could be found. So in the interim they had worked on a theory that Vennesla's murder was one individual's revenge after an arrest, a bout of jealousy, an inheritance or any of the standard motives. And Nilsen's murder was another individual with a different motive, but he had been clever enough to copy Vennesla's murder to fool the police into thinking a serial killer was at work and stop them looking in the obvious places. But then the police had done exactly that, searched in the obvious places as though these were two separate murders. And they didn't find anything there either.

So the police had gone back to square one. A police murderer. And the press had done the same and kept nagging: why can't the police catch the person who has killed two of their own?

Truls felt both satisfaction and anger when he saw these headlines. Mikael had probably been hoping that by Christmas and New Year the press would have forgotten the murders and started focusing on other things, allowing them to work in peace. Letting him continue to be the sexy new sheriff in town, the whizz-kid, the town's guardian. And not someone who failed, who messed up, who sat in front of the flashing cameras with a loser's face radiating dejected Norwegian Rail-style incompetence.

Truls didn't need to look at the papers, he had read them at home. He had laughed out loud at Mikael's feeble statement about where the investigation stood. "At this moment in time it's not possible to say . . ." and "There is no information regarding . . ." They were sentences taken directly from the chapter about handling the press in Bjerknes and Hoff Johansen's **Investigative Methods,** which had been a set text at Police College and in which it said police officers should use these generic quasi-sentences because journalists got so frustrated with "no comment." And also that they should avoid adjectives.

Truls had checked the photos for traces of desperation on Mikael's face, the expression he used to wear when the big boys in Manglerud reckoned it was time to shut the poncy upstart's gob, and Mikael needed help. Truls's help. And of course Truls stepped up. And he was the one who went home with black eyes and thick lips, not Mikael. No, his good looks were spared. For Ulla.

"Don't cut off **too** much," Truls said. He watched his hair falling from his pale, slightly protruding forehead in the mirror. The forehead and the sturdy underbite often led people to assume he was stupid. Which on occasion was an advantage. On occasion. He closed his eyes. Trying to decide whether Mikael's desperate expression was there in the press conference photos or if he saw it only because he wanted to see it.

Suspension. Expulsion. Rejection.

He was still getting his salary. Mikael had been apologetic. Placed a hand on his shoulder and said it was in everyone's best interest, Truls's too. Until it was decided what the consequences would be for a policeman who had received money he couldn't or wouldn't account for. Mikael had even made sure that Truls was entitled to keep some allowances. So it wasn't as if he had to go to cheap hairdressers. He had always come here. But he liked it even better now. He liked having exactly the same haircut as the Arab in the next chair. The terrorist cut.

"What are you laughing at, pal?"

Truls stopped abruptly when he heard his own grunted guffaws. Those which had given him the sobriquet Beavis. No, Mikael had given it to him. During the school party, to the amusement of everyone else, as they discovered, holy shit, that Truls Berntsen did indeed look and sound like the MTV cartoon character! Had Ulla been there? Or was Mikael sitting with his arm round another girl? Ulla with the gentle eyes, with the white sweater, with the slender hand she had once placed on his neck and drawn his head closer, shouted in his ear to drown the roars of the Kawasakis one Sunday in Bryn. She only wanted to ask where Mikael was. But he could still remember the warmth of her hand, it had felt as if it would melt him, make his knees buckle under him on the bridge over the motorway, then and there in the morning sun. And with her breath in his ear and on his cheek, his senses had been working overtime. Even surrounded by the stench of petrol, exhaust and burnt rubber from motorbikes below he could identify her toothpaste, tell her lip gloss was strawberry flavour and that her sweater had been washed in Milo. That Mikael had kissed her. Had had her. Or had he been imagining it? He definitely remembered he had answered he didn't know. Even though he did. Even though part of him had wanted to tell her. Had wanted to crush the gentleness, the purity, the innocence and the naivety in her eyes. To crush him, Mikael.

But of course he hadn't.

Why would he? Mikael was his best friend. His only friend. And what would he have achieved by telling her Mikael was up at Angelica's house. Ulla could get anyone she wanted, and she didn't want him, Truls. As long as she was with Mikael he would at least have a chance to be in her presence. He'd had the opportunity, but not the motive.

Not then.

"That do you, pal?"

Truls looked at the back of his head in the round plastic mirror the poof was holding.

Terrorist cut. Suicide bomber cut. He grunted. Got up, chucked a 200-krone note on the newspaper to avoid hand-to-hand contact. Went out into the March day that was still no more than a rumour that spring was on its way. Glanced up at Police HQ. Started walking towards the metro in Grønland. The haircut had taken nine and a half minutes. He lifted his head, walked faster. He had no deadlines. Nothing to do. Oh, yes, he did have something. But it didn't require much work, and he had his usual resources: time to plan, hatred, the determination to lose everything. He glanced at the shop window in one of the district's Asian food outlets. And confirmed he finally looked like what he was.

● ● ●

Gunnar Hagen sat gazing at the wallpaper above the Chief of Police's desk and empty chair. Focused on the darker patches from the photos that had hung there for as long as anyone could remember. There had been pictures of former police chiefs, probably meant as sources of inspiration, but Mikael Bellman was clearly able to do without them. Without the inquisitorial stares at their successor.

Hagen wanted to drum his fingers on the arm of the chair, but there weren't any arms. Bellman had changed the chairs as well. For hard, low wooden ones.

Hagen had been summoned, and the assistant in the anteroom had shown him in and said the Chief of Police would be along soon.

The door opened.

"There you are!" Bellman rushed round the desk and slumped into the chair. Interlaced his hands behind his head.

"Anything new?"

Hagen coughed. He knew Bellman was aware that there was nothing new, as Hagen had standing orders to pass on the smallest development in the two murder cases. But he did as he was asked, explained that they still didn't have any clues in the cases viewed in isolation, or a connection between the murders, beyond the obvious, that the victims were two policemen who had been found at scenes of earlier unsolved murders they themselves had investigated.

Bellman got up in the middle of Hagen's account

and stood by the window with his back to him. Rocked on his heels. Pretended to listen for a while before breaking in.

"You've got to fix this, Hagen."

Gunnar Hagen stopped. Waited for him to continue.

Bellman turned. There was a redness around the white patches on his face.

"And I have to query your judgement prioritising the twenty-four-hour guard at the Rikshospital when honest policemen are being killed. Shouldn't it be all hands on deck for this investigation?"

Hagen looked at Bellman in amazement. "It isn't my officers doing it; it's the City Centre Police Station and PHS students doing their practicals. I don't think the investigation is suffering, Mikael."

"Isn't it?" Bellman said. "I'd still like you to reconsider your decision. I can't see any impending danger of someone killing the patient after all the time that's passed. They know he'll never be able to testify anyway."

"The doctors say there are signs of improvement."

"The case no longer has priority." The Police Chief's answer came in a hurried, almost angry tone. Then he took a deep breath and turned on the charm. "But mounting a guard is of course your decision. I don't want to be involved. Understood?" he smiled.

It was on the tip of Hagen's tongue to answer no, but he managed to restrain himself and nodded briefly while trying to grasp what Mikael Bellman was after.

"Good," Bellman said, clapping his hands to signal

the meeting was over. Hagen was about to get up, as nonplussed as when he arrived, but instead stayed seated.

"We were thinking of trying a different procedure."

"Oh?"

"Yes," Hagen said. "Dividing the investigative unit into several smaller ones."

"How come?"

"To allow more space for alternative ideas. Big groups have the competence, but are not suitable for thinking outside the box in the same way."

"And we have to think outside . . . the box?"

Hagen ignored the sarcasm. "We're going round in circles and we can't see the wood for the trees."

He eyed the Police Chief. As a former detective Bellman knew the scenario well of course; a group could get stuck in a rut, assumptions hardened into facts and you're unable to see alternative hypotheses. Nevertheless, Bellman shook his head.

"In small groups you lose the ability to see a case through, Hagen. The responsibility is atomised, you get in each other's way and the same job is repeated. One big, well-coordinated group is always best. At least as long as it has a strong, decisive leader . . ."

Hagen felt the uneven surface of his molars as he ground his teeth and hoped the effect of Bellman's insinuation could not be seen in his facial expression.

"But—"

"When a leader starts changing tactics it can easily be interpreted as desperation and an admission that he's failed."

"But we **have** failed, Mikael. It's March now, which means it's six months since the first murder."

"No one will follow a leader who's failed, Hagen."

"My colleagues are neither blind nor stupid. They know we're in a rut. And they also know that good leaders must have the ability to change tack."

"Good leaders know how to inspire their teams."

Hagen swallowed. Swallowed what he wanted to say. That he was lecturing on leadership at the military academy while Bellman was running around with a catapult. That if Bellman was so bloody good at inspiring his subordinates, how about inspiring him—Gunnar Hagen? But he was too tired, too frustrated to swallow the words he knew would irritate Mikael Bellman most.

"We were successful with the independent group Harry Hole led, do you remember? The Ustaoset murders would never have been solved if—"

"I think you heard me, Hagen. I'd prefer to consider changes to the management of the investigation. Management is responsible for the culture among its employees, and now it seems it's not result-orientated enough. If there's nothing else, I have a meeting in a few minutes."

Hagen couldn't believe his ears. He staggered to his feet, as though the blood in his legs hadn't circulated during the short time he had been sitting on the low, narrow chair. Stumbled towards the door.

"By the way," Bellman said behind him and Hagen heard him stifle a yawn, "anything new in the Gusto Hanssen case?"

"As you yourself said," Hagen answered, without turning so as not to show Bellman his face, where—in contrast to his legs—the blood vessels felt as if they were under immense pressure, his voice trembling with fury, "the case no longer has priority."

Mikael Bellman waited until the door closed and he heard Hagen say goodbye to the secretary in the ante-room. Then he slumped into the high-backed leather chair and crumpled. He hadn't summoned Hagen to question him about the police murders, and he had a suspicion Hagen had realised that. The telephone call he had received from Isabelle Skøyen an hour ago had been the cause. She, of course, had rabbited on about how these unsolved murders were making them both look incompetent and impotent. And how, unlike him, she was dependent on the electorate's approval. He had been interspersing the monologue with **mm**s and **oh**s, waiting for her to finish so that he could put the phone down, when she dropped the bombshell.

"He's coming out of the coma."

Bellman sat with his elbows on the table, his head in his hands. Staring down at the desk's shiny varnish in which he could see the blurred contours of himself. Women thought he was good-looking. Isabelle had told him straight out that was why she had chosen him, she liked attractive men. That was why she'd had sex with Gusto. The Elvis lookalike. People often misunderstood when men were good-looking. Mikael thought of the Kripos officer, the one who had tried it on with him, who had wanted to kiss him. He thought of Isabelle. And Gusto. Imagined them together. The three of them together. He got up from the chair abruptly. Went back to the window.

Everything had been set in motion. She had used the expression. **Set in motion.** All he had to do was wait. It should have made him feel calmer, better disposed to the world around him. So why had he plunged the knife into Hagen and turned it? To watch him wriggle? Just to see another tormented face, as tormented as the one reflected in the desk? But soon it would be over. Everything was in her hands now. And when what had to be done was done, they could carry on as before. They could forget Asayev, Gusto and definitely the man no one could stop talking about, Harry Hole. Sooner or later it would all be forgotten, even these police murders, in time.

Mikael Bellman wanted to test if that was what he wanted. But decided against it. He knew it was what he wanted.

7

Ståle Aune inhaled. This was one of the crossroads in the therapy, where he would have to take a decision. He decided.

"There may be something unresolved about your sexuality."

The patient eyed him. Tight-lipped smile. Narrow eyes. The slender hands with the almost abnormally long fingers rose, appeared to be about to straighten the knot of his tie above the pinstriped jacket, but didn't. Ståle had noticed this movement a few times before, and it reminded him of patients who have succeeded in breaking a specific compulsive habit but who can't shake the initial gesture, the hand poised to do something, an uncompleted action, an involuntary though definitely interpretable action. Like a scar, a limp. An echo. A reminder that nothing disappears in its entirety, everything leaves a trace in some way, somewhere. Like childhood. People you have known. Something you ate and couldn't tolerate. A passion you had. Cellular memory.

The patient's hand fell back into his lap. He cleared his throat, and his voice sounded tight and metallic.

"What the hell do you mean? Are we starting on that Freud shit now?"

Ståle looked at the man. He had caught a glimpse of a TV crime series recently in which the police interpreted people's emotional lives: the body language was fine, but it was their voices that gave them away. The muscles in the vocal cords and throat are so finely tuned that they can create sound waves in the form of identifiable words. When Ståle had lectured at PHS he had always emphasised to students what a miracle this was in itself. And he had said there was an even more sensitive instrument—the human ear. Which could not only decode the sound waves as vowels and consonants but also expose the speaker's body temperature, level of tension and feelings. In interviews it was more important to listen than to watch. A tiny rise in key, or an almost imperceptible quiver, was a more significant signal than crossed arms, clenched fists, the size of the pupils and all the factors on which the new wave of psychologists conferred such importance, but which in Ståle's experience more often confused and misled a detective. It was true this patient swore in front of him, but it was still primarily the pattern of pressure on Ståle's eardrums that told him this patient was on his guard and angry. Normally that wouldn't worry the experienced psychologist. On the contrary, strong emotions often meant a breakthrough was imminent. But the problem with this patient was that things came in the wrong sequence. Even after several months of regular sessions Ståle hadn't made contact, there was no closeness, no trust. In fact it had been so unproductive that Ståle had considered recommending they broke off the treatment and perhaps referring the patient to a colleague. Anger in an otherwise secure atmosphere was good, but in this case it could mean the patient was closing himself off further, digging an even deeper trench.

Ståle sighed. He had obviously made the wrong decision, but it was too late, and he decided to plough on.

"Paul," he said. The carefully plucked eyebrows and the two small scars under the chin, suggesting a facelift, had allowed Ståle to categorise him within ten minutes of the first therapy session. "Repressed homosexuality is very normal even in our apparently tolerant society." Aune followed the patient closely to detect a reaction. "I'm often consulted by the police, and one officer told me he was open about his homosexuality in his private life, but he couldn't be open in his job because he would be frozen out. I asked if he was really so sure of that. Oppression often turns out to be the expectations we impose on ourselves and the expectations we interpret those around us as having. Especially those closest, friends and colleagues."

He stopped.

There was no widening of the patient's pupils, no colouring of the complexion, no resistance to eye contact, no evasive body language. On the contrary, a little contemptuous smile had appeared on his thin lips. But, to his surprise, Ståle Aune noticed that the temperature in his own cheeks had risen. My God, how he hated this patient! How he hated this job.

"And the policeman," Paul said, "did he follow your advice?"

"Our time's up," Ståle said without checking the clock.

"I'm curious, Aune."

"And I've taken an oath of confidentiality."

"So let's call him X then. And I can see from your face that you didn't like the question." Paul smiled. "He followed your advice, and there was an unhappy outcome, wasn't there?"

Aune sighed. "X went too far, misunderstood a situation and tried to kiss a colleague in the toilets. And was frozen out. The point is that it **might** have gone well. Would you at least give the matter some thought for next time?"

"But I'm not a homo." Paul raised a hand towards his throat, then lowered it again.

Ståle Aune nodded briefly. "Same time next week?"

"I don't know. I'm not getting better, am I?"

"It's going slowly, but we're making progress," Ståle said. The answer came as automatically as the patient's hand moving towards his tie.

"Yes, you've said that a few times," Paul said. "But I have a feeling I'm paying for nothing. And that you're just as useless as those detectives who can't even nail a bloody serial killer and rapist . . ." Ståle registered with some astonishment that the patient's voice had gone lower. Quieter. His voice and body language communicated something quite different from what he actually said. Ståle's brain had, as if on autopilot, begun to analyse why the patient had used precisely this example, but the answer was so obvious he didn't need to delve very deep. The newspapers lying on Ståle's desk since the autumn. They had always been open at the page describing the police murders.

"It isn't so easy to catch a serial killer, Paul," Ståle Aune said. "I know quite a bit about serial killers, in fact, it's my speciality. Just like this is. But if you feel like stopping the therapy, or you'd like to try one of my colleagues, it's up to you. I have a list of very capable psychologists and can help you—"

"Are you washing your hands of me, Ståle?" Paul had tilted his head to one side, the eyelids with the colourless lashes had closed and the smile was broader. Ståle was unable to decide whether this was a smirk at the homosexuality theory or Paul was showing a glimpse of his true self. Or both.

"Please don't misunderstand," Ståle said, knowing that he had not been misunderstood. He wanted to get rid of him, but professional therapists didn't kick out tricky patients. They just gritted their teeth harder, didn't they? He adjusted his bow tie. "I'd like to treat you, but it's important that we trust each other. And right now it doesn't seem—"

"I'm just having a bad day, Ståle." Paul splayed his hands in defence. "Sorry. I know you're good. You worked on the serial murders at Crime Squad, didn't you? You helped to catch the guy who was drawing pentagrams at crime scenes. You and that inspector."

Ståle studied the patient as he got up and buttoned his jacket.

"Yep, you're more than good enough for me, Ståle.

Next week. And I'll think about whether I'm a homo in the meantime."

Ståle didn't get up. He could hear Paul humming in the corridor while waiting for the lift. There was something familiar about the tune.

As indeed there was about some of the things Paul had said. He had used the expression "serial murders," a police preference, rather than the more common "serial killings." He had called Harry Hole an inspector and most people had no idea about police ranks. Generally they remembered the gory details from the newspaper reports, not insignificant details such as a pentagram carved into a beam beside the body. But what had particularly caught his attention—because it could turn out to be significant for the therapy—was that Paul had compared him to "those detectives who can't even nail a bloody serial killer and rapist . . ."

Ståle heard the lift come and go. But he had remembered what the tune was now. In fact, he had listened to **Dark Side of the Moon** to find out if there were any hints to interpreting Paul Stavnes's dream. The song was called "Brain Damage." It was about lunatics. Lunatics who were on the grass, who were in the hall. Who end up inside.

Rapist.

The murdered policemen hadn't been raped.

Of course the case might have interested him so little that he had confused the murdered policemen with the earlier victims at the crime scene. Or he had assumed as a general rule that serial killers rape. Or he dreamt about raped policemen, which naturally would reinforce the theory about repressed homosexuality. Or . . .

Ståle Aune froze mid-movement and stared in amazement at the hand poised to move towards his bow tie.

Anton Mittet took a sip of coffee and looked down at the man sleeping in the hospital bed. Shouldn't he also feel a certain pleasure? The same pleasure that Mona had expressed, which she had called "one of the small everyday miracles that make all the slog worthwhile"? Well, yes, of course it was good that a coma patient they assumed would die should suddenly change his mind and drag himself back to life and wake up. But the person in the bed, the pale, ravaged face on the pillow meant nothing to him. All it meant was that the job was coming to an end. It didn't necessarily mean it was the end of his relationship with Mona, of course. They hadn't spent their most intimate hours here anyway. On the contrary, now they didn't need to worry if their colleagues noticed the tender gazes they sent each other whenever she went in and out of the patient's room, or the conversations that were just a little too long, the chats that ended a little too abruptly when someone appeared. But Anton Mittet had a nagging feeling that precisely this had been the spark in their relationship. The secrecy. The illicit. The excitement of seeing but not being able to touch. Having to wait, having to sneak away from home, serving up the lie to Laura about another extra shift, a lie which had become easier and easier to perform and which nevertheless filled his mouth and he knew that sooner or later it would suffocate him. He knew that infidelity didn't make him a better man in Mona's eyes and that she could envisage him serving up the same excuses to her at some point in the future. She had told him it had happened to her before with other men, that they had deceived her. And then she had been younger and slimmer than she was now, so if he wanted to drop the fat, middle-aged woman she had become it wouldn't exactly shock her. He had tried to explain to her that she mustn't say things like that, not even if she meant them. It made her less attractive. It made **him** less attractive. Made him into a man who would take anything he could get, as it were. But now he was glad she had said it. It had to stop somewhere, and she had made it easier for him.

"Where did you get the coffee?" the new nurse asked, straightening the round glasses as he read the doctor's notes he unhooked from the end of the bed.

"There's an espresso machine down the corridor. I'm the only person who uses it but you can—"

"Thanks for the offer," the nurse said. Anton could hear there was something odd about his pronunciation. "But I don't drink coffee." The nurse had taken a sheet of paper from his jacket pocket and was reading it. "Let me see . . . he needs to have some propofol."

"I've no idea what that is."

"It means he'll sleep for a good while."

Anton scrutinised the nurse as he pierced the foil on a little bottle of a transparent liquid with a syringe. The nurse was short, slightly built and resembled a famous actor. Not one of the good-looking ones. One of the ones who had made it, though. The one with the ugly teeth and the Italian name it was impossible to remember. The way he had forgotten the name the nurse had given when he introduced himself.

"It's complicated with patients who come out of a coma," the nurse said. "They're extremely vulnerable and have to be carefully brought into a conscious state. One injection out of place and we risk sending them back to where they were."

"I see," Anton said. The man had shown him his ID card, produced the password and waited for Anton to ring the duty room to confirm that the person in question had been scheduled to do this shift.

"So you've had lots of experience with anaesthetics?" Anton asked.

"I worked in the anaesthetics department for long enough, yes."

"But you don't work there now?"

"I've been travelling for two or three years." The nurse held the syringe up to the light. Released a jet that dissolved into a cloud of microscopic drops. "This patient looks as if he's had a hard life. Why's there no name on the notes?"

"He's supposed to be anonymous. Didn't they tell you?"

"They haven't told me anything."

"They should have done. It's thought an attempt may be made on his life. That's why I sit out here in the corridor."

The man leaned down close to the patient's face. Closed his eyes. Looked as if he was inhaling the patient's breath. Anton shivered.

"I've seen him before," the nurse said. "Is he from Oslo?"

"I've taken an oath of confidentiality."

"And what do you think I've done?" The nurse rolled up the patient's sleeve. Flicked the inside of his forearm. There was something about the way the nurse spoke, something Anton couldn't quite put his finger on. He shivered again as the syringe slid into the skin, and in the total silence he thought he could **hear** a rasp, the friction of the needle against flesh. The flow of the liquid being squeezed through the syringe as the plunger was pressed.

"He lived in Oslo for several years before moving abroad," Anton said with a swallow. "But then he returned. Rumours say it was because of a boy. He was a junkie."

"That's a sad story."

"Yes, but it looks as if it will have a happy ending."

"That's a bit too early to say," the nurse said, pulling out the needle. "Lots of coma patients have sudden relapses."

Anton could hear it now. Hear what it was about the way he spoke. It was barely audible, but they were there, the **s**'s. He lisped.

After they had left the room and the nurse had

gone down the corridor, Anton went back in to the patient. He studied the heart monitor. Listened to the rhythmical beeps, like a submarine's sonar signals from the depths of the ocean. He didn't know what made him do it, but he did as the nurse had done, leaned over the man's face. Closed his eyes. And felt the breath on his cheek.

Altman. Anton had taken a close look at his name tag before he left. The nurse's name was Sigurd Altman. He had a gut feeling, that was all. But he had already decided that he would check him out the following day. He didn't want this to turn out like Drammen. He wasn't going to make any mistakes this time.

8

Katrine Bratt sat with her feet on the desk and a telephone pressed between her shoulder and ear. Gunnar Hagen was on another call. Her fingers ran across the keyboard in front of her. She knew that behind her, outside the window, Bergen was bathed in sunshine. That the wet streets were glistening from the rain that had been falling all morning until ten minutes ago. And that with the Bergen law of averages it would soon start to drizzle again. But right now there was a glimpse of sun, and Katrine Bratt hoped Gunnar Hagen would finish on the other line, so that he could resume the conversation he was having with her. She only wanted to hand over the information she had and get out of Bergen Police Station. Into the fresh Atlantic ozone that tasted so much better than the air her former boss was inhaling at that moment in his office in the east of the capital. Before he released it again in the form of an indignant shout:

"What do you mean we can't talk to him yet? Is he out of the coma or not? . . . Yes, I appreciate he's in a fragile state, but . . . What?"

Katrine hoped that what she had spent the last few days finding out would put Hagen in a better mood than he was obviously in now. She scanned the pages, just to check what she already knew.

"I don't give a **shit** what his solicitor says," Hagen said. "And I don't give a **shit** what the consultant says, either. I want him questioned **now**!"

Katrine Bratt heard him smack down the receiver. Then, at last, he was back.

"What was that all about?" she asked.

"Nothing," Hagen said.

"Is it him?" she asked.

Hagen sighed. "Yes, it's him. He's coming out of the coma, but they're doping him up and saying we have to wait at least two days before we can talk to him."

"Isn't it wise to tread warily?"

"Probably. But as you know we need some results now. The police murders have us on our knees."

"Two days won't make much difference."

"I know, I know. But I have to do a bit of barking. I mean, that's half the point of climbing your way to the top. Isn't it?"

Katrine Bratt had no answer to that. She'd never had any interest in becoming a boss. And even if she had, she had a suspicion that detectives who had done time in psychiatric wards would not be first in the queue when the big, spacious offices were being allocated. The diagnosis had shifted from manic depression via borderline personality disorder to bipolar and healthy. At least as long as she took the small pink pills to keep her on an even keel. They could criticise the use of pills in psychiatry as much as they liked, for Katrine they had meant a new and better life. But she noticed that her boss kept a watchful eye on her, and that she wasn't being given more work in the field than absolutely necessary. That was fine, though; she liked sitting in her cramped office with a high-spec computer and exclusive access to search engines even the police didn't know about. Looking, searching, finding. Tracking down people who had apparently vanished from the surface of the earth. Seeing patterns where others only see chance. That was Katrine Bratt's speciality and more than once it had been of benefit to Kripos and Crime Squad in Oslo. So they would have to put up with the walking psychosis.

"You said you had something for me."

"It's been quiet in the department for the last few weeks, so I've been having a look at the murdered police officers."

"Did your boss at Bergen tell you . . . ?"

"No, no, no. I thought it was better than gawping at Pornhub and playing patience."

"I'm all ears."

Katrine could hear that Hagen was trying to sound positive, but was unable to conceal his despair. He had probably got sick of his hopes being raised only to be dashed in the following months.

"I've gone through the data to see if there were any recurrent names in the original rapes and murders in Maridalen and by Lake Tryvann."

"Thanks, Katrine, but we've done that, too. Ad nauseam, one might say."

"I know. But I work in a slightly different way, you see."

Deep sigh. "Go on then."

"I noticed there were different teams on the two cases. Only two officers from Krimteknisk and three detectives were on both. And none of the five could have had a complete picture of who was brought in for questioning. As neither of the cases was cleared up, it was a protracted affair and the case file was enormous."

"Enormous—you can say that again. And naturally it's right that no one can remember everything that happened during the investigation. But everyone who was brought in for questioning is on the police central registration system. That goes without saying."

"That's exactly the point," Katrine said.

"What's exactly the point?"

"When people are brought in for questioning, they're registered and the interview is filed according to the case they're brought in for. But sometimes things fall between two stools, such as if the interviewee is already in prison—then the interview is an informal matter in the cell and the person isn't registered as he's already on the register."

"But the notes from the interview are still in the case file."

"Normally, yes. But not if this interview is primarily about another case for which he is the prime suspect, and for example, the murder in Maridalen was only a minor part of the interview, a routine long shot. Then the whole interview is filed under the first case and a search wouldn't link him to the second case."

"Interesting. And you've found . . . ?"

"A person who was questioned as a prime suspect in a rape case in Ålesund while he was inside for the assault and attempted rape of an underage girl at a hotel in Otta. During the interview he was also asked about the Maridal case, but afterwards the interview was filed under the Otta rape. The interesting thing is that this person was also hauled in for the Tryvann case, but on that occasion in the usual manner."

"And?" For the first time she could hear signs of genuine interest in Hagen's voice.

"He had an alibi for all three cases," Katrine said, and she felt rather than heard the air go out of the balloon she had inflated for him.

"I see. Any other amusing stories from Bergen you think I should hear today?"

"There's more," Katrine said.

"I have a meeting in—"

"I checked the man's alibi. It's the same for all three cases. A witness who confirmed he was at home. The witness was a young lady who at that time was regarded as reliable. No record, no connection with the suspect, apart from them lodging in the same house. But if you follow the link to her name into the future, interesting things happen."

"Such as?"

"Such as embezzlement, drug dealing and forging documents. If you look a bit more closely at the interviews she's been summoned to since then, there's a common theme running through them. Guess what it is."

"False statements."

"Unfortunately, we're not in the habit of looking at old cases in a new light. At least not cases that are as old and complex as the Maridalen and Tryvann ones."

"What's the woman's name, for goodness' sake?" The interest was back in his voice.

"Irja Jacobsen."

"Have you got an address for her?"

"Yes. She's in the police registration system, the national register and a couple of others—"

"Well, for goodness' sake, let's get her in now!"

"—such as the missing persons register."

There was a long silence coming from Oslo. Katrine felt like going for a walk, down to the fishing boats in Bryggen, buying a bag of cod heads, heading home to her flat in Møhlenpris and slowly making dinner and watching **Breaking Bad** while, hopefully, it started to rain again.

"Great," Hagen said. "Well, at least you've given us something to get our teeth into. What's the name of the guy?"

"Valentin Gjertsen."

"And where is he?"

"That's the point," Katrine Bratt said, and could hear she was repeating herself. Her fingers flitted across the keyboard. "I can't find him."

"Is he missing too?"

"He's not on the missing persons list. And that's strange because it's as if he's vanished off the face of the earth. No known address, no registered phones, no use of credit card, not even a registered bank account. Didn't vote at the last election, hasn't caught a train or a plane in the last year."

"Have you tried Google?"

Katrine laughed until she realised Hagen wasn't joking.

"Relax," she said. "I'll find him."

They rang off. And Katrine got up, put on her jacket and started to hurry; clouds were already on their way across the island of Askøy. She was about to switch off her computer when she remembered something. Something Harry Hole had once said to her. About how often you forget to check the patently obvious. She typed quickly. Waited for the page to come up.

She noticed heads turn in the open-plan office as she let rip with a few Bergen oaths. But she couldn't be bothered to reassure them that this was not a psychosis in full bloom. As usual, Harry had been right.

She picked up the phone and pressed redial. Gunnar Hagen answered on the second ring.

"Thought you had a meeting," Katrine said.

"Postponed. I'm detailing people to find this Valentin Gjertsen."

"You don't need to. I've just found him."

"Oh?"

"It's not so weird that he's vanished off the face of the earth. In fact he **has** vanished off the face of the earth, I think."

"Are you saying . . . ?"

"He's dead, yes. It's in black and white in the national register. Sorry for this ditsiness from Bergen. I'll go home and eat fish heads in shame."

By the time she put down the receiver, it was raining.

Anton Mittet looked up from his cup of coffee as Gunnar Hagen rushed into the almost deserted canteen on the sixth floor of Police HQ. Anton had been staring at the view for some time. Thinking. Of how it could have been. And reflecting on the fact that he had stopped thinking about how it could be. Perhaps this was what it was like getting old. He had lifted the cards he had been dealt, he had seen them. You didn't get new ones. So all that was left was to play the ones you had as well as you could. And dream about the cards you **might** have been given.

"Sorry I'm late, Anton," Gunnar Hagen said, slumping down in the chair opposite him. "A hare-brained call from Bergen. How's it going?"

Anton shrugged. "Don't stop working. I watch the young 'uns passing me on the way up. I try to give them some advice, but they don't see any reason to listen to a middle-aged man who hasn't made it. They seem to think life's a red carpet rolled out just for them."

"And at home?" Hagen asked.

Anton repeated the shrug. "Fine. Wife moans that I work too hard. But when I'm at home she moans just as much. Sound familiar?"

Hagen made a non-committal sound that could have meant whatever the listener wanted it to mean.

"Do you remember your wedding day?"

"Yes," Hagen said, casting a discreet glance at the clock. Not because he didn't know what the time was, but to give Anton a hint.

"The worst thing is that you really mean it when you're standing up there saying yes for all eternity." Anton gave a hollow laugh and shook his head.

"Was there something specific you wanted to talk to me about?" Hagen asked.

"Yes." Anton ran a forefinger down his nose. "There was a nurse there while I was on duty last night. He seemed a bit fishy. Dunno exactly what it was, but you know old hands like us notice these things. So I checked up on him. Turns out he was involved in some murder case several years ago. He was released, eliminated from inquiries. But nevertheless."

"I see."

"Thought it best to talk to you about it. You could talk to hospital management. Perhaps get him discreetly moved."

"I'll take care of the matter."

"Thank you."

"Thank **you.** Well done, Anton."

Anton Mittet half bowed. He was happy to hear Hagen thanking him. Happy because the monk-like Crime Squad boss was the only man in the force he felt any sort of gratitude towards. It had been Hagen who had saved Anton's skin after the Case. He had rung the Police Commissioner in Drammen and said they were being too hard on Anton and that if they didn't need his experience in Drammen they did at Police HQ in Oslo. And that was what had happened. Anton had worked on the first floor in Grønland, but lived in Drammen, which was the condition that Laura had set. And as Anton Mittet caught the lift down to the first floor, he could feel he had more of a spring in his step, a straighter back and even a smile on his lips. And he felt, yes he did, this could be the beginning of something good. He would buy some flowers for . . . He deliberated. For Laura.

Katrine stared out of the window as she tapped in the number. Her flat was on what Norwegians called the high ground floor. It was high enough for her not to see people passing outside, low enough to see the tops of their opened umbrellas. And behind the raindrops trembling on the windowpane in the gusting wind she could see Puddefjord Bridge linking the town with a hole in the mountain on the Laksevåg side. But right now she was looking at the fifty-inch TV screen, where a chemistry teacher and cancer victim was cooking up methamphetamine. Which she found strangely entertaining. She had bought the TV under her personal slogan, why should single men have the biggest TVs? And had her DVDs arranged and categorised according to highly subjective criteria under the Marantz player. The first and second places, furthest to the left on the classics shelf, were taken by **Sunset Boulevard** and **Singin' in the Rain** while more recent films on the shelf beneath had a surprising new leader: **Toy Story 3.** Shelf number three was devoted to the CDs that for sentimental reasons she hadn't given to the Salvation Army even though she had copied them onto her hard drive. She had narrow taste in music: exclusively glam rock and progressive pop, preferably British and often of the androgynous variety: David Bowie, Sparks, Mott the Hoople, Steve Harley, Marc Bolan, Small Faces, Roxy Music, with Suede as a contemporary bookend.

The chemistry teacher was having one of the recurrent arguing-with-the-wife scenes. Katrine put the DVD player on fast forward while ringing Beate.

"Lønn." The voice was high-pitched, girlish almost. And the response revealed no more than was necessary. In Norway, didn't answering with the surname imply there was a bigger family, that you had to specify which Lønn you wanted? However, in this case, Lønn was just Beate Lønn, the widow, and her son.

"Katrine here."

"Katrine! It's been a long time. What are you doing?"

"Watching TV. And you?"

"Being beaten at Monopoly by this young man. Comfort eating. Pizza."

Katrine racked her brain. How old was her son now? Old enough to beat his mum at Monopoly anyway. Another reminder how terrifyingly fast time went. Katrine was about to add she was comfort eating as well. Cod heads. But remembered it had become a cliché among women, a kind of ironic, quasi-depressed phrase single girls were expected to use rather than telling it like it was: that she didn't think she could live without total freedom. Over the years she had sometimes thought she should contact Beate just for a chat. Chat the way she used to do with Harry. She and Beate were both unattached police officers in their thirties, they had grown up with policemen as fathers, they were of above-average intelligence, realists without illusions or even the desire for a prince on a white charger. Well, maybe the horse, if it would take them where they wanted to go.

They could have had so much to talk about.

But she had never got round to ringing. Unless it was about work, of course.

They were similar in that respect as well.

"I'm ringing about one Valentin Gjertsen," Katrine said. "Deceased sex offender. Do you know anything about him?"

"Hang on," Beate said.

Katrine could hear a flurry of fingers on a keyboard and noted another thing they had in common. They were always online.

"Ah, him," Beate said. "I've seen him a few times."

Katrine realised that Beate had his picture on the screen. They said that Beate Lønn's fusiform gyrus, the part of the brain that recognises faces, contained all the people she had ever met. In her case, the line "I never forget a face" was quite literally true. It was said she had been examined by brain researchers as she was one of the thirty-odd people in the world who were known to have this ability.

"He was questioned about the Tryvann and Maridalen cases," Katrine said.

"Yes, I can recall that vaguely," Beate said. "But I seem to remember he had alibis for both."

"One of the people in the house where he lived swore he'd been at home on the nights in question. What I'm wondering is if you took his DNA?"

"I can't imagine we would do that if he had an alibi. In those days, analysing DNA was a complicated and expensive process. At most it would have been done for prime suspects, and only then if we had nothing else."

"I know, but once you got your own DNA-testing department at the Institute you started checking the DNA on cold cases, didn't you?"

"Yes, we did, but in fact there were no biological traces at Maridalen or Tryvann. And if I'm not mistaken, Valentin Gjertsen received his punishment, with interest."

"Oh?"

"Yes, he was killed."

"I knew he was dead, but not . . ."

"Yes, indeed. While serving his sentence at Ila. He was found in his cell. Beaten to a pulp. Inmates don't like people who've molested small girls. The guilty party was never caught. Not certain anyone tried hard to find out who it was anyway."

Silence.

"Sorry I couldn't help," Beate said. "And he's got me playing Try Your Luck now, so . . ."

"Let's hope it turns," Katrine said.

"What?"

"Your luck."

"Exactly."

"Just one last thing," Katrine said. "I'd like to have a chat with Irja Jacobsen, the woman who gave Valentin his alibi. She's down as a missing person. But I've been doing some research."

"Oh yes?"

"No changes of address, tax payments, social security payments or credit card purchases. No trips or mobile phone calls. If there's so little activity, a person generally falls into one of two categories. The most common is they're dead. But then I found something. Lotto. She'd registered for a flutter. Twenty kroner."

"She played lotto?"

"Maybe she was hoping her luck would turn. Anyway, it means she belongs to the second category."

"Which is?"

"Those actively trying not to be found."

"And now you want me to help you find her?"

"I've got her last known address in Oslo and the address of the kiosk where she filled in the numbers. And I know she was on drugs."

"OK," Beate said. "I'll check with our undercover guys."

"Thanks."

"OK."

Pause.

"Anything else?"

"No. Yes. What do you think of **Singin' in the Rain**?"

"I don't like musicals. Why?"

"Soulmates are hard to find, don't you think?"

Beate chuckled. "True. Let's talk about that some-time."

They hung up.

Anton was sitting with his arms crossed. Listening to the silence. He looked down the corridor.

Mona was in with the patient now, and soon she would be coming out. And giving him that mischievous smile. Perhaps laying a hand on his shoulder. Caressing his hair. Maybe a fleeting kiss, letting him feel her tongue, which always tasted of mint, and then she would be off down the corridor. Wiggling her voluptuous bottom in that teasing way. Perhaps she didn't mean to do it, but he liked to think she did. That she tightened her muscles, rolled her hips, strutted her stuff for him, for Anton Mittet. Yes, he had a lot to be grateful for, as they said.

He looked at his watch. Soon be change of shift. Was about to yawn when he heard a cry.

That was enough for him to jump to his feet. He tore open the door. Scanned the room from left to right, confirmed that Mona and the patient were the only two there.

Mona was standing beside the bed with her mouth open. She hadn't looked up from the patient.

"Is he . . . ?" Anton started to say, but he didn't complete the sentence when he heard it was still there. The sound of the heart monitor was so piercing—

and the silence was otherwise so total—he could hear the short, regular beeps from the corridor.

Mona's fingertips rested on the point where the collarbone meets the sternum, what Laura called the "jewel pit" because that was where it lay, the gold heart he had given Laura on one of the wedding anniversaries they had marked in their own way. Perhaps that was also where women's real hearts rose when they were scared, worked up or out of breath, for Laura put her fingers in exactly the same place. And it was as though this spot, so like Laura's, held his full attention. Even when Mona beamed at him and whispered, as if frightened to wake the patient, the words seemed to come from somewhere else.

"He spoke. **He spoke**."

It took Katrine no more than three minutes to slip through the familiar back alleys into the Oslo Police District system, but it was harder to find the interview tapes of the rape case at the Otta Hotel. The imposed digitalisation of all sound and film recordings was already well under way but it was a different matter with the indexing. Katrine had tried all the search words she could think of—Valentin Gjertsen, Otta Hotel, rape and so on—with no luck, and had almost given up when a man's high-pitched voice filled the room.

"She was asking for it, wasn't she?"

Katrine felt an electric shock go through her body, like when she and her father had been sitting in the boat and he calmly announced he had a bite. She didn't know why, she only knew this was the voice. This was him.

"Interesting," said another voice. Low, almost ingratiating. The voice of a policeman pushing for a result. "What makes you say that?"

"They do ask for it, don't they? In some way or another. And afterwards they're ashamed and report you to the police. But you know all that."

"So this girl at the Otta Hotel, she was asking for it, is that what you're saying?"

"She would have been."

"If you hadn't raped her before she had a chance?"

"If I'd been there."

"You admitted just now that you'd been there that night, Valentin."

"To get you to describe the rape in a bit more detail. It's pretty boring sitting in a cell, you know. You have to . . . spice up the day as best you can."

Silence.

Then Valentin's high-pitched laughter. Katrine shuddered and pulled her cardigan tighter around her.

"You look like someone's pissed . . . what is that expression, Officer?"

Katrine closed her eyes and recalled his face.

"Let's put the Otta case to one side for a moment. What about the girl in Maridalen, Valentin?"

"What about her?"

"It was you, wasn't it?"

Loud laughter this time. "You'll have to practise that one a bit harder, Officer. The confrontation stage of the interview has to have a punch like a piledriver, not a pat on the head."

Katrine could hear that Valentin's vocabulary extended beyond that of most inmates.

"So you deny it?"

"No."

"No?"

"No."

Katrine could hear the quivering excitement as the policeman took a deep breath and said with hard-won composure: "Does that mean . . . that you admit committing the rape and murder in Maridalen in September?" At least he was experienced enough to specify what he hoped Valentin would answer yes to, so that the defence counsel couldn't claim afterwards that the accused had misunderstood which case they were actually talking about. But she also heard the merriment in the interviewee's voice as he answered:

"It means I don't need to deny it."

"What the h—"

"It starts with an 'a' and finishes in an 'i.' "

Short pause.

"How can you tell me off the top of your head that you've definitely got an alibi for that night, Valentin? It's quite a long time ago."

"Because I was thinking about it when he told me. What I was doing at that very moment."

"Who told you what?"

"The guy who raped the girl."

Long pause.

"Are you messing us about, Valentin?"

"What do you think, Officer Zachrisson?"

"What makes you think that's my name?"

"Snarliveien 41. Am I right?"

Another pause. More laughter and Valentin's voice. "In your porridge, that's what it is. You look like someone's pissed in your porridge."

"Where did you find out about the rape?"

"This is a prison for pervs, Officer. What do you think we talk about? Thank you for sharing that with me, as we say. He didn't think he was giving that much away, but I read the papers, and I remember the case well."

"So who was it, Valentin?"

"So when will it be, Zachrisson?"

"When?"

"When can I count on being let out if I grass?"

Katrine felt an urge to fast-forward, past the repeated pauses.

"I'll be back in a while."

A chair scraped. A door was closed gently.

Katrine waited. She heard the man inhaling and exhaling. And felt something strange. She was having difficulty breathing. It was as if his breathing in the speakers was sucking the life out of her sitting room.

The policeman could hardly have been away for more than a couple of minutes, but it felt like half an hour.

"OK," he said with a scrape of the chair again.

"That was quick. And my sentence will be commuted as well?"

"You know we're not responsible for sentencing,

Valentin. But we'll talk to a judge, all right? So who's your alibi and who raped the girl?"

"I was at home all night. I was with my landlady and unless she's suffering from Alzheimer's she'll confirm that."

"How come you can remember just like that?"

"I have a thing about noting dates of rapes. If you don't find the lucky man at once I know that sooner or later you'll come asking me where I was."

"I see. And now for the sixty-four-thousand-dollar question. Who did it?"

The answer was articulated slowly and with overly precise diction. "Ju-das Jo-hansen. An old acquaintance of the police, as they say."

"Judas Johansen?"

"You work in Vice and you don't recognise the name of a notorious rapist, Zachrisson?"

The sound of shuffling feet. "What makes you think I don't recognise the name?"

"Your expression is as blank as outer space, Zachrisson. Johansen is the greatest rapist talent since . . . well, since me. And there's a murderer inside him. He doesn't know that yet himself, but it's just a question of time before the murderer wakes up, believe me."

Katrine imagined she heard the clunk of the salivating policeman's jaw as it fell. She listened to the crackling silence. She thought she could hear the officer's pulse racing, the sweat springing from his brow as he tried to rein in the excitement and the nerves now that he knew he was close to the moment, the great breakthrough, the feather in the detective's cap.

"How, how—" Zachrisson stammered, but was interrupted by a howl which was distorted in the speakers and which Katrine eventually realised was laughter. Valentin's laughter. The shrill howls mutated gradually into long, gasping sobs.

"I'm pulling your leg, Zachrisson. Judas Johansen is a homo. He's in the cell next to me."

"What?"

"Do you want to hear a story that's much more interesting than the one you came up with? Judas fucked a young lad and they were caught red-handed, so to speak, by the mother. Unfortunately for Judas the boy was still in the closet and the family was of the rich, conservative variety. So they reported Judas for rape. Judas! Who'd never hurt a fly. Or is it a flea? Fly, flea. Fly. Flea. Anyway, what do you think about taking up that case if you get a tip-off? I can tell you a thing or two about what the lad's been up to since then. I take it the offer of time off is still on the table?"

Chair legs scraped on the floor. The bang of a chair falling backwards. A click and silence. The tape recorder had been switched off.

Katrine sat staring at the computer screen. Noticed that darkness had fallen outside. The cod heads had gone cold.

"Yes, yes, yes," Anton Mittet said. "He **spoke**!"

Anton Mittet was standing in the corridor with the phone to his ear while checking the ID cards of two doctors who had arrived. Their faces showed a mixture of surprise and annoyance. Surely he could remember them?

Anton waved them through and they hurried in to the patient.

"But what did he say?" Gunnar Hagen asked on the phone.

"She only heard him mumble something, not what he said."

"Is he awake now?"

"No, there was just some mumbling and then he was gone again. But the doctors say he could wake up at any moment."

"I see," Hagen said. "Keep me posted, OK? Ring any time. Whenever."

"OK."

"Good. Good. The hospital has standing orders to contact me as well, as far as that goes, but . . . yes, well, they have their own things to think about."

"Of course."

"Yes, they do, don't they?"

"Yes, they do."

"Yes."

Anton listened to the silence. Was there something Gunnar Hagen wanted to say?

The head of Crime Squad rang off.

9

Katrine landed at Gardermoen at half past nine, got on the airport express, let it take her right through Oslo. Or, to be precise, beneath Oslo. She had lived here, but the few glimpses she caught of the town didn't evoke any sentimentality. A half-hearted skyline. Low, good-natured, soft, snowy ridges, tamed countryside. Inside the train, closed, expressionless faces, none of the spontaneous, casual communication between strangers she was used to in Bergen. Then there was a signal failure on one of the world's most expensive lines and the train came to a standstill in the pitch-black tunnel.

She had justified her application for a trip to Oslo with the fact that there were three unsolved rape cases in their own police district—Hordaland—which bore some resemblance to the cases that Valentin could conceivably have been behind. She had argued that if they could nab Valentin for these cases that might indirectly help Kripos and Oslo Police District with the murders of their officers.

"And why can't we leave it to Oslo Police to do this themselves?" the head of the Crime Squad in Bergen, Knut Müller-Nilsen, asked her.

"Because they have a crime clearance rate of twenty point eight per cent and we have one of forty point one."

Müller-Nilsen had laughed out loud, and Katrine knew the plane ticket was hers.

The train started with a jolt and the carriage resounded with sighs: of relief, irritation and desperation. She got out at Sandvika and caught a taxi to Eiksmarka.

It stopped outside Jøssingveien 33. She stepped into the grey slush. Apart from the high fence around the red-brick building there was little about Ila Prison and Detention Centre to betray the fact that it housed some of the country's worst killers, drug profiteers and sex offenders. Among others. The prison statutes said it was a national institution for male prisoners who . . . "needed special help."

Help, so that they wouldn't escape. Help, so that they wouldn't mutilate others. Help with what sociologists and criminologists for some reason believe is a wish the species as a whole shares: to be good human beings, to make a contribution in the flock, to function in society.

Katrine had spent enough time in the psychiatric ward in Bergen to know that as a rule even non-criminal deviants had no interest in society's welfare, and no experience of any company other than their own and their demons, they just wanted to be left in peace. Which did not necessarily imply they wanted to leave others in peace.

She went through the security channels, showed

her ID card and the permit she had received by email and was ushered into the reception room.

A prison officer waiting for her stood with legs apart, arms crossed and keys rattling. More swagger and feigned self-assurance because the visitor was police, the Brahmin caste in law and order, who receive special treatment from prison officers, security guards and even parking wardens.

Katrine behaved as she always did in such cases: she was politer and friendlier than her true nature craved.

"Welcome to the sewer," the prison warder said, a phrase Katrine was fairly sure he didn't use with his standard clientele, but which he had prepared carefully in advance, one that signalled the right mixture of black humour and realistic cynicism towards his job.

But the image was in a sense not inappropriate, Katrine thought, as they walked through the prison corridors. Or perhaps they ought to be called the bowels of the system. The place where the law's digestive tracts broke down individuals found guilty into a stinking brown mass, which at some point would have to be released. All the doors were closed, the corridors empty.

"Pervs unit," the warder said, unlocking an iron door at the end of the corridor.

"So they have their own unit?"

"Yes. If all the sex offenders are in one section there's less chance of their neighbours doing them in."

"Doing them in?" Katrine said, shamming surprise.

"Yes, sex offenders are hated as much here as in the rest of society. If not more. And we have killers here with less self-control than you or me. So on a bad day . . ." He drew a key across his throat in a dramatic gesture.

"They're **killed**?" Katrine exclaimed with horror in her voice, wondering for a moment if she had gone too far. But the warden didn't appear to notice.

"Well, maybe not killed. But they pay. There's a constant stream of pervs with broken arms and legs. Saying they fell down the stairs or slipped in the shower. Can't blow the whistle, can they?" He locked the door behind them and breathed in. "Can you smell that? It's sperm on hot radiators. Dries at once. The smell seems to eat into the metal and it's impossible to get rid of. Reeks like burnt flesh, doesn't it?"

"Homunculus," Katrine said, inhaling. All she could smell was fresh paint on the walls.

"Eh?"

"In the 1600s people believed sperm contained tiny people, homunculi," she said. Seeing the officer's glower, she guessed that had been a blunder, she should have pretended to be shocked.

"So," she hastened to add, "Valentin was safely banged up here with others of his ilk?"

The warder shook his head. "Someone started a rumour that he'd raped the girls in Maridalen and Tryvann. And it's different for inmates who've molested underage kids. Even a notorious rapist hates a child-fucker."

Katrine recoiled, and this time it wasn't put on.

It was mainly because of the casual way in which he pronounced the word.

"So Valentin got a going-over?"

"You could certainly say that."

"And this rumour. Any idea who started it?"

"Yes," the warder said, unlocking the next door. "You did."

"We did? The police?"

"A policeman came here purporting to question cons about the two cases. But I was told he leaked more info than he got."

Katrine nodded. She had heard about it, cases where the police were certain that an inmate was guilty of child abuse, but they couldn't prove it and so they made sure he got his punishment in other ways. You just had to inform the right prisoner. The one with the most power. Or the least control.

"And you accepted that?"

The warder shrugged. "What can we prison guards do?" And added in a lower voice: "And perhaps in this particular case we weren't so averse . . ."

They passed a recreation room.

"What do you mean?"

"Valentin Gjertsen was a sick bastard. Evil through and through. The sort of person you wonder what our Lord put him on this earth for. We had a female officer here he—"

"Oh, hello, there you are."

The voice was soft, and Katrine turned automatically to the left. Two men were standing by a dartboard. She met the smiling gaze of the man who had spoken, a thin man probably in his late thirties. The last remaining strands of blond hair were combed back across a red scalp. Skin disease, Katrine thought. Or maybe there was a solarium here since they needed special help.

"Thought you'd never get here." The man slowly pulled the darts from the board while holding her gaze. Took a dart, threw it into the flesh-red centre of the board, bullseye. Grinned as he wriggled the dart up and down, pushing it in deeper. Pulled it out. Made sucking noises with his lips. The other man didn't laugh as Katrine had expected. Instead he watched his partner with a concerned expression.

The warder caught Katrine gently under the arm to pull her away, but she raised her arm to free herself, her brain whirring at full speed searching for a retort. It rejected the obvious one about darts and organ size.

"Less Cillit Bang in your hair gel maybe?"

She strolled on, but was aware that if she hadn't hit bullseye, she had been close. A red tinge spread across the man's face; then he mounted an even broader smile and made a kind of salute.

"Did Valentin have anyone he could talk to?" Katrine asked as the warder opened the cell door.

"Jonas Johansen."

"Is he the one they call Judas?"

"Yep. Did time for raping a man. Not many of them around."

"Where is he now?"

"He hopped it."

"How?"

"We don't know."

"You don't know?"

"Listen, there are a lot of bad people here, but we're not a high-security unit. In this unit we have people with reduced sentences. There were lots of mitigating circumstances about Judas's verdict. And Valentin was only in for attempted rape. Serial offenders are kept elsewhere. So we don't waste resources guarding the ones we've got. We have a roll call every morning, and on the odd occasion there's someone missing, everyone has to go back to their cells so that we can find out who it is. But if the number tallies, things rumble along in the usual groove. So that was how we found out that Johansen was gone, and we reported it to the police. I didn't think much about it until afterwards when our hands were full with the other case."

"You mean . . . ?"

"Yes, the murder of Valentin."

"So Judas wasn't here when that happened?"

"Right."

"Who could have killed him, do you think?"

"I don't know."

Katrine nodded. The answer was a bit too pat, a bit too quick.

"I promise this won't go any further. I'm asking you who do **you** think killed Valentin?"

The warder sucked his teeth, scrutinising Katrine carefully. As though checking whether he had missed anything on first inspection.

"There were lots of people here who hated and feared Valentin. Some might have realised it was him or them—he had a thirst for revenge. The man who killed him definitely had some thirst in him, too. Valentin was . . . what shall I say?" Katrine watched the officer's Adam's apple go up and down above his collar. "The body was smashed to jelly. I've never seen anything like it."

"Hit with a blunt instrument perhaps?"

"I don't know anything about that, but he was definitely beaten until he was unrecognisable. The face was mincemeat. Had it not been for the terrible tattoo on his chest I don't know that we would have been able to identify him. I'm not overly sensitive, but I had hellish nightmares about it afterwards."

"What sort of tattoo was it?"

"What **sort**?"

"Yes, wh . . ." Katrine noticed she was slipping out of the friendly police officer role and pulled herself together, so as not to reveal her irritation. "What was the tattoo of?"

"Well, who knows? There was a face. Gruesome. Sort of drawn out at the sides. As if it was stuck and was struggling to break away."

Katrine nodded slowly. "Couldn't get away from the body it was trapped in?"

"Yes, that's it, yes. Do you know—?"

"No," Katrine said. But I know the feeling, she thought. "And you didn't ever find this Judas again?"

"**You** didn't ever find Judas again."

"No. Why **didn't** we, do you think?"

The warder shrugged. "How would I know? I do know, however, that Judas isn't top priority for you. As I said, there were mitigating circumstances, and the risk of any repetition was minimal. He would soon have done his time, but the idiot must have got the fever."

Katrine nodded. Demob fever. The date approaches, the prisoner starts thinking about freedom and suddenly being locked up for another day is intolerable.

"Is there anyone else here who can tell me about Valentin?"

The warder shook his head. "Apart from Judas, no one wanted anything to do with him. Shit, he intimidated people. Something seemed to happen to the air when he came into a room."

Katrine stood asking more questions until she realised she was trying to justify the time and her plane ticket.

"You started to tell me about what Valentin had done," she said.

"Did I?" he said quickly, looking at his watch. "Oops, I've got to . . ."

On the way back through the recreation room Katrine saw only the thin man with the red scalp. He was standing straight, his arms at his side, staring at the empty dartboard. No darts anyway. He turned slowly, and Katrine couldn't help but return his gaze. The grin was gone, and his eyes were matt and as grey as jellyfish.

He shouted something. Four words which were

repeated. Loud and piercing, like a bird warning others of danger. Then he laughed.

"Don't worry about him," the warder said.

The laughter behind them faded as they hurried down the corridor.

Then she was outside and breathing in the dank, rain-soaked air.

She took out her phone, switched off the voice recorder, which had been on all the time she had been inside, and called Beate.

"Finished at Ila," she said. "Got time now?"

"I'll put the coffee machine on."

"Agh, haven't you—?"

"You're police, Katrine. You drink machine coffee, OK?"

"Listen, I used to eat at Café Sara in Torggata, and you need to get out of your lab. Lunch. I'm paying."

"Yes, you are."

"Oh?"

"I've found her."

"Who?"

"Irja Jacobsen. She's alive. At least if we hurry."

They agreed to meet in three-quarters of an hour and rang off. While Katrine was waiting for a taxi she played the recording, winding forward to the end and Red Scalp's repeated warning cries.

"Valentin's alive. Valentin kills. Valentin's alive. Valentin kills."

• • •

"He woke up this morning," Anton Mittet said as he and Gunnar Hagen rushed down the corridor.

Silje got up from her chair when she saw them coming.

"You can go now, Silje," Anton said. "I'll take over."

"But your shift isn't for another hour."

"You can go, I said. Take the time off."

She sent Anton an appraising look. Observed the other man.

"Gunnar Hagen," he said, leaning forward with a hand outstretched. "Head of Crime Squad."

"I know who you are," she said, shaking his hand. "Silje Gravseng. I hope to work for you one day."

"Great," he said. "You can start by doing as Anton says."

She nodded to Hagen. "It's your name on my orders, so of course . . ."

Anton watched as she packed her things in her bag.

"By the way, this is the last day of my practical training," she said. "Now I have to start thinking about exams."

"Silje's a police trainee," Anton said.

"Student at Politihøyskole, PHS, it's called now," Silje said. "There was one thing I was wondering about, Politioverbetjent."

"Yes?" Hagen said, smiling wryly at the long words she used.

"This legend who worked for you, Harry Hole. They say he didn't make a single blunder. He solved all the cases he investigated. Is that true?"

Anton intervened with a cautionary cough and looked at Silje, but she ignored him.

Hagen's wry smile widened. "First of all, can you have unsolved cases on your conscience without it meaning you've made a **blunder**?"

Silje Gravseng didn't answer.

"As far as Harry and unsolved cases are concerned . . ." He rubbed his chin. "Well, they're probably right. But it depends how you look at it."

"How you look at it?"

"He returned from Hong Kong to investigate the murder for which his girlfriend's son had been arrested. And even though he managed to get Oleg released, and someone else confessed, the murder of Gusto Hanssen was never really solved. Not officially at any rate."

"Thank you," Silje said with a quick smile.

"Good luck with your career," Gunnar Hagen said.

He watched her as she made her way down the corridor. Not so much because men always like watching attractive, young women, Anton thought, but to defer what was to come for a few seconds. He had noticed the head of Crime Squad's nerves. Then Hagen turned to the closed door. Buttoned up his jacket. Rocked on the balls of his feet like a tennis player waiting for an opponent's serve.

"I'll go in then."

"Do that," Anton said. "I'll keep watch here."

"Right," Hagen said. "Right."

● ● ●

Halfway through lunch Beate asked Katrine if she and Harry had had sex that time.

To start with, Beate had explained how one of the undercover guys had recognised the picture of the woman who had given the false alibis, Irja Jacobsen. He had said that by and large she stayed indoors and lived in a house by Alexander Kiellands plass they had been keeping under surveillance because amphetamines were being sold there. But the police weren't interested in Irja, she didn't do any dealing, at worst she was a customer.

Then their conversation had meandered via work and their private lives, to the good old days. Katrine had mildly protested when Beate claimed that Katrine had given half the Crime Squad a crick in the neck as she swept through the corridors. At the same time Katrine reflected that this was the way women put each other in their place, by emphasising how beautiful they had **once** been. Especially if they weren't objects of beauty themselves. But even though Beate had never given anyone a crick in the neck she had never been the type to shoot poisoned darts either. She had been quiet, flushed, hard-working, loyal, someone who never resorted to dirty tactics. But something had obviously changed. Perhaps it was the glass of white wine they had allowed themselves. At any rate it was not like Beate to ask such direct, personal questions.

Katrine was glad her mouth was so full of pita bread that all she could do was shake her head.

"But OK," she said after she had swallowed, "I

admit it did cross my mind. Did Harry ever say anything?"

"Harry told me most things," Beate said, raising her glass with the last drops. "I was wondering if he was lying when he denied that you and he . . ."

Katrine waved for the bill. "Why did you think we might have been together?"

"I saw the way you looked at each other. Heard the way you spoke to each other."

"Harry and I **fought,** Beate!"

"That's what I mean."

Katrine laughed. "What about you and Harry?"

"Impossible. Much too good a friend. Then I got together with Halvorsen of course . . ."

Katrine nodded. Harry's partner, a young detective from Steinkjer. Halvorsen was the father of Beate's child and was later killed in the line of duty.

Pause.

"What is it?"

Katrine shrugged. Took out her phone and played the last part of the recording.

"Lots of crazy people at Ila," Beate said.

"I've done a bit of psychiatric myself so I know what's crazy," Katrine said. "But what I'm wondering is how he knew I was there because of Valentin."

Anton Mittet was sitting on a chair watching Mona come towards him. Enjoying the sight. Thinking it might be one of the last times.

She was smiling from a long way off. Heading straight for him. He watched her put one foot in front of the other, as if walking in an imaginary straight line. Perhaps that was how she walked. Or she was walking like that for him. Then she was there, automatically looking behind her to make sure no one was coming. Running her hand through his hair. Without getting up, he wrapped his arms around her thighs and looked up at her.

"Well?" he said. "You're on this shift too?"

"Yes," she said. "We let Altman go. He was ordered back to the cancer ward."

"Then we'll see all the more of you," Anton smiled.

"I wouldn't bet on it," she said. "The tests suggest he's coming round fast."

"But we'll meet anyway."

He said this in a joking tone. But it wasn't a joke. And she knew that. Was that why she seemed to stiffen, that her smile became a grimace, that she shoved him away while looking behind her as if to show she did this because someone might see them? Anton let go.

"The head of Crime Squad's in there now."

"What's he doing in there?"

"Talking to him."

"What about?"

"I can't say," he said. Instead of I don't know. God, he was so pathetic.

At that moment the door opened and Gunnar Hagen came out. He stopped, looked from Mona to Anton and back to Mona again. As though they had coded messages painted on their faces. Mona had, if nothing else, a tinge of red on hers as she darted through the door behind Hagen.

"Well?" Anton said, trying to appear unmoved. And realised that Hagen's look had not been of someone who understood, but of someone who didn't understand. He stared at Anton as if he were a Martian; it was the mystified look of a man who had just had all his beliefs turned upside down.

"The man in there . . ." Hagen said, jerking his thumb over his shoulder. "You keep a damn good eye on him, Anton. D'you hear me? You keep a damn good eye on him."

Anton heard him excitedly repeating the last words to himself as he launched into rapid strides down the corridor.

10

When Katrine saw the face in the door opening she thought at first they had come to the wrong place and that the old woman with grey hair and a drawn face could not possibly be Irja Jacobsen.

"What do you want?" she asked, glaring at them with suspicion.

"I rang you earlier," Beate said. "We'd like to talk about Valentin."

The woman slammed the door.

Beate waited until the sound of shuffling feet inside had faded. Then she pressed the handle and opened the door.

Clothes and plastic bags hung from the hooks along the corridor. Always plastic bags. Why was it that junkies always surrounded themselves with plastic bags? Katrine wondered. Why did they insist on everything they owned being stored, protected, transported in the flimsiest, most unreliable packaging there was? Why did they steal mopeds, hatstands and tea services, anything, and never suitcases and bags?

The flat was filthy, but still not as bad as most crack dens she had seen. Perhaps the woman of the house, Irja, had some standards and decided to do the cleaning herself. Katrine automatically assumed she she would be on her own in this endeavour. She followed Beate into the sitting room. A man was lying on an old divan, sleeping. Undoubtedly drugged. The room reeked of sweat, smoke, wood marinated in beer, and a sweet smell Katrine couldn't, or didn't want to, place. Along the wall were the obligatory stolen goods, pile upon pile of children's surfboards, all packed in transparent plastic, picturing the same snapping jaws of a great white shark and black bite marks on the tip, to suggest the shark had bitten off a chunk. God knows how they were going to convert these into cash.

Beate and Katrine continued into the kitchen, where Irja had taken a seat at the tiny table and was rolling herself a cigarette. The table was covered with a little cloth, and there was a sugar bowl with plastic flowers on the windowsill.

Katrine and Beate sat down opposite her.

"They never stop," Irja said, nodding to the traffic in Uelands gate. Her voice had the rasping huskiness that Katrine expected, having seen the flat and the face of the ancient woman in her thirties. "Always on the move. Where do they all go?"

"Home," Beate suggested. "Or they're leaving home."

Irja shrugged her shoulders.

"You've left home as well," Katrine said. "The address on the register . . ."

"I sold my house," Irja said. "I inherited it. It was too big. It was too . . ." She stuck out a dry, white tongue, ran it along a cigarette paper while Katrine mentally completed the sentence: too tempting to sell as her dole money was no longer enough for her dope consumption.

"There were too many bad memories."

"What sort of memories?" Beate asked, and Katrine shivered. Beate was a forensics expert, not an expert in questioning techniques, and she was casting too wide a net, asking for the whole tragedy of her life. And no one painted it with more detail or more slowly than a self-pitying junkie.

"Valentin."

Katrine sat up. Perhaps Beate knew what she was doing after all.

"What did he do?"

She shrugged her shoulders again. "He rented the basement flat. He . . . was there."

"Was there?"

"You don't know Valentin. He's different. He . . ."

She clicked the lighter, in vain. "He . . ." She clicked again and again.

"He was crazy?" Katrine suggested impatiently.

"No!" Irja threw the cigarette and lighter down in a fury.

Katrine cursed herself. Now she was the amateur asking leading questions.

"Everyone says Valentin was crazy! He **isn't**! It's just that he does something . . ." She looked through the window down onto the street. Lowered her voice. "He does something to the air. It frightens people."

"Did he hit you?" Beate asked.

Also a leading question. Katrine tried to get eye contact with Beate.

"No," Irja said. "He didn't hit me. He strangled me. If I contradicted him. He was so strong, he could just put one hand round my throat and squeeze. Hold it there until everything started spinning. It was impossible to remove his hand."

Katrine presumed the smile that had spread over Irja's face was a kind of gallows humour. Until she continued:

". . . and the strange thing was it made me high. And turned me on."

Katrine involuntarily pulled a face. She had read that a shortage of oxygen in the brain could have that effect on some people, but with a sex offender?

"And then you had sex?" Beate asked, bending down and picking the cigarette up from the floor. Lit it and passed it to Irja. Who quickly poked it between her lips, leaned forward and sucked at the unreliable flame. Let out the smoke again, sank back on the chair and seemed to implode, as though her body were a bag the cigarette had just burnt a hole in.

"He didn't always want a shag," Irja said. "Then he would go out. While I sat waiting, hoping he would be back soon."

Katrine had to pull herself together so as not to snort or show her contempt in some other way.

"What did he do outside?"

"I don't know. He didn't say anything, and I . . ." Again this shrug of the shoulders. A shrug of the shoulders as an attitude to life, Katrine thought. Resignation as an analgesic. ". . . I probably didn't want to know, I suppose."

Beate cleared her throat. "You gave him an alibi for the two nights the girls were killed. Maridalen and—"

"Yeah, yeah, yeah," Irja interrupted.

"But he wasn't at home with you as you stated in the interviews, was he?"

"I can't bloody remember. I had my orders, didn't I?"

"To do what?"

"Valentin told me the night we got together, sort of . . . well, you know, for the first time. The police would ask me these questions whenever anyone was raped, just because he'd been a suspect in a case they hadn't managed to pin on him. And if he didn't have an alibi in a new case they'd try and fit him up however innocent he was. He said the police usually do that with people they reckon have got away with other cases. So I had to swear he'd been at home, whatever time they asked about. Said he wanted to save us both loads of trouble and wasted time. Made sense to me."

"And you really thought he was innocent of all these rapes?" Katrine asked. "Even though you knew he'd raped before."

"Did I hell!" Irja shouted, and they heard low grunts coming from the sitting room. "I didn't know anything!"

Katrine was about to push her when she felt Beate's hand squeeze her knee under the table.

"Irja," Beate said gently, "if you didn't know anything, why did you want to talk to us now?"

Irja looked at Beate, picking imaginary threads of tobacco off the tip of her white tongue. Reflected. Made a decision.

"He was convicted, wasn't he? For attempted rape. And when I was cleaning the flat before renting it to someone else, I found these . . . these . . ." All of a sudden, without any warning her voice seemed to meet a brick wall and could go no further. ". . . these . . ." Tears were in her large, blood-dappled eyes.

"These photos."

"What kind of photos?"

Irja sniffled. "Girls. Young girls, little girls. Their mouths tied with something . . ."

"Gags?"

"Gagged, yes. They were sitting on chairs or beds. You can see blood on the sheet."

"And Valentin," Beate said. "Is he in the photos?"

Irja shook her head.

"So it could have been faked," Katrine said. "There are so-called rape photos circulating online made by pros for those interested in that sort of thing."

Irja shook her head again. "They were too frightened. You could see it in their eyes. I . . . recognised the fear there when Valentin was going to . . . wanted . . ."

"What Katrine is saying is that it doesn't have to be Valentin who took the pictures."

"The shoes," Irja sniffled.

"What?"

"Valentin had these long, pointed cowboy boots with buckles on the side. In one photo you can see the boots on the floor beside the bed. And then I knew it had to be true. He really could have done those rapes, as they said. But that wasn't the worst . . ."

"It wasn't?"

"You can see the wallpaper behind the bed. And it was that wallpaper, the same pattern. The picture had been taken in the basement flat. In the bed where he and I had . . ." She squeezed her eyes shut, forcing out two tiny drops of water.

"So what did you do?" Katrine asked.

"What do you think?" Irja hissed, wiping her forearm along her runny nose. "I went to you lot! To the people who are supposed to protect us."

"And **we** said?" Katrine asked, unable to conceal her repugnance.

"**You** said you would investigate the matter. So you went to Valentin with the photos, but of course he managed to talk his way out of it. He said it had been a game, there hadn't been any force, he didn't remember the names of the girls, he'd never seen them again and asked if anyone had reported him. They hadn't, so it stopped there. That is, it stopped for **you.** For me it had just begun . . ."

She carefully ran a bony forefinger under each eye, obviously believing she had put on make-up that might have smudged.

"Oh?"

"In Ila they're allowed one phone call a week. I received a message telling me he wanted to talk to me. So I went to visit him."

Katrine didn't need to hear the rest.

"I was sitting in the visitors' room waiting for him. And when he came in he just looked at me and it was as if he had his hand around my throat again. I couldn't bloody breathe. He sat down and said that if I ever said one word about the alibis to anyone he would kill me. And if I ever talked to the police, for whatever reason, he would kill me. And that if I thought he was going to be inside for long I was mistaken. Then he got up and left. And I was left in no doubt. As long as I knew what I knew he would kill me whatever happened, at the first opportunity. I went straight home, locked all the doors and wept with terror for three days. On the fourth a so-called friend rang wanting to borrow money. She used to do that pretty regularly, she was hooked on some heroin that had just come out, which later they dubbed violin. I used to hang up on her, but this time I didn't. The following night she was at my place helping me with the first shot of something I wished I'd had all my life. Oh God, how it helped. Violin . . . it fixed everything . . . it . . ."

Katrine could see the glint of a former love in the destroyed woman's eyes.

"And then you were hooked as well," Beate said. "You sold the house . . ."

"Not just for money," Irja said. "I had to escape. Had to hide from him. Everything that could lead back to me had to go."

"You stopped using a credit card, you moved without telling the authorities," Katrine said. "You didn't even collect your social security any more."

"Of course not."

"Not even after Valentin died."

Irja didn't answer. Didn't blink. Sat unmoving as the smoke curled upwards from the already burned-down stump between her nicotine-yellow fingers. Katrine was reminded of an animal caught in the headlights.

"You must have been relieved when you heard that?" Beate probed gently.

Irja nodded her head, mechanically, like a doll.

"He's not dead."

Katrine knew at once she meant it. What was the first thing she had said about Valentin? **You don't know Valentin. He's different.** Not was. Is.

"Why do you think I'm telling you this?" Irja stubbed out her cigarette on the table. "He's getting closer. Day by day, I can feel it. Some mornings I wake up, and I can feel his hand round my throat."

Katrine wanted to say that was called paranoia, the inseparable companion of heroin. But suddenly she wasn't so sure. And when Irja's voice sank to a low whisper as her eyes flitted between the dark corners of the room, Katrine could feel it too. The hand on her throat.

"You've got to find him. Please. Before he finds me."

Anton Mittet looked at his watch. Half past six. He yawned. Mona had been in to see the patient with a doctor a couple of times. Otherwise nothing had happened. You had a lot of time to think sitting there like that. Too much time actually. Because your thoughts had a tendency to become negative after a while. And that would have been fine if the negativity had been something he could have worked on. But he couldn't change the Drammen case or his decision not to report the baton he had found in the forest below the crime scene. He couldn't go back and unsay, undo, the times he had hurt Laura. And he couldn't undo his first night with Mona. Nor the second.

He gave a start. What was that? It seemed to come from the far end of the corridor. He listened intently. It was quiet now. But there had been a noise, and apart from the regular squawks from the heart monitor there **shouldn't** be any sounds here.

Anton got to his feet silently, loosened the strap over the butt of his gun and took out the weapon. Removed the safety catch. **You keep a damn good eye on him, Anton.**

He waited, but no one came. Then he began to walk slowly down the corridor. He shook all the doors on the way, but they were locked, as they were supposed to be. He rounded the corner and saw the next corridor stretch out before him. Illuminated the whole way down. And there was no one there. He stopped again and listened. Nothing. Perhaps he hadn't heard anything after all. He put the gun back in its holster.

Hadn't heard anything? Oh yes, he had. **Something** had created waves, which had met the sensitive membrane in his ear, made it react, only a little but enough for the nerves to receive it and transmit the signal to the brain. It was as good as a fact. But it could have been one of a thousand things that had caused it. A mouse or a rat. A bulb exploding with a bang. The temperature falling at night and making the woodwork in the building contract. A bird flying into a window.

It was only now—as he was calming down—that Anton noticed how high his pulse had been. He should start training again. Get into shape. Recover the body that was the real **him.**

He was about to go back when he thought now that he was here he might as well have a cup of coffee. He went over to the red espresso machine and picked up the solitary green capsule with a shiny lid bearing the name of Fortissio Lungo. And it struck him the noise could have been someone sneaking in and pinching their coffee. Hadn't there been plenty of capsules yesterday? He put the capsule in the machine, but suddenly noticed it had been perforated. Used, in other words. No, it can't have been, then the lid would have a kind of chess pattern after it had been squeezed. He switched on the machine. The humming started, and then he realised that for the next twenty seconds it would drown out any other noises. He stepped back two paces so that he wasn't in the middle of it.

When the cup was full he examined the coffee. Black, nice consistency; the capsule hadn't been used before.

As the last drop dripped into his cup he thought he heard it again. A noise. The same noise. But this time from the other side, towards the patient's room. Had he missed something on the way? Anton switched the cup to his left hand and took out his gun again. Walked back, taking long, even steps. Trying to balance the cup without looking at it, feeling the scalding hot coffee burning his hand. Rounded the corner. No one. He breathed out. Continued towards his chair. Was about to sit down. Then he froze. Went back to patient's room, opened the door.

It was impossible to see him; the duvet was covering him.

But the heart machine's sonar signal was as steady as ever, and he could see the line running from left to right on the green screen and jumping whenever there was a beep.

He was about to close the door.

But something made him change his mind.

He went in, left the door open and rounded the bed.

Looked down at the patient.

It was him.

He frowned. Leaned in close to his mouth. Was he breathing?

Yes, there it was. The movement in the air and the nauseous, sweet smell which perhaps emanated from the medication.

Anton Mittet went back out. Closing the door behind him. Looked at his watch. Drank the coffee. Looked at his watch again. Noticed that he was counting the minutes. That he wanted this shift to be over soon.

• • •

"How nice that he agreed to talk to me," Katrine said.

"Agreed?" the warder said. "Most of the men in this unit would give their right hand to spend a few minutes on their own with a woman. Rico Herrem is a potential rapist. Are you sure you don't want someone in there with you?"

"I know how to take care of myself."

"The dentist said that as well. But, OK, at least you're wearing trousers."

"Trousers?"

"She was wearing a skirt and nylon stockings. Sat Valentin down in the dentist's chair without having an officer present. You can imagine . . ."

Katrine tried to imagine.

"She paid the price for dressing like . . . OK, here we are!" He unlocked the door to the cell and opened it. "I'm right outside. Just shout if you need anything."

"Thank you," Katrine said, and went in.

The man with the red scalp was sitting at the desk and swivelled round on the chair.

"Welcome to my humble abode."

"Thank you," Katrine said.

"Take this." Rico Herrem got up, carried the chair over to her, walked back and sat on the neatly made bed. Good distance. She sat down and felt his body warmth on the chair. He moved further back on the bed as Katrine pulled the chair closer, and she wondered if he was one of those men who was actually afraid of women. And that was why he didn't rape them, he watched them. Exposed himself to them.

Rang them and said all the things he would like to do with them, but which of course he never dared to do. Rico Herrem's record was more unsavoury than actually frightening.

"You shouted to me that Valentin wasn't dead," she said, leaning forward. He shrank back even further. The body language was defensive, but the smile was the same: insolent, hate-filled. Obscene. "What did you mean by that?"

"What do you think, Katrine?" Nasal voice. "That he's alive, I reckon."

"Valentin Gjertsen was found dead in prison, right here."

"That's what everyone thinks. Did the guy outside tell you what he did to the dentist?"

"Something about a skirt and nylons. Apparently that ignites your imagination."

"It ignites Valentin's imagination. And I mean that literally. She used to be here two days a week. Lots of people complained about their teeth at that time. Valentin used one of her drills to force her to take off her nylon stockings and put them over her head. Then he fucked her in the dentist's chair. But as he said afterwards: 'She just lay there like a slaughtered animal.' She must have been given bad advice about what to do if something happened. Then Valentin took out his lighter and, yes, he set fire to the stockings. Have you seen how nylon melts when it burns? That got her going, I can tell you. Screaming and thrashing around, right? The stench of face fried in nylon was in the walls for weeks afterwards. I don't know what happened to her, but I would guess she doesn't have to be frightened of being raped again."

Katrine looked at him. Whipping-dog face, she thought. Been given so many beatings that the grin had become an automatic defence.

"If Valentin's not dead, where is he then?" she asked.

The grin grew wider. He pulled the duvet over his knees.

"Please tell me if I'm wasting my time here, Rico," Katrine sighed. "I've spent so much time at mental health institutions that crazy people bore me. All right?"

"You don't think I'm going to give you this information for nothing, do you, Officer?"

"My rank is Special Detective. What's the price? Reduced sentence?"

"I'm getting out next week. I want fifty thousand kroner."

Katrine burst into loud, hearty laughter. As hearty as she could make it. And saw the fury stealing into his eyes.

"I can't do anything for you then," she said, getting up.

"Thirty thousand," he said. "I'm skint and when I get out I'll need a plane ticket to take me a long way away."

Katrine shook her head. "We pay informers only when they have info that casts a whole new light on a case. A **big** case."

"And what if this is one?"

"Then I would have to talk to my boss about it. But I thought you had something you wanted to tell me. I'm not here to negotiate on something I don't have." She walked to the door and raised her hand to knock.

"Wait," Red Scalp said. His voice was thin. He had drawn the duvet up to his chin. "I can tell you something . . ."

"I've got nothing for you, I said." Katrine knocked on the door.

"Do you know what this is?" He held up a copper-coloured instrument that made Katrine's heart skip a beat. For a nanosecond she had thought it was a gun, but then saw that it was an improvised tattoo machine with a nail sticking out of the end.

"I'm the tattooist here in this joint," he said. "A bloody good one too. Do you know how they identified the body they found here as Valentin's?"

Katrine stared at him. At the small, hate-filled eyes. The thin, wet lips. The red skin glowing under the thinning hair. The tattoo. The demon face.

"I still haven't got anything for you, Rico."

"You could . . ." He pulled a face.

"Yes?"

"If you could unbutton your blouse so that I could see . . ."

Katrine looked down in disbelief. "You mean . . . these?"

As she placed her hands under her breasts she could almost feel the heat radiating out from the man in the bed.

She heard the key rattling in the lock outside.

"Officer," she said loudly without relinquishing Rico Herrem's gaze, "give us a couple more minutes, please."

She heard the rattling stop, heard him say something and then steps fading into the distance.

The Adam's apple in front of her looked like a little alien climbing up and down under the skin, trying to get out.

"Go on," she said.

"Not until . . ."

"Here's the deal. The blouse stays buttoned. But I'll squeeze one nipple so that you can see the outline. If what you tell me is good . . ."

"It is!"

"If you move the deal's off, OK?"

"OK."

"Right. Let me hear."

"I tattooed the demon face on his chest."

"Here? In the prison?"

He pulled a sheet of paper out from under the duvet.

Katrine moved towards him.

"Stop!"

She stopped. Looked at him. Raised her right hand. Groped for the nipple under the thin fabric of her bra. Caught it between forefinger and thumb. Squeezed. Didn't try to ignore the pain, welcomed it. Stood with her back arched. Knowing that blood was streaming to the nipple, that it was stiffening. Let him see. Heard his breathing accelerate.

He passed her the sheet of paper, and she stepped forward and snatched it. Sat down on the chair.

It was a drawing. She recognised it from the prison warder's description. Demon face. Drawn out to the sides as if it had hooks attached to the cheeks and forehead. Screaming with pain, screaming to get free.

"I thought it was a tattoo he'd had for many years before he died," she said.

"I wouldn't say that exactly."

"What do you mean?" Katrine studied the lines of the drawing.

"As he got it after he died, I mean."

She looked up. Saw his eyes still riveted on her blouse. "Did you tattoo Valentin **after** he died? Is that what you're saying?"

"Are you deaf, Katrine? Valentin isn't dead."

"But . . . who . . . ?"

"Two buttons."

"What?"

"Undo two buttons."

She undid three. Pulled her blouse to the side. Let him see her bra with the outline of the still stiff nipple.

"Judas." His voice was a whisper now, gruff. "I tattooed Judas. Valentin had him in his suitcase for three days. Locked in the suitcase, can you imagine!"

"Judas Johansen?"

"Everyone thought he'd escaped, but Valentin had killed him and hidden him in the suitcase. No one searches for a man in a suitcase, eh? Valentin had given him such a beating that even I wondered if it really could be Judas. Mincemeat. Could have been anyone. The only thing that was in one piece was the chest where I was supposed to do the tattoo."

"Judas Johansen. That was the body they found."

"Now I've told you, and I'm a dead man too."

"But why did he kill Judas?"

"Valentin was a hated man inside. Because he'd molested girls under ten, of course. Then there was the dentist business. Many people here liked her. The guards did as well. It was just a question of time before he had an accident. An overdose. Made it look like suicide. So he did something about it."

"He could have just escaped?"

"They would have found him. He had to make it seem as if he was dead."

"And his pal Judas was . . ."

"Useful. Valentin isn't like the rest of us, Katrine."

Katrine ignored his inclusive "us." "Why did you want to tell me this? You were an accessory."

"I only tattooed a dead man. Besides, you have to catch Valentin."

"Why?"

Red Scalp closed his eyes. "I've been dreaming so much recently, Katrine. He's coming. Coming back to join the living. But, first of all, he has to get rid of the past. Everyone in his way. Everyone who knows. And I'm one of them. I'm being released next week. You have to catch him . . ."

". . . before he catches you," Katrine completed, staring without seeing at the man in front of her. For it was as if it was being played out, the scene Rico had set, where he tattooed the three-day-old body.

And it was so unsettling that she was unaware of anything; she neither heard nor saw. Not until she felt a tiny droplet on her neck. Heard his low rattle and looked down. And jumped up from the chair. Stumbled towards the door, her nausea rising.

Anton Mittet woke up.

His heart was pounding wildly, and he was gulping down air.

Blinked for one confused moment before managing to focus.

Looked into the white wall in front of him. He was still sitting on the chair with his head lolling against the wall behind him. He had fallen asleep. Slept on the job.

It had never happened before. He lifted his left hand. It felt as if it weighed twenty kilos. And why was his heart beating as though he had run a half-marathon?

He looked at his watch. A quarter past eleven. He had been asleep for more than an hour! How could it have happened? He felt his heart gradually slowing down. It must have been all the stress over the past few weeks. The shifts, the daily rhythm out of sync. Laura and Mona.

What had woken him? Another noise?

He listened.

Nothing, just a quivering silence. And this vague dreamlike memory that the brain had registered something it found unsettling. It was like when he slept in their house in Drammen down by the river. He knew snarling boat engines raced past outside their open window, but his brain didn't register anything. A tiny creak of the bedroom door, on the other hand, and he jumped up. Laura claimed this was something he had started doing after the Drammen case, when they had found the young man, René Kalsnes, by the river.

He closed his eyes. Opened them wide again. Jesus, he had fallen asleep again! He got up. Felt so dizzy he had to sit down. Blinked. One hell of a mist, coating his senses.

He looked down at the empty coffee cup beside the chair. He would have to go and make himself a double espresso. Oh no, shit, it had run out of capsules. He would have to ring Mona and ask her to bring a cup for him; it wasn't long before her next visit. He picked up the phone. Her name was under GAMLEM CONTACT RIKSHOSPITAL. Which was no more than a safety precaution in case Laura checked the call log on his mobile phone and saw the frequent calls to this number. Of course he deleted the texts as he went. Anton Mittet was going to call when his brain identified it.

The wrong sound. The creak of the bedroom door.

It was the silence.

It was the sound that **wasn't** there that was wrong.

The sonar beep. The heart monitor.

Anton struggled to his feet. Staggered to the door, burst in. Tried to blink away the fuzziness. Stared at the machine's green shimmering screen. At the dead, flat line extending across it.

He ran to the bed. Looked down at the pallid face lying there.

He heard the sound of running footsteps approaching in the corridor. An alarm must have gone off in the duty office when the machine stopped registering heartbeats. Anton instinctively placed a hand on the man's forehead. Still warm. However, Anton had seen enough bodies to leave no room for doubt. The patient was dead.

Part Three

11

The funeral of the patient was a brief, efficient affair with an extremely meagre turnout. The priest didn't even try to suggest the man in the coffin was much-loved, had lived an exemplary life or was eligible to enter paradise. He therefore just went straight to Jesus, who, he maintained, had let all sinners off the hook.

There weren't even enough volunteers to carry the coffin, so it had to be left standing in front of the altar while the congregation walked out into the snow outside Vestre Aker Church. The majority of the assembled mourners were police officers—four to be precise—who got into the same car and drove to Kafé Justisen, which had just opened and where a psychologist was waiting for them. They stamped the snow off their boots, ordered a beer and four bottles of water, which was no cleaner or tastier than the water that came out of Oslo's taps. They **skål**ed, cursed the dead man, as was the custom, and drank.

"His death was premature," said the head of Crime Squad, Gunnar Hagen.

"Only a little premature," said the head of Krimteknisk, Beate Lønn.

"May he burn long and hot," said the red-haired

forensics officer in the suede jacket with a fringe, Bjørn Holm.

"As a psychologist I hereby diagnose you all as out of touch with your emotions," said Ståle Aune, raising his glass of beer.

"Thank you, Doctor, but the diagnosis is **police**," Hagen said.

"The autopsy," Katrine said. "I'm not sure that I quite understood it."

"He died of a cerebral infarction," Beate said. "A stroke. It can happen."

"But he came out of the coma," Bjørn Holm said.

"It can affect any of us, at any time," Beate said in flat voice.

"Thank you for that," Hagen grinned. "And now that we're done with the dead man, I suggest we move on."

"An ability to deal quickly with trauma is a sign of a person with low intelligence." Aune took a swig from his glass. "Just thought I would throw that in."

Hagen gazed at the psychologist for a second before continuing. "I think it would be good if we assembled here and not at HQ."

"Fine. Why are we here actually?" Bjørn Holm asked.

"To talk about the police murders." He turned. "Katrine?"

Katrine Bratt nodded. Cleared her throat.

"A brief summary so that Aune is also up to speed," she said. "Two police officers have been killed. Both at scenes of unsolved murders. Both were involved in those investigations afterwards. With respect to the police murders, as yet we do not have any clues, suspects or leads regarding the motive. With respect to the original murders, we assume they were sexually motivated. There were some clues, but none pointed towards particular suspects. That is, we had several in for questioning, but they were eliminated, either because they had an alibi or they didn't fit the profile. Now, however, one has had his eligibility revalidated . . ."

She took something from her bag and placed it on the table so that they could all see. It was a photograph of a man with his chest bared. The date and number showed it was a police mugshot.

"This is Valentin Gjertsen. Vice cases. Men, women and children. The first charge came when he was sixteen, interfering with a nine-year-old girl he had lured into a rowing boat. The following year his neighbour reported him for trying to rape her in the laundry room."

"And what ties him to Maridalen and Tryvann?" Bjørn Holm asked.

"For the moment, only that the profile fits and the woman who gave him an alibi for the times of the murders has just told us she was lying. She was doing what he ordered her to do."

"Valentin told her the police were trying to pin a false charge on him," Beate Lønn said.

"Aha," Hagen said. "That could be a basis for hating the police. What do you say, Doctor? Is it conceivable?"

Aune smacked his lips. "Absolutely. However, the rule of thumb I adhere to in matters concerning the human psyche is that absolutely everything conceivable is possible. Plus a goodly amount that is not conceivable."

"While Valentin Gjertsen was doing time for molesting a minor, he raped and disfigured a female dentist at Ila. He was sure revenge would follow and decided he would have to escape. Escaping from Ila is not exactly difficult, but Valentin wanted it to look as if he'd died so that no one would go after him. He killed a fellow inmate, one Judas Johansen, beat him to a pulp and hid the body so that when Judas didn't turn up for roll call he was listed as missing. Afterwards he forced the prison tattooist to do a copy of Valentin's demon face on the only place where Judas hadn't been beaten, his chest. He made it clear that he and his family would suffer a painful, premature death if he ever breathed a word to anyone, and then on the night Valentin escaped, he dressed Judas Johansen's dead body in his own clothes, placed him on the floor of his cell and left the door ajar. The next morning, when they found the body of the man they thought was Valentin, no one was especially surprised. The murder of the unit's most hated prisoner was more or less expected. It was so obvious they didn't even consider checking the fingerprints, even less running a DNA test."

There was silence around the table. Another customer came in, was about to sit at the neighbouring table, but one glance from Hagen was enough to make him move further away.

"So what you're saying is that Valentin escaped and is alive and well," Beate Lønn said. "He was behind the original murders and the police murders. The motive for the latter is revenge on the police in general. And he uses the earlier crime scenes to do it. But what precisely is he exacting revenge for? The police doing their job? In which case not many of us would be left alive."

"I'm not sure he's after the police in general," Katrine said. "The prison warder told me they'd been visited by a policeman at Ila, who spoke to some of the inmates about the murders of the girls at Maridalen and Tryvann. He said he spoke to prisoners in for murder, and rather than ask for information he leaked it. He fingered Valentin as a . . ." Katrine braced herself. ". . . child-fucker."

She saw them all, even Beate Lønn, recoil. It was strange how one word could seem stronger than even the worst crime-scene photographs.

"And if that's not meting out a straight death sentence, then it's not far off."

"And the policeman was?"

"The warder I was speaking to couldn't remember, and his name isn't recorded anywhere. But you can guess."

"Erlend Vennesla or Bertil Nilsen," Bjørn Holm said.

"A picture is emerging, don't you think?" Gunnar Hagen said. "This Judas was subjected to the same extreme physical violence as the police officers. Doctor?"

"Yes indeed," Aune said. "Murderers are creatures of habit who stick to tried and tested methods."

"But with Judas there was a specific purpose," Beate said. "To camouflage his escape."

"If that's really how it happened," Bjørn Holm said. "This inmate Katrine has spoken to ain't exactly the world's most reliable witness."

"Well," Katrine said, "I believe him."

"Why?"

Katrine gave a lopsided grin. "What was it Harry used to say? Intuition is only the sum of many small but specific things the brain hasn't managed to put a name to yet."

"What about digging up the body and checking?" Aune asked.

"Guess," Katrine said.

"Cremated?"

"Valentin had written a will the week before, in which it said that if he died the body should be cremated as soon as humanly possible."

"And since then no one's heard from him," Holm said. "Until he killed Vennesla and Nilsen."

"That's the hypothesis Katrine presented to me, yes," Gunnar Hagen said. "For now it's on the thin side and, to put it mildly, bold, but while our investigative unit is struggling to make any headway with other hypotheses, I'd like to give this one a chance. That's why I've gathered you here today. I want you to form a special little unit to follow this—and only this—trail. The rest you leave to the bigger unit. If you accept the assignment, you report to me . . ." He coughed, loud and brief, like a gunshot. "And only to me."

"Aha," Beate said. "Does that mean . . . ?"

"Yes, it means you'll be working in total secrecy."

"Secrecy from whom?" Bjørn Holm asked.

"Everyone," Hagen said. "Absolutely everyone except me."

Ståle Aune coughed. "And who in particular?"

Hagen rolled a bit of skin on his neck between his thumb and first finger. His eyelids had lowered, making him look like a lizard basking in hot sun.

"Bellman," Beate articulated. "The Chief of Police."

Hagen splayed his palms. "I just want results. We were successful with a small, independent group when Harry was with us. But the Chief of Police has put his foot down. He wants one big unit. But the one big unit has run out of ideas, and we **have** to catch this police killer. If we don't, all hell will be let loose. Were it to come to a confrontation with the Chief of Police, I would naturally take full and complete responsibility. I would say I hadn't told you he was unaware of this unit. But I appreciate the position I'm putting you in, so it's up to you whether you want to be in on this or not."

Katrine noticed how her eyes—like everyone else's—turned towards Beate Lønn. They knew the real decision lay with her. If she threw her hat in the ring, they all would. If not . . .

"The demon face on his chest," Beate said. She had picked up the photograph from the table and was studying it. "Looks like someone who wants out. Out of prison. Out of his own body. Or his own brain. Like the Snowman. Perhaps he's one of them." She looked up. Fleeting smile. "Count me in."

Hagen looked at the others. And received brief nods of confirmation.

"Good," Hagen said. "I'll be leading the investigative unit as before while Katrine will be the official leader of this one. As she comes under the Bergen and Hordaland Police District, technically you as a group don't have to report to Oslo Chief of Police."

"We're working for Bergen," Beate said. "Well, why not? **Skål** to Bergen, folks!"

They raised their glasses.

As they stood on the pavement outside Justisen, light drizzle was falling, emphasising the smell of rock salt, oil and tarmac.

"Let me take this opportunity to thank you for having me back," said Ståle Aune, buttoning up his Burberry.

"The untouchables ride again," Katrine smiled.

"Just like the old days," Bjørn said, contentedly patting his stomach.

"Almost," Beate said. "There's one person missing."

"Hey!" Hagen said. "We agreed we wouldn't talk about him again. He's gone and that's that."

"He'll never be completely gone, Gunnar."

Hagen sighed. Peered up at the sky. Shrugged.

"Maybe not. There was a PHS student doing a shift at the Rikshospital. She asked me if Harry Hole had ever **not** managed to solve a case. I thought at first she was just being nosy because she had studied one of his cases. I answered that the Gusto Hanssen case was never really solved. And today I heard that my secretary had received a call from PHS requesting copies of that very case file." Hagen smiled sadly. "Perhaps he's becoming a legend, after all."

"Harry will always be remembered," Bjørn Holm said. "Unsurpassed and unparalleled."

"Maybe," Beate said. "But we've got four people here who are close on his heels. Aren't we?"

They looked at each other. Nodded. Took their leave with brief, firm handshakes and headed off in three different directions.

12

Mikael Bellman saw the figure above his gunsights. He scrunched up one eye, slowly pulled the trigger, listening to his heartbeat. Calm but heavy. He felt the blood being pumped to his fingertips. The figure wasn't moving, he just had a sense it was. He let go of the trigger, took a deep breath and focused once more. Got the figure in the sights again. Pulled. Saw the figure twitch. Twitch in the right way. Dead. Mikael Bellman knew he had hit the head.

"Bring the body over and we'll do a post-mortem," he shouted, lowering his Heckler & Koch P30L. Tore off his ear and eye protectors. Heard the electric hum and the wires singing and saw the figure dance towards them. It came to a halt half a metre in front of him.

"Good," said Truls Berntsen, letting go of the switch. The humming stopped.

"Not bad," Mikael said, studying the paper target with the holes over half the torso and the head. Nodded to the target with the severed head in the lane beside his. "But not as good as yours."

"Good enough to pass the test. I heard ten point two per cent failed this year." With practised hands,

Truls changed his paper target, pressed the switch and a new figure sang its way back. It stopped at the flecked green metal plate twenty metres away. Mikael heard high-pitched laughter coming from a few lanes to the left. Saw two young women huddle together and glance over at them. Probably PHS students who had recognised him. All the sounds here had their own frequencies, so that even over the gunfire Mikael could hear the thwack of paper and the clunk of lead on metal. Followed by the tiny click as the bullet fell into the box for collecting the compressed shells beneath the target.

"In practice, more than ten per cent of the force are incapable of defending themselves or anyone else. What does the Chief of Police say to that?"

"Not all officers can train as much as you do, Truls."

"Have so much time to spare, you mean?"

Truls laughed his irritating grunted laugh as Mikael looked at his subordinate and childhood friend. At the higgledy-piggledy jumble of teeth his parents had never seen fit to have checked, at the red gums. Everything was apparently as before, yet something had changed. Perhaps it was just the recent haircut. Or was it the suspension? That kind of thing had a tendency to affect people you hadn't thought were so sensitive. Perhaps especially them, those who were not in the habit of venting their emotions, who kept them hidden, hoping they would pass with time. Those were the ones who could crack. Put a bullet through their temples.

But Truls seemed content. He was laughing. Mikael had once told Truls that his laughter made people panic. He should try to change it. Practise to find a more normal, more pleasant laugh. Truls had only laughed even louder. And pointed at Mikael. Pointed a finger at him without saying a word, only this eerie snorted laugh.

"Aren't you going to ask?" Truls enquired, pushing cartridges into the magazine of his gun.

"What about?"

"About the money in my account."

Mikael shifted his weight. "Was that why you invited me here? For me to ask you?"

"Do you want to know how the money got there?"

"Why should I harass you now?"

"You're the Chief of Police."

"And you took the decision not to say anything. I thought it was stupid of you, but I respect it."

"Do you?" Truls clicked the magazine into place. "Or are you leaving me alone because you already **know** where it came from, Mikael?"

Bellman eyed his childhood friend. He could see it now. See what had changed. It was the sick gleam. The one from their childhood, the one he got when he was angry, when the older kids in Manglerud were threatening to beat up the loudmouth with the girlie good looks who had taken Ulla, and Mikael had had to push Truls in front of him. Set the hyena on them. The mangy, whipped hyena who had already had to take so many beatings. So many that one more didn't make much difference. And when Truls had that gleam in his eye, the hyena gleam, it meant he was willing to die, and if he got his teeth into you, he would never, ever let go. He would lock his jaws and stay there until you went down on your knees or he was pulled off. But Mikael had seen the gleam only rarely as time went on. More recently there had of course been the time when they had dealt with the homo in the boiler room, and also, when Mikael had told him about the suspension. What had changed now, though, was that the gleam didn't go. It was there all the time, as if he had some kind of fever.

Mikael slowly shook his head in disbelief. "What are you talking about, Truls?"

"Maybe the money came indirectly from you. Maybe you were paying me the whole time. Maybe you led Asayev to me."

"I think you've inhaled too much gun smoke, Truls. I never had anything to do with Asayev."

"Maybe we should ask him about that?"

"Rudolf Asayev's dead, Truls."

"Bloody convenient, eh? Everyone who could talk happens to have snuffed it."

Everyone, Mikael Bellman thought. Except you.

"Except me," Truls grinned.

"I've got to go," Mikael said, pulling down his target and folding it.

"Oh yes," Truls said. "The Wednesday date."

Mikael froze. "What?"

"I remember you always used to leave the office at this time on Wednesdays."

Mikael studied him. It was odd—even after knowing Truls Berntsen for thirty years Mikael still wasn't sure how stupid or smart he was. "Right. But let me just say you'd better keep that kind of speculation to yourself. As things stand, it can only hurt you, Truls. And it might be best not to say too much. It could put me in a tricky spot if I'm summoned as a witness. Understand?"

But Truls had already put the protectors over his ears and turned to the target. Staring eyes behind the glasses. One flash. Two. Three. The gun seemed to try to detach itself, but Truls's grip was too tight. The hyena grip.

In the car park Mikael felt the phone vibrate in his trouser pocket.

It was Ulla.

"Did you manage to talk to pest control?"

"Yes," Mikael said, who hadn't given it a thought, let alone spoken to anyone.

"What did they say?"

"They said the smell you think is coming from the terrace could well be a dead mouse or a rat somewhere in there. But since it's concrete we can't do much. Whatever it is will rot and the smell will go of its own accord. They advised us not to break up the terrace. OK?"

"You should have had professionals do the terrace, not Truls."

"He did it in the middle of the night, without asking me. I've told you before. Where are you, darling?"

"I'm meeting a girlfriend. Will you be home for dinner?"

"Oh, yes. And don't worry about the terrace. All right, darling?"

"All right."

He hung up. Thinking he had said darling twice, and that was one time too many. Made it sound as if it was a lie. He started the car, pressed the accelerator, released the clutch and felt the wonderful pressure of the seat rest against his head as the new Audi surged across the car park. Thought about Isabelle. How he felt. Felt his blood pumping already. And thought about the strange paradox that had not been a lie. His love for Ulla never felt more real than just before he was going to fuck another woman.

Anton Mittet sat on the terrace. His eyes were closed and he could feel the sun warming his skin, just. Spring was fighting, but for the moment winter had the upper hand. Then he opened his eyes, and again his gaze fell on the letter on the table by him.

The Drammen Health Centre logo was embossed in blue.

He knew what it was, the result of his blood test. He was about to tear it open, but deferred it again and instead looked up and across the River Drammen. When they had seen the brochure for the new flats in Elveparken, to the west in Åssiden, they hadn't hesitated. The children had flown the nest and taming the stubborn garden had not become an easier job over the years, and nor had maintaining the old, much too big, timber house in Konnerud they had inherited from Laura's parents. Selling the whole lot and buying a modern, manageable flat was supposed to give them more time and money to do what they had spoken about for so many years. Travelling together. Visiting distant lands. Experiencing the things this short life on earth still had to offer.

So why hadn't they travelled after they made the move? Why had he deferred that as well?

Anton straightened his sunglasses, shuffled the letter around. Fished the phone from his baggy trouser pocket instead.

Was it everyday life that was so hectic with the days just coming and going, coming and going? Was it the view of Drammen that was so blissfully comforting? Was it the thought of having to spend so much time together, the fear of what it could reveal about both of them, about their marriage? Or was it the Case, the Fall, that had drained his energy, his initiative, leaving him in a state of mind in which daily routine appeared to be the sole escape from total collapse? And then Mona happened . . .

Anton looked at the display. GAMLEM CONTACT RIKSHOSPITAL.

There were three options beneath. Call. Send text. Edit.

Edit. Life should have that button as well. Everything could have been so different. He would have reported the baton. He wouldn't have invited Mona for coffee. He wouldn't have fallen asleep.

But he **had** fallen asleep.

Fallen asleep while on duty, on a hard wooden chair.

Him, someone who usually struggled to fall asleep in his own bed after a long day. It was incomprehensible. And he had wandered around half dazed for a long time afterwards as well, even the dead man's face and the ensuing commotion hadn't been enough to wake him; he had stood there like a zombie with this fog in his brain, incapable of doing anything or even answering questions clearly. Not that it would have necessarily saved the patient if he had stayed awake. The autopsy hadn't shown anything other than that the patient might have died of a stroke. But Anton hadn't done his job. Not that anyone would ever find out; he hadn't said a word. But **he** knew. Knew that he had screwed up again.

Anton Mittet looked down at the buttons.

Call. Send text. Edit.

It was time. Time to do something. Do something right. Just do it. Don't put it off.

He pressed Edit. Another option appeared.

He chose. Chose correctly. Delete.

Then he took the envelope and tore it open. Took the letter out and read. He had gone to the health centre early in the morning after the patient had been found dead. Explained he was a police officer on his way to work, he had taken a pill, but didn't know what it contained, he felt strange and was worried about going to work in case it had side effects. At first the doctor had wanted him to call in sick, but Anton had insisted they take a blood sample.

His eyes ran down the letter. He didn't understand all the words and names or what the numbers by

them signified, but the doctor had added two sum-
marising sentences to clarify:

**. . . nitrazepam is found in strong hypnotic
drugs. You MUST NOT take any more of these
tablets without consulting a doctor first.**

Anton closed his eyes and sucked in air through
clenched teeth.

Shit.

He had been right about his suspicion. He had
been doped. Someone had doped him. Not only that,
he had an inkling how. The coffee. The noise in the
corridor. The container with only one capsule left.
He had wondered if the lid had been perforated. The
solution must have been injected through the lid with
a syringe. Then the perpetrator only had to wait for
Anton to go and brew his own Mickey Finn, espresso
with nitrazepam.

They said the patient had died of natural causes.
Or rather, there was no evidence to suggest anything
suspicious had taken place. But a substantial part
of their conclusion was of course Anton's statement
that no one had been to see the patient subsequent to
the previous doctor's visit two hours before the heart
stopped beating.

Anton knew what he had to do. He had to report
this. Now. He lifted the phone. He had to report the
blunder. Explain why he hadn't told them straight
out that he had fallen sleep. He looked at the display.
This time not even Gunnar Hagen could save him.
He put the phone down. He **would** ring. Not right
now though.

• • •

Mikael Bellman knotted his tie in the mirror.

"You were good today," a voice from the bed said.

Mikael knew it was true. He watched Isabelle Skøyen get up behind him and pull on her stockings. "Is that because he's dead?"

She threw the reindeer-skin bedspread over the duvet. Above the mirror hung an impressive set of antlers and the walls were decorated with pictures by Sami painters. This wing of the hotel had rooms that were designed by female artists and bore their names. Their room had the name of a female joik singer. The only problem they had with the room was that Chinese tourists had stolen the ram horns, obviously firmly of the belief that the horn extract had a libido-boosting effect. Mikael had considered it himself the last couple of times. But not today. Perhaps she was right, perhaps it was the relief that the patient was finally dead.

"I don't want to know how it happened," he said.

"I wouldn't have been able to tell you anyway," she said, pulling on her skirt.

"Let's not even talk about it."

She was standing behind him. And bit him on the neck.

"Don't look so worried," she sniggered. "Life's a game."

"For you maybe. I've still got these bloody murders to deal with."

"You don't have to be elected. I do. But do I look worried?"

He shrugged. Reached for his jacket. "Are you going first?"

He smiled as she smacked his head. Heard her shoes click-clacking towards the door.

"I may have a problem with next Wednesday," she said. "The council meeting has been moved."

"Fine," he said, noticing that it was exactly that, fine. Well, more than that, he was relieved. Yes, he was.

She stopped by the door. Listened as usual for any noise in the corridor, making sure the coast was clear. "Do you love me?"

He opened his mouth. Saw himself in the mirror. Saw the black hole in the middle of his face with no sound emerging. Heard her low chuckle.

"I'm joking," she whispered. "Did I frighten you? Ten minutes."

The door opened and then closed softly behind her.

They had a deal that the second person would wait ten minutes before leaving the room. He couldn't remember if it had been his idea or hers. At the time they must have felt that the risk of bumping into a curious reporter or some familiar face in reception loomed large, but so far it hadn't happened.

Mikael took out his comb and groomed his slightly too long hair. The ends were still wet after the shower. Isabelle never showered after they had made love; she said she liked to walk around with the smell of him on her all day. He looked at his watch. Everything had worked today, he hadn't needed to think about Gusto and he had even prolonged it. So much so that if he waited here for the full ten minutes he would be late for the meeting with the chairman of the City Council.

Ulla Bellman looked at her watch. It was a Movado, 1947 design, and had been an anniversary present from Mikael. Twenty minutes past. She leaned back in the armchair and scanned the lobby. Wondering if she would recognise him. Strictly speaking they hadn't met more than twice. Once when he had held the door open for her as they were going to see Mikael at Stovner Police Station and he had introduced himself. A charming, smiling Nordlander. The second time, at a Christmas dinner at Stovner, they had danced and he had pressed her closer to him than he should have. Not that she had minded, it was an innocent flirtation, an acknowledgement she was happy to indulge, anyway Mikael was sitting somewhere in the room, and the other wives were also dancing with partners who weren't their husbands. And there was someone else apart from Mikael following her with a watchful eye. He had been standing on the dance floor with a drink in his hand. Truls Berntsen. Afterwards Ulla had asked Truls if he wanted to dance, but he had grinned and said no. He was no dancer, he had said.

 Runar. That was his name, it had slipped her mind. She had never heard or seen anything of him again. Until he had rung and asked if she could meet him here today. At first she had turned him down, saying she had no time, but he'd said he had something important to tell her. His voice was curiously distorted, she couldn't quite remember him sounding like that, but perhaps it was just that he was caught somewhere between his old Nordland dialect and Østland Norwegian. It often happened with people from the provinces when they had lived in Oslo for a while.

So she had said yes, a quick cup of coffee would be fine as she was going into town that morning anyway. It wasn't true. Like the answer she had given Mikael when he had asked where she was, and she had said she was on her way to meet a girlfriend. She hadn't meant to lie, but the question had caught her on the hop, and she realised she should have told Mikael she was having a coffee with an ex-colleague of his. So why hadn't she? Because deep down she suspected that what she was going to be told had something to do with Mikael? Already she regretted being here. She looked at her watch.

The receptionist had glanced at her a couple of times, she noticed. Ulla had removed her coat, and underneath she was wearing a sweater and trousers, which emphasised her slim figure. Going to the city centre was not something she did a lot, and she had spent a bit more time on her make-up and her long blonde hair, which had caused the Manglerud boys to drive past her to see if her front fulfilled what her back promised. And she could see from their faces that for once it had. Mikael's father had once told her she looked like the good-looking one in the Mamas & the Papas, but she didn't know who that was and had never tried to find out.

She shot a glance at the swing door. More and more people were streaming in, but not the person with darting eyes she was expecting.

She heard a muffled ping from the lift doors and then a tall woman in a fur coat stepped out. It struck Ulla that if a journalist asked the woman if the fur was genuine, she would probably deny it. Socialist politicians preferred to tell the majority of voters what they wanted to hear. Isabelle Skøyen. The City Councillor for Social Affairs. She had been to their house for the party after Mikael's appointment. Actually it had been a house-warming party, but instead of friends Mikael had by and large invited people who were important for his career. Or "their" career, as he called it, his and hers. Truls Berntsen had been one of the few present she had known, and he wasn't exactly the type of person you can talk to for the whole evening. Not that she'd had time; she had been kept very busy playing the hostess.

Isabelle Skøyen sent her a look and was about to walk on, but Ulla had already noticed the brief hesitation. The little hesitation that meant she had recognised Ulla and was now faced with the choice of pretending she hadn't or being obliged to go over and exchange a few words with her. And she would have preferred to avoid the latter. Ulla often felt exactly the same. For example, with Truls. In a way she liked him: they had grown up together and he was kind to her and loyal. Nevertheless. She hoped Isabelle would choose the former and make it easier for them both. And saw to her relief that she was already heading for the swing door. But then she evidently changed her mind, did a U-turn, big smile and sparkling eyes. Sailed over towards her, yes, indeed she did sail. Isabelle Skøyen reminded Ulla of a dramatic, oversized galleon figurehead as she rushed over.

"Ulla!" she cried, several metres away, as though this was a reunion of two long-lost friends.

Ulla got up, already somewhat uneasy about having to answer the next, inevitable question: what are you doing here?

"Nice to see you again, my dear! What a **lovely** little party that was!"

Isabelle Skøyen had placed a hand on Ulla's shoulder and proffered her cheek in such a way that Ulla had to rest hers against it. Little party? There had been thirty-two guests.

"Sorry I had to leave so early."

Ulla remembered that Isabelle had been a bit the worse for wear. While she had been serving the guests the tall, attractive councillor and Mikael had gone onto the terrace for a while. For a moment Ulla had actually been a bit jealous.

"That didn't matter. We were just honoured you could come." Ulla hoped her smile wasn't as stiff as it felt. "Isabelle."

The councillor looked down at her. Studying her. As though searching for something. The answer to the question she still hadn't asked: what are you doing here, my dear?

Ulla decided to tell the truth. As she would with Mikael later.

"I must be off," Isabelle said without making a move to go or taking her eyes off Ulla.

"Yes, I suppose you must be busier than me," Ulla said, and to her irritation heard the stupid titter she had been determined to drop. Isabelle was still looking at her, and all of a sudden Ulla felt that this stranger was trying to force it out of her without asking: what are you, the wife of the Chief of Police, doing here in the reception area of the Grand Hotel? My God, did she imagine Ulla was meeting a lover here? Was that why she was so discreet? Ulla could feel the stiffness of her smile dissipating, it was becoming easier, now she was smiling the way she actually smiled, the way she **wanted** to smile. She knew the smile had reached her eyes now. She was on the point of laughing in Isabelle Skøyen's face. And the strange thing was that Isabelle looked as if she wanted to laugh as well.

"I hope to see you again before too long, my dear," Isabelle said, pressing Ulla's hand between her big, strong fingers.

Then she turned and surged back through reception where one of the doormen was already hurrying to assist her. Ulla caught a glimpse of her pulling out a mobile phone before rushing through the swing door.

Mikael was standing by the lift only a few rapid strides from the Sami woman's room. Glanced at his watch. Just four or five minutes had passed, but that would have to be enough; after all, the vital element was that they shouldn't be seen **together.** Isabelle always booked the room and arrived ten minutes before him. Lying in bed, ready and waiting. That was how she liked it. Was that how he liked it?

Fortunately it was only three minutes' fast walk from the Grand to City Hall, where the chairman was waiting.

The lift doors opened, and Mikael stepped in. He pressed 1 for the ground floor. The lift started and stopped on the next floor down. The doors opened.

"Guten Tag."

German tourists. An elderly couple. Old camera in a brown leather case. He could feel he was smiling. He was in a good mood. He made room for them. Isabelle was right: he **was** relieved that the patient was dead. He felt a drop fall from his long hair, felt it roll down his neck, wetting his shirt collar. Ulla had suggested he should have his hair cut shorter for his new post, but why? His youthful looks, didn't they just underline the point? That he—Mikael Bellman— was Oslo's youngest ever Chief of Police?

The couple looked at the lift buttons with concern. It was the same old problem. Was floor number 1 street level or the floor above it? What system did they have in Norway?

"It's the ground floor," Mikael said in English, pressing the button and closing the doors.

"Danke," the woman murmured. The man had closed his eyes and was breathing audibly. **Das Boot,** Mikael thought.

They sank down through the building in silence.

As the doors opened and they exited into reception, a tremble seemed to go through Mikael's thigh. His phone picked up a signal again. He saw there was a missed call from Isabelle. He was about to ring back when it vibrated again. It was a text.

Met your wife in reception. :)

Mikael came to an abrupt halt. Glanced up. But it was too late.

Ulla was sitting in an armchair directly in front of him. She looked attractive. Had taken more care than usual. Attractive and turned to stone in her chair.

"Hello, darling," he exclaimed, hearing at once how shrill and false it sounded. Saw in her face how it sounded.

Her eyes were fixed on him, with the remnants of a confusion that was quickly giving way to something else. Mikael Bellman's brain was churning. Absorbing and processing data, looking for connections, drawing a conclusion. He knew the wet tips of his hair could not be explained satisfactorily. She had seen Isabelle. Her brain, like his, was processing at lightning speed. That is how the human brain is. Mercilessly logical as it assembles all the tiny bits of information, which suddenly fit. And he saw that the something else had already ousted the confusion. The certainty. She lowered her gaze, so that when he was standing in front of her, she was looking straight at his midriff.

He hardly recognised her voice as she whispered: "You got her text a little too late then."

• • •

Katrine turned the key in the lock and pulled the door, but it was jammed.

Gunnar Hagen stepped forward and shook it open.

A stale, heated damp atmosphere met them.

"Here," Gunnar Hagen said. "We've left it untouched since the last time it was used."

Katrine went in first and pressed the light switch. "Welcome to Bergen's Oslo branch office," she drawled.

Beate Lønn crossed the threshold. "So this is where we're to be hidden."

Cold, blue light from the neon tube fell on a square concrete room with greyish-blue lino on the floor and nothing on the walls. The windowless room boasted three desks with a computer on each and a chair. On one desk there was a brown-stained coffee machine and a large jug of water.

"We've been allocated an office in the **basement** of Police HQ?" Ståle Aune exclaimed, stupefied.

"Officially speaking, you are in fact on Oslo Prison property," Gunnar Hagen said. "The corridor outside goes under the car park. If you go up the iron stairs outside the door you'll end up in the reception area of the prison."

By way of response, the first notes of Gershwin's **Rhapsody in Blue** sounded. Hagen took out his mobile phone. Katrine glanced over his shoulder. And saw the name Anton Mittet light up on the display. Hagen pressed Reject and put the mobile back in his pocket.

"The investigative unit has a meeting now, so I'll leave you to it," he said.

The others stood looking at one another after Hagen had left.

"It's bloody hot in here," Katrine said, unbuttoning her jacket. "But I can't see any radiators."

"That's because the prison boilers are in the room next door," Bjørn Holm laughed, hanging his suede jacket over a chair back. "We called it 'The Boiler Room.'"

"So you've been here before, have you?" Aune loosened his bow tie.

"Yes, we have. We had an even smaller group then." He nodded towards the desks. "Three, as you can see. Solved the case anyway. But then Harry was in charge . . ." He shot Katrine a quick glance. "I didn't mean to—"

"It's OK, Bjørn," Katrine said. "I'm not Harry, and I'm not in charge either. It would be fine with me if you reported to me formally, so that Hagen could wash his hands of the whole business, but I've got more than enough to do just managing myself. Beate's the boss. She has the seniority and management experience."

The others looked at Beate. Who shrugged her shoulders. "If that's what you'd all like I can be boss, if there's any need for it."

"There **is** a need for it," Katrine said.

Aune and Bjørn nodded.

"Good," Beate said. "Let's get started. We've got mobile phone coverage. An Internet connection. And we've got . . . coffee cups." She took a white one from behind the coffee machine. Read the writing in felt pen. "Hank Williams?"

"Mine," said Bjørn.

She lifted another. "John Fante?"

"Harry's."

"OK, so let's detail the jobs," Beate said, putting down the cup. "Katrine?"

"I'll keep watch online. Still no sign of life from either Valentin Gjertsen or Judas Johansen. You need to be smart to hide from the electronic eye for so long, and that reinforces the theory that it wasn't Judas Johansen who escaped. Judas is not exactly top priority for the police, and it seems unlikely he would restrict his freedom by going into total blackout just to escape a couple of months in prison. Valentin has more to lose of course. Anyway, if either of them is alive and so much as moves a muscle in the electronic world, I'm on them."

"Good. Bjørn?"

"I'll go through the files of various cases Valentin and Judas have been involved in and see if I can find any links to Tryvann or Maridalen. Names that come up again and again or forensic evidence we've missed. I'm making a list of people who know them and may be able to help us find them. The ones I've spoken to so far are willing to open up about Judas Johansen. Valentin Gjertsen, on the other hand . . ."

"They're frightened?"

Bjørn nodded.

"Ståle?"

"I'll examine the Valentin and Judas cases as well, but to make a profile of each of them. I'll write an assessment of them as potential serial killers."

The room went silent at once. It was the first time anyone had spoken the words.

"In this case, serial killer is no more than a technical, mechanical term, not a diagnosis," Ståle Aune hastened to add. "It describes an individual who has killed more than one person and may conceivably kill again. All right?"

"All right," Beate said. "As for me, I'll go through all the visual material we have from CCTV cameras around the crime scenes. Petrol stations, all-night shops, photo booths. I've already seen quite a few shots of the police murders, but not everything. And there are the original murders as well."

"Enough to do then," Katrine said.

"Enough to do," Beate repeated.

The four of them stood looking at one another. Beate raised the John Fante cup and put it back behind the coffee machine.

13

"All right?" Ulla said, leaning back against the kitchen worktop.

"Oh, yes," Truls said, shifting uneasily on the chair and lifting the coffee cup from the narrow worktop. He took a swig. Looked at her with the eyes she knew so well. Frightened and hungry. Embarrassed and searching. Rejecting and imploring. No and yes.

She had immediately regretted allowing him to visit her. But she hadn't been prepared when he had suddenly rung and asked how things were going with the house, was there anything that needed fixing? As he was suspended now, the days were long, and he had nothing to do. No, there was nothing that needed fixing, she had lied. Oh, right. What about a cup of coffee then? A little chat about old times? Ulla had said she didn't know if . . . but Truls acted as if he hadn't heard, said he was passing by, a coffee would be nice. And she had answered, OK, why not, drop in, Truls.

"I'm still alone, as you know," he said. "Nothing new there."

"You'll find someone. Of course you will." She made a show of looking at the clock, had considered saying the children had to be picked up. But even a bachelor like Truls would realise it was too early.

"Maybe," he said. Looking into his cup. And instead of putting it down he took another swig. Like taking courage, he thought with dread.

"As you probably know, I've always liked you, Ulla."

Ulla clutched the worktop.

"So you know if you have a problem and you need . . . er, someone to talk to, you can always count on me."

Ulla blinked. Had she heard him correctly? **Talk?**

"Thank you, Truls," she said. "But I've got Mikael, haven't I?"

He put his cup down slowly. "Yes, of course. You've got Mikael."

"By the way, I have to start cooking dinner for him and the children."

"Yes, of course you have to. You're in the kitchen cooking for him while he . . ." He stopped.

"He what, Truls?"

"Has dinner elsewhere."

"Now I don't understand what you mean, Truls."

"I think you do. Listen, I'm only here to help you. I have your best interests at heart, Ulla. And the children's, of course. The children are important."

"I'm going to make them something nice. And these family meals take time, Truls, so . . ."

"Ulla, there's one thing I want to say."

"No, Truls. No, don't say it, please."

"You're good to Mikael. Do you know how many other women he—?"

"No, Truls!"

"But—"

"I want you to go now, Truls. And I don't want to see you here again for a while."

Ulla stood by the worktop watching Truls go out of the gate to the car parked beside the gravel drive winding between the newly built houses in Høyenhall. Mikael had said he would pull a few strings, make a few calls to the right people on the council, get the tarmac laid, but so far nothing had happened. She heard the brief chirp as Truls pressed the key and the car alarm switched itself off. Watched him get into the car. Watched him sit motionless, staring into the distance. Then his body seemed to twitch and he started pummelling the steering wheel so hard she saw it give. Even from a distance it was so violent she shuddered. Mikael had told her about his anger, but she had never witnessed it. If Truls hadn't become a policeman, according to Mikael he would have been a criminal. He said the same about himself when he was acting tough. She didn't believe him. Mikael was too straight, too . . . adaptable. But Truls . . . Truls was made of something else, something darker.

Truls Berntsen. Simple, naive, loyal Truls. She'd had a suspicion, no doubt about that, but she couldn't believe Truls could be so sly. So . . . imaginative.

The Grand Hotel.

They had been the most painful seconds of her life. Not that she hadn't considered the idea that he could have been unfaithful. Especially after he had stopped having sex with her. But there could be several explanations for that, the stress of the police murders . . . but Isabelle Skøyen? Sober, in a hotel in the middle of the day? And it had also struck her that the whole scenario had been a set-up. The fact that someone could know the two of them would be there suggested it was a regular occurrence. She wanted to throw up whenever she thought about it.

Mikael's suddenly pale face in front of her. The frightened, guilty eyes, like a boy caught apple scrumping. How did he manage it? How did he, the faithless swine, how did he make it seem as if it was a minor issue requiring his protective hand? The man who had trodden all over everything they had that was good, the father of three children. Why did **he** look as if he was the one carrying the cross?

"I'll be home early," he had whispered. "We can deal with it then. Before the children . . . I have to be in the council chairman's office in four minutes." Had he had a tear in the corner of his eye? Had the bastard had the temerity to shed a tear?

After he had gone she had pulled herself together surprisingly quickly. Perhaps that is what people do when there is no alternative, when a nervous breakdown is not an option. With numb composure she rang the number the man claiming to be Runar had used. No answer. She had waited for another five minutes, then she had left. When she got home she checked out the number with one of the women she knew at Kripos. And she told Ulla it was a pay-as-you-go mobile. The question was: who would go to such lengths to send her to the Grand so that she could witness it with her own eyes? A journalist from the celebrity gossip press? A more or less well-meaning woman friend? Someone on Isabelle's side, a vengeful rival of Mikael's? Or someone who didn't want to separate him and Isabelle but him and her, Ulla? Someone who hated Mikael or her? Or someone who loved her? Who thought it would give him a chance if he could drive a wedge between her and Mikael. She knew only one person who loved her more than was good for anyone.

She didn't mention her suspicions to Mikael when they spoke later in the day. He clearly thought her presence in reception had been a coincidence, one of those lightning strikes that happen in everyone's lives, that improbable concurrence of events that some call fate.

Mikael hadn't tried to lie and say he hadn't been there with Isabelle. She had to give him that. He wasn't so stupid. He had explained she didn't need to ask him to finish the affair; he had terminated it on his own initiative before Isabelle had left the hotel. That was the word he had used: affair. Probably advisedly, it made it sound so small, unimportant and sordid, something that could be swept under the carpet, as it were. A "relationship," on the other hand, that would have been a different matter. She didn't believe for a second that he had "terminated it" at the hotel. Isabelle had seemed too elated for that. But what he said next was true. If this came out, the scandal would not only hurt him, but also their children and her. It would, furthermore, come at the worst possible moment. The council chairman had wanted to talk to him about politics. And he wanted him to join the party. Mikael was someone they had been considering as an interesting candidate for a political post in the not too distant future. He was exactly what they were after: young, ambitious, popular and successful. Until these police murders, of course. But after he had solved them, they should sit down and discuss his future, where it lay, in the police or in politics, where Mikael thought he could have the most impact. Not that Mikael had decided what he wanted, but it was obvious that any kind of scandal would close that door.

And then of course there was her, and the children. What happened to his career was a minor issue compared to what this loss would mean. She interrupted him before his self-pity had gone too far and said she had thought the matter through and that her calculations matched his. His career. Their children. The life they had together. She said quite simply that she forgave him, but he would have to promise never, ever to have any more contact with Isabelle Skøyen. Except as the Chief of Police at meetings where others were present. Mikael had almost seemed disappointed, as though he had been armed for a battle and not a tame skirmish, which had fizzled out in an ultimatum that wouldn't cost him much. Ulla watched Truls start the car and drive off. She hadn't told Mikael about her suspicions and had no intention of doing so either. What purpose would it serve?

If she was right, Truls could continue to be the spy who sounded the alarm if the pact regarding Isabelle Skøyen was not kept.

The car disappeared and the residential silence mingled with the clouds of dust. And a thought went through her mind. A wild, totally unacceptable thought, of course, but the mind isn't so strict on censorship. Her and Truls. In the bedroom, here. Just as revenge, of course. She rejected the idea as soon as it had appeared.

The sleet that had oozed across the windscreen like grey spit had been superseded by rain. Vertical, heavy rain. The windscreen wipers fought a desperate battle against a wall of water. Anton Mittet drove slowly. It was pitch black, and the water was making everything blur and distort as though he were drunk. He glanced at the clock in his VW Sharan. When they had decided to buy a new car three years ago, Laura had insisted on this seven-seater, and he had jokingly enquired if she was planning a big family, even though he knew it was because she didn't want to be in a tiny car if they crashed. Well, Anton didn't want a crash either. He knew these roads well and also knew the chances of meeting oncoming traffic at this time of night were slim, but he didn't take any risks.

The pulse in his temple was pounding. Mostly because of the telephone call he had received twenty minutes ago. But also because he hadn't had his coffee today. He had lost his taste for it after reading the result of the test. Stupid, that went without saying. And now the caffeine-accustomed blood vessels had narrowed so much that his headache lay there like unpleasant, throbbing background music. He had read that coffee addicts' withdrawal symptoms took two weeks to disappear. But Anton didn't want to renounce his addiction. He wanted coffee. He wanted it to taste good. Good like the mint taste of Mona's tongue. But all he could taste now when he drank coffee was the bitter aftertaste of sleeping tablets.

He had plucked up the courage to ring Gunnar Hagen to tell him that he had been doped when the patient died. That he had been asleep while someone had been in the room. That even if the doctors said it had been a natural death, that could not have been the case. That they would have to do another, more thorough autopsy. Twice he had rung. Without getting an answer. He had tried. He had. And he would try again. Because it always catches up with you. Like now. It had happened again. Someone had been killed. He braked, turned off and took the gravel road up to Eikersaga, accelerated again and heard the small stones hitting the wheel arches.

It was even darker here, and there was already water lying in the hollows in the road. Midnight soon. It had been around midnight when it had happened the first time as well. As the location was close to the border of the neighbouring district, Nedre Eiker, an officer from that police force had been first on the crime scene after receiving a call from someone who had heard a crash and thought a car must have landed in the river. As if it wasn't bad enough that the officer had entered the district without permission, he had also made a mess, gouging up the site with his car and obliterating potential clues.

Anton passed the bend where he had found it. The baton. It had been the fourth day after the murder of René Kalsnes and Anton had finally had a day off, but he had got restless and had gone for a walk in the forest on his own to continue the search. After all, murder wasn't the kind of crime they had every day— or every year—in Søndre Buskerud Police District. He had left the area the search party had gone over with a fine-tooth comb. And that was where it had been, under the spruce trees behind the bend. That was where Anton had taken the decision, the stupid decision that had ruined everything. He decided not to report it. Why? First of all, it was such a long way up to the crime scene in Eikersaga that the baton could hardly have had anything to do with the murder. Later they had asked him why he had been searching there if he had really thought it was too far away to be of any relevance. But at the time he had just thought that a standard police baton would only lead to unnecessary and negative attention for the force. The injuries inflicted on René Kalsnes could have been caused by any heavy instrument or by being tossed around in the car when it had fallen off the precipice into the river forty metres below. And it wasn't the murder weapon anyway. René Kalsnes had been shot in the face with a 9mm calibre handgun, and that had been the end of the story.

But Anton had told Laura about the baton a couple of weeks later. And it was she who ultimately persuaded him it should be reported and that it wasn't up to him to assess how important the find was. So he had done it. He had gone to his boss and told him what he had found. "A serious miscalculation," the Chief of Police had called it. And the thanks he had received for spending his day off trying to help a murder investigation had been that they dropped him from active service and put him in an office answering a phone. In one fell swoop he had lost everything. For what? No one said it aloud, but René was generally known as a cold, unscrupulous bastard who had cheated friends and strangers alike, a person most considered the world was better off without. But the most mortifying part of the whole business had been that Krimteknisk hadn't found any traces on the baton to link it with the murder. After three months of being incarcerated in the office Anton had the choice of going insane, resigning or getting himself moved. So he rang his old friend and colleague Gunnar Hagen, and he got him a job with Oslo Police. Professionally, what Gunnar offered him was a step backwards, but at least Anton was among people, and villains, in Oslo, and anything was better than the stale air of Drammen, where they tried to copy Oslo, calling their little station "Police HQ," and even the address sounded plagiarised: Grønland 36 as compared with Oslo's Grønlandsleiret.

Anton came over the brow of the hill, and his right foot automatically jumped on the brake when he saw the light. The tyres chewed gravel. Then the car came to a standstill. Rain was hammering down on the car, almost drowning the sound of the engine. A torch twenty metres ahead was lowered. The headlights picked up the reflectors on the orange-and-white tape and the yellow police vest of the person who had just lowered the torch. He waved him closer, and Anton drove on. This was where, behind the barrier, René's car had driven off. They had used a breakdown truck with a crane and steel cables to drag the wreck up the river to the disused sawmill, where they'd managed to haul it onto land. They'd had to wriggle the body of René Kalsnes free as the engine had been knocked through into the car at hip height.

Anton pressed the button to open the window. Damp, chilly night air. Great, heavy raindrops hit the edge of the window, sending a fine spray over his neck.

"Well," he said. "Where . . . ?"

Anton blinked. He wasn't sure if he had completed the sentence. It was like a tiny jump in time, a bad edit in a film, he didn't know what had happened, just that he was absent. He looked down at his lap, at the fragments of glass there. He looked up again and discovered that the top part of the window was smashed. Opened his mouth, was about to ask what was going on. Heard something whistle through the air, sensed what it was, wanted to raise his arm, but was too slow. Heard a crunch. Realised it came from his own head, something breaking into pieces. Raised his arm, screamed. Got his hand on the gearstick, tried to put it in reverse. But it wouldn't go. Everything was moving in slow motion. Wanted to slip the clutch, accelerate, but that would only send them forwards. Towards the edge. To the precipice. Straight down into the river. Forty metres. This was . . . This was . . . He shook the gear lever and pulled at it. Heard the rain more clearly and felt the chilly night air down the whole of the left side of his body now. Someone had opened the door. The clutch. Where was his foot? This was a carbon copy. Reverse gear. There we are.

Mikael Bellman stared up at the ceiling. Listened to the reassuring patter of rain on the roof. Dutch tiles. Guaranteed to last forty years. Mikael wondered how many tiles they sold just as a result of this guarantee. More than enough to pay for the ones that **didn't** last that long. If there was one thing people wanted it was a guarantee that things would last.

Ulla lay with her head on his chest.

They had spoken. Spoken at length. For the first time he could remember. She had cried. Not the painful tears he hated but the others, the gentle tears that denoted less pain, more loss, the loss of something that had been and could never return. The tears that told him something in their relationship had been so precious it was worth the loss. He didn't feel the loss until she cried. It was as though he needed her tears to show him. They removed the curtain that was normally there; the curtain between what Mikael Bellman thought and what Mikael Bellman felt. She was crying for them both, she always had done. She had laughed for them both as well.

He had wanted to comfort her. Had stroked her hair. Allowed her tears to wet the light blue shirt she had ironed for him the day before. Then he had, almost inadvertently, kissed her. Or had it been consciously? Had it been out of curiosity? The curiosity to know how she would react, the same kind of curiosity he had felt when he, as a young detective, had questioned suspects according to the Inbau, Reid and Buckley nine-step model, the step where they press the emotional button just to see what reaction they get.

At first Ulla had not reacted to the kiss, she had just stiffened. Then she had responded gently. He knew her kisses but not this one. The tentative, hesitant one. Then he had kissed her with more hunger. And she had taken off. Dragged him into bed. Torn off his clothes. And in the darkness he'd had the thought again. That she wasn't him. Gusto. And his erection had subsided even before they were under the duvet.

He had explained that he was too tired. He'd had too much to think about. The situation was too confusing, the shame of what he had done too great. Hastening to add that **she,** the other woman, had nothing to do with it. And he was able to tell himself that this was actually true.

He closed his eyes again. But it was impossible to sleep. There was the unrest, the same unrest he had woken to over recent months, a vague feeling that something terrible had happened or was about to happen, and for some time he hoped it was just the lingering effect of a dream until he remembered it.

Something made him open his eyes again. A light. A white light on the ceiling. From the floor beside his bed. He turned and looked down at the display on his phone. On silent, but always on. He had agreed with Isabelle that they should never send messages at night. What **her** reason was, he had never asked. And she had appeared to take it well when he explained that they wouldn't be able to see each other for a while. Even though he thought she had understood what he meant. That the bit about "a while" should be deleted.

Mikael was relieved when he saw the text was from Truls. Then taken aback. Drunk probably. Or maybe the wrong number, maybe it was meant for a woman he hadn't mentioned. The text consisted of two words:

Sleep well.

Anton Mittet woke up.

The first thing he registered was the sound of rain, which was now no more than a light mumble on the windscreen. Then that the engine was switched off, his head ached and he couldn't move his hands.

He opened his eyes.

The headlamps were still on. They shone down along the ground, through the rain and into the darkness where the land suddenly vanished. The wet wind-screen prevented him from seeing the spruce forest on the other side of the gorge, but he knew it was there. Uninhabited. Silent. Blind. They hadn't been able to find witnesses that time. Not that time either.

He looked at his hands. The reason he couldn't move them was that they were bound to the wheel with plastic ties. The ties had almost completely taken over from handcuffs in the police force now. You just put the narrow bands around the wrists of the arrestee and tightened them, they restrained even the strongest suspects; the most anyone who struggled could achieve was deep cuts into the skin and the flesh. To the bone, if they didn't give up.

Anton gripped the wheel, with no feeling in his fingers.

"Awake?" The voice sounded strangely familiar. Anton turned to the passenger seat. Stared into the eyes peering through the holes of a balaclava. Same type Delta, the special forces, used.

"Let's release this, shall we?"

The gloved left hand gripped the handbrake between them and lifted it. Anton had always liked the rasp of the old handbrakes, it gave him a sense of the mechanics, of cogs and chains, of what was actually happening. This time it was lifted and released with barely a murmur. Just a slight crunch. The cogs. They rolled forward. But only a metre or two. Anton had instinctively stamped his foot on the brake pedal. He'd had to stamp hard as the engine was not switched on.

"Good reactions, Mittet."

Anton stared through the windscreen. The voice. That voice. He took his foot off the brake. It creaked like an unlubricated door hinge, the car moved and he stamped his foot back down. And held it there this time.

The interior light came on.

"Do you think René knew he was going to die?"

Anton Mittet didn't answer. He had just caught a glimpse of himself in the mirror. At least he thought it was him. His face was covered with glistening blood. His nose was swollen on one side, probably broken.

"How does it feel, Mittet? Knowing? Can you tell me that?"

"Wh . . . why?" Anton's question was almost an automatic response. He wasn't even sure if he wanted to know why. Just knew he was freezing cold. And that he wanted to get away. He wanted to go to Laura. To hold her. To be held by her. Smell her fragrance. Feel her warmth.

"Haven't you worked it out, Mittet? It's because you didn't solve the case, of course. I'm giving you all another chance. An opportunity to learn from earlier mistakes."

"L . . . learn?"

"Did you know that psychological research has shown that slightly negative feedback enhances your performance? Not very negative and not positive, but just a **bit** negative. Punishing all of you, killing just one detective from the group at a time, is like a series of slightly negative reports, don't you think?"

The wheels creaked, and Anton stamped on the pedal again. Staring at the edge. It felt as though he would have to press even harder.

"It's the brake fluid," the voice said. "I punctured the pipe. It's running out. Soon it won't help however hard you press. Do you think you'll be able to think while you're falling? Or regret what you've done?"

"Regret wha . . . ?" Anton wanted to go on, but no more words came, his mouth seemed to be filled with flour. Fall. He didn't want to fall.

"Regret taking the baton," the voice said. "Regret not helping to find the murderer. It could have saved you from this, you know."

Anton had a feeling he was squeezing the fluid out via the pedal, that the harder he pressed, the quicker the fluid was being drained from the system. He eased the pressure with his foot. The gravel under the tyres crunched, and in his panic he pushed his back against the seat and straightened his legs against the floor and the brake pedal. The car had two separate hydraulic brake systems; maybe just one of them had been punctured.

"If you repent perhaps your sins will be forgiven, Mittet. Jesus is magnanimous."

"I . . . I repent. Get me out."

Low laughter. "But, Mittet, I'm talking about heaven. **I'm** not Jesus. You won't get any forgiveness from me." Little pause. "And the answer is yes, I punctured both systems."

For a moment Anton thought he could **hear** the brake fluid dripping from under the car until he noticed that it was his own blood dripping from the tip of his chin into his lap. He was going to die. It was suddenly such an inalienable fact that a chill washed through his body and it became more difficult to move, as though rigor mortis had already set in. But why was the murderer still sitting beside him?

"You're frightened of dying," the voice said. "It's your body; it's secreting a scent. Can you smell it? Adrenalin. It smells of medicine and urine. It's the same odour you smell in old people's homes and slaughterhouses. The smell of mortal fear."

Anton gasped for air; there didn't seem to be enough for both of them.

"As for me, I'm not at all afraid of dying," the voice said. "Isn't it strange? That you can lose something so fundamentally human as the fear of dying. Of course, it's partly to do with the desire to live, but only partly. Many people spend their whole lives somewhere they don't want to be out of fear that the alternative is worse. Isn't that sad?"

Anton had a sense he was being suffocated. He had never had asthma himself, but he had seen Laura when she had an attack, seen the desperate, imploring expression on her face, felt the despair at not being able to help, at being no more than a spectator of her panic-stricken struggle to breathe. But a part of him had also been curious, wanting to know, to feel what it was like to be there, to feel you were on the verge of dying, to feel there was nothing you could do, it was something that was being done **to** you.

Now he knew.

"I believe death is a better place," the voice intoned. "But I can't join you now, Anton. You see, I have a job to do."

Anton could hear the crunching of gravel again, like a hoarse voice slowly introducing a sentence with this sound that would soon go faster. And it was no longer possible to press the pedal any further, it was on the floor.

"Goodbye."

He felt the cold air from the passenger's side as the door was opened.

"The patient," Anton groaned.

He stared ahead at the edge, where everything disappeared, but felt the person in the passenger seat turn towards him.

"Which patient?"

Anton stuck out his tongue, ran it along his top lip, sensing something moist that tasted sweet and metallic. Licked the inside of his mouth. Found his voice. "The patient at the Rikshospital. I was drugged before he was killed. Was that you?"

There was a couple of seconds' silence as he listened to the rain. The rain out there in the darkness, was there a more beautiful sound? If he could have chosen he would have sat there listening to the sound day after day. Year after year. Listening and listening, enjoying every second he was given.

Then the body beside him moved, he felt the car rise as it was relieved of the man's weight. The door closed softly. He was alone. The car was moving. The sound of tyres rolling slowly on gravel was like a husky whisper. The handbrake. It was fifty centimetres away from his right hand. Anton tried to pull his hands away. Didn't even feel the pain as the skin burst. The husky whisper was louder and quicker now. He knew he was too tall and too stiff to get a foot under the handbrake, so he leaned down. Opened his mouth. Held the tip of the handbrake, felt it pressing against the inside of his upper teeth, pulled, but it slipped out. Tried again, knowing it was too late, but he preferred to die like this, fighting, desperate, alive. He twisted, held the brake lever in his mouth again.

Now it was totally still. The voice had gone quiet and the rain had come to a sudden stop. No, it hadn't stopped. It was him. He was falling. Weightless, as he swirled round in a slow waltz, like the one he had danced that time with Laura while everyone they knew stood around watching. Rotated on his own axis, slowly, swaying, step-two-three, only now he was all alone. Falling in this strange silence. Falling with the rain.

14

Laura Mittet looked at them. She had come down to the front of the block in Elveparken when they rang, and now she was standing with her arms crossed, freezing in her dressing gown. The first rays of sun glittering on the River Drammen. Something had flickered in her mind; for a couple of seconds she wasn't there, she didn't hear them, didn't see anything, except for the river behind them. For a few seconds she was alone thinking that Anton had never been the right one. She had never met Mr. Right, or at least had never got him. And the one she had got, Anton, had cheated on her the same year they got married. He had never found out that she knew. She'd had too much to lose for that. And he'd probably been having another affair now. He'd had the same expression on his face of exaggerated normality when he delivered the same rotten excuses. Overtime shifts imposed from above. Traffic jam on the way home. Mobile off because the battery was dead.

There were two of them. A man and a woman, both in uniforms without a wrinkle or a stain. As though they had just taken them out of the wardrobe and put them on. Serious, almost frightened eyes.

Called her "fru Mittet." No one else did. And she wouldn't have appreciated it, either. It was his name and she had regretted taking it many times.

They coughed. They had something to tell her. So what were they waiting for? She already knew. They had already told her with those idiotic, hammed-up tragic faces of theirs. She was furious. So furious that she could feel her face writhing, distorting into some- one she didn't want to be, who had also been forced into a role in this comic tragedy. They had said some- thing. What was it? Was it Norwegian? The words made no sense.

She had never wanted to have Mr. Right. And she had never wanted his name.

Until now.

15

The black VW Sharan slowly rose in circles towards the blue sky. Like a rocket in super slow motion, Katrine thought, watching the trail, which was not fire and smoke but water running from the doors and boot of the crushed car, dissolving into drops and glistening in the sun on its way down to the river.

"We hauled the car up here last time," the local police officer said.

They were standing by the disused sawmill with the peeling red paint and smashed panes in the small windows. The withered grass lay on the ground like a Hitler fringe, combed in the direction the rain had fallen the previous night. In the shadows lay grey flecks of slushy snow. Doomed, a prematurely returning migratory bird sang optimistically, and the river gurgled with contentment.

"But this one was stuck between two rocks, so it was easier to raise it straight up."

Katrine's gaze followed the river downstream. Above the sawmill, there was a dam, where the water trickled between the enormous grey rocks that had embraced the vehicle. She saw the sun glinting on the scattered fragments of glass. Then her eyes were drawn up the vertical rock face. Drammen granite. It was a concept apparently. She glimpsed the tail of the truck and the yellow crane protruding over the edge of the precipice high up. Hoped someone had worked out the weight versus jib ratio correctly.

"But if you're detectives, why aren't you up there with the others?" said the policeman who let them through the cordon after carefully examining their ID cards.

Katrine shrugged. She couldn't exactly say they were apple scrumping, four people with no real authorisation, on the kind of mission that meant they should keep their distance from the official investigation unit.

"We can see what we need to see from here," Beate Lønn said. "Thanks for letting us look."

"No problem."

Katrine Bratt switched off her iPad, which was still logged into the Norwegian Prisons site, then hurried after Beate Lønn and Ståle Aune, who had already crossed the cordon and were on their way back to Bjørn Holm's forty-year-old-plus Volvo Amazon. Its owner came sauntering down the steep gravel road from the top and caught them up at the old-timer with no air conditioning, airbag or central locking, but with two chequered speed stripes over the hood, roof and tail. Katrine concluded from Holm's heaving chest that he would hardly satisfy the current PHS entrance requirements.

"Well?" Beate said.

"The face is partly smashed, but they reckon the

body's probably one Anton Mittet," Holm said, removing his Rasta hat and using it to wipe the sweat from his round face.

"Mittet," Beate said. "Of course."

The others turned to her.

"A local officer. He took over from Simon in Maridalen. Do you remember, Bjørn?"

"No," Holm said, without any visible shame. Katrine assumed he had got used to the idea that his boss was from Mars.

"He used to be in the Drammen force. And he was tangentially involved in the investigation of the previous murder here."

Katrine shook her head in astonishment. It was one thing for Beate to react as soon as the message about a car in the river had appeared on the police log and she had ordered them all to Drammen because she remembered that it was the exact spot where René Kalsnes had been murdered several years ago. And quite another for her to remember the name of a Drammen man who had been **tangentially** involved in the investigation.

"He was easy to remember because he made such a blunder," said Beate, obviously having noticed Katrine shaking her head. "He kept quiet about a baton he found because he was frightened it could implicate the police. Did they say anything about the probable cause of death?"

"No," Holm said. "It's pretty clear he would have been killed by the fall. The handbrake went through his mouth and out the back of his head. But he must have been beaten while he was alive because his face was bruised."

"Could he have driven off the cliff himself?" Katrine asked.

"Maybe. But his hands were attached to the wheel with cable ties. There were no brake marks, and the car hit the rocks close to the cliff, so it can't have been going very fast. Must have just rolled over."

"Handbrake in his mouth?" Beate said with a frown. "How did that happen?"

"His hands were tied and the car was rolling towards the edge," Katrine said. "He must have been trying to pull it with his mouth."

"Perhaps. Anyway, this is a policeman. He was killed at an old crime scene."

"On a murder that was never cleared up," Bjørn Holm added.

"Yes, but there are some important differences between that murder and the murders of the girls in Maridalen and Tryvann," Beate said, waving the report they had printed at breakneck speed before leaving the basement office. "René Kalsnes was a man and there were no signs of sexual abuse."

"There's an even more important difference," Katrine said.

"Oh?"

She patted the iPad under her arm. "I was just checking criminal records and the lists of prisoners as we were coming here. Valentin Gjertsen was serving a short sentence in Ila when René Kalsnes was killed."

"Shit!" That was Holm.

"Now now," Beate said. "That doesn't rule out Valentin killing Anton Mittet. He might have broken the pattern here, but it's still the same madman behind it. Isn't it, Ståle?"

The three of them turned to Ståle Aune, who had been unusually quiet. Katrine noticed that the plump man was also unusually pale. He was leaning on the door of the Amazon, and his chest was rising and falling.

"Ståle?" Beate repeated.

"Sorry," he said, making an unsuccessful attempt to smile. "The handbrake . . ."

"You'll get used to it," Beate said with an equally unsuccessful attempt to hide her impatience. "Is this our cop killer or not?"

Ståle Aune straightened up. "Serial killers can break the pattern, if that's what you're asking me. But I don't think this is a copycat continuing where the first . . . er, cop killer left off. As Harry was wont to say, a serial killer is a white whale. So, a serial killer of police officers is a white whale with pink dots. There aren't two of them."

"So we agree this is the same murderer," Beate stated. "But the prison sentence pulls the carpet from under the theory that Valentin is visiting his old haunts and repeating the murders."

"Nevertheless," Bjørn said, "this is the only murder where the murder itself is also a copy. The blows to the face, the car in the river. That may have some significance."

"Ståle?"

"It might mean that he feels he's becoming more skilled, that he's perfecting the murders by making them polished replicas."

"Come on," Katrine bridled. "You're making him sound like an artist."

"Really?" Ståle said, sending her a quizzical look.

"Lønn!"

They turned. From the top of the hill came a man with a flapping Hawaiian shirt, quivering belly and dancing curls. The relatively high speed appeared to be more a consequence of the steep gradient of the hill than any enthusiasm on the body's part.

"Let's get going," Beate said.

They had piled into the Amazon, and Bjørn was making a third stab at starting the car when a bony index finger tapped on the window at the front where Beate was sitting.

She gave a low groan and wound down the window.

"Roger Gjendem," she said. "Does **Aftenposten** have any questions I can answer with 'no comment?'"

"This is the third policeman to be murdered," the man in the Hawaiian shirt gasped, and Katrine was able to confirm that, fitness-wise, Bjørn Holm had met his inferior. "Have you got any leads?"

Beate Lønn smiled.

"N-O C-O-M . . ." Roger Gjendem spelt out, while pretending to write in his notebook. "We've been keeping an ear open. Picking up little things. A garage owner says Mittet filled up at his place late last night. He thought Mittet was alone. Does that mean . . . ?"

"No . . ."

". . . comment. I reckon your police chief will have to make you carry loaded guns from now on."

Beate raised an eyebrow. "What do you mean?"

"The gun in Mittet's glove compartment." Gjendem bent down and cast a suspicious look at the others, to see if they really hadn't got this basic information. "Empty, even though there was a box of ammo there. If he'd had his gun loaded it might have saved his life."

"Do you know what, Gjendem?" Beate said. "You can just add ditto marks after the first answer you got. Actually, I'd prefer it if you didn't mention this little meeting to anyone."

"Why's that?"

The engine growled into life.

"Have a nice day, Gjendem." Beate began to wind up the window. But not quickly enough to avoid the next question.

"Are you missing you-know-who?"

Holm let go of the clutch.

Katrine watched Roger Gjendem shrinking in the mirror.

But waited until they had passed Liertoppen before she said what everyone was thinking.

"Gjendem's right."

"Yes," Beate sighed. "But he's no longer available, Katrine."

"I know, but we have to try!"

"Try what?" Bjørn Holm asked. "Digging up a man declared dead and buried?"

Katrine stared out at the monotonous trees as they glided along the motorway. Thinking how once she had flown in a police helicopter above here, the most densely populated part of Norway, and how it had struck her that even here there was just so much forest and wilderness. Places people didn't go. Places to hide. That even here houses were tiny dots in the night, the motorway a thin stripe through the impenetrable darkness. That it was impossible to see everything. That you had to be able to smell. To listen. To know.

They had almost arrived in Asker, but they had travelled in a silence so impenetrable that when Katrine did answer no one had forgotten the question.

"Yes," she said.

16

Katrine Bratt crossed the open square in front of Chateau Neuf, the headquarters of the Norwegian Student Society. Great parties, cool gigs, heated debates. That was how she remembered the place. And in between they had passed their exams.

The dress code had changed surprisingly little since she was here: T-shirts, sagging trousers, nerdy glasses, retro Puffa jackets and retro army jackets, security of style trying to camouflage insecurity, the avarege social climber signalling "smart slacker," the fear of failing socially and professionally. At any rate, though, they were glad not to be the poor buggers on the other side of the square, which was where Katrine was heading.

Some of them were coming towards her now from the prison-like gate in front of the college grounds: students in black police uniforms that always looked a bit too big however well they fitted. From afar she could pick out the first years; they looked as if they were standing in the middle of the uniform, and the peak of the cap came too far down their foreheads. Either to conceal their insecurity or to avoid meeting the slightly contemptuous or even sympathetic looks from students across the square, the proper students, the free, independent, socially critical, thinking intellectuals. Who were grinning behind long, greasy hair, lying on the steps in the sun, exalted in their supine states, inhaling what they knew the police trainee knew **might** be a reefer.

For they were the real youth, the cream of society with a right to make mistakes, those who still had life choices ahead of them, not behind.

Perhaps it was only Katrine who had felt like this when she was here, who felt the desire to shout that they didn't know who she was, why she had chosen to become a police officer, what she had decided to do with the rest of her life.

The old duty officer, Karsten Kaspersen, still stood in the office inside the door, but if he did remember Katrine Bratt, his face didn't show it as he examined her ID card and gave a quick nod. She walked down the corridor to a lecture room. Passing the door of the crime-scene room which was furnished like a flat with partition walls and had a gallery from where they could watch one another practising searches, finding clues and interpreting the course of events. Then the door to the fitness room, with training mats and the smell of sweat, where they drilled the fine art of wrestling people to the ground and applying handcuffs. At the end of the corridor she slipped into auditorium 2. The lecture was in full flow, so she crept along to a free seat in the back row. She sat down so quietly she wasn't noticed by the two girls excitedly whispering in front of her.

"She's weird, I'm telling you. She's got a picture of him on her bedsit wall."

"**Has** she?"

"I've seen it myself."

"My God, he's so old. And ugly."

"Do you think?"

"Are you blind?" She nodded to the board where the lecturer was writing with his back to the class.

"Motive!" The lecturer had turned to them and repeated the word he had written on the board. "The psychological cost of killing is so high for rationally thinking people with normal feelings that there has to be an extremely good motive. Extremely good motives are as a rule easier and quicker to find than murder weapons, witnesses or forensic evidence. And they point you straight to a potential perp. That is why every detective should start with the question 'why.'"

He paused to scan the audience, a bit like a sheepdog circling and keeping the flock together, Katrine thought.

He raised his forefinger. "A rough simplification: find the motive and you've got the murderer."

Katrine Bratt didn't think he was ugly. Not attractive though, of course, not in the conventional meaning of the word. More what the British call an acquired taste. And the voice was the same deep, warm voice with the slightly worn, hoarse edge that appealed not only to young student fans.

"Yes?" The lecturer had hesitated for a moment before giving the floor to a female student waving her arm.

"Why do we send out large, costly forensics units if a brilliant detective like you can crack the case with a few questions and a bit of deduction?"

There was no audible irony in the girl's intonation, only an almost childlike sincerity plus a lilt that revealed she must have lived in the north.

Katrine saw the emotions flicker across the lecturer's face—embarrassment, resignation, annoyance—before he collected himself and gave an answer: "Because it's never enough to **know** who the lawbreaker is, Silje. During the bank robbery wave in Oslo ten years ago the Robberies Unit had a female officer who could recognise masked robbers by the shape of their faces."

"Beate Lønn," said the girl he had called Silje. "The boss of Krimteknisk."

"Exactly. And so in eight out of ten cases the Robberies Unit knew who the masked men on the CCTV videos were. But they didn't have any proof. Fingerprints are proof. A used gun is proof. A convinced detective is **not** proof, however brilliant he or she may be. I've used a number of simplifications today, but here is the last: the answer to the question 'why' is worthless unless we find out how and vice versa. But now that we've got a bit further in the process Folkestad is going to talk about forensic investigation." He glanced at his watch. "We'll talk more in depth about motives next time, but here's something to get your brains working. Why do people kill one another?"

He scanned the audience again with an encouraging expression. Katrine saw that in addition to the scar that ran like a channel from the corner of his mouth to his ear he had two new scars. One looked like a slash with a knife to the neck; the other could have been made by a bullet at the side of his head, level with his eyebrows. But otherwise he looked better than she had ever seen him. The 1.92-metre figure looked tall and supple; the blond, cropped brush of hair still didn't have any flecks of grey. And she could see he was toned beneath his T-shirt. There was meat back on his bones. And, most important of all, life in his eyes. The alert, energetic, bordering on manic, look was back. Laughter lines and expansive body language she had never seen before. You could almost suspect him of leading a good life. Which, if this was the case, would be a first.

"Because they have something to gain by it," a boy's voice answered.

The lecturer nodded good-naturedly. "You would think so, wouldn't you? But murder as a crime for profit is not that usual, Vetle."

A barking Sunnmøre voice: "Because they hate someone?"

"Elling is suggesting crimes of passion," he said. "Jealousy. Rejection. Revenge. Yes, definitely. Anything else?"

"Because they are deranged." The suggestion came from a tall, stooped boy.

"Deranged's not the word, Robert." It was the girl again. Katrine could only see a blonde ponytail over the back of the seat in the front row. "It's called—"

"It's fine. We know what he means, Silje." The lecturer had sat down at the front of the desk, stretched out his long legs and crossed his arms over the Glasvegas logo on his T-shirt. "And personally I think 'deranged' is an excellent word. But not in fact a particularly usual reason for murder. There are of course those who are of the opinion that murder in itself is proof of insanity, but most murders are rational. Just as it's rational to seek material gain, it's rational to seek emotional relief. The murderer may have some idea that murder will dull the pain that comes with hatred, fear, jealousy, humiliation."

"But if murder is so rational . . ." The first boy. "Can you tell us how many satisfied murderers you've met?"

The class smart-arse, Katrine hazarded a guess.

"Very few," the lecturer said. "But the fact that the murder is felt to be a disappointment doesn't mean it's not a rational act so long as the murderer **believes** he will obtain relief. But revenge is generally sweeter in your imagination; the fury of a murder motivated by jealousy is followed by regret, the moment that the serial killer builds up to so carefully is invariably an anticlimax, so he has to keep trying. In short . . ." He got up and went back to the board. "As far as murder is concerned, there is something in the claim that crime doesn't pay. For the next session I want each of you to think of a motive that could drive you to murder. I don't want any politically correct bullshit. I want you to examine your darkest, innermost recesses. Well, the next darkest will do perhaps. And then I want you to read Aune's thesis on the personality of a murderer and profiling, OK? And, yes,

I'm going to ask follow-up questions. So be afraid, be ready. Off you go."

There was a cacophony as seats sprang back.

Katrine stayed where she was, watching the students passing her. In the end, there were only three people left. Her, the lecturer wiping the board and the blonde ponytail who was standing right behind him, legs together, notes under her arm. Katrine could see she was slim. And that her voice sounded different now from when she had been speaking in class.

"Do you think the serial killer you caught in Australia achieved satisfaction after killing the women?" Affected little girl's voice. Like a young girl trying to get into her father's good books.

"Silje . . ."

"I mean, he raped them. And that must have been pretty good."

"Read the thesis and we can come back to it in the next session, OK?"

"OK."

Still she hung around. Rocking up and down on her feet. As if stretching up on her toes, Katrine thought. Up to him. While the lecturer shuffled his papers into a leather case without taking any notice of her. Then she turned on her heel and went up the stairs to the exit. Slowed down when she saw Katrine and eyeballed her, then sped up and was gone.

"Hi, Harry," Katrine said quietly.

"Hi, Katrine," he said without looking.

"You look good."

"Same to you," he said, zipping up his case.

"Did you see me arrive?"

"I **sensed** you arrive." He looked up. And smiled. Katrine had always been surprised at the metamorphosis his face went through when he smiled. At how the smile could blow away the hard, dismissive, life-weary expression he wore like a shabby coat. At how, suddenly, he could look like a playful, overgrown boy with the sun radiating from him. Like a sunny July day in Bergen. As welcome as it was rare and short.

"What does that mean?"

"That I've been half expecting you to turn up."

"Oh, you have, have you?"

"Yes. And the answer's no." He stuffed the case under his arm, ran up the stairs to her in four long strides and hugged her.

She squeezed him, drawing in his aroma. "No to what, Harry?"

"No, you can't have me," he whispered in her ear. "But you knew that, didn't you?"

"Hey!" she said, trying to free herself from his grip. "If it hadn't been for Miss Ugly Bug it wouldn't have taken me five minutes to have you at my feet, sunshine. And I didn't say you looked **that** good."

He laughed, let her go and Katrine felt herself thinking he could have held her for a bit longer. She had never worked out whether she really wanted Harry; maybe it had always been so unrealistic she refrained from forming an opinion on it. And in time it had become a joke and the waters were muddied. Besides he was back with Rakel. Or Miss Ugly Bug as he allowed Katrine to call her as the notion was so absurd it only emphasised Rakel's annoying beauty.

Harry rubbed his badly shaven chin. "Hm, if it's not my irresistible body you're after, then it must be . . ." He raised a forefinger. "I've got it. My brilliant mind!"

"You haven't got any funnier over the years, either."

"And the answer's still no. And you knew that too."

"Have you got an office where we can discuss this?"

"Yes and no. I have an office, but not one where we can discuss whether I can help you with the murder case."

"Murder cases."

"It's one case, as far as I've been informed."

"Fascinating, isn't it?"

"Don't you try that one on me. I've finished with that kind of life, and you know it."

"Harry, this case needs you. And you need it."

The smile didn't reach his eyes this time. "I need a murder case like I need a drink, Katrine. Sorry. Save yourself some time and try an alternative."

She looked at him. Thinking the analogy with drink came without any hesitation. It confirmed what she had suspected, that he was simply afraid. Afraid that if he so much as looked at a case it would have the same result as a drop of booze. He wouldn't be able to stop; he would be swallowed up, consumed. For a moment her conscience pricked her, the pusher's unbidden attack of self-loathing. Until she started visualising the crime scene again. Anton Mittet's crushed skull.

"There are no alternatives for you, Harry."

"I can give you a couple of names," Harry said. "There's a guy I was on the FBI course with. I can ring and—"

"Harry . . ." Katrine grabbed him under the arm and led him to the door. "Has this office of yours got any coffee?"

"It has, but as I said—"

"Forget the case. Let's just have a chat about the old days."

"Have you got the time for it?"

"I need some distraction."

He looked at her. Was about to say something, then changed his mind. Nodded. "OK."

They went up a staircase and down a corridor to the offices.

"I can hear you've nicked bits of Ståle Aune's psychology lectures," Katrine said. As usual she had to jog to keep up with Harry's giant strides.

"I nick as much as I can. After all, he was the best."

"Like 'deranged' being one of the few words in medicine which is exact, intuitively comprehensible and poetic all at once. But precise words always end up on the scrapheap because stupid professionals think linguistic obfuscation is best for patients' welfare."

"Yep," Harry said.

"That's why I'm no longer a manic-depressive. Not borderline, either. I'm bipolar type II."

"Two?"

"Do you understand? Why doesn't Aune lecture? I thought he loved it."

"He wanted a better life. Simpler. More quality time with his nearest and dearest. A wise decision."

She eyed him. "You should persuade him. No one in society should be allowed to stop using such a superior talent when there is most need for it. Don't you agree?"

Harry chuckled. "You're not going to give up, are you? I think there's a need for me here, Katrine. And the college won't contact Aune because they want to see more uniformed lecturers, not civilians."

"You're wearing civvies."

"And that's my point. In fact, I am no longer in the police force, Katrine. It was a choice. Which means that I, we, are in different places now."

"How did you get that scar on your temple?" she asked and noticed Harry almost imperceptibly but instantly flinch. Before he could answer, a sonorous voice in the corridor called out.

"Harry!"

They stopped and turned. A short, bulky man with a full red beard came out of one of the doors and approached them with an uneven rolling gait. Katrine followed Harry as he went to meet the older man.

"You've got a visitor," the man roared long before they had reached a normal speaking distance.

"Indeed," Harry said. "Katrine Bratt. This is Arnold Folkestad."

"I mean you have a visitor in your office," Folkestad said, stopping to take a couple of deep breaths before passing Katrine a large, freckled hand.

"Arnold and I co-lecture on murder investigation," Harry said.

"And since he's been given the entertaining side of the subject, naturally he's the more popular of us two," Folkestad growled. "While I have to bring them down to earth with methodology, forensics, ethics and regulations. The world is unjust."

"On the other hand, Arnold knows a bit about pedagogy," Harry said.

"The whelp's making progress," Folkestad chortled.

Harry frowned. "This visitor, it's not . . . ?"

"Relax, it's not frøken Silje Gravseng, just old colleagues. I gave them some coffee."

Harry eyed Katrine sharply. Then he turned and marched towards the door. Katrine and Folkestad watched him leave.

"Er, did I say something wrong?" Folkestad asked in amazement.

"I know this might be construed as a pincer movement strategy," Beate said, lifting the cup of coffee to her mouth.

"Do you mean by that it's **not** a pincer movement?" Harry said, leaning back on his chair as far as it was possible to go in the tiny office. On the other side of the desk, behind the towering piles of paper, Beate Lønn, Bjørn Holm and Katrine Bratt were squeezed into chairs. The round of greetings was soon over.

Brief handshakes, no hugs. No clumsy attempts at small talk. Harry Hole was not the type. Harry Hole was the type to get to the point. And, of course, they knew he already knew what that was.

Beate took a sip, winced inevitably and put the cup down with a disapproving mien.

"I know you've made up your mind not to do any more active investigation," Beate said. "And I also know you have better reason than most. The question, however, is whether you can make an exception here or not. You are, after all, our sole specialist in serial killings. The state invested money and trained you with the FBI—"

"—which, as you know, I paid back with blood, sweat and tears," Harry broke in. "And not just my own blood and tears."

"I haven't forgotten that Rakel and Oleg ended up in the firing line on the Snowman case, but—"

"The answer's no," Harry said. "I've promised Rakel that none of us will go back there. And for once I intend to keep a promise."

"How's Oleg?" Beate asked.

"Better," Harry said, keeping a weather eye on her. "As you know, he's in a detox clinic in Switzerland."

"I'm glad to hear that. And Rakel got the job in Geneva?"

"Yes."

"Does she commute?"

"Four days in Geneva, three at home. It's good for Oleg to have his mother close by."

"I can understand that," Beate said. "In a way

they're out of every firing line there, aren't they? And you're alone during the week. Days when you can do what you like."

Harry laughed quietly. "My dear Beate, perhaps I didn't make myself clear enough. **This** is what I want. To lecture. To pass on my knowledge."

"Ståle Aune's with us," Katrine said.

"Good for him," Harry said. "And for you. He knows as much about serial murders as I do."

"Sure he doesn't know more?" Katrine said with a hint of a smile and a raised eyebrow.

Harry laughed. "Nice try, Katrine. OK. He knows more."

"My God," Katrine said, "what's happened to your competitive streak?"

"The combination of you three and Ståle Aune is the best possible start for this case. I have another lecture, so . . ."

Katrine slowly shook her head. "What's happened to you, Harry?"

"Good things," Harry said. "Good things have happened to me."

"Message received and understood," Beate said, getting up. "But I'd still like to ask if we can consult you now and then."

She saw he was going to shake his head. "Don't answer no," she hastened to add. "I'll ring you later."

In the corridor, three minutes later, as Harry was striding towards the auditorium, where the students had already gathered, it struck Beate that perhaps it was true, perhaps the love of a woman **could** save a man. And she doubted in this case that another woman's sense of duty would be enough to whisk him back into the jaws of hell. But that was her task. He had looked shockingly healthy and happy. She would so much have liked to let him go. But she knew they would soon reappear, the ghosts of colleagues that had been killed. And she formulated the next thought: they won't be the last.

She rang Harry as soon as she was back in the Boiler Room.

Rico Herrem woke with a start.

He blinked in the darkness until his eyes could focus on the white screen three rows in front of him, where a fat woman was sucking off a horse. Felt his racing pulse slow down. No reason to panic, he was still in Fiskebutikken; it was just the vibration of a new arrival that had woken him. Rico opened his mouth and tried to inhale some oxygen from the air that stank of sweat, tobacco and something that might have been fish, but wasn't. It was forty years since Moen's Fiskebutikk had sold the original combination of relatively fresh fish over the counter and relatively fresh porn mags under the counter. After Moen had sold up and gone into retirement—so that he could drink himself to death more systematically—the new owners had opened a twenty-four-hour cinema in the basement showing straight porn. But when VHS and DVDs had taken their customers they specialised in procuring and showing films you couldn't get online, at least not without the police knocking at your door.

The sound was on so low Rico could hear the wanking in the darkness around him. He had been told that was the idea, that was why the sound was on so low. He had long grown out of the boyhood fascination with group wanking, that wasn't why he was sitting here. It wasn't why he had headed here straight after his release, sat here for two solid days, broken only by emergency trips to eat, shit and get more booze. He still had four Rohypnol pills in his pocket. He had to make them last.

Of course, he could spend the rest of his life in Fiskebutikken. But he had persuaded his mother to lend him ten thousand kroner, and until the Thai Embassy had sorted out his extended tourist visa Fiskebutikken offered the darkness and anonymity he required to avoid being found.

He inhaled, but it was as though the air consisted entirely of nitrogen, argon and carbon dioxide. He looked at his watch. The luminous hand was on six. In the evening or the morning? It was perpetual night in here, but it had to be evening. The feeling of suffocation came and went. He mustn't get claustrophobic, not now. Not until he was out of the country. Gone. Far, far from Valentin. God, how he longed for his cell. For the security. The loneliness. The air you could breathe.

The woman on the screen was working hard, but

had to follow the horse as it took a few steps forward, causing the picture to blur for a second.

"Hi, Rico."

Rico froze. The voice was low, a whisper, but the sound was like an icicle being driven into his ear.

"**Vanessa's Friends.** A real eighties classic. Did you know that Vanessa died during the recording? Stamped on by a mare. Jealousy, do you think?"

Rico wanted to turn, but was stopped by a hand squeezing the top of his neck, holding it in a vise-like grip. He wanted to shout, but a gloved hand was already over his mouth and nose. Rico breathed in the smell of pungent, wet wool.

"It was disappointingly easy to find you. Pervs' cinema. Rather obvious, don't you think?" Low chortle. "What's more it illuminates your red skull like a lighthouse. Looks like your eczema's bad at the moment, Rico. It flares up during periods of stress, isn't that correct?"

The hand over his mouth slackened the pressure so that he could get some air. There was a smell of chalk dust and ski grease.

"There are rumours going round that you spoke to a policewoman at Ila, Rico. Did you have anything in common?"

The woollen glove over his mouth was removed. Rico breathed heavily as his tongue searched for saliva.

"I didn't say anything," he gasped. "I swear. Why would I? I was getting out in a few days anyway."

"Money."

"I've **got** money!"

"You spent all your money on rope, Rico. I bet you've got some pills in your pocket now."

"I'm not joking! I'm off to Thailand the day after tomorrow. You won't have any trouble with me, I promise."

Rico could hear that sounded like the pleading of a petrified man, but he couldn't care less. He **was** petrified.

"Relax, Rico. I don't intend to do anything to my tattooist. You trust a man you've let stick needles in your skin. Don't you?"

"You . . . you can trust me."

"Good. Pattaya sounds good."

Rico didn't answer. He hadn't said he was going to Pattaya. How . . . ? Rico was tipped back slightly as the other man grabbed the seat to help him stand up.

"Gotta go. I've got a job to do. Enjoy the sun, Rico. It's good for eczema, I've heard."

Rico turned and looked up. The man had masked the bottom half of his face with a scarf, and it was too dark for him to see the eyes properly. He suddenly bent down to Rico.

"Did you know that when they did the autopsy on Vanessa they found sexual diseases medical science didn't know existed? Stick to your own species, that's my advice."

Rico watched the figure hurry to the exit. Watched him take off the scarf. Glimpsed the face in the green light of the exit sign as it disappeared behind the black felt curtain. The oxygen seemed to pour back into the room, and Rico sucked it in greedily as he blinked at the running stick man on the exit sign.

He was confused.

Confused that he was still alive and confused about what he had just seen. Not confused that pervs were busy checking out escape routes. They had always done that. But that it wasn't him. The voice had been the same, the laugh too. But the man he had seen in the green light for a fraction of a second was **not** him. It wasn't Valentin.

17

"So you've moved in here, have you?" Beate said, looking around the spacious kitchen. Outside the window, darkness had descended over Holmenkollen Ridge and the neighbouring houses. None of the houses was the same, but they were all twice the size of the house Beate had inherited from her mother in East Oslo and they had hedges that were double the height, double garages and double-barrelled names on the letter boxes. Beate knew she was prejudiced about West Oslo, but it was still strange to see Harry Hole in these surroundings.

"Yes," Harry said, pouring coffee for both of them.

"Isn't it . . . lonely?"

"Mm. Don't you and the littl'un live on your own as well?"

"Yes, but . . ." She didn't continue. What she wanted to say was that she lived in a cosy yellow house erected in the Einar Gerhardsen socialist spirit of the reconstruction period after the Second World War, sober and practical, with none of the national-romantic fashion that caused the affluent to build log-cabin-like fortresses such as this. With black-stained timbers, which even on sunny days gave an atmosphere of eternal darkness and melancholy to the house Rakel had inherited from her father.

"Rakel comes home at the weekends," he said, lifting his cup to his mouth.

"So things are good?"

"Things are very good."

Beate nodded and studied him. The changes. He had laughter lines around his eyes, but still looked younger. The titanium prosthesis replacing his middle finger on the right hand clinked against the cup.

"What about you?" Harry asked.

"Good. Busy. The little one's off school staying with his grandmother in Steinkjer."

"Really? Scary how quickly . . ." He half closed his eyes and chuckled.

"Yes," Beate said, sipping her coffee. "Harry, I wanted to meet you because I'd like to know what happened."

"I know," Harry said. "I meant to contact you. But I had to sort things out with Oleg. And myself."

"Come on then."

"OK," Harry said, putting down his cup. "You were the only person I informed while it was going on. You helped me, and I owe you a great debt of thanks, Beate. And you're the only person who'll ever know. But are you sure you want to know? It could put you in a bit of a dilemma."

"I was an accessory the moment I started helping you, Harry. And we got rid of violin. It's not on the streets any more."

"Fantastic," Harry said drily. "The market's back on heroin, crack and speedballs."

"And the man behind violin's gone. Rudolf Asayev's dead."

"I know."

"Oh? You **knew** he was dead? Did you know he was in a coma under a false name at the Rikshospital for more than a year before he died?"

Harry raised an eyebrow. "Asayev? I thought he died in a room at Hotel Leon."

"He was found there. With blood from wall to wall. But they managed to keep him alive. Until now. How do you know about Hotel Leon? All of that was kept under wraps."

Harry didn't answer, just twirled the cup in his hand.

"Oh no . . ." Beate groaned.

Harry shrugged his shoulders. "I said you might not want to know."

"It was you who stabbed him?"

"Would it help if I said it was in self-defence?"

"We found a bullet in the wooden bed frame. But the wound from the knife was big and deep, Harry. The pathologist said the blade must have been twisted round several times."

Harry looked down into his cup. "Well, I obviously didn't do a thorough enough job."

"Honestly, Harry . . . you . . . you . . ." Beate wasn't used to raising her voice, and it sounded like a quivering saw blade.

"He turned Oleg into a junkie, Beate." Harry's voice was low, and he spoke without looking up from the cup.

They sat in silence listening to the expensive Holmenkollen silence.

"Was it Asayev who shot you in the head?" Beate asked at length.

Harry ran his finger over the new scar at the side of his forehead. "What makes you think it's a bullet wound?"

"Well, what do I know about gunshot wounds? I'm just a forensics officer."

"OK. It was a guy who had worked for Asayev," Harry said. "Three shots at close range. Two in the chest. The third in the head."

Beate looked at Harry. Knowing he was telling the truth. But it wasn't the whole truth.

"And how did you survive that?"

"I'd been walking round with a bulletproof vest on for two days. So it was about time it did something useful. But the shot to the head knocked me out. And would have killed me if . . ."

"If . . . ?"

"If the guy who shot me hadn't run to the A&E in Storgata. He badgered a doctor to come along, and he saved me."

"What? Why haven't I heard any of this?"

"The doctor bandaged me up on the spot and wanted to send me to hospital, but I woke up in time and made sure I was sent home instead."

"Why?"

"I didn't want any fuss. How's Bjørn these days? Got himself a girl?"

"This guy . . . first of all he tried to shoot you and then he saved your life? Who—?"

"He didn't try to shoot me, it was an accident."

"Accident? Three shots is no accident, Harry."

"If you're going cold turkey and holding an Odessa, it can happen."

"Odessa?" Beate knew the weapon. The cheap copy of the Russian Stechkin. In pictures the Odessa looked like it had been welded together by a schoolboy of average skill in a metalwork class, the clumsy, illegitimate progeny of a pistol and a machine gun. But it was popular with Russian Urkas and professional criminals because it could fire both single shots and salvos. The slightest pressure on an Odessa and you had suddenly let off two rounds. Or three. It struck her that the Odessa had the rare Makarov 9x18mm calibre bullets, the same ammunition that had killed Gusto Hanssen.

"I'd like to see that weapon," she said slowly, watching Harry's eyes automatically wander around the living room. She turned. She couldn't see anything there, just an ancient black corner cupboard.

"You didn't say who the guy was," Beate said.

"It's not important," Harry said. "He's long been outside your jurisdiction."

Beate nodded. "You're protecting someone who almost took your life."

"All the more credit to him that he saved it."

"Is that why you're protecting him?"

"How we choose who we protect is often a riddle, don't you think?"

"Yes," Beate said. "Take me for example. I protect police officers. As I'm handy at facial recognition I questioned the bartender at Come As You Are, the place where this drug dealer of Asayev's was killed by a tall blond guy with a scar running from his mouth to his ear. I showed the bartender some photos and talked and talked. And as you know, the visual memory is child's play to manipulate. Witnesses no longer remember what they thought they remembered. In the end, the bartender was sure the man in the bar wasn't the Harry Hole I showed him in the photos."

Harry looked at her. Then he nodded slowly. "Thanks."

"I was going to say no thanks were necessary," Beate said, lifting the cup to her mouth. "But they are. And I have a suggestion as to how you could thank me."

"Beate . . ."

"I protect police officers. You know it's a personal matter for me when officers die on active duty. Jack. And my father." She noticed she automatically touched her earring. The button off her father's uniform jacket, which she'd had recast. "We don't know whose turn it is next, but I intend to do whatever I can to stop this bastard, Harry. Whatever I can. Do you understand?"

Harry didn't answer.

"Sorry, of course you understand," Beate said under her breath. "You have your own dead to grieve for."

Harry rubbed the back of his right hand against

the coffee cup as if he was cold. Then he got up and walked to the window. Stood there for a while before he spoke.

"As you know, a murderer came here and tried to kill Oleg and Rakel. And it was my fault."

"That's a long time ago, Harry."

"It was yesterday. It will always be yesterday. Nothing has changed. But I'm trying anyway. To change **myself.**"

"And how's it going?"

Harry shrugged. "Up and down. Have I told you I never remembered to buy Oleg a birthday present? Even though Rakel reminded me weeks in advance. There was always some case or other supressing my memory. Then I would come up here, find the place all done up for a party and have to leave at once, the old trick as always." Harry drew one corner of his mouth into half a smile. "I said I had to go and buy some cigarettes, so I jumped in the car, raced to the nearest petrol station, bought a couple of CDs or something. Rakel and I had a deal. When I came in the door Oleg stood there looking at me with those dark, accusatory eyes of his. But before he could search me, Rakel hurried over to give me a hug, as if she hadn't seen me for years. And while she had her arms round me she tugged the CDs, or whatever the present was, from the back of my trousers, hid it and left the room while Oleg frisked me. Ten minutes later Rakel had wrapped the present, attached a gift tag, the whole caboodle."

"And?"

"And this year Oleg got a properly wrapped present from me. He said he didn't recognise the writing on the tag. I said that was because it was mine."

A smile flitted across Beate's face. "Sweet story. Happy ending and all that."

"Listen, Beate. I owe those two people everything, and I still need them. And I'm so lucky that they need me, too. As a mother, you know what a blessing and a curse it is to be needed."

"Yes. And what I'm trying to say is we need you, too."

Harry walked back. Leaned across the table to her. "Not like these two do, Beate. And no one is irreplaceable at work, not even . . ."

"No, that's true, we'll manage to replace the ones that have been killed. One was retired anyway. And we'll find enough people to take over after the next officers have been butchered as well."

"Beate . . ."

"Have you seen these?"

Harry didn't look down at the pictures she had taken from her bag and laid on the kitchen table.

"Crushed, Harry. Not a bone left intact. Even I had problems identifying them."

Harry stayed standing. Like a party host signalling that it was late. But Beate stayed where she was. Sipped from her cup. Didn't budge. Harry sighed. She took another sip.

"Oleg's going to study law when he gets back from the clinic, isn't he? And afterwards apply to Police College."

"Where did you get that from?"

"From Rakel. I spoke to her before coming here."

Harry's bright blue eyes darkened. "You **what**?"

"I rang her in Switzerland and told her what this was about. It was quite improper and I apologise. But, as I said, I will do whatever it takes."

Harry's lips moved, muttering silent imprecations. "And what did she answer?"

"That it was up to you."

"Yes, she probably did."

"So now I'm asking you, Harry. I'm asking you for Jack Halvorsen's sake. Ellen Gjelten's sake. I'm asking you for all the dead officers' sakes. But above all I'm asking you for those who are still alive. And for those who may become police officers."

She watched Harry's jaw muscles flexing furiously.

"I didn't ask you to manipulate witnesses for my sake, Beate."

"You never ask for anything, Harry."

"Well, it's late, so I'm asking you to—"

"—leave now." She nodded. Harry had a look that made people obey. Then she got up and went into the hall. Put her coat on, buttoned it. Harry stood in the doorway watching her.

"I'm sorry," she said. "I shouldn't intervene in your life. We do a job. It's only a job." She could hear her voice was about to fail her and hurried to add the rest: "And of course you're right. There must be rules and limits. Goodbye."

"Beate . . ."

"Sleep well, Harry."

"Beate Lønn."

Beate had already opened the front door, trying to get out, out before he could see the tears in her eyes. But Harry stood right behind her holding a hand against the door. His voice was next to her ear.

"Have you wondered how the murderer got the officers to go voluntarily to their old crime scenes on the same date as the murder was committed?"

Beate let go of the door handle. "What do you mean?"

"I mean I read newspapers. I read that Nilsen had gone to Tryvann in a Golf that was left in the car park, and they were his footprints in the snow down to the ski-lift hut. And that you had CCTV images from a petrol station in Drammen showing Anton Mittet alone in his car before his murder. They knew police had been killed in exactly this way. Yet they still went."

"Of course we've wondered about that," Beate said. "But we haven't found the right answer. We know they were called from phone booths not far from the crime scenes, so our guess is they knew who it was and this was their chance to catch the murderer on their own."

"No," Harry said.

"No?"

"Forensics found an empty gun and a box of ammo in Anton Mittet's glove compartment. If he had thought the murderer was there he would have at least loaded the gun first."

"He might not have had the time and the murderer struck before he could open the glove compartment and—"

"He was called at 22:31, but he filled up with petrol at 22:35. So he had time **after** he'd received the call."

"Perhaps he ran out of petrol?"

"Nope. **Aftenposten** has put the petrol station video online under the heading: THE LAST IMAGES OF ANTON MITTET BEFORE HE WAS EXECUTED. It shows a man filling up for only thirty seconds before the pump trigger clicks, meaning the tank is full. So Mittet had plenty of petrol to get to the crime scene and back home, which in turn means he wasn't in any hurry."

"Right. So he could have loaded the gun, but he didn't."

"Tryvann," Harry said. "Bertil Nilsen also had a gun in the glove compartment of his car. Which he didn't take with him. Accordingly we have two officers with experience of murder cases who turn up at unsolved crime scenes even though they know a colleague has recently been murdered in this way. They could have armed themselves, but they didn't and apparently they had plenty of time to do so. Veteran policemen who have stopped playing the hero. What does all this tell you?"

"OK, Harry," Beate said, turning, leaning back against the door and shutting it, "what **should** it tell us?"

"It should tell you that they didn't think they were going to catch a murderer there."

"Well, so they didn't think that. Perhaps they

thought it was a rendezvous with a beautiful woman who got a kick out of having sex at crime scenes."

Beate meant this as a joke, but Harry answered without batting an eyelid. "Not enough notice."

Beate considered the matter. "What if the murderer pretended to be a journalist interested in talking about other unsolved cases in the wake of these? And told Mittet he wanted to talk late at night to get the right atmosphere for the photographs?"

"It takes a bit of an effort to get to the crime scenes. At least to Tryvann it does. I read that Bertil Nilsen drove from Nedre Eiker, which is a thirty-minute drive. And serious police officers don't volunteer their time in order to give the press another shocking murder headline."

"When you say they don't volunteer their time, do you mean . . . ?"

"Yes, I do. My guess is they thought it was work."

"And it was a colleague ringing?"

"Mm."

"The murderer rang them, pretending to be a policeman working at the crime scene because . . . because it was a potential scenario for the cop killer to strike next time and . . . and . . ." Beate rubbed the uniform button in her ear. ". . . and said he needed their help to reconstruct the original murder!"

She could feel herself smiling like a schoolgirl who had just given the teacher the right answer, and she blushed like one when Harry laughed.

"We're getting warmer. But with the restrictions on overtime I'd imagine Mittet would have been surprised to be summoned in the middle of the night and not during working hours."

"I give up."

"Oh?" Harry said. "What kind of call from a colleague would make you go anywhere at all in the middle of the night?"

Beate smacked her forehead. "Of course," she said. "We've been such idiots!"

18

"What are you saying?" Katrine said, shivering in the cold gusts of wind as they stood on the steps outside the yellow house on Bergslia. "He rings his victims and says the police murderer has struck again?"

"It's as simple as it's brilliant," Beate said, confirming the key fitted, turning it and opening the door. "They get a call from someone pretending to be a detective. He says he wants them at the crime scene right away because they know all about the previous murder and they need information to see if it can help them to make the correct decisions while the evidence is still fresh."

Beate went in first. She knew her way around of course. It was more than a cliché to say forensics officers never forgot a crime scene. She came to a halt in the living room. The sunlight fell from the window and lay in crooked rectangles on the bare, evenly faded wooden floor. It must have been sparsely furnished for years. The family had probably taken most of it with them after the murder.

"Interesting," said Ståle Aune, who had taken up a position by a window overlooking the forest between the house and what he assumed to be Berg School.

"The murderer uses the hysteria he has created himself as bait."

"If I got a call like that I would consider it very plausible," Katrine said.

"And that's why they go there unarmed," Beate continued. "They think the danger's over. That the police are already in position, so they can take their time and fill up with petrol on the way."

"But," Bjørn said with his mouth full of Wasa cracker and caviar, "how does the murderer know the victim won't ring a colleague and find out there isn't any murder?"

"Presumably the murderer has told them not to talk to anyone until further notice," Beate said, eyeing the crumbs falling on the floor with disapproval.

"Also plausible," Katrine said. "Experienced police officers wouldn't be taken aback by that. They know it's important to keep a suspicious death quiet for as long as possible."

"Why is it important?" Ståle Aune asked.

"The murderer might drop his guard when he thinks the body hasn't been found," Bjørn said and sank his teeth into another bit of the crispbread.

"And Harry reeled all this off just like that?" Katrine asked. "After reading the newspapers?"

"He wouldn't be Harry otherwise," Beate said, hearing the tram rattle past across the road. From the window she could see the roof of Ullevål Stadium. The windows were too thin to shut out the drone of traffic from Ring 3. And she remembered how cold it had been, how they had frozen in their white overalls. But also how she had formulated the idea that it hadn't only been the temperature that had made it impossible to be in this room without shivering. Perhaps that was why it had been vacant for so long. Potential tenants or buyers could still feel the cold. The chill of the stories and rumours circling at that time.

"Fair enough," said Bjørn. "He's worked out how the murderer lures the victim. But we already knew they'd gone there willingly, under their own steam. So it's not exactly a quantum leap in the investigation, is it?"

Beate went over to the second window and her gaze scanned the area. It would be easy to hide the Delta team in the forest, in the dip in the ground by the metro rails and perhaps in the neighbouring houses on both sides. In short, surround this house.

"He always did come up with such simple ideas you scratched your head afterwards wondering why you hadn't thought of them," she said. "The crumbs."

"Eh?" Bjørn said.

"The crispbread crumbs."

Bjørn looked down at the floor. Back up at Beate. Then he tore a sheet from his notepad, crouched down and brushed the crumbs onto the paper.

Beate looked up and met Katrine's enquiring eyes.

"I know what you're thinking," Beate said. "Why the fuss? This isn't a crime scene. But it is. Every place where an unsolved crime has been committed is and remains a crime scene with the potential to reveal evidence."

"Are you counting on finding clues from the Saw Man here?" Ståle asked.

"No," Beate said, examining the floor. "They must have planed it off. There was so much blood, and it must have stained so deep into the wood, that scrubbing would have made no difference."

Ståle glanced at his watch. "I've got a patient soon, so what about telling us Harry's suggestion?"

"We never informed the press," Beate said, "but when we found the body in this room we first had to ascertain whether it really was human."

"Oooh," Ståle said, "do we want to hear any more?"

"Yes," Katrine said firmly.

"The body had been sawn up into such small parts that at first sight it wasn't easy to tell. He had put the breasts on a shelf in the glass cabinet there. The only evidence we found was a broken jigsaw blade. And . . . yes, those of you who are interested can read the rest in this report." Beate patted her shoulder bag.

"Oh, thank you," Katrine said with a smile she must have felt was too sweet, as she quickly replaced it with her serious expression.

"The victim was a young girl at home on her own," Beate said. "And we were also aware then that the methods used bore similarities to those in the Tryvann murder. But what is crucial for us is that it's an unsolved murder. And it was committed on the seventeenth of March."

It was so quiet in the room that they could hear joyful shouts from the school playground on the other side of the trees.

Bjørn was the first to break the silence. "That's in three days' time."

"Yes," Katrine said. "And Harry, the sicko, has suggested we set a trap, hasn't he?"

Beate nodded.

Katrine slowly shook her head. "Why did none of **us** think of that?"

"Because none of us knew exactly how the murderer lured the victims to the crime scene," Ståle answered.

"Harry could still be wrong," Beate said. "Both with regard to how the murderer operates and that this is the next crime scene. Since the first officer died we've passed several dates for unsolved murders in Østland and nothing has happened."

"But," Ståle said, "Harry's seen a similarity between the Saw Man and the other murders. Disciplined planning combined with apparently unbridled brutality."

"He called it gut instinct," Beate said. "But by that he meant—"

"Analysis based on non-systematised facts," Katrine said. "Also known as Harry's method."

"So he says it will happen in three days," Bjørn said.

"Yes," Beate said. "And he had another prediction. He pointed out, like Ståle, that the last murder was even more like the original with him putting the victim in a car and rolling him over a cliff. That the murderer was continuing to perfect the killings. The next logical step would be for him to choose the identical murder weapon."

"A jigsaw," Katrine gasped.

"That would be typical of a narcissistic serial killer," Ståle said.

"And Harry was sure it would take place here?" Bjørn asked, looking around him with a grimace.

"In fact, that was where he was least sure of himself," Beate said. "The murderer had easy access to all the other crime scenes. This house has stood vacant for many years as no one has wanted to live where the Saw Man had been. But nevertheless it is locked. It's true the Tryvann hut was broken into, but this house has neighbours. Luring a policeman here would involve much greater risk. So Harry thinks he might change the pattern and entice the victim somewhere else. But we'll set the trap for the cop killer here, and see if he rings."

There was a tiny pause as they all appeared to be chewing on the fact that Beate had used the name the press had adopted, the cop killer.

"And the victim . . . ?" Katrine asked.

"I have here," Beate said, patting her shoulder bag again, "everyone who worked on the Saw Man case. They'll be told to stay at home with the phone switched on. Whoever is called will act cool and just confirm they're on their way. Then he will ring the Ops Room, say where he's going and then we'll swing into action. If it's not Berg but somewhere else, Delta will be moved there."

"So we have to act cool when a serial killer calls?" Bjørn queried. "I dunno if my acting's up to that."

"They don't need to conceal their trepidation,"

Ståle said. "Quite the contrary, it would be suspicious if a policeman's voice **didn't** quiver when he got a call about the murder of a colleague."

"I'm more concerned about Delta and the Ops Room," Katrine said.

"Yes, I know," Beate said. "Too much going on to avoid Bellman's attention. Hagen is informing him as we speak."

"And what happens to our group when he finds out?"

"If this has a chance of succeeding, that's a minor matter, Katrine." Beate impatiently rubbed the button dangling from her ear. "Let's make a move. No point hanging around here and being seen. And don't leave anything behind."

Katrine had taken a step towards the door when she froze.

"What's the matter?" Ståle asked.

"Didn't you hear it?" she whispered.

"Hear what?"

She raised one foot and sent Bjørn a narrow-eyed look. "The crunching noise."

Beate laughed her surprisingly light laugh while, with a deep sigh, the Skreia native took out his notebook and crouched down again.

"Well, I'll be . . ."

"What?"

"It's not crumbs," he said, leaning forward and peering under the table. "Old chewing gum. The rest is stuck under here. It's probably so desiccated that bits crumble off."

"Perhaps it's the murderer's?" Ståle suggested with

a yawn. "People stick chewing gum under their seats in cinemas and on buses, but not under their own dining-room table."

"Interesting theory," Bjørn said, holding up a piece to the window. "I reckon for months we could have found DNA in the spit of a lump like that. But this is all dried out."

"Come on, Sherlock," Katrine grinned. "Chew it and tell us what brand—"

"That's enough, you lot," Beate interrupted. "Out now."

Arnold Folkestad set down his teacup and looked at Harry. He scratched his red beard. Harry had seen him plucking spruce needles from it when he came to work, after cycling from the little house he had somewhere in the forest that was still so bizarrely close to the city centre. But Arnold had made it clear that colleagues who pigeonholed him as a progressive environmental activist because of his long beard, bicycle and house in the forest were wrong. He was only a tight-fisted weirdo who liked the silence.

"You'd better tell her to rein herself in," Harry said. "It would seem more . . ." He couldn't find the word. Didn't know if it existed. If so, it was somewhere between "correct" and "less embarrassing for all concerned."

"Is Harry Hole frightened of a little girl in the front row who's got a bit of a crush on her lecturer?" Arnold Folkestad chuckled.

"More correct and less embarrassing for all concerned."

"You're going to have to sort this out yourself, Harry. Look, there she is . . ." Arnold nodded towards the square outside the canteen window. Silje Gravseng was standing on her own a few metres from a throng of students chatting and laughing. She looked up at the sky, followed something with her eyes.

Harry sighed. "Perhaps I should wait a bit. Statistically speaking, I suppose these teacher infatuations are short-lived in a hundred per cent of cases."

"Speaking of stats," Folkestad said, "I've heard they're claiming that that patient Hagen had under guard at the Rikshospital died of natural causes."

"So they say."

"The FBI ran some statistics on that. They examined all the cases where the prosecution's key witness had died in the period between the official summons as a witness and the start of the trial. In serious trials, where the accused faced more than ten years' prison, witnesses died of so-called unnatural causes in seventy-eight per cent of cases. The stats led to several witnesses being given a second post-mortem, after which the figure rose to ninety-four."

"So?"

"Ninety-four is high, don't you think?"

Harry stared out at the square. Silje was still looking at the sky. The sun was shining on her upturned face.

He cursed under his breath and drank the rest of his coffee.

• • •

Gunnar Hagen, balancing on one of the spindle-back chairs in Bellman's office, looked up in surprise at the Chief of Police. Hagen had just told him about the small working group he had set up, in direct conflict with the Chief's instructions, and the plan to set a trap in Berg. The surprise was caused by the fact that the Chief's unusually good mood had not appeared to be upset by the news.

"Excellent," Bellman exclaimed, clapping his hands. "Finally something proactive. May I pass on the plan and the map, so that we can get cracking?"

"We? Do you mean that you personally—?"

"Yes, I think it would be only natural for me to lead this, Gunnar. Such a big operation involves top-level decisions—"

"There's just one house and one man who—"

"Then it's right that I, as the most senior ranking officer, involve myself when there is so much at stake. And it is of paramount importance that the operation is kept secret. Do you understand?"

Hagen nodded. Secret if it doesn't bear fruit, he thought. If, on the other hand, it leads to success and an arrest, publicity will be of paramount importance, and Mikael Bellman can take the credit and tell the press he was personally in charge of the operation.

"Understood," Hagen said. "I'll get going then. My understanding is therefore that the group in the Boiler Room can also resume their work?"

Mikael Bellman laughed. Hagen wondered what

could have caused such a shift in mood. The Police Chief seemed ten years younger, ten kilos lighter and free from the frown he had carried like a deep gash in his forehead since the day he had been appointed.

"Don't push it, Gunnar. Liking the idea you've come up with doesn't mean I like my subordinates defying my orders."

Hagen shrugged, but still tried to capture the Police Chief's cold, mocking gaze.

"I'm freezing all activity in your group until further notice, Gunnar. Then we'd better have the requisite chat after this operation. And if in the meantime I find out you've so much as run one computer search or made a single phone call regarding this case . . ."

I'm older than him, and I'm a better man, Gunnar Hagen thought, keeping his eyes raised and knowing a mixture of defiance and shame were causing his cheeks to flush.

It's just decoration, he reminded himself, the gold braid on a uniform.

Then he lowered his gaze.

It was late. Katrine Bratt stared down at the report in front of her. She shouldn't have done. Beate had just rung to say that Hagen had asked them all to stop their work, direct orders from Bellman. So Katrine should have been at home, lying in bed with a big cup of camomile tea and a man who loved her, or alternatively watching a TV series she loved. Instead of sitting here in the Boiler Room, reading case files and searching for possible flaws, hints of something that didn't sit right and any vague connections. And this connection was so vague it verged on the inane. Or did it? It had been relatively easy to gain access to the reports on the Anton Mittet murder via the police's own system. The summarised search of the car had been as detailed as it was soporific. So why had she stopped at this particular sentence? Among all the potential evidence they had removed from Mittet's car was an ice scraper and a lighter plus some chewing gum stuck to the underside of the driver's seat.

The contact information for Anton Mittet's widow, Laura Mittet, was in the report.

Katrine hesitated, then dialled the number. The voice of the woman who answered sounded weary, dulled by pills. Katrine introduced herself and asked her question.

"Chewing gum?" Laura Mittet repeated slowly. "No, he never chewed gum. He drank coffee."

"Was there anyone else who drove the car and chewed—?"

"No one ever drove the car apart from Anton."

"Thank you," Katrine said.

19

It was evening and the kitchen windows in the yellow wooden house in Oppsal where Beate Lønn had just finished her daily conversation with her son were brightly lit. Afterwards she had talked to her mother-in-law and agreed that if the boy still had a temperature and was coughing, they would have to postpone the journey home for a few days. The in-laws would love to have him for a bit longer in Steinkjer. Beate unhooked the plastic leftovers bag in the cupboard under the sink and was putting it in one of the white rubbish bags when the phone rang. It was Katrine, and she didn't waste any time on pleasantries.

"There was a piece of chewing gum under the driver's seat in Mittet's car."

"Right . . ."

"It was removed, but it hasn't been sent for DNA testing."

"I wouldn't have sent it either if it was under the driver's seat. It was Mittet's. Listen, if you tested every single thing you found at a crime scene, the queue would make waiting times—"

"But Ståle was right, Beate! People don't stick gum under their own dining-room tables. Or in their own cars. According to Mittet's wife, he didn't even chew gum. And no one else drove the car except him. I think the person who left the gum was leaning across the driver's seat when he did it. And according to the report the murderer was sitting in the passenger seat and leaned across Mittet to fasten his hands to the wheel with the ties. The car has been in the river, but according to Bjørn the DNA in the spit can—"

"Yes, I know where you're going," Beate interrupted. "You'll have to ring someone in Bellman's investigative unit and tell them."

"But don't you understand?" Katrine said. "This could lead us straight to the murderer."

"Yes, of course I understand, and the only place this is leading us is straight to hell. We've been taken off the case, Katrine."

"I can just drop by the Evidence Room and have the chewing gum sent for testing," Katrine said. "Check it against the register. If there's no match, no one needs to know. If there's a match we've solved the case. No one's going to say a bloody word about how we did it. Yes, I'm all ego now. For once we could get the credit, Beate. **You and I.** The women. And we deserve it, for Christ's sake."

"Yes, it's tempting, and it won't ruin anyone else's work, but—"

"No buts! For once we can take the liberty of using our elbows. Or do you want to see Bellman standing there with that smug smile being honoured for our work again?"

Silence. A long silence.

"You say no one needs to know anything," Beate said. "But all requisition orders for potential forensic clues from the Evidence Room have to be registered at the requests hatch. If they discover we've been sticking our noses into the Mittet file, it won't be long before a note lands on Bellman's desk to that effect."

"Hm, I hear you," Katrine said. "Unless my memory's playing tricks on me, the Krimteknisk boss—who on occasion needs to test evidence outside of the Evidence Room's opening hours—has her own key."

Beate groaned aloud.

"I promise there won't be any trouble," Katrine hastened to add. "Listen, I'll pop round to yours now, borrow the key, find the gum, cut off a tiny chunk, put everything back nicely and tomorrow morning the chunk's tested at the Institute. If they ask, I'll say it's for another case. Yes? OK?"

The head of Krimteknisk weighed up the pros and cons. It wasn't hard. It wasn't OK at all. She took a deep breath.

"As Harry used to say," Katrine said. "**Just get the ball,** for Christ's sake."

Rico Herrem lay in bed watching TV. It was five o'clock in the morning, but he had lost track of time and couldn't sleep. The programme was a repeat of one he saw yesterday. A Komodo dragon was lolloping across a beach. The long lizard tongue flashed out, swept round and was retracted. It was following a water buffalo it had given an apparently harmless bite. Had been following it for several days. Rico had turned down the sound so that all that could be heard was the wheeze of the air-conditioning unit which couldn't make the hotel room cold enough. Rico had already felt the sniffles coming on the flight. Classic. Air conditioning and summer clothes on the way to a hot country, and the holiday becomes a headache, a runny nose and a high temperature. But he had time; he didn't have to go home for a long while. Why should he? He was in Pattaya, the paradise of all pervs and criminals on the run. Everything he wanted was here, outside his hotel door. Through the mosquito net by the window he could hear the traffic and voices gabbling away in a foreign language. Thai. He couldn't understand a word. He didn't need to. Because they were there for him, not vice versa. He had seen them when he was driven here from the airport. They lined up outside the go-go bars. The young. The very young. And further down the alleys, behind the trays they sold chewing gum from, the much too young. But they would still be there when he was back on his feet. He listened for waves breaking, even though he knew the cheap hotel he had moved into was a long way from the beach. But they were out there as well. Them and the scorching hot sun. And the drinks and the other **farangs** who were there on the same mission as him and could give him some tips about how to go about things. And about the Komodo dragon.

Last night he had dreamt about Valentin again.

Rico stretched out his hand for the bottle of water

on the bedside table. It tasted of his own mouth, death and contagion.

He had been given two-day-old Norwegian newspapers with the Western breakfast he'd hardly touched. There hadn't been anything about Valentin being arrested yet. It wasn't difficult to surmise why. Valentin wasn't Valentin any more.

Rico had wondered whether he should tell them. Ring, get hold of that policewoman, Katrine Bratt. Tell her he had changed. Rico had seen that down here you could get that kind of thing done for a few thousand Norwegian kroner at one of the private clinics. Ring Bratt, leave an anonymous message that Valentin had been seen near Fiskebutikken and that he'd had comprehensive plastic surgery. Without asking for anything in return. Just to help them catch him. To help him sleep at night without dreaming about him.

The Komodo dragon had crouched a few metres from the waterhole where the water buffalo had settled down in the cooling mud, apparently unaffected by the three-metre-long, carnivorous monster just lying in wait.

Rico could feel the nausea rising and swung his legs out of bed. His muscles ached. Jesus, this was full-blown flu.

When he returned from the bathroom it was with bile acid still burning in his throat and two decisions made. He would visit one of those clinics and get himself some of that strong medicine they wouldn't give you in Norway. The second was that when he had it and felt a bit better, he would ring Bratt. Give her a description. So that he could sleep.

He turned up the volume with the remote control. An enthusiastic voice explained in English that it had long been thought that the Komodo dragon killed through the bacteria-infected spit that was injected into the victim's bloodstream with a bite, but now it had been discovered that in fact the poison in the lizard's glands stopped the victim's blood from coagulating so it slowly bled to death from what seemed to be an innocent wound.

Rico shivered. Closed his eyes to sleep. Rohypnol. The thought had occurred to him. That this wasn't flu at all, but withdrawal symptoms. And Rohypnol was probably something they had on the room-service menu here in Pattaya. His eyes opened wide. He couldn't breathe. For a moment in sheer, utter panic, Rico writhed around as if fighting an invisible attacker. It was just the same as at Fiskebutikken; there was no oxygen in the room! Then his lungs got what they wanted, and he fell back onto his bed.

He stared at the door.

It was locked.

There was no one else here. No one. Just him.

20

Katrine walked up the hill under cover of night. A wan, anaemic moon hung low in the sky behind her, but Police HQ's facade didn't reflect any of the little light the moon cast, it swallowed it like a black hole. She glanced at the compact, professional wristwatch she had inherited from her father, a fallen policeman with the fitting nickname of Iron Rafto. A quarter past eleven.

She tugged open the front door of Police HQ with its strange, staring porthole and hostile weight. As though the suspicion started right here.

She waved in the direction of the duty officer, who sat hidden on the left, but could see her. And unlocked the door to the atrium. Walked past the unmanned reception desk and went over to the lift, which she took down to the lower ground floor. Exited and crossed the concrete floor in the meagre light, hearing her own footsteps as she listened for others.

During the day the iron door to the Evidence Room opened on to a counter. She fished out the key Beate had given her, put it in the lock, twisted and opened. Stepped inside. Listened.

Then she locked the door behind her.

Switched on the light, lifted the hinged section of the counter and advanced into the darkness, which was so dense the torchlight seemed to need time to bore its way through, to find the rows of broad shelves filled with boxes made of frosted plastic through which you could only just make out the objects inside. The person in charge must have had an orderly mind because the boxes were lined up on the shelves with such precision that the short sides formed an unbroken surface. Katrine strode along reading the case numbers stuck to the boxes. They were numbered chronologically from the far left of the room inwards, where they took the place of evidence from time-restricted cases once the stored material was returned to the owners or destroyed.

She had almost reached the end of the middle row when the torch beam fell on the box she was after. It was on the lowest shelf and scraped against the brick floor as she pulled it out. She whipped off the lid. The contents tallied with the report. An ice scraper. A seat cover. A plastic bag containing some strands of hair. A plastic bag containing some chewing gum. She put down the torch, opened the bag, removed the gum with tweezers and was about to cut off a bit when she felt a draught in the clammy air.

She looked down at her forearm, which was caught in the torchlight, and saw the shadow of fine hairs standing up. Then she raised her eyes, grabbed the torch and shone it at the wall. Beneath the ceiling there was an inset hatch fan. But as it was only inset it was unlikely it could have caused on its own what she was fairly certain was a movement in the air.

She listened.

Nothing. Absolutely nothing. Just the throbbing of blood in her ears.

She concentrated on the hard piece of chewing gum again. Cut off a tiny piece with the Swiss army knife she had brought along. And froze.

It came from somewhere by the door, so far away the ear hadn't been able to identify what it was. The rattle of a key? The banging of a counter? It was probably nothing; perhaps you just get strange sounds in a large building.

Katrine switched off the torch and held her breath. Blinked into the darkness as though that might help her to see. It was quiet. As quiet as the . . .

She tried not to continue that train of thought.

Instead she tried another train of thought, one that would slow her heart down: what was actually the worst that could happen? She was caught exceeding the call of duty and they were all reprimanded? Perhaps she would be sent home to Bergen? Tedious, but not exactly a reason for her heart to pound like a pneumatic drill inside her chest.

She waited, listening.

Nothing.

Still nothing.

And that was when she realised. Pitch black. If someone had really been there they would of course have switched on the light. She grinned at her own stupidity, felt her heart slowing down. Switched the torch on, put the evidence back in the box and replaced it. Made sure it was exactly in line with the other boxes, and walked towards the exit. A thought flashed through her mind. A stray thought that caught her by surprise. She was looking forward to ringing him. Because that was what she was going to do. Ring him and tell him what she had done. She came to an abrupt halt.

The torch beam had caught something.

Her first instinct was to keep walking; a small, cowardly voice that told her to get out as fast as she could.

But she shone the light back.

An unevenness.

One of the boxes wasn't in line.

She went closer. Shone the torch on the label.

Harry thought he heard a door slam. He pulled out his earphones on the sound of Bon Iver's new recording, which so far had lived up to the hype. Listened. Nothing.

"Arnold?" he called.

No answer. He was used to having this wing of PHS to himself so late in the evening. Of course it could have been a member of the cleaning staff who had forgotten something. But a quick look at his watch confirmed it was not evening but night. Harry glanced to the left of the pile of uncorrected assignments on his desk. Most students had printed them on the rough recycled paper they used at the library, and it was so dusty that Harry went home with nicotine-yellow fingertips, which Rakel told him to wash before he was allowed to touch her.

He looked out of the window. The moon hung in the sky, big and round, reflecting on the windows and the roofs of the blocks towards Kirkeveien and Majorstuen. To the south he saw the green, shimmering silhouette of the KPMG financial services building beside the Colosseum cinema. It wasn't magnificent, beautiful or even picturesque. But it was the town he had lived and worked in almost all his life. There were some mornings in Hong Kong when he had put a bit of opium in a cigarette and gone up onto the roof of Chungking Mansions to see the day break. Sitting there in the darkness wishing the town, which would soon come to life, were his. A modest town with low, self-effacing buildings instead of these intimidating steel steeples. Wishing he could see Oslo's soft, green ridges instead of Hong Kong's brutally steep, black mountainsides. Hear the sound of a tram clanking and braking or the Denmark ferry entering the fjord and whistling, elated that today too it had succeeded in crossing the sea between Frederikshavn and Oslo.

Harry looked down at the paper centred in the beam from the reading lamp, the only light in the room. He could, of course, have taken everything with him to Holmenkollveien. Coffee, a babbling radio, the fragrance of fresh trees through an open window. But he had decided not to mull over why he preferred to sit here alone instead of there alone. Presumably because he had an inkling what the response would be. That there he wasn't alone. Not quite. The black timber fortress with three locks on the door and sprinklers in front of all the windows still couldn't keep the monsters out. The ghosts were sitting in the dark corners watching him through their empty eye sockets. His phone vibrated in his pocket. He took it out and saw the text on the illuminated screen. It was from Oleg and there were no letters, only numbers. 665625. Harry smiled. Naturally it was a long way off Stephen Krogman's legendary Tetris world record of 1,648,905 points in 1999, but Oleg had long smashed Harry's best scores in the slightly antiquated computer game. Ståle Aune had maintained there was a line where Tetris records went from being impressive to just being sad. And that Oleg and Harry had crossed it a long time ago. But no one else knew of the other line they had crossed. The one to death and back. Oleg on a chair beside Harry's bed. Harry feverish as his body fought against the damage Oleg's bullets had caused, Oleg crying as his body shook with cold turkey. Not much was said, but Harry had a vague memory of them holding hands so hard at one point that it had hurt. And this image, two men clinging to each other, not wanting to let go, would always be with him.

Harry texted **I'll be back** in return. A number answered with three words. It was enough. Enough to know that the other person was **there,** even if the next time they saw each other could be weeks away. Harry put the earphones back and searched for the music Oleg had sent over without any comment. The band was the Decemberists and was more Harry than Oleg, who preferred harder stuff. Harry heard a lone Fender guitar with the pure, warm twang, which was only a pipe amplifier and not a fixed box, or perhaps a deceptively **good** box, and leaned over the next sheet. The student had written that after a sudden hike in the murder rate in the 1970s, the figure had stabilised at the new, higher level. There were around fifty murders a year in Norway, so about one a week.

Harry noticed that the air had become close and he ought to open a window.

The student remembered that the clear-up rate was around ninety-five per cent. And concluded that there had to be approximately fifty unsolved murders over the last twenty years. Seventy-five over the last thirty years.

"Fifty-eight."

Harry jumped in his chair. The voice had reached his brain before the perfume. His doctor had explained that his sense of smell—or more specifically the olfactory cells—had been damaged by years of smoking and alcohol abuse. But that wasn't why it took him a minute to place the scent. It was called Opium, made by Yves Saint Laurent, and stood by the bath at home in Holmenkollveien. He tore out his earphones.

"Fifty-eight over the last thirty years," she said. She had put on make-up. Sported a red dress and was barefoot. "But Kripos's statistics don't include Norwegian citizens killed abroad. For that you would have to use Statistics Norway. And then the figure is seventy-two. Which means that the clear-up rate in Norway is higher. Which the Chief of Police regularly uses in his publicity."

Harry pushed his chair away from her. "How did you get in?"

"I'm the class rep. I have keys." Silje Gravseng perched on the edge of the desk. "But the point is that the majority of murders abroad are assaults, so we can assume the perp doesn't know the victim." Harry registered suntanned knees and thighs where her skirt rode up. She must have been on holiday recently. "And for that type of murder the clear-up rate in Norway is lower than in countries we ought to be comparing ourselves with. It is frighteningly low, actually." She had angled her head down to one shoulder so that damp blonde hair fell across her face.

"Oh yes?" Harry said.

"Yes. There are in fact only four detectives in Norway with a hundred per cent clear-up rate. And you're one of them . . ."

"I'm not sure that's correct," Harry said.

"But I am." She smiled at him, squinting as though she had the low afternoon sun in her eyes. Dangling her bare feet as though she were sitting on the edge of a jetty. Holding his eyes as though she thought she could suck the eyeballs out of the sockets.

"What are you doing here so late?" Harry asked.

"I've been doing some training in the fitness room." She pointed to the rucksack on the floor and flexed her right arm. A pronounced biceps muscle appeared. He remembered the combat instructor mentioning something about her flooring several of the boys.

"Training on your own so late?"

"Got to learn as much as I can. But perhaps you could show me how to bring down a suspect?"

Harry looked at his watch. "Tell me, shouldn't you be . . . ?"

"Asleep? I can't sleep, Harry. I just think about . . ."

He looked at her. She pouted. Placed a finger against her bright red lips. He could feel a certain irritation mounting. "It's good you use your brain, Silje. Keep doing it. And I'll keep . . ." He pointed to the pile of papers.

"You haven't asked **what** I think about, Harry."

"Three things, Silje. I'm your lecturer and not your confessor. You've no business to be in this wing without an appointment. And to you I'm Hole, not Harry. OK?" He knew his voice had been sterner than necessary, and when he looked up again he discovered her eyes were big and round with disbelief. She dropped the finger from her lips. She dropped the pout as well. And when she spoke again her voice was hardly more than a whisper.

"I was thinking about you, Harry."

Then she laughed a loud, shrill laugh.

"I suggest we stop right there, Silje."

"But I **love** you, Harry." More laughter.

Was she high? Drunk? Had she come straight from a party perhaps?

"Silje, don't . . ."

"Harry, I know you've got obligations. And I know there are rules for lecturers and students. But I know what we can do. We can go to Chicago. Where you did the serial killer course. I can apply to do it and you can—"

"Stop!"

Harry heard his shout echo down the corridor. Silje had hunched up as if he'd hit her.

"Now I'll accompany you to the door, Silje."

She blinked at him in astonishment. "What's the matter, Harry? I'm the second-best-looking girl in the year. I could have whoever I want in this place. Including the lecturers. But I've saved myself for you."

"Come on."

"Do you want to know what I've got under my dress, Harry?"

She put a bare foot on the desk and opened her thighs. Harry was so quick she didn't have a chance to react when he knocked her foot off the desk.

"No one puts their feet on my desk except me, thank you."

Silje crumpled. Hid her face in her hands. Ran them over her head, as though she wanted to creep into a hiding place under her long, muscular arms. She cried. Sobbed quietly. Harry let her sit like this until the sobbing had subsided. He was about to put his hand on her shoulder, but then changed his mind.

"Listen, Silje," he said. "Perhaps you're on something, I don't know. That's fine. Happens to all of us.

This is my suggestion: you go now, we pretend this never happened and neither of us breathes a word about it ever again."

"Are you afraid someone will find out about us, Harry?"

"There is no us, Silje. And listen to me. I'm giving you a chance here."

"Are you thinking that someone will find out that you're shagging a student?"

"I'm not shagging anyone. I'm thinking of your own good."

Silje lowered her arm and raised her head. Harry was shocked. Her make-up had run like black blood, her eyes had a wild gleam to them and the sudden hungry-predator grin made him think of an animal he had seen on one of those nature programmes.

"You're lying, Harry. You're shagging that bitch. Rakel. And you don't think about me. Not the way you say, you hypocritical bastard. But you do think about me, all right. Like a piece of meat you can shag. Like you're **going** to shag."

She had slid off the desk and taken a step towards him. Harry sat there, sunk in his chair with his legs stretched out in front of him, as always. He was looking up at her with this sense that he was part of a scene that was going to be acted out, no, had already been acted out, for Christ's sake. She stretched forward, gracefully, her hand rested on his knee, she stroked upwards, up over his belt as she leaned over him and her hand disappeared under his T-shirt. The voice purred: "Mmm, nice six-pack, teacher." Harry grabbed her hand, twisting her wrist round as he shot out of the chair. She screamed as he forced her arm up behind her back and pushed her head down towards the floor. Then he turned her towards the door, grabbed her rucksack and shoved her out of the room and down the corridor.

"Harry!" she groaned.

"This hold is called the half-nelson, or by many, the police grip," Harry said without stopping, propelling her down the stairs. "Handy to learn for the exam. That is, if you get as far as the exam. Because I hope you realise you've put me in a position where I'll have to report this."

"Harry!"

"Not because I feel I've been harassed particularly, but because I question whether you have the psychological stability to work in the police force, Silje. I'll leave it to the authorities to evaluate. So you'll have to convince them that this was just a bit of a slip-up. Does that sound fair to you?"

He opened the front door with his free hand, and as he shoved her out she swung round and eyeballed him. It was a glare of such naked fury and ferocity it confirmed what Harry had been thinking for a while about Silje Gravseng. She was not someone who should be given police powers and unleashed on the general public.

Harry watched her as she tottered through the gate, across the square to Chateau Neuf, where a student was having a smoke and a break from the dull pounding of the music inside. He stood leaning against a street lamp, wearing an army jacket, Cuba 1960 style. Watched Silje with studied indifference until she'd passed, whereupon he turned and stared after her.

Harry stood in the corridor. Cursing loudly. Felt his pulse slowing. Took out his phone, rang one of the contacts from a list which was so short some people were entered with only one letter.

"Arnold here."

"This is Harry. Silje Gravseng just turned up at my office. This time it went too far."

"Oh yes? Spill the beans."

Harry gave his colleague the edited highlights.

"This is not good, Harry. Worse, maybe, than you imagine."

"She might have been on something. Looked as if she'd come from a party. Or she just has problems controlling her impulses. But I need some advice here about what to do. I know I ought to report it but—"

"You don't understand. Are you still down by the front door?"

"Yes. So?" Harry said, surprised.

"The guard must have gone home. Can you see anyone else?"

"Anyone else?"

"Anyone?"

"Well, there's a guy in the square outside Chateau Neuf."

"Would he have seen her leave?"

"Yes."

"Perfect! Go over to him now. Talk to him. Get his

name and address. Keep him occupied until I come and pick you up."

"You what?"

"I'll explain later."

"Am I supposed to sit on the back of your bike?"

"I have to confess I have a kind of car here somewhere. I'll be there in twenty minutes."

"Good . . . er, morning?" Bjørn Holm mumbled. He peered at his watch, but wasn't sure if he was still in dreamland.

"Were you asleep?"

"No, no," Bjørn Holm said, leaning back against the headboard and pressing the phone to his ear. As though it would bring her even closer.

"I just wanted to tell you I've got a bit of the chewing gum stuck under Anton Mittet's car seat," Katrine Bratt said. "I reckon it's the murderer's. But of course it's a long shot."

"Yes," Bjørn said.

"You mean it's a waste of time?"

Bjørn thought she sounded disappointed. "You're the detective," he answered and immediately regretted not saying anything more encouraging.

In the ensuing silence he wondered where she was. At home? Was she also in bed?

"Oh well," she sighed. "By the way, something odd happened while I was in the Evidence Room."

"Oh yes?" Bjørn said and could hear he was overdoing the enthusiasm.

"I thought I heard someone else in there. I may have been mistaken, but on the way out it looked as if someone had moved one of the evidence boxes on the shelf. I checked the label . . ."

Bjørn Holm thought she was lying down; her voice had that lazy softness.

"It was the René Kalsnes case."

Harry closed the heavy door and locked out the gentle morning light behind him.

He walked through the cool darkness of the timber house to the kitchen. Slumped down onto a chair. Unbuttoned his shirt. It had taken time.

The guy in the army jacket had seemed fairly alarmed when Harry went over to him and asked him to wait until a police colleague arrived.

"This is normal tobacco, you know!" he had said, passing Harry the cigarette.

When Arnold came they took the student's signed testimony and then got into a dust-covered Fiat of indeterminate vintage and went straight to Krimteknisk where people were still working because of the latest police murder. There, Harry undressed, and while someone took his clothing for examination, two of the male officers went over his genitals and hands with a light and contact paper. Then he was given an empty plastic beaker.

"Give it your best shot, Hole. If there's enough room. Toilet's down the corridor. Think about something nice, OK?"

"Mm."

Harry had sensed rather than heard the suppressed laughter as he left them.

Think about something nice.

Harry fingered the copy of the report lying on the kitchen worktop. He had asked Hagen to send it. Privately. Discreetly. It consisted largely of medical terms in Latin. He understood some of them though. Enough to know that Rudolf Asayev had died in the same mysterious, inexplicable way that he had lived. And, lacking anything to suggest criminal activity, they had been obliged to conclude that it had been a cerebral infarction. A stroke. The kind of thing that happens.

As a detective, Harry could have told them that this kind of thing doesn't happen. A Crown witness doesn't "happen to" die. What was it that Arnold had said? In ninety-four per cent of cases it was murder if someone had enough to lose as a result of the witness's testimony.

The paradox was of course that Harry himself would have had something to lose if Asayev had testified. A lot to lose. So why bother? Why not just show gratitude, bow and move on with his life? There was a simple answer to that. His system had a malfunction.

Harry slung the report down to the end of the long oak table. And decided he would shred it in the morning. Now he needed to get some sleep.

Think about something nice.

Harry got up and undressed on his way to the bathroom. Stood under the shower, turned the dial to burning hot. Felt his skin tingle and smart, punishing him.

Think about something nice.

He dried himself, lay down under the clean white bedlinen in their double bed, closed his eyes and tried to hurry the process. But the thoughts reached him before sleep did.

He had thought about her.

When he had been standing in the toilet cubicle with his eyes closed, concentrating, trying to think of something nice, he had thought about Silje Gravseng. Thought of her soft, suntanned skin, her lips, her burning breath on his face, the wild fury in her eyes, the muscular body, the curves, the firm flesh, all the unjust beauty of the young.

Shit!

Her hand over his belt, on his stomach. Her body on its way down to meet his. The half-nelson. Her head almost on the ground, the protesting groans, the arched back with her bottom raised towards him, as slender as a doe.

Shit, shit!

He sat up in bed. Rakel was smiling warmly at him from the photo on the bedside table. Warm, clever and knowing. But did she actually know? If she had been allowed to spend five seconds in his head, to see who he actually was, would she have run off screaming? Or are we all equally sick? Is the difference only who lets the monster loose and who doesn't?

He had thought about her. Thought that he had done exactly what she'd wanted, there, on the desk, knocked the pile of students' work flying, sending the sheets fluttering around the room like faded butterflies, which stuck to their skin, rough paper with small, black letters that became categories of murder: sex, alcohol, crimes of passion, family feuds, honour killings and greed. He had thought about her as he stood there in the toilet. And he had filled the beaker to the brim.

21

Beate Lønn yawned, blinked and stared out of the tram window. The morning sun had started its work burning away the mist over Frogner Park. The dewy tennis courts were empty. There was just one emaciated, elderly man standing lost in thought on a shale court where they still hadn't put up the nets for the new season. Staring at the tram. Thin thighs protruding from antiquated shorts, blue office shirt buttoned up wrongly, racket dragging on the ground. Waiting for a partner who wasn't coming, Beate thought. Perhaps because the arrangement was for this time last year, and he was no longer alive. She knew how he felt.

She glimpsed the Monolith as they glided past the main park gate to where the tram stopped.

In fact, she had a partner, she had visited him last night, after Katrine had collected the key for the Evidence Room. That was why she was on this tram on this side of town. He was an ordinary man. That was how she classified him. Not the kind of man you dreamt about. Just the kind of man you needed once in a while. His children were at the ex's, and now that her little one was staying with her mother-in-law in Steinkjer they had the time and opportunity to meet a little more. Nevertheless, Beate noticed that she limited it. Basically it was more important for her to know he was there as an option rather than for them to spend time together. He hadn't been able to replace Jack, but that didn't matter. She didn't want a replacement, she wanted this. Something else, something non-committal, something that wouldn't cost her much if it was taken from her.

Beate stared through the window, at the tram going the opposite way sliding in beside them. In the silence she could hear low music coming from the headphones of the girl sitting next to her and recognised an irritating pop hit from the nineties. From the time when she had been the quietest girl at Police College. Pale with an embarrassing tendency to blush as soon as anyone looked in her direction. Though fortunately not many did. And those who did forgot her at once. Beate Lønn had the type of face and charisma that made her a non-event, an aquarium fish, visual Teflon.

But she remembered them.

Every single one of them.

And that was why she could look at the faces on the tram alongside her and remember where she had seen them and when. Perhaps on the same tram the day before, perhaps in a school playground twenty years ago, perhaps on CCTV footage of a bank robbery, perhaps on an escalator at Steen & Strøm where she went to buy a pair of tights. And it didn't make any difference if they had grown older, put on make-up, grown a beard, had a haircut, Botox or silicone implants, it was as though the face, their **real** face, shone through, as though it was a constant, something unique, an eleven-figure number in a DNA code. And this was her blessing and curse, which some psychiatrists wanted to label Asperger's syndrome, others minor brain damage, for which her fusiform gyrus—the brain's centre for facial recognition—tried to compensate. And which others, wiser counsels, didn't call anything at all. They just stated that her brain stored the uniqueness of every face like a computer stores the numbers of a DNA code for later identification.

And that was why it was not unusual for Beate Lønn's brain to be whirring already, trying to place the face of the man in the other tram.

What was unusual was that she couldn't place it straight away.

Only a metre and a half separated them, and her attention had been drawn to him because he was writing in the condensation on the window and therefore had his face turned to her. She had seen him before, but the name, the numbers of the DNA code markers that linked the face to the name, was concealed.

Perhaps it was the reflection on the glass, perhaps a shadow covering his eyes. She was about to give up when her tram lurched into motion, the light fell differently and he raised his gaze and met hers.

An electric shock went through Beate Lønn.

His gaze was that of a reptile.

The cold gaze of a murderer who knew who she was.

Valentin Gjertsen.

And she also knew why she hadn't recognised him at once. How he had managed to stay hidden.

Beate Lønn got up from her seat. Tried to get out, but the girl beside her had her eyes closed and was nodding her head. Beate nudged her and the girl looked up with annoyance.

"Out," Beate mouthed.

The girl raised a pencilled eyebrow, but didn't stir.

Beate grabbed her headphones.

"Police. I'm getting off."

"We're moving," the girl said.

"Shift your fat arse now!"

The other passengers turned towards Beate Lønn. But she didn't blush. She wasn't that quiet girl any longer. Her figure was as petite, her skin pale to the point of transparency, her hair colourless and dry like uncooked spaghetti. But that Beate Lønn no longer existed.

"Stop the tram! Police! Stop!"

She ploughed her way through to the driver and the exit. Heard the thin scream of brakes. She was there, had flashed her ID at the driver, waited impatiently. They came to a halt with a final jerk, the standing passengers lunged forward and hung onto the straps as the doors banged open. Beate was outside in one leap, and running up the tramway that divided the road. Felt the dew on the grass through the thin fabric of her shoes. The other tram was moving, she heard the low, rising song of the rails, and she ran as fast as she could. There was no reason to assume that Valentin was armed, and he would never escape from a

packed tram with her waving police ID, shouting that
he was under arrest. If she could only catch the tram.
Running wasn't her strong suit. That was what the
doctor who'd thought she had Asperger's had said.
People like her tended to be physically uncoordinated.

She slipped on the wet grass, but managed to stay
on her feet. Just a few more metres. She caught up
with the end of the tram. Slapped her hand against
it. Screamed, waved her ID, hoping the driver would
see her in the mirror. And perhaps he did. Saw a
commuter who had overslept desperately waving her
monthly ticket. The song of the rails rose another
quarter of a tone and the tram left her standing.

Beate stopped and watched the tram disappear up
Majorstuen. She turned and saw her tram heading
for Frogner plass.

Cursing quietly, she took out her mobile, crossed
the road, leaned against the wire fence of the tennis
courts and tapped in a number.

"Holm."

"It's me. I've just seen Valentin."

"Eh? Are you sure?"

"Bjørn . . ."

"Sorry. Where?"

"On the tram passing Frogner Park up towards
Majorstuen. Are you at work?"

"Yes."

"It's a number 12. Find out where it goes and have
it cut off. He mustn't get away."

"Fine. I'll find the stops and send a description of
Valentin to all the patrol cars."

"That's no good."

"What's no good?"

"The description. He's changed."

"What d'you mean?"

"Plastic surgery. Radically enough to be able to move around undetected in Oslo, for example. Tell me where the tram has been stopped and I'll make my way there and point him out."

"Received and out."

Beate put the phone back in her pocket. It was only now that she noticed how out of breath she was. In front of her the morning rush-hour traffic inched past as if nothing had happened. As if the fact that a murderer had just been exposed made no difference one way or the other.

"What's happened to them?"

Beate pushed herself off the fence and turned to the creaky voice.

The old man looked at her with enquiring eyes.

"Where are they all?" he reiterated.

And when Beate saw the pain there she quickly had to swallow the lump in her throat.

"Do you think . . ." he said, attempting a tentative swing of the racket, "they're on the other court?"

Beate nodded slowly.

"Yes, they probably are," he said. "I shouldn't be here. They're on the other court. They're waiting for me there."

Beate watched his narrow back as he tottered towards the gate.

Then she hurried off to Majorstuen. And even as

her mind raced, wondering where Valentin could be going, where he was coming from and how close they might be to arresting him, she still couldn't shake off the echo of the old man's whisper.

They're waiting for me there.

Mia Hartvigsen watched Harry Hole.

She had crossed her arms and half turned her shoulder to him. Around the pathologist lay blue plastic tubs of severed body parts. The students had left the room at the Institute of Forensic Medicine on the ground floor of the Rikshospital, and then this blast from the past had marched in with the pathology report on Asayev under his arm.

The dismissive body language was not because Mia Hartvigsen disliked Hole, but that he spelt trouble. When he'd worked as a detective Hole had always meant extra work, tighter deadlines and an increased chance of being pilloried for blunders for which they were hardly responsible.

"We've done a post-mortem on Rudolf Asayev," Mia said. "A thorough one."

"Not thorough enough," Harry said, putting the report down on one of the shiny metal tables where the students had just been cutting into human flesh. A muscular arm, severed at the shoulder, hung out from under a blanket. Harry read the letters of the faded tattoo on the upper arm. **Too young to die.** Well. Maybe one of the Los Lobos bikers, a rival gang Asayev was determined to eliminate.

"And what makes you think we haven't been thorough enough, Hole?"

"First of all, you couldn't show any cause of death."

"Sometimes the body simply doesn't give us any clues. You know that. It doesn't necessarily mean there isn't a perfectly natural cause."

"And the most natural cause in this case would be that someone murdered him."

"I know he was a potential Crown witness, but a post-mortem follows certain fixed routines which are not influenced by such circumstances. We find what we find, and nothing else. Pathology isn't a hunch science."

"With regard to the science," Hole said, sitting on her desk. "It's based on hypothesis testing, isn't it? You form a theory and then you test it, true or false. Right?"

Mia Hartvigsen shook her head. Not because it wasn't right, but because she didn't like the direction this conversation was taking.

"My theory," Hole continued with an innocent smile, making him look like a boy trying to persuade his mother he should have an atomic bomb for Christmas, "is that Asayev was killed by someone who knows exactly how you work and what is required to ensure you don't find anything."

Mia shifted feet, turning the other shoulder to him. "So?"

"So how would you have done that, Mia?"

"Me?"

"You know all the tricks. How would you have fooled yourself?"

"Am I a suspect?"

"Until further notice."

She stopped herself reacting when she saw him smiling.

"Murder weapon?" she asked.

"Syringe," Hole said.

"Oh? Why's that?"

"Something to do with anaesthesia."

"I see. We can trace almost all drugs, especially when we have access as quickly as we did in this case. The only option I can see is . . ."

"Yes?" He smiled as though he had already got his way. Irritating man. The kind you can't decide whether to slap or kiss.

"An air injection."

"Which is?"

"The oldest and still the best trick in the book. You fill a syringe with enough air to put air bubbles into the blood vessel and block it. If it's blocked for long enough the blood doesn't reach vital parts of the body such as the heart or the brain and you die. Fast and without any chemical residue. A blood clot can form inside the body without any external intervention. Case closed."

"But the needle mark would be visible."

"Not if you use a thin enough needle. You'd have to examine every centimetre of skin to reveal a mark."

Hole brightened up. The boy opened the present and thought it was an atomic bomb.

Mia was happy.

"Then you'll have to examine——"

"We did." Smack. "Every millimetre of it. We even checked the intravenous drip. It's possible to inject air bubbles there as well, you see. There wasn't so much as a mozzie bite anywhere." She watched the feverish light in his eyes die. "Sorry, Hole, but we were aware the death was suspicious." She stressed **were.**

"Now I have to prepare the next lecture, so maybe—"

"What about somewhere that wasn't skin?" Hole said.

"What?"

"What about if he injected the needle somewhere else? Orifices. Mouth, rectum, nostrils, ears."

"Interesting idea, but in the nose and ears there are very few blood vessels which would be suitable. The rectum is a possibility, but the odds of isolating vital organs in those regions are lower, and furthermore you have to know your way around extremely well to find a vein blind. The mouth may be feasible as it has veins with a short route to the brain and would have led to a quick, certain death, but we always check the mouth. And it's full of mucous membranes where an injection would have caused swelling, and that would be easy to see."

She looked at him. Sensed his brain still churning round for a solution, but he gave a resigned nod.

"Nice to see you again, Hole. Pop by if you fancy giving it another shot."

She turned and walked over to one of the tubs and pushed a pale, grey arm with outstretched fingers down into the alcohol.

"Another . . . shot," she heard Harry muttering. She heaved a deep sigh. **Very** irritating man.

"He could have tried another shot," Hole said.

"Where exactly?"

"You said a short route to the brain. From behind. He could have hidden the shot from behind."

"Behind what . . . ?" She stopped. Looked where he was pointing. Closed her eyes and sighed again.

"Sorry," Harry said. "But FBI statistics show that in cases where a post-mortem has been performed on witnesses, the percentage of murders rises from seventy-eight to ninety-four with a second post-mortem."

Mia Hartvigsen shook her head. Harry Hole. Trouble. Extra work. An increased chance of being pilloried for blunders not of their own making.

"Here," Beate Lønn said, and the taxi pulled into the curb.

The tram was at the Welhavens Café gate stop. There was one police car parked in front and two behind. Bjørn Holm and Katrine Bratt were leaning against the Amazon.

Beate paid and jumped out.

"Well?"

"Three officers are in the tram and no one has been allowed to leave. We were waiting for you."

"It says number 11 on this tram. I said 12."

"It changes number after the Majorstuen crossing, but it's the same tram."

Beate hurried over to the front door, knocked hard

and held up her ID. The door opened with a snort and she climbed in. Nodded to the uniformed policeman standing there. He was holding a Heckler & Koch P30L.

"Follow me," she said and started walking through the packed tram.

She scrutinised all the faces as she made her way to the middle of the carriage. Felt her heart beating faster as she approached, saw the doodlings in the condensation on the window. She signalled to the officer before addressing the man in the seat.

"Excuse me! Yes, you."

The face turned up to her bore angry red pimples and a terrified expression.

"I . . . I didn't mean to. I left my travel card at home. Won't happen again."

Beate closed her eyes and swore under her breath. Nodded to the officer to keep following her. When they had reached the end of the carriage without any success, she called to the driver to open the back door and clambered out.

"Well?" Katrine said.

"Gone. Question the passengers to see if they saw him. In an hour they'll have forgotten, if they haven't already. As a reminder, he's a man in his forties, about one eighty tall with blue eyes. But the eyes are a bit slanted now. He's got short brown hair, high, pronounced cheekbones and thin lips. And no one touch the window where he was writing. Take fingerprints and photos. Bjørn?"

"Yes?"

"Take all the stops between here and Frogner Park, talk to people working in nearby shops, ask if they know anyone of this description. When people catch trams early in the morning it's often part of a routine. They're going to work, school, the gym, a regular coffee bar."

"We've got a few more bites at the cherry then," Katrine said.

"Yes, but be careful, Bjørn. Make sure the people you talk to aren't likely to warn him. Katrine, see if we can borrow some officers to take the tram early in the morning. Get a couple of men on the trams from here to Frogner Park for the rest of the day, in case Valentin should return the same way. OK?"

While Katrine and Bjørn joined the police officers and allocated tasks, Beate looked up at the window of the tram. The lines he had drawn in the condensation had run. There was a recurrent pattern, a bit like frilly lace. A vertical line followed by a circle. After one row there was another, forming a square matrix.

It wasn't necessarily important.

But as Harry used to say: "It might not be important or relevant, but everything means **something.** And we start searching where there is light, where we can see **something.**"

Beate took out her mobile and photographed the window. And remembered something.

"Katrine! Come here!"

Katrine heard her and left the briefing to Bjørn.

"How did it go last night?"

"Fine," Katrine said. "I took the chewing gum for

testing this morning. Registered it with the file number of a shelved rape case. They're prioritising the police murders, but they promise to look at it asap."

Beate nodded pensively. Ran a hand across her face. "How soon is asap? We can't let what **might** be the murderer's DNA end up last in the queue just to get the bouquets for ourselves."

Katrine put a hand on her hip and eyed Bjørn, who was gesticulating to the officers. "I know one of the women up there," she lied. "I'll ring her and do some pushing."

Beate looked at her. Hesitated. Nodded.

"And you're sure you didn't just **want** it to be Valentin Gjertsen?" Ståle Aune said. He was standing by the window and staring down at the busy street beneath the office. At the people hurrying hither and thither. At the people who could be Valentin Gjertsen. "Optical illusions are common among those suffering from a lack of sleep. How much sleep have you had in the last forty-eight hours?"

"I'll count them up," Beate Lønn answered, in a way that made it clear to Ståle that she didn't need to. "I'm ringing because he drew something on the window inside the tram. Did you get my text?"

"Yes," Aune said. He had just started a therapy session when Beate's text shone up at him from his open desk drawer.

See pic. Urgent. I'll ring.

And he had felt an almost perverse sense of pleasure when he had looked straight into Paul Stavnes's astonished face, said there was a call he absolutely **had** to take and saw the subtext had been received: it's much more important than your bloody whingeing.

"You told me once that you psychologists can analyse the scribbles of sociopaths and deduce something about their subconscious."

"Well, what I said was probably that Granada University has developed a method for studying psychopathological personality disorders through art. But then individuals are told what they have to draw. And this looks more like writing than drawing," Ståle said.

"Does it?"

"At least I can see i's and o's. That's much more interesting than a drawing."

"In what way?"

"Early in the morning on a tram, still half asleep, your writing is governed by your subconscious. And the thing about the subconscious is that it likes codes and rebuses. Sometimes they're incomprehensible, at others they're astonishingly simple, downright banal even. I had a patient once who walked around terrified of being raped. She had a recurrent dream about being woken up by the gun barrel of a tank coming through her bedroom window and stopping at the foot of her bed. And hanging from the end of the barrel was a note, on which was written P plus N plus 15. It may seem odd that she herself was unable to crack the childishly simple code, but the brain often camouflages its real thoughts. For reasons of comfort, guilt, terror . . ."

"What do the i's and o's mean?"

"It might mean trams bore him. Don't overestimate my abilities, Beate. I entered the field of psychology when it was seen as a good option for those too stupid to be doctors or engineers. Let me ruminate and get back to you. I have a patient with me now."

"OK."

Aune rang off and looked down at the street again. There was a tattoo parlour on the other side, a hundred metres down Bogstadveien. The number 11 tram went down Bogstadveien, and Valentin had had a tattoo. A tattoo that would identify him. Unless he'd had it removed. Or modified at a tattoo parlour. An image could be changed radically by adding a couple of simple lines. Like tacking a semicircle onto a vertical line to make a D. Or placing a diagonal line across an O to make an Ø. Aune breathed on the window.

Behind him he heard the sound of an irritated cough.

He drew a vertical line and a circle in the condensation the way he had seen it on the picture message.

"I refuse to pay the full fee if you—"

"Do you know what, Paul?" Aune said, adding a semicircle and a diagonal line. He read it. **DØ,** meaning die. Rubbed it out. "You can have this session free."

22

Rico Herrem knew he was going to die. He had always known. What was new was that he knew he was going to die within the next thirty-six hours.

"Anthrax," the Thai doctor repeated. With a proper "r" and an American accent. The slit-eye must have studied medicine there. And qualified for a job at this private clinic which probably had only ex-pats and tourists as patients.

"I'm so sorry."

Rico breathed into the oxygen mask; even that was difficult. Thirty-six hours. He had said thirty-six hours. Had asked if Rico had wanted them to contact any next of kin. They might be able to make it to Thailand if they caught a plane right away. Or a priest. Was he Catholic?

The doctor must have seen from Rico's bewildered expression that further explanation was necessary.

"Anthrax is a disease caused by bacteria. It's in your lungs. You probably inhaled it a few days ago."

Rico still didn't understand.

"If you'd digested it or got it on your skin, we might have been able to save you. But in the lungs . . ."

Bacteria? Was he going to die of bacteria? That he'd breathed in? Where could that have been?

The thought was repeated like an echo by the doctor.

"Any idea where? The police will want to know to prevent other people from being exposed to the bacteria."

Rico Herrem closed his eyes.

"Mr. Herrem, please try to think back. You might be able to save other people . . ."

Other people. But not himself. Thirty-six hours.

"Mr. Herrem?"

Rico wanted to nod to show he'd heard, but he couldn't. A door opened. Several pairs of shoes click-clacked in. A woman's breathless voice, low.

"Kari Farstad, Norwegian Embassy. We came as soon as we could. Is he . . . ?"

"His blood's stopped circulating. He's going into shock now."

Where? In the food he'd eaten when the taxi stopped at the lousy roadside restaurant between Bangkok and Pattaya? From the stinking hole in the ground they called a toilet? Or at the hotel? Wasn't that how bacteria were often spread, through the air conditioning? But the doctor had said the initial symptoms were the same as with a cold, and he'd had those on the flight. But if these bacteria had been in the air on the plane, the other passengers would have been ill too. He heard the woman's voice, lower and in Norwegian this time:

"Anthrax. My God, I thought that only existed as a biological weapon."

"Not at all." Man's voice. "I googled it on the way here. **Bacillus anthracis.** Can lie dormant for years. It's a tough little bugger. Spreads by forming spores. Same spores as in the powder posted to the Americans, do you remember? Ten or so years ago."

"Do you think someone sent him a letter containing anthrax?"

"He may have caught it anywhere, but the most common scenario is close contact with livestock. We'll probably never find out."

But Rico knew. Knew with a sudden clarity. He put a hand to his oxygen mask.

"Did you track down his next of kin?"

"Yes, I did."

"And?"

"They said he could rot."

"Right. Paedophile?"

"No. But the list was long enough. Hey, he's moving."

Rico had managed to remove the mask and was trying to speak. But all that came out was a hoarse whisper. He tried again. Saw that the woman had blonde curls and was staring down at him with a mixture of concern and disgust.

"Doctor, is it . . . ?"

"No, it isn't contagious between humans."

Not contagious, so it was just him.

Her face came closer. And even dying—or perhaps precisely because he was—Rico Herrem greedily inhaled her perfume. Inhaled it the way he had inhaled that day in Fiskebutikken. From the woollen glove, smelling of wet wool and tasting of chalk. Powder. The man with a scarf in front of his nose and mouth. Not to hide his face. Tiny spores flying through the air. **"Might have been able to save you. But in the lungs . . ."**

He strained to speak, and with great difficulty pronounced the words. Three words. It flashed through his mind that they were his last. Then—like the curtain falling after a pathetic, tormented performance lasting forty-two years—a great darkness descended over Rico Herrem.

The intense, brutal rain hammered on the car roof, as if it were trying to get in, and Kari Farstad gave an involuntary shudder. Her skin was perpetually covered with a layer of sweat, but they said it would be better when the rainy season was over, sometime in November. She longed to be home in the embassy flat, she hated these trips to Pattaya, and this was not the first. She hadn't chosen this career path to work with human detritus. The opposite, in fact. She had envisaged cocktail parties with interesting, intelligent people, lofty conversation about politics and culture; she had expected personal development and greater understanding of the big issues. Instead of this confusion surrounding the small issues. Like how to get a Norwegian sexual predator a good lawyer, possibly have him deported and sent to a Norwegian prison with the standards of a three-star hotel.

As suddenly as it had started, the rain stopped and they raced through the clouds of steam hovering above the hot tarmac.

"What was it you said Herrem said again?" the embassy secretary asked.

"Valentin," Kari replied.

"No, the rest."

"It was very unclear. A long word. May have been two. Sounded like something to do with a commode."

"Commode?"

"Something like that."

Kari stared at the rows of rubber trees planted alongside the motorway. She wanted to go home. Home as in home home.

23

Harry ran down the corridor of PHS past the Frans Widerberg painting.

She was standing in the doorway of the gym. Ready for battle in tight-fitting sports gear. Her arms crossed, leaning against the door frame, she followed him with her eyes. Harry was about to nod, but someone shouted "Silje!" and she went inside.

On the first floor Harry popped his head round the door to see Arnold.

"How did the lecture go?"

"Not bad, but they probably missed your gruesome, if irrelevant, examples from the so-called real world," Arnold said, continuing to massage his bad foot.

"Anyway, thanks for covering my slot," Harry smiled.

"No problem. What was so important?"

"Had to go up to the Pathology Unit. The pathologist has agreed to exhume the body of Rudolf Asayev and do a second post-mortem. I used your FBI stats on dead witnesses."

"Glad I could be of use. By the way, you have another visitor."

"Not . . ."

"No, neither frøken Gravseng nor any of your ex-colleagues. I said he could wait in your office."

"Who . . . ?"

"Someone you know, I believe. I gave him some coffee."

Harry met Arnold's gaze. Nodded quickly and left.

The man in the chair in Harry's office hadn't changed much. Bit more meat on the bones, a touch of grey around the temples. But he still had the boyish fringe befitting the suffix "junior," a suit that looked borrowed and the sharp-eyed, quick-witted gaze that could read a document page in four seconds flat and quote every word, if necessary, in a court of law. Johan Krohn was, in brief, the law's answer to Beate Lønn, the lawyer who won even when Norwegian law was his opponent.

"Harry Hole," he said in his youthful voice, got up and proffered his hand. "Been a long time," he said in English.

"Not long enough," Harry said, shaking his hand. Squeezing his titanium finger against Krohn's palm. "You've always been bad news, Krohn. Coffee all right?"

Krohn squeezed back. Hard. The additional kilos must be muscle.

"Your coffee's good," he smiled knowingly. "My news as usual is bad."

"Oh?"

"I'm not in the habit of showing up in person, but

I wanted to have a tête-à-tête before putting anything into writing. This is about Silje Gravseng, who is your student."

"My student," Harry repeated.

"Is that not the case?"

"In a sense. You made it sound as if she were personally mine."

"I'll do my best to be as precise as possible," Krohn said, puckering his lips into a smile. "She came straight to me instead of going to the police. Out of fear you would back one another up."

"You?"

"The police."

"I'm not—"

"You were employed by the police for years and, as a PHS employee, you're part of the system. The point is she's frightened the police would try to dissuade her from reporting this sexual assault. And that in the long term it would damage her career if she set herself against them."

"What are you talking about, Krohn?"

"Am I still not making myself clear? You raped Silje Gravseng here in this office last night, just before midnight."

Krohn observed Harry during the ensuing silence.

"Not that I can use this against you, Hole, but your absence of visible surprise is eloquent and reinforces my client's credibility."

"Does it need reinforcing?"

Krohn placed the tips of his fingers together. "I

hope you're aware of the seriousness of this matter, Hole. The very fact that this rape has been reported and made public will turn your life upside down."

Harry tried to imagine him in his lawyer's gown. The trial. The accusatory finger pointing at Harry in the dock. Silje bravely drying a tear. The lay judges' open-mouthed expressions of indignation. The cold front from the public gallery. The ceaseless scratching of the court sketcher's lead pencil on his pad.

"The only reason I'm sitting here, instead of two policemen with handcuffs ready to usher you out through the corridors, past your colleagues and your students, is that this approach would have a cost for my client as well."

"Which is?"

"I'm sure you know. She would always be the woman who sent a colleague to prison. Grassed up, it would be said. I understand this is frowned upon in police circles."

"You've seen too many films, Krohn. The police like to see rape cases cleared up, whoever the suspect is."

"And the trial would be a strain for a young girl, of course. Especially with important exams looming. As she didn't dare to go to the police, and had to think hard before she came to me, much of the forensic and biological evidence will already be lost. And that means the trial might drag on for longer than it would otherwise."

"And what evidence **have** you got?"

"Bruising. Scratch marks. A torn dress. And if I

have to ask for this office to be gone through with a fine-tooth comb, I'm sure we'll find bits of the same dress."

"If?"

"Yes. I'm not just bad news, Harry."

"Oh?"

"I have an alternative to offer you."

"The devil's, I assume."

"You're an intelligent man, Hole. You know we don't have damning evidence. This is a typical rape case, isn't it? It'll be one person's word against another's and we'll end up with two losers. The victim is suspected of loose morals and making false accusations, and everyone assumes the man who has been acquitted got off lightly. Given this potential lose–lose situation, Silje Gravseng has presented me with a wish, a suggestion, which I have no hesitation in supporting. Let me for a moment step out of my role as your adversary's lawyer, Hole. I advise you to support it too. For the alternative is she reports you. She's absolutely clear about that."

"Oh?"

"Yes. As someone who wants to maintain law and order as her profession, she sees it as her civic duty to ensure that rapists are punished. But, fortunately for you, not necessarily by a judge."

"So, principled in a way?"

"If I were you, I would be less sarcastic and a little more grateful, Hole. I **could** have recommended she report you to the police."

"What do you two want, Krohn?"

"In brief, for you to resign from your post at PHS and never again work for, or be in any way connected with, the police. Leaving Silje to continue her studies here in peace without any interference from you. The same applies when she takes up a job. One negative word from you and the agreement is declared null and void, and the rape will be reported."

Harry placed his elbows on the table, put his head in his hands. Massaging his forehead.

"I'll set up a written agreement in the form of a settlement," Krohn said. "Your resignation in exchange for her silence. Secrecy is a prerequisite on both sides. You will, however, hardly be able to damage her if you did break secrecy. Her decision will be met with sympathetic understanding."

"While I'll be seen as guilty because I went along with this settlement."

"View it as damage limitation, Hole. A man with your background will easily be able to find work. As an insurance investigator, for example. They pay better than PHS, believe me."

"I believe you."

"Good." Krohn flipped up the lid of his phone. "How's your calendar for the next few days?"

"I can do it tomorrow as a matter of fact."

"Good. My office at two o'clock. Can you remember the address from the last time?"

Harry nodded.

"Excellent. Have a marvellous day, Hole!"

Krohn jumped from his chair. Knee-lifts, pull-ups and bench press, Harry guessed.

After he had gone, Harry looked at his watch. It was Thursday and Rakel was coming a day earlier this weekend. Due to land at 17:30 and he had offered to collect her from the airport, which—after two of the standard "oh no, you don't need to's"—she had accepted gratefully. He knew she loved the three-quarters of an hour in the car home. The chat. The calm. The prelude to a wonderful evening. Her excited voice explaining what it **actually** meant that only states could be parties to the Statute of the Court at the International Court of Justice in The Hague. About the UN's legal powers or lack of them, as the countryside rolled past them. Or they talked about Oleg, about how he was doing, how he looked better by the day, how the old Oleg was returning. About the plans he had made. Studying law. PHS. And how lucky they had been. And how fragile happiness was.

They talked about everything that came into their heads, no beating around the bush. Almost everything. Harry never said how frightened he was. Frightened of making promises he couldn't keep. Frightened of not being the person he wanted to be, had to be, for them. Frightened that he didn't know if they could be the same for him. That he didn't know how someone could make him happy.

The fact that he was now together with her and Oleg was almost an exceptional circumstance, something he only half believed in, a suspiciously wonderful dream he was constantly expecting to wake up from.

Harry rubbed his face. Perhaps it was close now. The awakening. The pitiless, stinging daylight. Reality. Where everything would be as before. Cold, hard and lonely. Harry shivered.

Katrine Bratt looked at her watch. Ten past nine. Outside, it might have been a sudden mild spring evening. Down in the basement it was a chilly, damp winter evening. She watched Bjørn Holm scratching his red sideburns. Ståle Aune scribbling on a pad. Beate Lønn stifling a yawn. They were sitting around a computer looking at the photo Beate had taken of the tram window. They had talked a bit about the drawing, and concluded that whatever it was meant to signify, it was unlikely to help them catch Valentin.

Then Katrine had told them again about her feeling that someone else had been in the Evidence Room.

"It must have been someone working there," Bjørn said. "But, well, OK, it is strange they didn't switch on the light."

"The key would be easy to copy," Katrine said.

"Perhaps they aren't letters," Beate said. "Perhaps they're numbers."

They turned to her. She was still staring at the computer.

"Ones and zeros. Not i's and o's. Like a binary code. Don't ones mean yes and zeros no, Katrine?"

"I'm not a programmer," Katrine said. "But yes, that's right. And one means on and zero means off."

"One means action, zero means do nothing," Beate said. "Do. Don't. Do. Don't. One. Zero. Row after row."

"Like petals on an ox-eye daisy," Bjørn said.

They sat in silence; the computer fan was all that could be heard.

"The matrix ends in a zero," Aune said. "Don't."

"If he was finished," Beate said. "He had to get off at his stop."

"Sometimes serial killers just stop killing," Katrine said. "Disappear. Never to be seen again."

"That's the exception," Beate said. "Zero or no zero. Who thinks the cop killer intends to stop? Ståle?"

"Katrine's right, that does happen, but I'm afraid this one will keep going."

Afraid, Katrine thought, close to blurting out what she was thinking, which was that she was afraid of the opposite, now that they were so close, that he would stop, disappear from view. That it was worth the risk. Yes, that in a worst-case scenario she would be willing to sacrifice one colleague to catch Valentin. It was a sick thought, but it was there anyway. Another police death was tolerable. Letting Valentin get away wasn't. And she mouthed a silent incantation: one more time, you bastard. Strike one more time.

Katrine's mobile rang. She saw from the number it was the Pathology Unit.

"Hi. We checked this chunk of chewing gum from the rape case."

"Yes?" Katrine could feel her blood pumping round faster. To hell with all the little theories, this was hard evidence.

"I'm afraid we can't find any DNA."

"What?" It was like someone dousing you with a bucket of ice-cold water. "But . . . but it has to be crammed with spit."

"That's the way it goes sometimes, I'm afraid. Of course we could check it again, but with these police murders . . ."

Katrine rang off. "They didn't find anything in the chewing gum," she said in a low voice.

Bjørn and Beate nodded. Katrine thought she detected a certain air of relief in Beate.

There was a knock at the door.

"Yes!" Beate shouted.

Katrine stared at the iron door, suddenly sure it was him.

The tall blond man. He had changed his mind. He had come to save them all from this misery.

The iron door opened. Katrine cursed. It was Gunnar Hagen. "How's it going?"

Beate stretched her arms above her head. "No Valentin on trams 11 or 12 this afternoon, and the questioning didn't produce anything of interest. We've got officers on the tram this evening, but our hopes are higher for early tomorrow morning."

"I've been fielding queries from the Investigation Unit about the use of officers on the tram. They're wondering what's going on and if it has any connection with the police murders."

"Rumours spread quickly," Beate said.

"Bit too quickly," Hagen said. "This is going to get to Bellman's ears."

Katrine stared at the screen. Patterns. This was her strength, this was; it was how they had managed to trace the Snowman that time. So. One and zero. Two numbers in pairs. Ten maybe? A pair of numbers that go together several times. Several times. Several . . .

"For this reason I'll have to inform him about Valentin this evening."

"What does that mean for our group?" Beate asked.

"Valentin turning up on a tram isn't our fault. It's obvious we had to act. However, with that our group has completed its mission. It has established that Valentin is alive and given us a main suspect. And if we don't catch him, there's a chance he'll turn up at the house in Berg. Now other officers will take over, folks."

"What about poly-ti?" Katrine said.

"I beg your pardon," Hagen answered in a soft voice.

"Ståle says that you write what's going on in your subconscious. Valentin has written lots of tens, one after the other. Another way of saying 'many' is 'poly.' So, **poly-ti**. As in **politi.** Police. That might mean he's planning to murder more police officers."

"What's she blathering about?" Hagen asked, turning to Ståle.

Ståle Aune shrugged. "We're trying to interpret

his doodles on the tram window. My own doodle suggested that he was writing 'die.' But what if he's content to use ones and zeros? The human brain is a four-dimensional labyrinth. Everyone's been there; no one knows the way."

As Katrine walked through Oslo's streets on her way to the police flat in Grünerløkka, she wasn't aware of life around her, the laughing, excited people hurrying to celebrate the short spring, the short weekend, life before it was over.

She knew now. Why they had been so obsessed with this idiotic "code." Because they were desperately hoping that things would cohere, have some meaning. But more importantly, because they had nothing else to go on. So they flogged a dead horse.

Her gaze was fixed on the pavement in front of her, and she was banging her heels on the tarmac in time to the incantation she kept repeating: "One more time, you bastard. Strike one more time."

Harry had taken her long hair in his hand. It was still dark and shiny and so thick it felt like you were holding coiled rope. He pulled it towards him, tipping her head back, and looked down at her slender, arched back, her spine winding like a snake beneath her glowing, perspiring skin. Thrust again. Her groan was like a low-frequency growl coming from the depths of her chest, an angry, frustrated sound.

Sometimes their lovemaking was quiet, calm, lazy like a slow dance, a shuffle. At other times it was like fighting. As it was tonight. It was as though her wanton lust bred greater lust, like now; it was like trying to extinguish a fire with petrol, it escalated, burned out of control, and often he thought, Jesus, this can't end well.

Her dress was lying on the floor beside the bed. Red. She was so attractive in red it was almost a sin. Barefoot. No, she hadn't been barefoot. Harry leaned over and breathed in her aroma.

"Don't stop," she groaned.

Opium. Rakel had told him the bitter smell was sweat from the bark of an Arab tree. No, not sweat, it was tears. The tears of a princess who fled to Arabia because of a forbidden love. Princess Myrrha. Myrrh. Her life ended in grief, but Yves Saint Laurent paid a fortune per litre of tears.

"Don't stop, hold . . ."

She had taken his hand, pressed it against her neck. He squeezed carefully. Felt the blood vessels and the tensed muscles in her slender neck.

"Harder! Har—"

Her voice was cut off as he did what she said. Knowing that now he had stopped the flow of oxygen to her brain. This had been her thing, something he did and got a kick out of because he knew she got a kick out of it. But something was different now. The thought that she was in his power. That he could do with her as he wished. He stared down at her dress. The red dress. Felt it building up inside him and that he wouldn't be able to hold it back. He closed his eyes and imagined her. On all fours as she slowly turned over, looked at him, while her hair changed colour, and he saw who she was. Her eyes had rolled backwards and her neck was covered in bruises, which became visible as the forensics officer's flash went off.

Harry let go and pulled his hand away. But Rakel was already there. She had tensed up and was shaking like a deer the second before it hits the ground. Then she died. Slumped with her forehead against the mattress, a bitter sob came from her mouth. She lay like that, kneeling as if in prayer.

Harry pulled out. She whimpered, turned and eyed him accusingly. Usually he waited before pulling out until she was ready for the separation.

Harry kissed her quickly on the neck, slid out of bed and fished around for the Paul Smith underpants she had bought him at some airport. Found his pack of Camels in the Wranglers hanging over the chair. Went downstairs to the living room. Sat in a chair and looked out of the window, where the night was at its darkest and yet not so dark that he couldn't see the silhouette of Holmenkollen Ridge against the sky. Lit a cigarette. Immediately afterwards he heard the patter of her feet behind him. Felt a hand stroking his hair and neck.

"Is there something wrong?"

"No."

She sat down on the arm of the chair and snuggled her nose up against his neck. Her skin was still hot and smelt of Rakel and lovemaking. And Princess Myrrha's tears.

"Opium," he said. "Quite a name for a perfume."

"Don't you like it?"

"Yes, I do." Harry blew smoke at the ceiling. "But it's quite . . . pronounced."

She lifted her head. Looked at him. "And you're telling me that now?"

"I hadn't thought about it before. I didn't really now, either."

"Is it the booze?"

"What?"

"The alcohol in the perfume. Is it that . . . ?"

He shook his head.

"But there's something," she said. "I know you, Harry. You're troubled, restless. Look at the way you're smoking. You're sucking it out as if it were the last drop of water in the world."

Harry smiled. Stroked the gooseflesh on her back. She kissed him lightly on the cheek. "So if it's not alcoholic abstinence, it's the other variety."

"The other variety?"

"The police variety."

"Oh, that," he said.

"It's the police murders, isn't it?"

"Beate came here to persuade me. She said she'd talked to you first."

Rakel nodded.

"And that you'd given the impression it was fine by you," Harry said.

"I said it was up to you."

"Had you forgotten our promise?"

"No, but I can't force you to keep a promise, Harry."

"And what if I'd said yes and joined the investigation?"

"Then you would have broken your promise."

"And the consequences?"

"For you, me and Oleg? Greater chance that we would be doomed. For the investigation into the murders of the three officers? Greater chance of success."

"Mm. The former is definite, Rakel. The latter highly doubtful."

"Maybe. But you know very well that we could be doomed anyway, whether you work for the police or not. There are several pitfalls. One is that you start climbing the walls because you can't do what you feel you were born to do. I've heard of men whose relationships break down just in time for the autumn hunt."

"Elk. Rather than birds of the featherless variety, you mean?"

"Yes, that does have to be said in their favour."

Harry inhaled. Their voices were lowered, calm, as though they were discussing the shopping. That was how they talked, he thought. That was what she was like. He pulled her to him. Whispered in her ear.

"I want to keep you, Rakel. I want to keep this."

"Yes?"

"Yes. This is good. This is the best I've ever known. And you know what makes me tick, you remember Ståle's diagnosis. An addictive personality bordering on OCD. Booze or hunting, it makes no difference, my mind starts whirring in the same grooves. As soon as I open the door, I'm there, Rakel. And I don't want to be there. I want to be **here.** Hell, I'm on the way there now, only talking about it! I'm not doing this for Oleg and you; I'm doing it for me."

"There, there." Rakel stroked his hair. "Let's talk about something else then."

"Yes. So they said Oleg would be out early?"

"Yes. There are no more withdrawal symptoms. And he seems more motivated than ever. Harry?"

"Yes."

"He told me what happened that night." Her hand continued to stroke him. He wanted it to be there forever.

"Which night?"

"You know. The night the doctor patched you up."

"Oh, he told you, did he?"

"You told me you were shot by one of Asayev's dealers."

"In a sense that's true. Oleg was one of them."

"I preferred the old version. The one about Oleg appearing at the crime scene afterwards, seeing how badly hurt you were and running along the Akerselva to A&E."

"But you never really believed it, did you?"

"He told me he burst in and forced a doctor at gunpoint to go with him."

"The doctor forgave Oleg when he saw my state."

Rakel shook her head. "He would have liked to tell me the rest as well, but he says he doesn't remember much from those months."

"Heroin does have that effect."

"But I thought you might fill in the gaps for me now. What do you say?"

Harry inhaled. Waited a second. Let out the smoke. "I prefer to say as little as possible."

She tugged his hair. "I believed you that time because I **wanted** to. My God, Harry, Oleg shot you. He should be in prison."

Harry shook his head. "It was an accident, Rakel. All that's behind us now, and as long as the police don't find the Odessa gun no one can link Oleg to the murder of Gusto Hanssen or anyone else."

"What do you mean? Oleg has been acquitted of that murder. Are you saying he had something to do with it after all?"

"No, Rakel."

"So what are you telling me, Harry?"

"Are you sure you want to know, Rakel? Really?"

She looked at Harry hard without answering.

Harry waited. Stared out of the window. Saw the silhouette of the ridge surrounding this quiet, secure town where nothing happened. Which was actually the edge of a dormant volcano, where the town had been built. Depending on how you looked at it. Depending on what you knew.

"No," she whispered in the darkness. Taking his hand and putting it to her cheek.

It was easy to live a happy life of ignorance, Harry thought. It was just a question of repression. Repressing an Odessa lying, or not lying, locked in a cupboard. Repressing three murders that were not your responsibility. Repressing the image of the hate-filled eyes of a rejected student with a red dress pulled up over her waist. Wasn't it?

Harry stubbed out his cigarette.

"Shall we go to bed?"

At three o'clock in the morning Harry woke with a start.

He had dreamt about her again. He had gone into a room and found her there. She was lying on a filthy mattress on the floor, cutting up the red dress she was wearing with a big pair of scissors. Beside her was a portable TV broadcasting her and what she was doing with a two-second delay. Harry looked around, but he couldn't see a camera anywhere. Then she placed one shiny blade against the inside of her white thigh, opened her legs and whispered:

"Don't do it."

And Harry fumbled behind him and found the handle of the door that had closed after him, but it was locked. Then he discovered that he was naked and was moving towards her.

"Don't do it."

It sounded like an echo from the TV. A two-second delay.

"I just have to get the key," he said, but it sounded like he was talking underwater, and he knew she hadn't heard. Then she put two, three, four fingers inside her vagina, and he stared as the whole of the slim hand slipped inside. He took another step towards her. Then the hand came back out holding a gun. Pointed at him. A shiny, dripping gun with a cable leading back inside her like an umbilical cord. "Don't do it," she had said, but he was already kneeling in front of her, leaning forward. Felt the gun, cool and pleasant, against his forehead. And then he whispered:

"Do it."

24

The tennis courts were unoccupied as Bjørn Holm's Volvo Amazon pulled up in front of Frogner Park and the police car by the main gate.

Beate jumped out, wide awake despite having slept hardly a wink. It was hard to sleep in a stranger's bed. Yes, she still thought of him as a stranger. She knew his body, but his mind, habits and thinking were still a mystery she wondered whether she had enough patience or interest to explore. So every morning she woke in his bed, she asked herself the question: are you going to carry on?

Two plainclothes policemen leaning back against the car straightened and came to meet her. She saw two uniformed officers sitting in the front seats of the car and another man in the back.

"Is that him?" she asked, feeling her heart beat wonderfully fast.

"Yes," said one of the plainclothes men. "Great police sketch. He's the spitting image."

"And the tram?"

"We sent it on, it was packed to the brim. But we took one woman's details as there was a bit of drama."

"Oh?"

"He tried to make a run for it when we showed our ID and said he had to come along with us. He leapt into the aisle and grabbed a pram to block our way. Yelled for the tram to stop."

"A pram?"

"Yes, you can't believe it, can you? Bloody criminal."

"I'm afraid he's committed worse."

"I mean, taking a pram on the tram during the morning rush hour."

"OK. But then you arrested him?"

"The baby's mother screamed and held onto his arm so that I could get a punch in." The policeman showed the bleeding knuckles on his right fist. "No point brandishing a shooter when this works, is there?"

"Good," Beate said, trying to sound as if she meant it. She bent down and looked into the back of the car, but all she could see was a silhouette beneath the reflection of herself in the morning sun. "Can someone lower the window?"

She tried to breathe calmly as the window slid soundlessly down.

She recognised him at once. He didn't look at her, he stared straight ahead, stared into the Oslo morning with half-closed eyes, as though still in the dream he hadn't wanted to wake up from.

"Have you searched him?" she asked.

"Close encounter of the third kind," the plainclothes man grinned. "No, he didn't have a weapon on him."

"I mean, have you searched him for drugs? Checked his pockets?"

"Well, no. Why would we?"

"Because this is Chris Reddy, also known as Adidas, several convictions for selling speed. He tried to run, so you can bet your life he's got something on him. So strip him."

Beate Lønn straightened up and went back to the Amazon.

"I thought she did fingerprints," she heard the plainclothes man say to Bjørn Holm, who had come to join them. "Not that she recognised junkies."

"She recognises anyone who's ever been in Oslo Police archives," Bjørn said. "Look a bit closer next time, OK?"

When Bjørn got in the car and glanced at her, Beate knew she looked like a grumpy old cow, with her arms crossed, fuming as she stared ahead.

"We'll collar him on Sunday," Bjørn said.

"Let's hope so," Beate said. "Everything set up in Bergslia?"

"Delta's done a recon and found their positions. They said it was simple with all the forest around. But they're in the neighbouring house as well."

"And everyone who investigated the original crime has been informed?"

"Yes. Everyone will be near a phone all day and report in if they receive a call."

"That goes for you too, Bjørn."

"And you. By the way, why wasn't Harry on that case? He was an inspector in Crime Squad then."

"Mm, he was indisposed."

"On the booze?"

"How are we using Katrine?"

"She's got a position in Berg Forest, with a good view of the house."

"I want regular mobile contact with her all the time she's there."

"I'll tell her."

Beate glanced at her watch. 09:16. They drove down Thomas Heftyes gate and Bygdøy allé. Not because it was the shortest way to Police HQ, but because it was the most scenic. And because it killed some time. Beate glanced at her watch again. 09:22. D-Day in two days. Sunday.

Her heart was still beating fast.

Was already beating fast.

Johan Krohn kept Harry waiting in reception the usual four minutes past the time of the appointment before coming out. Gave a couple of obviously super-fluous messages to the receptionist before directing his attention to the two people sitting there.

"Hole," he said, fleetingly studying the policeman's face to diagnose mood and attitude before proffering his hand. "You've brought your own lawyer, have you?"

"This is Arnold Folkestad," Harry said. "He's a colleague, and I've asked him to join me so that I have a witness to what is said and agreed."

"Wise, very wise," said Johan Krohn, without anything in his tone or expression suggesting he meant it. "Come in, come in."

He led the way, looked quickly at a surprisingly petite, feminine wristwatch and Harry took the hint: I'm a busy lawyer with limited time for this relatively minor matter. The office was executive size and smelt of leather, which Harry assumed came from the bound chronological volumes of **Norsk Rettstidende** filling the shelves. And a perfume he recognised. Silje Gravseng was sitting in a chair, half turned towards them, half turned towards Johan Krohn's massive desk.

"Endangered species?" Harry asked, running a hand across the desk before taking a seat.

"Standard teak," Krohn said, occupying the driving seat behind the rainforest.

"Standard yesterday, endangered today," Harry said, nodding briefly to Silje Gravseng. She answered by slowly lowering her eyelids and opening them again, as if she mustn't move her head. Her hair was tied in a ponytail so tight it made her eyes narrower than usual. She was wearing a suit that could easily suggest she worked in the office. She seemed calm.

"Shall we get down to business?" said Johan Krohn, who had adopted his customary pose with his fingertips pressed together. "Frøken Gravseng has testified that she was raped in your office at the Politihøyskole at around midnight on the night in question. The evidence so far: scratch marks, bruises and a torn dress. All this has been photographed and can be used as proof in a court of law."

Krohn shot Silje a quick glance to ensure she was bearing up under the strain before continuing.

"The medical examination at the Rape Crisis Centre didn't, it is true, reveal any tears or bruising, but it rarely does. Even in brutal attacks we're only talking about fifteen to thirty per cent of cases. There is no sign of semen as you had enough presence of mind to ejaculate externally, on frøken Gravseng's stomach to be precise, before you told her to get dressed, dragged her to the door and threw her out. Shame she didn't have the same presence of mind as you did in retaining some of the sperm as evidence. Instead, she cried in the shower for hours and did her utmost to wash away all the signs of her defilement. Not so surprising, perhaps, a very understandable and normal reaction for a young girl."

Krohn's voice had acquired a slightly indignant quiver, which Harry assumed wasn't genuine, but rather designed to demonstrate how effective this testimony could be in court.

"But the staff at the Rape Crisis Centre are required to describe the victim's psychological state in a few lines. We are talking here about professionals with long experience of rape victims' behaviour, and accordingly these are descriptions that the court would set great store by. And, believe me, in this case the psychological observations support my client's statement."

An almost apologetic smile flitted across the lawyer's face.

"But before going over the evidence in any more detail let's establish whether you have given my proposal any more thought, Hole. If you have concluded that accepting my offer is the right path—and I hope for everyone's sake you have—I have the written contract here. Which, I hardly need say, will remain confidential."

Krohn passed a black leather document case to Harry while sending eloquent glances to Arnold Folkestad, who nodded slowly.

Harry opened the case and scanned the A4 sheet.

"Mm. I resign from PHS and waive any work in, or in connection with, the police force. And I do not talk under any circumstances with or about Silje Gravseng. Ready for signature, I can see."

"It's not exactly complicated, so if you've already done your own calculations and come to the correct solution . . ."

Harry nodded. Looked across at Silje Gravseng, who was sitting there, as stiff as a post, staring back at him, her face pale and expressionless.

Arnold Folkestad coughed quietly, and Krohn turned his attention to him with a friendly gaze while straightening his wristwatch in a studied casual manner. Arnold held out a yellow folder.

"What's this?" Krohn asked, taking it with one raised eyebrow.

"Our suggestion for an agreement," Folkestad said. "As you'll see, we suggest Silje Gravseng terminates her course at PHS with immediate effect and does not apply under any circumstances for a job in, or in connection with, the police force."

"You are joking . . ."

"And she does not try under any circumstances to contact Harry Hole again."

"This is preposterous."

"In return, we will—out of consideration for all parties—refrain from legally pursuing this false accusation and attempted blackmail of a PHS employee."

"In that case, see you in court," Krohn said, managing to avoid the cliché sounding like one. "And even if you suffer as a result I am looking forward to conducting the prosecution."

Folkestad shrugged. "Then I'm afraid you're going to be a bit disappointed, Krohn."

"Let's see who will be disappointed." Krohn had already risen to his feet and done up one button of his jacket, a sign he was on his way to the next meeting, when he caught Harry's eye. He hesitated.

"What do you mean?"

"If you wouldn't mind taking the trouble," Folkestad said, "I would suggest you read the documents behind the proposed agreement."

Krohn opened the file again. Flicked through. Read.

"As you can see," Folkestad continued, "your client has followed the lectures at PHS about rape, in which, among other things, there is a description of how rape victims tend to react psychologically."

"That doesn't mean—"

"May I ask you to wait with your objections until the end and now flick over to the next page, Krohn? There you will find a signed, and for the moment unofficial, witness statement from a male student who was standing outside the front entrance where he saw frøken Gravseng leaving PHS at the time in question. He states that she looked angry rather than frightened. He doesn't mention anything about a torn dress. On the contrary, he says she appeared to be both dressed and unhurt. And he admits to studying her very closely." He turned to Silje Gravseng. "A compliment to you, I assume . . ."

She sat as still as before, but her cheeks had coloured up and her eyes were blinking non-stop.

"As you can see, Harry Hole went over to him a maximum of one minute, so sixty seconds, after frøken Gravseng had passed him. Hole stayed with the witness until I arrived and took Hole to Krimteknisk, which is—" Folkestad motioned with his hand—"on the next page, there, yes."

Krohn read it, and slumped back in his chair.

"The report says that Hole has none of the things you would expect a man who has just committed rape to have. No skin under the nails, no genital secretions or pubic hairs from other persons on his hands or his genitals. And this gives the lie to frøken Gravseng's statement about scratching and penetration. Furthermore, there are no marks on Hole's body to suggest she had been fighting him at all. The only suggestion of contact is two hairs on his clothes, but they are no more than one would expect after she had leaned across him, see page three."

Krohn flicked through without looking up. His eyes danced down the page, his lips forming a profanity after three seconds, and Harry knew the myth was true: no one in Norwegian justice circles could read an A4 document faster than Johan Krohn.

"Finally," Folkestad said, "if you look at the volume of Hole's ejaculate only half an hour after the alleged rape, it shows four millimetres. A second ejaculation within the same half an hour would produce less than ten per cent of that. In short, unless Harry Hole's testicles are made of something very special he did not have an ejaculation at the time frøken Gravseng claims."

In the ensuing silence Harry could hear a car horn outside, shouting, then laughter and swearing. The traffic was at a standstill.

"It's not exactly complicated," Folkestad said, tentatively smiling into his beard. "So if you've done your calculations and—"

The hydraulic snort of brakes being released. And then the bang as Silje Gravseng got up from her chair immediately followed by the bang of the door as she left the room.

Krohn sat with his head lowered for some time. When he raised it again, his gaze was directed at Harry.

"I apologise," he said. "As a defence counsel we have to accept that our clients lie to save their skins. But this . . . I should have read the situation better."

Harry shrugged. "You don't know her, do you?"

"No," Krohn said. "But I know you. **Should** know you after so many years, Hole. I'll get her to sign your agreement."

"And if she won't?"

"I'll explain to her the consequences of making a false accusation. And an official expulsion from PHS. She's not stupid, you know."

"I know," Harry said, getting up with a sigh. "I know."

Outside, the traffic had started again.

Harry and Arnold Folkestad walked up Karl Johans gate.

"Thank you," Harry said. "But I'm still wondering how you grasped everything so quickly."

"I have some experience of OCD," Arnold smiled.

"Sorry?"

"Obsessive compulsive disorder. When a person with that predisposition has made a decision, she stops at nothing. Action is in itself more important than the consequences."

"I know what OCD is. I have a psychologist pal who has accused me of being halfway there myself. What I meant was, how did you twig so fast that we needed a witness and that we had to get ourselves to Krimteknisk?"

Arnold Folkestad chuckled. "I don't know if I can tell you that, Harry."

"Why not?"

"What I can tell you is that I was involved in a case where two policemen were about to be reported by someone they'd beaten senseless. But by doing something similar to what we've just done they got one over on him. One of them burnt the evidence that counted against them. And what was left wasn't enough, so the man's lawyer advised him to drop the charge because they wouldn't get anywhere. I reckoned the same would happen here."

"Now you're making it sound as if I really did rape her, Arnold."

"Sorry." Arnold laughed. "I had been half expecting that something like this would happen. The girl's a ticking time bomb. Our psychological tests should have disqualified her before she was offered a place on the course."

They walked across Egertorget. Images flickered through Harry's brain. A smile from a laughing girlfriend one May when he was young. The body of a Salvation Army soldier in front of the Christmas kettle. A town full of memories.

"So who were the two policemen?"

"One pretty high up."

"Is that why you won't tell me? And you were part of it? Guilty conscience?"

Arnold Folkestad shrugged. "Anyone who doesn't dare to stand up for justice should have a guilty conscience."

"Mm. A policeman with a history of violence and a predilection for burning evidence. There aren't many of them. We wouldn't by any chance be talking about an officer by the name of Truls Berntsen, would we?"

Arnold Folkestad said nothing, but the wince that recoiled through his short, round body was more than enough to tell Harry what he wanted to know.

"Mikael Bellman's shadow. That's what you mean by pretty high up, isn't it?" Harry spat on the tarmac.

"Shall we talk about something else, Harry?"

"Yes, let's do that. Lunch at Schrøder's?"

"Schrøder's? Do they really have . . . er, lunch?"

"They have burgers on bread. And room."

"That looks familiar, Rita," Harry said to the waitress who had just placed two burnt burgers covered with pale fried onions in front of them.

"Nothing changes here, you know." She smiled and left them.

"Truls Berntsen, yes," Harry said, looking over his shoulder. He and Arnold were almost alone in the single, square room which despite years of anti-smoking legislation still felt smoky. "I think he's been operating as a burner inside the police for many years."

"Oh?" Folkestad studied the animal cadaver in front of them with scepticism. "And what about Bellman?"

"He was responsible for narcotics during that time. I know he had some deal with one Rudolf Asayev, who was selling a heroin-like substance called violin," Harry said. "Bellman granted Asayev the monopoly in Oslo in return for an assurance that visible signs of drug trafficking, junkies in the streets and of course ODs went down. That made Bellman look good."

"So good that he got his hands on the Police Chief job?"

Harry chewed tentatively on the first bite of burger and shrugged his shoulders to suggest a "maybe."

"And why haven't you passed on what you know?" Arnold Folkestad cut carefully into what he hoped was meat. Gave up and looked at Harry, who returned a blank stare as he chewed and chewed. "A blow for justice?"

Harry swallowed. Wiped his mouth with a paper serviette. "I had no proof. Besides, I was no longer a policeman. It wasn't my business. It isn't my business now either, Arnold."

"No, I suppose not." Folkestad speared a chunk on his fork and raised it for inspection. "But if this isn't your business, and you're no longer a policeman, why has the pathologist sent you a post-mortem report on this Rudolf Asayev?"

"Mm. So you saw it?"

"Only because I usually collect your post as well when I'm by the pigeonholes. And because I'm a nosy parker, of course."

"What's it like?"

"I haven't tried it yet."

"Go for it. It won't bite."

"Same to you, Harry."

Harry smiled. "They searched behind the eyeball. And found what we'd been searching for. A little pin-prick in the large blood vessel. Someone could have pushed Asayev's eyeball to the side while he was in the coma and injected air bubbles into the corner of the eye. The result would have been instant blindness followed by a blood clot in the brain which couldn't be traced."

"Now I really feel like eating this," Folkestad grimaced and put down his fork. "Are you saying you've proved that Asayev was murdered?"

"Nope. The cause of death is still impossible to determine. But the mark proves what **might** have happened. The conundrum is of course how anyone got into the hospital room. The duty officer insisted he didn't see anyone pass during the period when the injection must have been made. Neither a doctor nor anyone else."

"The mystery of the locked room."

"Or something simpler. Like the officer leaving his post or falling asleep and, quite understandably, not admitting it. Or he was in on the murder, directly or indirectly."

"If he went AWOL or fell asleep the murder would have depended on serendipity, and surely we don't believe in that?"

"No, Arnold, we don't. But he could have been lured away from his post. Or doped."

"Or bribed. You'll have to get the officer in for questioning!"

Harry shook his head.

"Why on earth not?"

"First of all, I'm not a policeman any more. Secondly, the officer's dead. He was the one killed in the car outside Drammen." Harry nodded as if to himself, raised his coffee cup and took a sip.

"Damn!" Arnold had leaned forward. "And thirdly?"

Harry signalled to Rita for the bill. "Did I say there was a thirdly?"

"You said 'secondly,' not 'and secondly.' As though you were in the middle of reeling off a list."

"Right. I'll have to sharpen up my Norwegian."

Arnold tilted his head. And Harry saw the question in his colleague's eyes. If this is a case you're not going to follow up, why are you telling me about it?

"Come on, eat up," Harry said. "I've got a lecture."

The sun slipped across a pale sky, made a gentle landing on the horizon and coloured the clouds orange.

Truls Berntsen sat in his car half listening to the police radio while waiting for darkness to fall. Waiting for the lights in the house above him to be switched on. Waiting to see her. A fleeting glimpse would be enough.

Something was brewing. He could hear it in the style of communication, something was happening alongside the usual, subdued, routine normality. Short, intense reports came sporadically, as though they had been told not to use the radio more than necessary. And it wasn't what was said, more what wasn't said. The way it wasn't said. The staccato sentences on the surface about surveillance and transport, but without addresses, times or individual names being mentioned. People used to say the police frequency was the fourth most popular local radio in Oslo, but that was before it had been encrypted. Nevertheless, they were talking this evening as though they were terrified of revealing something.

There they were again. Truls turned up the volume.

"Zero one. Delta two zero. All quiet."

Delta, the elite force. An armed operation.

Truls picked up his binoculars. Focused on the living-room window. It was harder to see her in the new house; the terrace in front of the living room was in the way. With the old house, he had been able to stand in the trees and see straight into the room. See her sitting on the sofa with her feet tucked up underneath her. Barefoot. Stroking the blonde curls away from her face. As though she knew she was being watched. So beautiful he could cry.

The sky above Oslo Fjord changed from orange to red and then violet.

It had been all black the night he had parked by the mosque in Åkebergveien. He had walked down to Police HQ, clipped on his ID card in case the duty officers saw him, unlocked the door to the atrium and sauntered downstairs to the Evidence Room. Unlocked the door with the copy he'd had for three years now. Put on his night-vision goggles. He'd started doing that after the time he'd switched on the lights and aroused the suspicions of a security guard during one of Asayev's burner jobs. He had been quick, found the box by date, opened the bag containing the 9mm bullet taken from Kalsnes's head and replaced it with the one he had in his jacket pocket.

The only oddity had been that he hadn't felt alone.

He watched Ulla. Did she feel that too? Was that why she kept looking up from her book towards the window? As though there was something outside. Something waiting for her.

They were talking on the radio again.

He knew what they were talking about.

Understood what they were planning.

25

D-day was drawing to an end.

The walkie-talkie crackled quietly.

Katrine Bratt twisted on the thin ground sheet. Raised her binoculars again and focused on the house in Bergslia. Dark and silent. As it had been for almost twenty-four hours.

Something had to happen soon. In three hours it would be another date. The wrong date.

She shivered. But it could have been worse. About nine degrees during the day and no rain. But after the sun went down the temperature had plummeted and she had begun to feel cold, even with the full complement of winter underwear and the padded jacket which, according to the salesman, was "eight hundred on the American scale, not the European one, that is." It had something to do with insulation. Or was it feathers? Right now she wished she had something warmer than eight hundred. Like a man she could snuggle up to . . .

There was no one posted in the house itself; they hadn't wanted to risk being seen going in or out. Even for the recon they had parked a long way away, then sneaked around at some distance from the house, never more than two people at once and always out of uniform.

The spot she had been allocated was a little hill in Berg Forest, set back from where the Delta troops were deployed. She knew their positions, but even when she scanned them with the binoculars she couldn't see anything. She knew there were four marksmen, though, covering every side of the house, as well as eleven men ready to storm the place in under eight seconds.

She looked at her watch again. Two hours and fifty-eight minutes to go.

To the best of their knowledge the original murder had taken place at the end of the day, but it was hard to determine the moment death occurred when the body was cut into bits of no more than two kilos. Anyway, the timings of the copycat murders had so far matched the originals, so the fact that nothing had happened as yet was in a sense expected.

Clouds were moving in from the west. Dry weather had been forecast, but it would get darker and visibility would worsen. On the other hand, perhaps it might become milder. She should have brought a sleeping bag with her. Katrine's mobile vibrated. She answered it.

"What's happening?" It was Beate.

"Nothing to report here," Katrine said, scratching her neck. "Except that global warming is a fact. There are midges here. In March."

"Don't you mean mosquitoes?"

"No, midges. They . . . well, we have a lot of them in Bergen. Any interesting phone calls?"

"No. Just Cheez Doodles, Pepsi Max and Gabriel Byrne. Tell me, is he hot or **just** a tad too old?"

"Hot. Are you watching **In Treatment?**"

"First season. Disc three."

"Didn't know you'd succumbed to calories and DVDs. Trackie bottoms?"

"With very loose elastic. Have to go for some hedonism when the little one's not here."

"Shall we swap?"

"Nope. I'd better call off in case the prince rings. Keep me posted."

Katrine put the phone next to the walkie-talkie. Lifted the binoculars and studied the road in front of the house. In principle he could come from any direction. It was unlikely he would cross the fences on either side of the tracks where the metro had just clattered past, of course, but if he came from Damplassen he could come through the forest on any one of the many paths. He could walk through the neighbouring gardens alongside Bergslia, especially now that it was clouding over and getting darker. But if he felt confident there was no reason why he wouldn't come on the road. Someone on an old bike was pedalling uphill, staggering from side to side, perhaps he wasn't quite sober.

Wonder what Harry's doing tonight.

No one ever quite knew what Harry was doing,

even when you were sitting opposite him. Secret
Harry. Not like anyone else. Not like Bjørn Holm,
who wore his heart on his sleeve. Who had told
her yesterday he would play several Merle Haggard
records while waiting by the phone. Eat home-made
elk burgers from Skreia. And when she had screwed
up her nose he had said, heck, when this was over he
would invite her to eat his mother's elk burgers with
fries and initiate her into the secrets of the Bakers-
field sound. Which was probably all the music he
had. No wonder the guy was single. He'd looked as
if he regretted making the offer when she politely
refused.

Truls Berntsen drove through Kvadraturen. The way
he did almost every night now. Slowly cruising up
and down, here, there and everywhere. Dronnin-
gens gate, Kirkegata, Skippergata. Nedre Slottsgate,
Tollbugata. This had been his town. And it would
become his town again.

They were prattling away on the radio. Codes
which were meant for him, Truls Berntsen, it was
him they wanted to keep on the outside. And the
idiots probably thought they were succeeding and
that he didn't understand. But they didn't fool him.
Truls Berntsen straightened the mirror, glanced at
the service pistol lying on his jacket on the front seat.
It was, as usual, the other way round. It was he who
would fool them.

The women on the street ignored him; they recognised the car, knew he wasn't going to buy their services. A boy wearing make-up and trousers that were far too tight swung round the pole of a No Parking sign like a pole dancer, jutting out a hip and pouting at Truls, who responded by giving him the finger.

The darkness felt as if it had become a touch denser. Truls leaned into the windscreen and looked up. Clouds were on their way in from the west. He stopped at the lights. Glanced back down at the seat. He had fooled them time after time and was about to fool them again. This was his town, no one could come here and take it away from him.

He shifted the gun into the glove compartment. The murder weapon. It was so long ago, but he could still see his face. René Kalsnes. The weak lady-boy features. Truls smacked the wheel with his fist. Turn green, for Christ's sake!

He had hit him first with the baton.

Then he had taken his gun.

Even with his face bleeding, smashed to pieces, Truls had seen the pleading look, heard the begging wheeze, like a punctured cycle tyre. Wordless. Useless.

He had put the gun in the guy's nose, fired, seen the jerk, as if it were in a film. Then he had rolled the car over the cliff and driven off. Further down the road he had wiped the baton and thrown it into the forest. He had several more in the bedroom cupboard at home. Weapons, night-vision goggles, bulletproof vest, even a Märklin rifle which they thought was still in the Evidence Room.

Truls drove down the tunnels and into Oslo's belly. The car lobby, on the political right, had called the recently constructed tunnels the capital's vital arteries. A representative of the environment lobby had responded by calling them the town's bowels. They might be vital but they still carried shit.

He manoeuvred his way through the spur roads and roundabouts, signposted in the Oslo tradition, so that you had to be a local not to fall foul of the Department of Transport's practical jokes. Then he was high up. East Oslo. His part of town. On the radio they were rabbiting away. One of the voices was drowned out by a rattling sound. The metro. The idiots. Did they think he couldn't work out their childish codes? They were in Bergslia. They were outside the yellow house.

Harry lay on his back watching cigarette smoke slowly curling up to the bedroom ceiling. It formed figures and faces. He knew whose. He could mention them by name, one by one. The Dead Policemen's Society. He blew on them and they disappeared. He had made a decision. He didn't know exactly when he'd decided, he only knew it was going to change everything.

For a while he had tried to convince himself that it didn't have to be such a risk, that he was exaggerating, but he had been an alcoholic for too many years not to recognise the fool's ill-judged disdain of the cost. After he'd said what he was going to say now, it would change everything in his relationship with the woman he was lying next to. He was dreading it. Rolled some of the phrases around in his mouth. It was now or never.

He took a deep breath, but she intervened.

"Can I have a drag?" Rakel murmured, snuggling closer to him. Her naked skin had that tiled-stove glow he could begin to long for at the most astonishing times. It was warm underneath the duvet, cold on top. White bedlinen, always white bedlinen, nothing else got cold in the same, authentic way.

He passed her the Camel. Watched her hold it in that clumsy manner of hers, her cheeks hollowing as she squinted at the cigarette, as though it was safest to keep an eye on it. He reflected on all he had.

All he had to lose.

"Shall I run you to the airport tomorrow?" he asked.

"You don't need to."

"I know. But my first lecture isn't until late."

"Drive me then." She kissed him on the cheek.

"On two conditions."

Rakel rolled over onto her side and eyed him with a quizzical look.

"The first is you never stop smoking like a teenager at a party."

She sniggered quietly. "I'll try. And the second?"

Harry swallowed. Knowing he could come to regard this as the last happy moment of his life.

"I expect . . ."

Oh, shit.

"I'm considering breaking a promise," he said. "A promise I'd made primarily to myself, but I'm afraid it affects you as well."

He sensed rather than heard her breathing change in the darkness. Shorten, quicken. Fear.

Katrine yawned. Looked at her watch. At the luminous second hand counting down the time. None of the detectives on the original case had reported receiving a call.

She should have felt the tension mounting as the deadline approached, but instead it was the opposite, she had already started to work on her disappointment by forcing herself to think positively. Of the hot bath she would have when she got back to her flat. Of the bed. Of the coffee early tomorrow. Another day with new possibilities. There was always something new, there had to be.

She could see the car headlights on Ring 3: life in Oslo incomprehensibly following its inexorable course. The darkness deepening after the clouds had drawn a curtain in front of the moon. She was about to turn when she froze. A noise. A crack. A twig. Here.

She held her breath and listened. The position she had been allocated was surrounded by dense bushes and trees, well hidden from any of the paths he might choose. But there hadn't been any twigs on the paths.

Another crack. Closer this time. Katrine instinctively opened her mouth, as though the blood, which was pounding through her veins, needed more oxygen.

Katrine reached for the walkie-talkie. But never got that far.

He must have moved like greased lightning, yet the breath she felt on her neck was quite calm and the whispering voice by her ear unruffled, cheerful almost.

"What's happening?"

Katrine turned to him and released her breath in a long hiss. "Nothing."

Mikael Bellman took her binoculars and studied the house below. "Delta has two positions inside the railway line there, don't they?"

"Yes. How—?"

"I was given a copy of the ops map," Bellman said. "That's how I found this observation post. Well hidden, I must say." He smacked himself on the forehead. "Well I never. Mosquitoes in March."

"Midges," Katrine said.

"Wrong," said Mikael Bellman, who was still holding the binoculars to his eyes.

"Well, we're both right. Midges are similar to mosquitoes, just much smaller."

"You're wrong about—"

"Some of them are so small that they don't suck the blood of humans but other insects. Or their bodily fluids." Katrine knew she was babbling out of nervousness, without really knowing why she was nervous. Perhaps because he was the Chief of Police. "Of course, insects don't have—"

"—nothing happening. A car has stopped outside the house. Someone's getting out and approaching the house."

"And if a midge . . . What did you say?"

She took the binoculars from him. Chief of Police or not, this was her post. And he was right. In the light from the street lamps she saw someone who had already walked through the gate and was heading for the front door. He was dressed in red and carrying something she couldn't identify. Katrine felt her mouth going dry. It was him. It was happening. It was happening **now.** She grabbed her mobile phone.

"And I don't break promises lightly," Harry said. Staring at the cigarette she had passed back to him. Hoping there was enough for at least one big drag. He was going to need it.

"And which promise is that?" Rakel's voice sounded small, helpless. Alone.

"It's a promise I made to myself . . ." Harry said, pressing his lips round the filter. Inhaled. Tasted the smoke, the end of the cigarette which for some strange reason has a completely different flavour from the beginning. ". . . about never asking you to marry me."

In the silence that followed he could hear a gust

of wind rustling through the deciduous trees, like an excited, shocked, whispering audience.

Then came her answer. Like a short walkie-talkie message.

"Repeat."

Harry cleared his throat. "Rakel, will you marry me?"

The wind had moved on. And all that remained was silence, calm. Night. In the midst of it, Harry and Rakel.

"Are you pulling my leg?" She had moved away from him.

Harry closed his eyes. He was in free fall. "I'm not joking."

"Quite sure?"

"Why would I joke? Do you **want** this to be a joke?"

"First off, Harry, you have a very bad sense of humour."

"Agreed."

"Second, I have Oleg to consider. And you do, too."

"When I think about us getting married, Oleg is a big plus."

"Third, even if I had wanted to, getting married has a number of legal implications. My house—"

"I had been thinking of separate estates. I'm damned if I'm going to hand over my fortune to you on a silver platter. I can't promise much, but I can promise the world's most pain-free divorce."

She chuckled. "But we're getting on well as we are, aren't we, Harry?"

"Yes, we've got everything to lose. And fourth?"

"Fourth, that's not how you propose, Harry. In bed, over a cigarette."

"Well, if you want me on my knees, I'll have to put my trousers on first."

"Yes."

"Yes, I should put my trousers on? Or yes, I—?"

"Yes, you idiot! Yes! I want to marry you."

Harry's reaction was automatic, rehearsed over a long life as a policeman. He turned to the side and checked his watch. Noted the time. 23:11. The nitty-gritty for when he had to write the report. When they arrived at the crime scene, when the arrest was made, when the shot was fired.

"Oh good lord," he heard Rakel mumble. "What am I saying?"

"Cooling-off period expires in five seconds," Harry said, turning back to her.

Her face was so close to his that all he saw was a hazy sparkle in her wide eyes.

"Time's up," he said. "And what kind of a grin is that supposed to be?"

And now Harry could feel it himself, the smile that just kept spreading across his face like a freshly cracked egg in the pan.

Beate was lying with her legs on the arm of the sofa watching Gabriel Byrne wriggle uncomfortably in the chair. She had worked out it had to be the eyelashes and the Irish accent. The eyelashes of a Mikael Bellman, the lilt of a poet. The man she was seeing had none of these things, but that wasn't the problem. There was something odd about him. For starters, there was the intensity; he hadn't understood why he couldn't visit her if she was by herself this evening. And then there was his background. He had told her things she had gradually discovered didn't tally.

Perhaps that wasn't so unusual: you want to make a good impression and so you lay it on a bit thick.

On the other hand, perhaps there was something wrong with **her.** After all, she had tried to google him. Without finding anything. So she had googled Gabriel Byrne instead. Reading with interest that he'd worked as a teddy bear eye-installer before she found what she was really looking for. Spouse: Ellen Barkin (1988–1999). For a moment she'd thought Gabriel was widowed, left behind, like her, until she realised it was probably the marriage that was deceased. And if so Gabriel must have been single for longer than her. Or maybe Wikipedia wasn't up to date?

On the screen the female patient flirted at will. But Gabriel wasn't fooled. He sent her a brief, troubled smile, fixed his gentle eyes on her and said something trivial, which he made sound like a Yeats poem.

A light flashed on the table and her heart stopped.

Her mobile. It was ringing. It could be him. Valentin.

She lifted the phone, looked at the caller. Sighed.

"Yes, Katrine?"

"He's here."

Beate could hear from her colleague's excitement that it was true, they had a bite.

"Tell . . ."

"He's standing on the doorstep."

Doorstep! That was more than a bite. That was fish for supper. Christ, they had the whole house surrounded.

"He's just standing there, hesitating."

She heard the activity on the walkie-talkie in the background. Get him now, get him now. Katrine answered her prayers. "The orders have been given to move in."

Beate heard another voice in the background say something. It was familiar, but she couldn't place it.

"They're storming the house now," Katrine said.

"Details, please."

"Delta. All wearing black. Automatics. God, the way they're running . . ."

"Less colour, more content."

"Four men running up the path. Blinding him with light. The others are hidden, waiting to see if he has any backup. He's dropped what he's holding . . ."

"Has he got a weap—?"

A shrill, high-pitched ring. Beate groaned. Doorbell.

"He hasn't got time. They're on him already. They've wrestled him to the ground."

Yes!

"Searching him, so it seems. They're holding something up."

"Weapon?"

The doorbell again. Hard, insistent.

"Looks like a remote control."

"Ooh! A bomb?"

"Don't know. But they've got him now anyway. They're signalling the situation is under control. Wait . . ."

"I've got to open the door. I'll ring you back."

Beate jumped up off the sofa. Jogged to the door. Wondering how to explain to him that this wasn't acceptable, that if she said she wanted to be alone she meant it.

And as she opened the door she thought about how far she had come. From the quiet, shy, self-sacrificing girl, who had graduated from the same police college her father had attended, to the woman who not only knew what she wanted but did what she had to do to achieve it. It had been a long and at times hard road, but the reward was worth every single step.

She looked at the man opposite her. The reflected light from his face hit her retina, was converted into visual signals and fed her fusiform gyrus with the data.

Behind her she heard Gabriel Byrne's reassuring voice; she thought it said: "Don't panic now."

By which time her brain had recognised the face before her.

Harry could feel the orgasm coming. His own. The sweet, sweet pain, the muscles in his back and abdomen tensing. He closed the door on what he could see and opened his eyes. Looked down at Rakel, who was staring up at him with glassy eyes. The blood vessel on her forehead bulged. A jerk went through her body and face every time he thrust. She seemed to be trying to say something. And he became aware that this was not the suffering, offended look she generally wore before she came, this was something else, a terror in her eyes he could only once remember having seen before, also here in this room. He became aware she had both hands around his wrist, trying to drag his hand off her neck.

He waited. Not knowing why, but he wouldn't slacken his grip. Felt the resistance in her body, saw her eyes bulge. Then he let go.

Heard the hiss as she inhaled air.

"Harry . . ." Her voice was hoarse, unrecognisable. "What were you doing?"

He looked down at her. He had no answer.

"You . . ." She coughed. "You mustn't hold on so long!"

"Sorry," he said. "I got a bit carried away."

Then he felt it come. Not the orgasm, but something similar. A pain in his chest that rose into his throat and spread to behind his eyes.

He slumped down beside her. Buried his face in the pillow. Felt the tears come. Rolled to the side, away from her, took deep breaths, fought them. What the hell was going on with him?

"Harry?"

He didn't answer. Couldn't.

"Is something wrong, Harry?"

He shook his head. "Just tired," he said into the pillow.

He felt her hand on his neck, caressing him gently, then it lay over his chest and she snuggled up to his back.

And he thought what he had always known at some point he was going to think: how could he ask someone he loved so much to share her life with someone like him?

Katrine lay with her mouth open, listening to the furious communication on the walkie-talkie. Behind her Mikael Bellman was cursing. It wasn't a remote control the man on the step had in his hand.

"It's a payment terminal," a breathless voice rasped.

"And what's in his bag?"

"Pizza."

"Repeat?"

"Looks like the guy's a bloody delivery boy. Says he works for Pizzaexpressen. Got an order for this address three-quarters of an hour ago."

"OK, we'll check that out."

Mikael Bellman leaned forward and took the walkie-talkie.

"Bellman here. He's sent this guy out to clear the mines. Which means he's in the area and can see what's happening. Have we got any dogs?"

Pause. Crackling noise.

"U05 here. No dogs. We can have them here in fifteen."

Bellman cursed again under his breath, then pressed the talk button. "Get them here. And the helicopter with floodlights and thermal imaging. Confirm."

"Received. Request helicopter. But I don't think it has thermal imaging."

Bellman closed his eyes and whispered "idiot" before answering: "It does, it's fitted, so if he's in the forest we'll find him. Use the whole team to spread a net north and west of the forest. If he makes a run for it, it'll be that way. What's your mobile number, U05?"

Bellman let go of the talk button and signalled to Katrine, who was holding the phone ready. Keyed in the numbers as U05 said them. Passed the phone to Bellman.

"U05? Falkeid? Listen, we're losing this one, and we haven't got enough officers to do an effective search of the forest, so let's try a long shot. As he clearly suspected we were here, he may also have access to our frequencies. It's true we don't have thermal imaging, but if he now believes we do and we're spreading a net to the north and west, then . . ." Bellman listened. "Exactly. Position your men on the east side. But keep a couple back in case he still comes to the house to check it out."

Bellman broke the connection and handed the phone over.

"What do you think?" Katrine asked. The screen went off and it was as though the light from the white, pigmentless stripes on his face was pulsating in the darkness.

"I think," Bellman said, "we've been out-manoeuvred."

26

They left Oslo at seven o'clock.

The incoming rush-hour traffic was at a standstill, and mute. As it was in their car, where both were adhering to the long-established pact of no unnecessary talking before nine.

On the way through the tollbooths a light drizzle fell, which the windscreen wipers seemed to absorb rather than remove.

Harry switched on the radio, listened to yet another news broadcast, but it wasn't there, either. The item that should have been on every website and station this morning. The arrest in Berg, the news that a suspect had been detained in connection with the police murders. After the sport, which was about Norway's match against Albania, Pavarotti and some pop star sang a duet and Harry hurriedly switched off the radio.

Through the hills up to Karihaugen, Rakel rested her hand on Harry's, which was on the gearstick, as usual. Harry waited for her to say something.

Soon they would be apart for a whole working week, and Rakel still hadn't said a word about his proposal of the night before. Was she having doubts?

She didn't usually say things she didn't mean. At the turn-off to Lørenskog it struck him that perhaps she was thinking **he** had doubts. That if they acted as if it hadn't happened, burying it in an ocean of silence, then it hadn't happened. At worst it would be remembered as an absurd dream. Shit, perhaps he **had** dreamt it. In his opium-smoking days he would speak to people about things he was convinced had happened and would receive quizzical looks in return.

At the turn-off to Lillestrøm he broke the pact. "What about June? The twenty-first is a Saturday."

He glanced at her, but she was looking at the rolling landscape of fields. Silence. Oh shit, she was having regrets. She—

"June's fine," she said. "But I'm pretty sure the twenty-first is a Friday." He could hear the smile in her voice.

"Big do or . . . ?"

"Or just us and witnesses?"

"You reckon?"

"You can decide, but maximum ten people in total. We haven't got the crockery for any more. And with five each you can invite everyone in your contacts list anyway."

He laughed. This could be good.

"And if you're thinking of Oleg as best man, he's busy," she said.

"I see."

Harry parked in front of the departures terminal and kissed Rakel with the boot still open.

On his way back, he rang Øystein Eikeland. Harry's

taxi-driving drinking pal and sole childhood friend sounded plastered. On the other hand, Harry didn't know how he sounded when he wasn't.

"Best man? Shit, Harry, I'm touched. You asking **me.** Shit, got a smile on the clock now."

"Twenty-first of June. Anything on your calendar then?"

Øystein chuckled at the joke. The chuckling morphed into coughing. Which morphed into the gurgle of a bottle. "I'm touched, Harry. But the answer's no. What you need is someone who can stand up straight in the church and speak with moderately clear diction at the meal. And what I need is an attractive woman at the table, free booze and no responsibility. I promise to wear my finest suit."

"Liar, you've never worn a suit, Øystein."

"That's why they stay in such good shape. Not used much. Just like your pals, Harry. You could ring once in a while, you know."

"I suppose I could."

They rang off and Harry drove bumper to bumper to the city centre, running through the short list of remaining candidates for best man. To be precise, one. He dialled Beate Lønn's number. Got voicemail after five seconds and left a message.

The queue moved forward at snail's pace.

He dialled Bjørn Holm's number.

"Hiya, Harry."

"Is Beate at work?"

"Off today."

"Beate? She's never off. Got a cold?"

"Dunno. She texted Katrine last night. Ill. Did you hear about Berg?"

"Oh, I'd forgotten all about that," Harry lied. "Well?"

"He didn't strike."

"Shame. You keep at it. I'll try her at home."

Harry hung up and called her landline.

After letting the phone ring for two minutes without success, he glanced at his watch. Plenty of time before his lecture, and Oppsal was on the way. He turned off at Helsfyr.

Beate had inherited her house from her mother, and it reminded Harry of the house in Oppsal where he had grown up: a typical 1950s timber house, the kind of sober box for a burgeoning middle class who thought apple orchards were no longer an upper-class preserve.

Apart from the rumble of a dustcart working its way up the road from bin to bin, all was quiet. Everyone was at work, school, kindergarten. Harry parked the car, went through the gate, passed a child's bike locked to the fence, a dustbin bulging with black bags, a swing, leapt up the steps to a pair of Nike trainers he recognised. Rang the bell under the ceramic sign bearing Beate's name and her son's.

Waited.

Rang again.

On the first floor there was an open window to what he assumed had to be one of the bedrooms. He called her name. Perhaps she couldn't hear because of the lorry's steel piston loudly crushing and compacting rubbish as it came ever closer.

He tried the door. Open. He entered. Called up to the first floor. No answer. And could no longer ignore the unease he knew had been there the whole time.

From when the news didn't come.

From when she didn't answer her mobile phone.

He strode upstairs, went from room to room.

Empty. Undisturbed.

He ran back down the stairs and headed for the sitting room. Stood in the doorway and let his gaze wander. He knew exactly why he didn't go right in, but didn't want to think the thought aloud.

Didn't want to tell himself he was looking at a possible crime scene.

He had been here before, but it struck him that the room seemed barer now. Perhaps it was the morning light, perhaps it was just that Beate wasn't here. His gaze stopped at the table. A mobile phone.

He heard himself breathe out and realised how much relief he felt. She had nipped down to the shop, left the phone, not even bothering to lock up. To the chemist for some aspirin or something. Yes, that's what must have happened. Harry thought of the Nike trainers on the doorstep. So? A woman would have more than one pair of shoes. If he waited for a couple of minutes she would be back.

Harry shifted his weight from one foot to the other. The sofa looked tempting, but still he didn't go in.

His gaze had fallen on the floor. There was a darker patch around the coffee table by the TV.

She had obviously got rid of the rug.

Recently.

Harry felt his skin itch inside his shirt, as if he had just been rolling, naked and sweaty, in the grass. He crouched down. Smelt a faint aroma of ammonia from the parquet floor. Unless he was mistaken, wooden floors didn't like ammonia. Harry stood up, straightened his back. Strode through the hall into the kitchen.

Empty, tidy.

Opened the tall cupboard beside the fridge. It was as though houses built in the 1950s had these unwritten rules about where to keep everything: food, tools, important documents and, in this case, cleaning equipment. At the bottom of the cupboard there was a bucket with a cloth neatly folded over the edge; on the first shelf were three dusting cloths, one sealed and one opened roll of white bin bags. A bottle of Krystal green soap. And a tin of Bona polish. He bent down and read the label.

For parquet floors. Did not contain ammonia.

Harry got up slowly. Stood quite still listening. Scenting the air.

He was rusty, but he tried to absorb it and memorise everything he had seen. The first impression. He had emphasised it in his lectures again and again, how the first impressions at a crime scene were often the most important and correct, the collection of data while your senses were still on high alert, before they were blunted and counteracted by the forensics team's dry facts.

Harry closed his eyes, tried to hear what the house was telling him, which details he had overlooked, the one that would tell him what he wanted to know.

But if the house was talking it was drowned by the noise of the dustcart outside the open front door. He heard the voices of the men on the lorry, the gate opening, the happy laughter. Carefree. As though nothing had happened. Perhaps nothing had happened. Perhaps Beate would soon be back, sniffling as she tightened her scarf around her neck, would brighten up, surprised but happy to see him. And even more surprised and happy when he asked her if she wanted to be a witness at his wedding to Rakel. Then she would laugh and blush to the roots as she did if anyone looked her way. The woman who used to immure herself in the House of Pain, the video room at Police HQ, where she would sit for twelve hours at a stretch and with infallible accuracy identify masked robbers caught on bank CCTV. Who became the head of Krimteknisk. A well-liked boss. Harry swallowed.

It sounded like notes for a funeral speech.

Pack it in, she's on her way! He took a deep breath. Heard the gate slam, the dustcart start churning.

Then it came to him. The detail. That didn't tally.

He stared into the cupboard. A half-used roll of white bin bags.

The bags in the dustbin had been black.

Harry was out of the blocks.

Sprinted through the hall, out of the door, down towards the gate. Ran as fast as he could, yet his heart was running ahead of him.

"Stop!"

One dustman looked up. He was standing with one leg on the rear platform of the lorry, which had already started moving towards the next house. The crunch of the steel jaws as they chewed seemed to come from inside Harry's head.

"Stop the butchery!"

He jumped over the gate and landed on the tarmac with both feet. The dustman reacted at once, hit the red stop button and banged the side of the lorry, which pulled up with an angry snort.

The crusher was quiet.

The dustman stared.

Harry walked slowly over to him, looking at the same place, the open iron jaws. There was a pungent stench, but Harry didn't notice it. He saw only the half-crushed, split rubbish bags, leaking and seeping out liquid, and staining the metal red.

"Folk are not right in the head," the dustman whispered.

"What's up?" It was the driver; he had stuck his head out of the cab.

"Looks like someone's chucked their dog in again," his colleague shouted. And looked at Harry. "Is it yours?"

Harry didn't answer, just stepped up onto the platform and into the half-open hydraulic jaws.

"Hey! You can't do that! It's danger—"

Harry shook off the man's hand. Slipped on the red mess, hitting his elbow and cheek on the slippery steel floor, noticed the familiar taste and smell of day-old blood. Struggled to his knees and tore open a bag.

The contents poured out and slipped down the sloping flatbed.

"Jesus Christ!" the dustman behind him gasped.

Harry tore open a second. And a third.

Heard the dustman jump off and puke, the splash on the tarmac.

In the fourth bag Harry found what he was looking for. The other parts of her body could have belonged to anyone. But not this. Not this blonde hair, not this pale face that would never blush again. Not these vacant, staring eyes that had recognised everyone she had ever seen. The face had been hacked to pieces, but Harry was in no doubt. He put a finger on the earring forged from a uniform button.

It was so painful, so, so painful that he couldn't breathe, so painful that he was doubled up, like a dying bee with its sting removed.

And he heard a sound cross his lips, as though from a stranger, a long, drawn-out howl that echoed around the quiet neighbourhood.

Part Four

27

Beate Lønn was buried in Gamlebyen Cemetery, beside her father. He hadn't been buried there because it was his parish but because the cemetery was the closest one to Police HQ.

Mikael Bellman adjusted his tie. Held Ulla's hand. It had been the PR consultant's suggestion that she went along. The situation for him as the most senior officer had become so precarious after the latest killing that he needed help. The consultant had explained that it was important for him as Chief of Police to show more personal commitment, empathy, that so far he had appeared slightly too professional. Ulla had stepped up. Of course she had. Stunningly beautiful in the mourning outfit she had chosen with such meticulous care. She was a good wife to him. He would not forget it. Not for a long time.

The priest went on and on about what he called the big questions, about what happens when we die. But of course they weren't the big questions; those were what had happened before Beate died and who had killed her. Her and three other officers in the course of the last six months.

They were the big questions for the press, who had spent recent days paying homage to the brilliant head of Krimteknisk and criticising the new and shockingly inexperienced Chief of Police.

They were the big questions for Oslo Council, who had summoned him to a meeting where he would have to account for his handling of the murders. They had indicated that they would not pull their punches.

And they were the big questions for the investigation groups, both the large one and the small one Hagen had set up without telling him, but which Bellman had now accepted, as at least it had found a concrete lead to work on, Valentin Gjertsen. Its weakness was that the theory that this ghost might be behind the murders was based on a single witness's claim that she had seen him alive. And she was now in the coffin by the altar.

In the reports from the forensics team, the police investigation and the pathologist, there hadn't been enough detail to give a full picture of what had happened, but everything they did know matched the old reports of the murder in Bergslia.

So if you assumed the rest was identical, Beate Lønn had died in the worst way imaginable.

There wasn't a trace of anaesthetic in any of the body parts they had examined. The pathologist's report contained the phrases "massive internal bleeding in muscles and subcutaneous tissue," "an inflammatory reaction to infection in the tissue," which, translated, meant that Beate Lønn had been alive not only at the time the relevant parts of her body had been cut off, but unfortunately also some time afterwards.

The severed surfaces suggested a bayonet saw rather than a jigsaw had been used for the carving up of the body. The forensics officers guessed a so-called bimetal blade had been used, that is, a fourteen-centimetre, fine-toothed blade that could cut through bone. Bjørn Holm said this was the one hunters where he came from called the elk blade.

Beate Lønn might have been cut up on the coffee table as it was made of glass and could be cleaned effectively afterwards. The killer had probably taken ammonia with him and black bin bags as none of these had been found at the crime scene.

In the dustcart they had also found the remains of a rug drenched in blood.

What they didn't find were fingerprints, footprints, fabric, hairs or other DNA material that didn't belong to the house.

Or any signs of a break-in.

Katrine Bratt had explained that Beate Lønn had finished the call because the doorbell had rung.

It seemed very unlikely that Beate Lønn would have voluntarily let in a stranger, and definitely not in the middle of an operation. So the theory they were working on was that the killer had forced his way in, threatening her with a weapon.

And then, of course, there was the second theory. That it wasn't a stranger. Because Beate Lønn had a chain on the solid door. And there were plenty of scratch marks, suggesting that it was used regularly.

Bellman looked down the rows. Gunnar Hagen. Bjørn Holm and Katrine Bratt. An elderly lady with a small boy he assumed was Lønn's son, at any rate the similarity was striking.

Another ghost, Harry Hole. Rakel Fauke. Brunette, with these dark, glinting eyes, almost as beautiful as Ulla, incomprehensible that a guy like Hole could have got his paws on her.

And a bit further back, Isabelle Skøyen. Oslo City Council had to be represented, of course, the press would make a point of it if not. Before they entered the church she had taken him aside, ignoring the fact that Ulla was there, and asked how long he was intending to avoid her phone calls. And he had repeated it was over. And she had regarded him in the way you regard an insect before you tread on it and said she was a leaver, not a leavee. Which he would soon find out. He had felt her eyes on his back as he had walked over to Ulla and offered her his arm.

Otherwise the rows were filled with what he assumed was a mixture of relatives, friends and colleagues, most of them in uniform. He had overheard them consoling one another as best they could: there were no signs of torture and loss of blood had hopefully meant she would have been unconscious in no time.

For a fraction of a second his eyes met someone else's. And moved on as if he hadn't seen him. Truls Berntsen. What the hell was he doing here? He hadn't exactly been on Beate Lønn's Christmas card list. Ulla pressed his hand lightly, looked at him enquiringly, and he flashed her a quick smile. Fair enough; in death we are all colleagues, he supposed.

Katrine had been wrong. She wasn't all cried out.

A few times since Beate had been found she had thought there were no tears left. But there were. And she had squeezed them out of a body that was already sore from long bouts of weeping.

She had cried until her body refused and she had thrown up. Cried until she fell asleep from pure exhaustion. And cried from the moment she awoke. And she was crying again now.

And in the hours she slept she was plagued by nightmares, haunted by her own devilish pact. The one where she was willing to sacrifice a colleague in return for the arrest of Valentin. The one she had ratified with her incantation: one more time, you bastard. Strike one more time.

Katrine sobbed aloud.

The loud sob jolted Truls Berntsen upright. He had been falling asleep. The cheap suit was so damned slippery on the worn church pew there was a good chance he would slide right off.

He fixed his eyes on the altarpiece. Jesus with rays of sun coming out of his head. A headlight. Forgiveness of sins. It was a stroke of genius what they had done. Religion hadn't been selling so well; it was so hard to obey all the commandments once you had the money to succumb to more temptations. So they had come up with this idea that was good enough to believe. A sales idea that did as much for turnover as credit, it almost felt like redemption was free. But, just like with credit, things got out of control, people didn't care, they sinned for their dear lives, because all you had to do was believe. So around the Middle Ages they had to tighten up, implement debt collection. So they thought up hell and the stuff about the soul burning. And hey presto—you frightened the sinners back into the church and this time they settled their accounts. The church became very wealthy, and good for them, they had done such a fantastic job. That was Truls's genuine opinion on the matter. Even though he believed he would die and that would be that, no forgiveness of sins, no hell. But if he was mistaken, he was in deep trouble, that much was obvious. There had to be limits to what you could forgive, and Jesus would hardly have the imagination to conjure up a couple of the things Truls had done.

● ● ●

Harry was staring straight ahead. Was somewhere else. In the House of Pain with Beate pointing and explaining. He didn't come to until he heard Rakel's whisper.

"You have to help Gunnar and the others, Harry."

He recoiled. Looked at her in surprise.

She nodded to the altar where the others had already taken up positions by the coffin. Gunnar Hagen, Bjørn Holm, Katrine Bratt, Ståle Aune and Jack Halvorsen's brother. Hagen had said Harry had to carry the coffin alongside the brother-in-law, who was the second tallest.

Harry got up and walked quickly down the aisle.

You have to help Gunnar and the others.

It was like an echo of what she had said the night before.

Harry exchanged imperceptible nods with the others. Took up the unoccupied position.

"On the count of three," Hagen said softly.

The organ tones intensified, swelled.

Then they carried Beate Lønn outside into the light.

Justisen was packed with people from the funeral.

Over the loudspeakers blared a song Harry had heard there before. "I Fought the Law" by the Bobby Fuller Four. With the optimistic continuation . . . "and the law won."

He had accompanied Rakel to the airport express,

and in the meantime several of his former colleagues had managed to get very drunk. As a sober outsider Harry was able to observe the almost frantic drinking, as if they were sitting on a sinking ship. At many of the tables they were howling along with Bobby Fuller that the law won.

Harry signalled to the table where Katrine Bratt and the other coffin-bearers sat that he would be back soon and went to the toilet. He had started peeing when a man appeared at his side. He heard him unzip.

"This is a place for police officers," a voice snuffled. "So what the hell are you doing here?"

"Pissing," Harry said, without looking up. "And you? Burning?"

"Don't you try it with me, Hole."

"If I did, you wouldn't be walking around a free man, Berntsen."

"Mind your own business," groaned Truls Berntsen, leaning against the wall above the urinal with his unoccupied hand. "I can stick a murder on you, and you know it. The Russian in Come As You Are. Everyone in the police knows it was you, but I'm the only one who can prove it. And that's why you don't dare to mix with me."

"What I know, Berntsen, is that the Russian was a dope dealer who tried to dispatch me into the beyond. But if you think your chances are better than his, go ahead. You've beaten up policemen before."

"Eh?"

"You and Bellman. A gay officer, wasn't it?"

Harry could hear the head of steam Berntsen had worked up fizzle and fade.

"Are you on the booze again, Hole?"

"Mm," Harry said, buttoning up. "This must be the season for police haters." He went to the sink. Saw in the mirror that Berntsen still hadn't got the tap flowing again. Harry washed his hands and dried them. Went to the door. Heard Berntsen hiss:

"Don't you try anything, I'm telling you. If you take me down, I'll take you with me."

Harry went back into the bar. Bobby Fuller had almost finished. And it made Harry think of something. How full of coincidences our lives were. Bobby Fuller was found dead in his car in 1966, soaked in petrol, and some thought he had been killed by the police. He had been twenty-three years old. The same as René Kalsnes.

A new song started. Supergrass and "Caught by the Fuzz." Harry smiled. Gaz Coombes singing about being caught by the fuzz, who want him to spill the beans, and twenty years later the police are playing the song as a tribute to themselves. Sorry, Gaz.

Harry looked around the room. Thought about the long conversation he and Rakel had had yesterday. About all the things you could evade, avoid, elude in life. And what you couldn't escape. Because this **was** life, the meaning of existence. All the rest—love, peace, happiness—was what followed, for which this was a prerequisite. By and large, she had done the talking, had explained that he had to. The shadows of Beate's death were already so long that they covered the June day, however hysterically the sun might shine. He had to. For them both. For them all.

Harry ploughed his way to the table of coffin-bearers.

Hagen got up and pulled out the chair that they had reserved for him. "Well?" he said.

"Count me in," Harry said.

Truls stood by the urinal, still semi-paralysed by what Harry had said. This must be the season for police haters. Did he know anything? Rubbish! Harry knew nothing. How could he? If he did, he wouldn't have blurted it out like that, like a provocation. But he knew about the homo in Kripos, the one they had beaten up. And how could he know about that?

The guy had tried it on with Mikael, had tried to kiss him in the toilets. Mikael thought someone might have seen. They had pulled a hood over his head in the boiler room. Truls had hit him. Mikael had just watched. As usual. Had only intervened when it was on the point of going too far and told him to stop. No. It had already gone too far. The guy was still lying on the ground when they left.

Mikael had been afraid. The guy was badly hurt, he might get it into his head to report them. So that had been Truls's first job as a burner. They had used the blue light to race down to Justisen where they had pushed their way through the queue at the bar and demanded to pay for the two Munkholms they'd had half an hour before. The bartender had nodded, said it was good there were honest folk about and Truls had given him such a hefty tip he was sure the guy would remember. Took the receipt displaying the time and date of purchase, drove with Mikael up to Krimteknisk where there was a newcomer Truls knew really wanted a job as a detective. Explained to him it was possible that someone would try to pin an assault on them and he would have to check they were clean. The newcomer had performed a quick, superficial examination of their clothes and hadn't found any DNA or blood, he said. Then Truls had driven Mikael home and afterwards returned to the boiler room at Kripos. The fudge-packer wasn't there any more, but the trail of blood indicated he had managed to crawl out under his own steam. So perhaps there wasn't a problem. But Truls had removed any potential evidence and afterwards driven down to the Havnelager building and dropped the baton in the sea.

The next day a colleague rang Mikael and said the fudge-packer had contacted him from hospital and talked about reporting them for GBH. So Truls had gone up to the hospital, waited until the doctor had done his rounds and then told the guy there was no evidence and no career if he ever so much as breathed a word or turned up for work again.

They never saw or heard anything again from the guy at Kripos. Thanks to him, Truls Berntsen. So fuck Mikael Bellman. Truls had saved the bastard's skin. At least until now. For now Harry knew about the little matter. And he was a loose cannon. He could be dangerous, Hole could. Too dangerous.

Truls Berntsen observed himself in the mirror. The terrorist. Dead right. He was.

And he had only just started.

He went out to join the others. In time to catch the last part of Mikael Bellman's speech.

". . . that Beate Lønn was made of the sterner stuff we hope is typical of our force. Now it is up to us to prove it. In the only way we can honour her memory as she would have wanted it honoured. By catching him. **Skål!**"

Truls stared at his childhood pal as they all raised their glasses to the ceiling, like warriors raising their spears at the chieftain's command. Saw their faces glowing, serious, determined. Saw Bellman nod as though they were of one mind, saw that he was moved, moved by the moment, by his own words, by what motivated them, the power they had over others in the room.

Truls went back to the hall by the toilets, stood beside the slot machine, pressed a coin into the slot of the phone and lifted the receiver. Dialled the switchboard number.

"Police."

"I've got an anonymous tip-off. It's about the bullet in the René Kalsnes case. I know which gun it was fried . . . fl . . ." Truls had tried to speak clearly, knowing it would be recorded and played back afterwards. But his tongue wouldn't obey his brain.

"Then you should talk to the detectives in Crime Squad or Kripos," the operator said. "But they're all at a funeral today."

"I know!" Truls answered, hearing his voice was unnecessarily loud. "I just wanted to give you a tip-off."

"You know?"

"Yes. Listen—"

"I can see you're ringing from Kafé Justisen. You should find them there."

Truls glared at the phone. Realised that he was drunk. That he had made a huge blunder. That if this was followed up, and they knew the call came from Justisen, they could just summon the officers who had been there, play the tape and ask if anyone recognised the voice. And that would be too big a risk to take.

"Just kidding," Truls said. "Sorry, we've had a bit too much beer here."

He rang off and left. Straight through the room without looking to either side. But when he opened the front door and felt the cold blast of rain he stopped. Turned. Saw Mikael with his hand on a colleague's shoulder. Saw a group standing round Harry Hole, the piss artist. One of them, a woman, was even hugging him. Truls turned back. Watched the rain.

Suspended. Excluded.

He felt a hand on his shoulder. Looked round. The face blurred, as though he was peering through water. Was he really that drunk?

"That's fine," said the face with the gentle voice as

the hand squeezed his shoulder. "Slip away. We all feel like that today."

Truls reacted instinctively, flicked the hand off and headed into the night. Stomped down the street feeling the rain soak through the shoulders of his jacket. To hell with them. To hell with all of them.

28

Someone had stuck a piece of paper on the grey metal door. BOILER ROOM.

Inside, Gunnar Hagen saw from his watch that it had just gone 7 a.m. and confirmed that all four of them were present. The fifth person wasn't going to come, and her chair was unoccupied. The new member had taken a chair from one of the conference rooms higher up in Police HQ.

Gunnar Hagen examined each of them in turn.

Bjørn Holm looked as though the previous day had hit him hard, ditto Katrine Bratt. Ståle Aune was as usual impeccably dressed in tweed and bow tie. Gunnar Hagen studied the new member extra carefully. The Crime Squad boss had left Justisen before Harry Hole, and at that point Harry had still been on the coffee and soft drinks wagon. But sitting there, slumped into his chair, pale, unshaven, eyes closed, Hagen wasn't sure if Harry had gone the distance. What this group needed was Harry Hole the detective. What no one needed was the drinker.

Hagen looked up at the whiteboard where, together, they had given Harry a résumé of the case so far. Names of the victims along one timeline, crime scenes, the name Valentin Gjertsen, arrows leading to earlier murders with dates.

"So," Hagen said, "Maridalen, Tryvann, Drammen and the last one at the victim's home. Four officers from the investigations of earlier unsolved murders, the same date and—in three of the cases—the same crime scene. Three of the original murders were typical sexually motivated killings, and though they are distant from one another in time, they were connected even then. The exception is Drammen where the victim was a man, René Kalsnes, and there was no indication of any sexual abuse. Katrine?"

"If we assume that Valentin Gjertsen was behind all four of the original murders and the four police murders, Kalsnes is an interesting exception. He was homosexual, and the people Bjørn and I spoke to at the club in Drammen describe Kalsnes as a promiscuous schemer. Not only did he have deeply infatuated older partners, whom he exploited like sugar daddies, but he also sold his body for sex at the club whenever the opportunity offered itself. He was up for most things if there was any money in it."

"So someone with the kind of behaviour and line of work that put you most at risk of being murdered," Bjørn Holm said.

"Exactly," Hagen said. "But that makes it likely that the perpetrator was also a homosexual. Or bisexual. Ståle?"

Ståle Aune coughed. "Sexual predators like Valentin Gjertsen often have a complicated relationship with their sexuality. The trigger for such individuals tends to be a need for control, sadism and a desire to push limits rather than the gender and the age of the victim. But the murder of René Kalsnes could also be about jealousy. The fact that there was no sign of any sexual abuse may suggest that. As well as the fury. He's the only one of the victims from the original four murders who was hit with a blunt instrument in the same way as the police officers."

There was a silence as everyone looked at Harry Hole, who had sunk into a semi-recumbent posture in the chair, still with his eyes closed and his hands folded over his stomach. Katrine Bratt thought for a moment he had fallen asleep until he coughed.

"Has anyone found a link between Valentin and Kalsnes?"

"Not so far," Katrine said. "No phone contact, no credit card records at the club or in Drammen or any electronic trails showing Valentin had been near René Kalsnes. And no one who knew Kalsnes had heard of Valentin or seen anyone resembling him. That doesn't mean they haven't . . ."

"No, of course," Harry said, pinching his eyes shut. "Just wondering."

Silence fell in the Boiler Room as they all stared at Harry.

He opened one eye. "What?"

No one answered.

"I'm not going to rise and walk on water, or turn water into wine," he said.

"No, no, no," Katrine said. "It's enough if you can give these four blind souls sight."

"Can't do that either."

"I thought a leader was supposed to make his followers believe everything was possible," Bjørn Holm said.

"Leader?" Harry smiled, pulling himself up in the chair. "Have you told them about my status, Hagen?"

Gunnar Hagen cleared his throat. "Harry no longer has the status or the powers of a police officer, so he's been brought in solely as a consultant, just like Ståle. That means, for example, that he can't apply for warrants, carry weapons or undertake arrests. And it also means he can't lead a police operation. It is in fact important that we abide by these rules. Imagine if we catch Valentin, have bags full of evidence, but the defence counsel discovers we haven't proceeded by the book."

"These consultants . . ." Ståle Aune said, tamping his pipe with a grimace. "I've heard they have hourly rates that make psychologists look like dimwits. So let's make the most of our time here. Say something smart, Harry."

Harry shrugged.

"Right," Ståle Aune said, with a wry smile, putting the unlit pipe in his mouth. "Because we've already said the smartest things we can come up with. And we've been in a rut for a while."

Harry looked down at his hands. And at length took a deep breath.

"I don't know how smart this is, it's pretty half-baked, but here's what I've been thinking . . ." He raised his head and met four pairs of round eyes.

"I'm aware Valentin is a suspect. The problem is we can't find him. So I suggest we find a new suspect."

Katrine Bratt could hardly believe her ears. "What? We have to suspect someone we **don't** think did it?"

"We don't think," Harry said. "We suspect with various degrees of probability. And weigh the probability against how resource-intensive it would be to have the suspicion confirmed or rejected. We consider it less likely that there is life on the moon than on Gliese 581d, which is a perfect distance from its sun, where the water doesn't boil or freeze. Yet we check the moon first."

"Harry Hole's fourth commandment," Bjørn Holm said. "Start searching where there is light. Or was it the fifth?"

Hagen coughed. "Our mandate is to find Valentin. Everything else is the responsibility of the larger investigative unit. Bellman won't allow anything else."

"With all due respect," Harry said. "To hell with Bellman. I'm no smarter than any of you, but I'm new and that gives us a chance to look at this with fresh eyes."

Katrine snorted. "Bollocks. You didn't mean that 'no smarter' stuff."

"No, I didn't, but let's pretend I did," Harry said, without batting an eyelid. "Let's start from the beginning again. Motive. Who would want to kill police officers who have failed to solve cases? Because that's the common denominator here, isn't it? Come on, you tell me."

Harry folded his arms, slipped down in his chair and closed his eyes. Waiting.

Bjørn Holm was the first to break the silence. "Relatives of the victims."

Katrine weighed in. "Rape victims who aren't believed by the police or whose cases aren't properly investigated. The murderer punishes the police for not clearing up other sexually motivated murders."

"René Kalsnes wasn't raped," Hagen said. "And if I thought my case hadn't been investigated properly I would have confined myself to killing the officers concerned, not all the others."

"Keep the suggestions coming and we can shoot them down afterwards," Harry said, sitting up. "Ståle?"

"Those who have been wrongfully convicted," Aune said. "They've served their time, they're stigmatised, they've lost their job, respect for themselves and the respect of others too. The lions that have been expelled by the pride are the most dangerous. They don't feel any responsibility, only hatred and bitterness. And they're willing to take risks to avenge themselves as their lives have been devalued anyway. As herd animals they feel they haven't got a lot to lose. Inflicting suffering on those who have inflicted suffering on them is what makes them get out of bed in the morning."

"Avenging terrorists then," Bjørn Holm said.

"Good," Harry said. "Make sure we check all rape cases where there is no confession from the accused and the case wasn't cut and dried. And where time has been served and the individual concerned is out of prison."

"Or perhaps it isn't the accused," Katrine said. "The accused could be still inside or could have taken his life in desperation. And the girlfriend or brother or father has vowed to wreak revenge."

"Love," Harry said. "Good."

"Heck, you can't mean that," Bjørn came in.

"Why not?" Harry said.

"Love?" His voice was metallic, his face distorted into a strange grimace. "You can't think that this bloodbath has anything to do with **love**?"

"In fact I do," Harry said, slipping back down in his chair and closing his eyes.

Bjørn got up, red-faced. "A psychopathic serial killer who, out of love, does . . ." His voice cracked and he nodded to the empty chair. ". . . this."

"Look at yourself," Harry said, opening one eye.

"Eh?"

"Look at yourself and feel. You're furious, you hate, you want to see the miscreant dangle by the neck, die, suffer, don't you? Because you, like us, loved the woman who sat there. So the mother of your hatred is love, Bjørn. And it's love, not hatred, that makes you willing to do whatever it takes, go to any lengths to get your hands on the guilty party. Sit down."

Bjørn sat down. And Harry got up.

"That's what strikes me about these murders too. The lengths he goes to to reconstruct the original crimes. The risks the murderer is willing to take. I'm not sure, bearing in mind all the work involved, that behind everything is sheer bloodlust or hatred. The bloodthirsty murderer kills prostitutes, children or other easy targets. Someone who hates without love is never so extreme in his efforts. I think we should look for someone who loves more than he hates. And so the question is, from what we know about Valentin Gjertsen, has he really got the capacity to love so much?"

"Maybe," Gunnar Hagen said. "We don't know everything about Valentin Gjertsen."

"Mm. When's the date for the next unsolved murder?"

"There's a bit of a gap now," Katrine said. "May. There was a case nineteen years ago."

"That's more than a month away," Harry said.

"Yes, and there was no sexual element. It was more like a family feud. So I took the liberty of examining a missing persons case that looks like murder. A girl disappeared in Oslo. She was reported missing after no one had seen her for more than two weeks. The reason no one reacted earlier was that she had texted several friends that she was off on a cheap flight to the sun and needed some time and space. A few friends answered her text but didn't get a reply, so they concluded that getting away from it all included her phone. When she was reported missing the police checked all the airlines, but she hadn't been on any of them. In short, she vanished without a trace."

"The phone?" Bjørn Holm asked.

"Last signal to the base station was in Oslo city centre, then it stopped. The battery may have died."

"Mm," Harry said. "The text. Leaving a message that she's ill . . ."

Bjørn and Katrine nodded slowly.

Ståle Aune sighed. "Possible to have this spelt out?"

"He means the same thing happened to Beate," Katrine said. "I got a text saying she was ill."

"Of course," Hagen said.

Harry nodded slowly. "He might for example check the recent calls and then send a short message to those contacts to delay the chase."

"Which means it's harder to find clues at the crime scene," Bjørn added. "He's in the loop."

"What date was the message sent?"

"The twenty-fifth of March," Katrine said.

"That's today," Bjørn said.

"Mm." Harry rubbed his chin. "We have a possible sexually motivated murder and a date, but no location. Which detectives were involved?"

"No investigation was set up as it remained a missing persons case and was never upgraded to murder." Katrine looked at her notes. "But in the end it was sent to Crime Squad and put on the list of one of the inspectors. You, in fact."

"Me?" Harry frowned. "I usually remember my cases."

"This was straight after the Snowman. You'd buggered off to Hong Kong and never reappeared. You ended up on the missing persons list yourself."

Harry shrugged. "Fine. Bjørn, you check with the

Missing Persons Unit afterwards to see what they have on this case. And alert them to the danger of someone ringing their doorbell or receiving mysterious call-outs during the day, OK? I think we should follow this one up, despite the fact that we don't have a body or a crime scene." Harry clapped his hands. "So, who makes the coffee round here?"

"Mm," Katrine said in a deeper, hoarse voice, slumped in her chair, legs stretched out, eyes closed and rubbing her chin. "I reckon that has to be the new consultant."

Harry pursed his lips, nodded, jumped up, and for the first time since they found Beate there was the sound of laughter in the Boiler Room.

The gravity of the occasion hung heavy in the chamber at City Hall.

Mikael Bellman sat at the far end of the table, the chairman at the top. Mikael knew the names of most of the councillors; it was one of the first things he did as the Chief of Police, learn names. And faces. "You can't play chess without knowing the pieces," the outgoing Police Chief had told him. "You have to know what they can and can't do."

It had been a well-meant piece of advice from an experienced Chief. But why was this retired officer sitting here now, in this room? Had he been brought in as a kind of consultant? Whatever his experience with chess, he doubted he'd played with pieces like the tall blonde sitting two places from the chairman.

The person who was speaking at this moment. The queen. The Councillor for Social Affairs. Isabelle Skøyen. The leavee. Her voice had that cold administrative timbre of someone who knows that minutes are being taken.

"With increasing unease we have seen how Oslo Police appear to be unable to stop these murders on their own. For some time the media have naturally been applying considerable pressure for us to do something drastic, but it is of greater significance that the city's inhabitants have also lost their patience. We simply cannot have this growing lack of trust in our institutions, in this case the police and the City Council. And since this is my area of responsibility I have initiated this informal hearing so that the council can react to the Chief of Police's solution, which we have to assume exists, and thereafter evaluate the alternatives."

Mikael Bellman was sweating. He hated sweating in his uniform. In vain he had tried to catch the eye of his predecessor. What the hell was he doing here?

"And I think we should be as open and innovative as possible with regard to alternatives," Isabelle Skøyen's voice intoned. "We, of course, understand that this may be an excessively demanding issue for a young, newly appointed Police Chief. It is indeed unfortunate that a situation requiring experience and knowledge of procedure should come so early in his period of office. It would have been better if this had landed on the desk of the previous Police Chief, given his long years of experience and his many achievements. I'm sure that's what everyone in this room would have wished for, including the two Police Chiefs."

Mikael Bellman wondered if he had heard what he thought he had heard. Did she mean . . . was she about to . . . ?

"Isn't that right, Bellman?"

Mikael Bellman cleared his throat.

"Excuse me for interrupting, Bellman," Isabelle Skøyen said, placing a pair of Prada reading glasses on the tip of her nose and peering down at the sheet of paper in front of her. "I'm reading from the minutes of the previous meeting we had on this matter and in which you said, quote: 'I can assure the council that we have this case under control and we have every confidence that there will be a speedy resolution.'" She removed her glasses. "To save ourselves and you the time, which apparently we are short of, perhaps you could skip the repetition and tell us what you're intending to do now that differs from and is more fruitful than what you were doing before?"

Bellman rolled his shoulders in the hope his shirt would come loose from his back. Bloody sweat. Bloody bitch.

It was eight o'clock in the evening, and Harry felt tired as he unlocked the door to PHS. He was obviously out of practice at concentrating for longer periods. And they hadn't got much further. They had skimmed through reports, thinking thoughts they had thought a dozen times before, gone in circles, banged their heads against the wall hoping that the wall would give sooner or later.

The ex-inspector nodded to the cleaner and ran up the stairs.

Tired, and yet astonishingly alert. Elated. Ready for more.

He heard his name being called as he passed Arnold's office, turned and poked his head round. His colleague interlaced his fingers behind his dishevelled hair. "Just wanted to hear how it feels to be a real policeman again."

"Good," Harry said. "I just have to correct the last criminal investigation tests."

"Don't worry about it. I've got them here," Arnold said, tapping his finger on the pile of papers in front of him. "Just make sure you catch the guy."

"OK, Arnold. Thanks."

"By the way, we've had a break-in."

"Break-in?"

"In the gym. The equipment cupboard was broken into, but all that was taken were two batons."

"Oh shit. Front door?"

"No signs of forced entry there. So that suggests it must have been an inside job. Or someone who works here let them in or lent them their pass."

"Is there no way of finding out?"

Arnold shrugged. "We haven't got much here that's worth stealing, so we don't spend any of the budget on complex check-in procedures, CCTV or a twenty-four-hour security guard."

"We may not have weapons, dope or a safe, but surely we have more cash-convertible things than batons?"

Arnold smirked. "You'd better check to see if your computer is still there."

Harry walked on to his office, saw that it appeared to be intact, sat down and wondered what to do. The evening had been set aside for marking tests, and at home only shadows were waiting. In answer to his question, his mobile began to vibrate.

"Katrine?"

"Hi. I've got something." She sounded excited. "Do you remember me telling you that Beate and I had spoken to Irja, the woman who rented out the basement flat to Valentin?"

"The one who gave him a false alibi?"

"Yes. She said she'd found some photos in the flat. Photos of rape and abuse. In one of the photos she recognised his shoes and the wallpaper from the bedroom."

"Mm. You mean . . ."

". . . that it's not very likely, but it **may** be the scene of a crime. I contacted the new owners and it turns out they're living with family nearby while the house is being done up. But they didn't mind if we borrowed the key and had a scout round."

"I thought we agreed we weren't looking for Valentin now."

"I thought we agreed to search where there was light."

"Touché, bright Bratt. Vinderen is practically round the corner. Have you got an address?"

Harry was given it.

"That's walking distance. I'll head there right away. Are you coming?"

"Yes, but I've been so tense I forgot to eat."

"OK. Come when you're ready."

It was a quarter to nine when Harry walked up the flagstone path to the empty house. Close to the wall were used paint pots, rolls of plastic and planks sticking out from under tarpaulins. He walked down the little stone steps, as instructed by the owners, and across the flagstones at the back. He unlocked the basement flat and immediately the smell of glue and paint assailed him. But also another smell, one the owners had spoken about and which was one of the reasons they had decided to do some renovation work. They had said they couldn't work out where it was coming from; the smell was all over the house. They'd had a pest controller in, but he had said that such a strong smell had to come from more than one dead rodent and they would probably have to take up the floor and open up the walls to find out.

Harry switched on the light. Spread across the hall floor was a transparent plastic sheet, covered with grey heavy-duty boot marks and wooden boxes filled with tools, hammers, crowbars and paint-stained drills. Some boards had been removed from the wall so that you could see through to the insulation. In addition to the hall the flat consisted of a small kitchen, bathroom and sitting room with a curtain concealing the bedroom. The renovation project obviously hadn't got as far as the bedroom yet; it was being used to store the furniture from the other rooms. To protect the furniture from the dust, the bead curtain had been pulled aside and replaced with a thick, matt plastic curtain which reminded Harry of slaughterhouses, cold-storage rooms and cordoned-off crime scenes.

He inhaled the smell of solvents and decay. And concluded, like the pest controller, that this was not a single tiny rodent.

The bed had been pushed into the corner to make more space for the furniture, and the room was so full it was hard to form an impression of exactly how the rape had been committed and the girl photographed. Katrine had said she would visit Irja in case she could give them any more information, but if this Valentin was their cop killer, Harry already knew one thing: he hadn't left evidence implicating him lying around. Harry scanned the room from the floor to the ceiling and back down again to his reflection in the window, looking out on the darkness in the garden. There was something claustrophobic about the room, but if it really was the scene of a crime it wasn't talking to him. Anyway, too much time had passed, too many other things had happened here in the meantime and all that was left was the wallpaper. And the smell.

Harry let his gaze wander back up to the ceiling. Held it there. Claustrophobic. Why did it feel like that here and not in the sitting room? He stretched his full height of one ninety-two, plus arm, to the ceiling. His fingertips could just reach. Plasterboard. He went back into the sitting room and did the same. Without touching the ceiling.

So, the bedroom ceiling must have been lowered. Typical of the 1970s when people were trying to reduce heating costs. And in the space between the old and the new ceiling there would be room. Room to hide something.

Harry went into the hall, took a crowbar from a toolbox and returned to the bedroom. Froze when his gaze met the window. Knowing the eye automatically reacts to movement. He stood still for two seconds staring and listening. Nothing.

Harry concentrated on the ceiling again. There was nowhere to insert a crowbar, but it was easy with plasterboard, all you had to do was cut out a big section and afterwards replace the piece, use a bit of filler and paint the whole ceiling. He reckoned it could be done in half a day if you were efficient.

Harry stepped onto a chair and took aim at the ceiling with the crowbar. Hagen was right: if a detective, without a blue chit, the search warrant, tore down a ceiling without the owner's consent, a court would certainly overrule any evidence that this may unearth.

Harry aimed a blow. The crowbar went through the ceiling with a lifeless groan and white gypsum sprinkled down over his face.

And Harry was not even a detective, just a civil-

ian consultant, not part of the investigation, a private
individual who could accordingly be held to account
and found guilty of hooliganism. And Harry was
willing to pay the price.

He closed his eyes and bent the crowbar back. Felt
bits of plaster fall on his shoulders and forehead. And
caught the stench. It was worse here. He smashed the
crowbar in again, making the gap bigger. He hunted
around for something he could put on the chair so
that he could get his head through the opening.

There it was again. A movement by the window.
Harry jumped down and raced over to the window, shading his eyes to keep out the light and leaning
against the glass. But all he could see out there in the
darkness were the silhouettes of apple trees. Some of
the branches were swaying. Had the wind picked up?

Harry turned back into the room, found a large
plastic IKEA box, which he put on the chair, and
he was about to clamber up when he heard a sound
from the hall. A click. He stood waiting, listening.
But no further sounds reached him. Harry shrugged
it off; it was just the creaking of an old wooden house
when the wind starts blowing. He balanced on top of
the plastic box, stretched up gingerly, put the palms
of his hands against the ceiling and poked his head
through the cavity in the plasterboard.

The stench was so intense that his eyes instantly
filled with water and he had to concentrate on holding his breath. The stench was familiar. Flesh in
that phase of the decomposition process when inhaling the gas seems dangerous to your health. He had

only smelt such an intense stench once before, when they'd found a body that had been wrapped in plastic for two years in a dark cellar and they'd poked holes in it. No, this was not a rodent, not even from the rodent family. It was dark inside, and his head was blocking all the light, but he could glimpse something lying right in front of him. He waited for his pupils to dilate slowly to make the most of the little light there was. And then he saw it. It was a drill. No, a jigsaw. But there was something else, further back, something he couldn't quite see; he just felt a physical presence. Something . . . He felt his throat constrict. A sound. Of footsteps. Beneath him.

He tried to retract his head, but it was as if the opening had become too narrow, as if it was growing smaller around his neck, closing with him inside the atmosphere of death. He felt the panic rise, he forced his fingers between his throat and the mangled ceiling and tore off chunks. And pulled his head out.

The footsteps had stopped.

Harry's pulse was throbbing in his throat. He waited until he was perfectly calm. Took the lighter from his pocket, put his hand through the opening, the flame leapt up, and he was about to stick his head back in when he noticed something. The plastic curtain separating the two rooms. Something was outlined against it. A figure. Someone was watching him from behind the curtain.

Harry coughed. "Katrine?"

No answer.

Harry's eyes sought the crowbar he had left somewhere on the floor. Found it, stepped down as quietly as he could. Got one foot on the floor, heard the curtain being moved to the side and realised he wouldn't have time to reach it. The voice sounded almost cheerful.

"So we meet again."

He looked up. In the dim light it took him a few seconds to recognise the face. He cursed under his breath. His brain searched for conceivable scenarios for how the next few seconds would play out, tossing around the question: what the hell's going to happen now? But found no answer.

29

She had a bag over her shoulder, which she let slide down. It hit the floor with a surprisingly heavy thud.

"What are you doing here?" Harry asked gruffly, aware this was a repeat performance. The same as her answer.

"I've been doing some training. Martial arts."

"That's no answer, Silje."

"Yes, it is," Silje Gravseng said, thrusting one hip forward. She was wearing a thin tracksuit top, black leggings, trainers, a ponytail and a sly smile. "I'd finished my training and saw you leaving the college. I followed you."

"Why?"

She shrugged. "To give you another chance perhaps."

"A chance to do what?"

"To do what you want."

"Which is?"

"I don't think I need to spell it out, do I?" She tilted her head. "I saw it on your face in Krohn's office. You don't exactly have a poker face, Harry. You want to shag me."

Harry nodded towards the bag. "Your training, is

it the ninja stuff with a cane sword?" His voice rasped from the dryness in his mouth.

Silje Gravseng's gaze took in the room. "Something like that. We even have a bed here." She grabbed her bag, walked past him and pulled out a chair. Put the bag on the bed and tried to move a large sofa which was in the way, but it was stuck. Leaned forward, held the back of the sofa and pulled. Harry looked at her bottom, where her tracksuit top had ridden up, the muscles tightening in her thighs and heard her low groan. "Aren't you going to help me?"

Harry swallowed.

Shit, shit, shit.

Watched the blonde ponytail dancing on her back. Like a bloody handle. The material pulled up between her buttocks. She had stopped moving, just stood there, as though she had noticed something. Noticed it. Noticed what he was thinking.

"Like this?" she whispered. "Do you want me like this?"

He didn't answer, his erection grew; like delayed pain from a punch to the stomach, it spread from a point in his groin. His head began to fizz, bubbles rose and burst with a rushing noise that grew and grew. He took a step forward. Stopped.

She half turned her head, but cast her eyes down, looking at the floor.

"What are you waiting for?" she whispered. "Do you . . . do you want me to put up some resistance?"

Harry swallowed. He wasn't on autopilot. He

knew what he was doing. This was him. This was the kind of person he was. Even though he was talking to himself aloud now, he was going to do it. Didn't he want to?

"Yes," he heard himself say. "Stop me."

He saw her raise her bottom now; it struck him this was like a ritual from the animal world, perhaps he was programmed to do this after all. He placed a hand on the small of her back, on the arch, felt bare, sweaty skin where her leggings finished. Two fingers under the elastic. All he had to do was pull them down now. She had one hand resting on the back of the chair and the other on the bed, on the bag. The bag was open.

"I'll try," she whispered. "I'll try."

Harry drew a long, quivering breath.

Noticed a movement. It happened so fast he hardly had time to react.

"What's up?" Ulla asked as she was hanging up Mikael's coat in the inbuilt cupboard.

"What should be up?" he asked, rubbing his face with the palms of his hands.

"Come on," she said, leading him into the living room. Placed him on the sofa. Stood behind him. Rested her fingers on the transition behind the shoulders and his neck, let the tips find the middle of the trapezius and squeezed. He groaned aloud.

"Well?" she said.

He sighed. "Isabelle Skøyen. She's proposed that the old Police Chief should assist us until the present case is solved."

"I see. Is there anything wrong with that? You said yourself you need more resources."

"In practice it would mean he would be the de facto Chief of Police and I'd be brewing the coffee. It would be a vote of no confidence, which I couldn't accept. Surely you can see that."

"But it's only temporary, isn't it?"

"And afterwards? When the case is solved with him at the helm? Will the council say now it's all over you can have your job back? Ow!"

"Sorry, but it's just here. Try to relax, darling."

"It's her revenge, of course, you know. Dumped women . . . ouch!"

"Oh dear, did I hit the sore spot again?"

Mikael wriggled out of her hands. "The worst of it is that there's nothing I can do. She's good at this game; I'm just a beginner. If I'd only had a bit of time, time to build some alliances, see who was scratching whose back."

"You'll have to use the alliances you've got," Ulla said.

"All the important alliances are in her half of the court," Mikael said. "Sodding politicians, they don't think about outcomes like we do. For them it's all about votes, how things **look** to the stupid voters."

Mikael lowered his head. Her hands started to work again. Gentler this time. Massaged him, stroked his hair. And as he was about to let his mind float away, it seemed to apply the brakes and returned to what she had said. Use the alliances you've got.

Harry was blinded. He had automatically let go of Silje and turned. The plastic curtain had been drawn to one side and he stared into white light. Harry raised his hand above his eyes.

"Sorry," said a familiar voice and the torch was lowered. "Brought a torch along. Didn't think you . . ."

Harry drained his lungs with a groan. "Jesus, Katrine, you frightened me! Er . . . us."

"Oh, yes, isn't that the student . . . I saw you at PHS."

"I'm not there any more." Silje's voice sounded completely unruffled, almost as though she was bored.

"Oh? So what are you doing . . . ?"

"Moving furniture," Harry said, with a quick sniff, pointing to the gap in the ceiling. "Trying to find something more robust to stand on."

"There's a stepladder outside," Katrine said.

"Is there? I'll go and fetch it." Harry dashed past Katrine and through the sitting room. Shit, shit, shit and bugger.

The stepladder was leaning against the wall between the paint pots.

There was total silence when he returned, pushed away the armchair and positioned the aluminium ladder beneath the opening. No suggestion that they had spoken either. Women with arms crossed and faces devoid of expression.

"What's the stink?" Katrine asked.

"Pass me the torch," Harry said, climbing up the ladder. Tore off a chunk of plasterboard, poked the torch inside, then his head. Reached for the green jigsaw. The blade was broken. He held it between two fingers and passed it to Katrine. "Careful. There may be fingerprints."

He shone the torch inside again. Stared. The dead body lay on its side, squeezed between the old and the new ceiling. Harry was thinking he bloody deserved to be here inhaling the stench of death and rotting flesh, no, he deserved to be the rotting flesh. He was a sick man, a very sick man. And if he wasn't shot on the spot, he needed help. He had been about to do it, hadn't he? Or had he stopped? Or was the idea that he **might** have stopped something he invented to sow doubt?

"Can you see anything?" Katrine asked.

"I can indeed," Harry said.

"Do we need a forensics team?"

"That depends."

"On what?"

"Whether Crime Squad wants to investigate this death."

30

"This is a bit tricky to talk about," Harry said, stubbing out the cigarette on the windowsill, leaving the window overlooking Sporveisgata open and going back to his chair. Ståle Aune had said he could come before the first patient at eight when Harry had rung him at six and said he was in a mess again.

"You've been here before to talk about tricky matters," Ståle said. For as long as Harry could remember he had been the psychologist the officers in Crime Squad went to when things got tough. Not just because they had his phone number, but because Ståle Aune was one of the few psychologists who knew what their everyday working life was like. And they knew they could rely on him keeping his mouth shut.

"Yes, but that was about drinking," Harry said. "This is . . . quite different."

"Is it?"

"Don't you think it is?"

"I think that since the first thing you did was to ring me, you think it may be more of the same."

Harry sighed, leaned forward in the chair and rested his forehead against his folded hands. "Maybe it is. I always had the feeling I chose the worst possible times to drink. I always succumbed when it was important to be at my most alert. As though there was a demon inside me who wanted everything to go down the Swanee. Wanted **me** to go down the Swanee."

"That's what demons do, Harry." Ståle concealed a yawn.

"In that case, this one has done a good job. I was about to rape a girl."

Ståle was no longer yawning. "What did you say? When was this?"

"Last night. The girl's an ex-student of mine at PHS. She turned up while I was searching a flat where Valentin had lived."

"Oh?" Ståle removed his glasses. "Did you find anything?"

"A jigsaw with a broken blade. Must have been there for years. Of course, the builders may have left it there when they were lowering the ceiling, but they're checking the serrated edge against what they found in Bergslia."

"Anything else?"

"No. Yes. A dead badger."

"Badger?"

"Yes. Looked as if it had been hibernating there."

"Heh heh. We had a badger once, but fortunately it stayed in the garden. It has a fearsome bite on it. Did it die during its hibernation then?"

Harry smirked. "If you're interested I can get forensics on the case."

"Sorry, I . . ." Ståle shook his head and put his

glasses back on. "The girl arrived and you felt tempted to rape her, is that how it was?"

Harry raised his arms over his head. "I've just proposed to the woman I love more than anything else in the world. I want nothing more than for us to have a good life together. And just as I've articulated the thought, the devil jumps out and . . . and . . ." He lowered his arms again.

"Why have you stopped?"

"Because I'm sitting here and making up a devil and I know what you'll say. I'm absolving myself of all responsibility."

"Aren't you?"

"Of course I am. It's the same guy in new clothes. I thought he was called Jim Beam. I thought he was called the mother who died young or the pressure of the job. Or testosterone or booze genes. And perhaps all of that's true too, but when you undress him he's still called Harry Hole."

"And you're saying Harry Hole almost raped this girl last night."

"I've been dreaming about it for a long time."

"Rape? In general?"

"No. This girl. She asked me to do it."

"Rape her? Strictly speaking, that's not rape, is it?"

"The first time she just asked me to fuck her. She provoked me, but I couldn't. She was a student at PHS. And afterwards I began to fantasise about raping her. I . . ." Harry ran a hand across his face. "I didn't think I had it in me. Not a rapist. What's happening to me, Ståle?"

"So you had the inclination and the opportunity to rape her, but you chose to desist?"

"Someone interrupted us. Was it rape? I don't know, but she invited me to take part in a role play. And I was willing to take the role, Ståle. Very willing."

"Yes, but I still can't see that as rape."

"Perhaps not in a legal sense, but . . ."

"But what?"

"But if we'd got going and she'd asked me to stop, I don't know whether I would have done."

"You don't know?"

Harry shrugged. "Have you got a diagnosis, Doctor?"

Ståle looked at his watch. "I need you to tell me a bit more, but my first patient's waiting for me now."

"I haven't got any time for therapy, Ståle. We've got a murderer to catch."

"In that case," Aune said, rocking his podgy stomach to and fro in his chair, "you'll have to make do with me shooting from the hip. You've come to me because you feel something you can't identify, and the reason you can't identify it is that the feeling is trying to disguise itself as something which it is not. Because what the feeling really is, is something you don't **want** to feel. It's classic denial, just like men who refuse to accept they're homosexual."

"But I'm not denying that I'm a potential rapist! I'm asking you straight out."

"You're not a rapist, Harry, you don't become one overnight. I think this may be about one of two things. Or perhaps both. One is, you may feel some form of aggression towards this girl. And what it's really about is you exercising control. Or to use layman's language, a punishment fuck. Am I close?"

"Mm. Maybe. What was the other one?"

"Rakel."

"Sorry?"

"What you're being drawn towards is neither rape nor this girl, but being unfaithful. Unfaithful to Rakel."

"Ståle, you—"

"Easy now. You've come to me because you need someone to tell you what you've already realised. To say it loud and clear. Because you're unable to tell yourself. You don't want to have to feel like that."

"Like what?"

"That you're petrified of committing yourself to her. The thought of marriage has driven you to the edge of panic."

"Oh? Why's that?"

"Since I may venture to claim that I know you a bit after all these years, I believe that in your case this is more about the fear of taking responsibility for other people. You've had bad experiences . . ."

Harry gulped. Felt something growing in his chest, like a cancerous tumour on fast forward.

". . . you start drinking when the world around you is dependent on you and because you can't take the responsibility, you **want** things to go down the pan. It's like when a house of cards is almost finished and the pressure's so great you can't cope, so instead of persisting you knock it down. To get the defeat over with. And I think that's what you're doing now. You want to fail Rakel as quickly as possible because you're convinced it's going to happen anyway. You can't bear the long-drawn-out torment, so you're proactive; you knock down the damned house of cards, which is how you see your relationship with Rakel."

Harry wanted to say something. But the lump had reached his throat and blocked the way for words, so he made do with one: "Destructive."

"Your basic attitude is **con**structive, Harry. You're just scared. Scared it will hurt too much. You and her."

"I'm a coward. That's what you're saying, isn't it?"

Ståle eyed Harry, took a breath, as though on the point of correcting him, then seemed to change his mind.

"Yes, you're a coward. You're a coward because I think you want this. You **want** Rakel, you want to be in the same boat, you want to tie her to the mast, to sail in this boat or go down in the process. That's how it is with you, Harry, on those rare occasions when you make a promise. How does that song go again?"

Harry mumbled something about not retreating or surrendering.

"There you have it, that's you."

"That's me," Harry repeated softly.

"Give it some thought. We can talk again after the meeting in the Boiler Room this afternoon."

Harry nodded and got up.

In the corridor sat a man impatiently shuffling his

feet and sweating in training gear. He looked at his watch and glared at Harry.

Harry set off down Sporveisgata. He hadn't slept all night, and he hadn't had breakfast either. He needed something. He took stock. He needed a drink. He dismissed the thought and went into the cafe just before Bogstadveien. Asked for a triple espresso. Tossed it back at the counter and asked for another. Heard low laughter behind him, but didn't turn. Drank number two slowly. Picked up the newspaper lying there. Saw the front-page teaser and leafed through.

Roger Gjendem was speculating that the City Council, in light of the police murders, was going to have a reshuffle at Police HQ.

After letting in Paul Stavnes, Ståle resumed his position behind the desk while Stavnes went into the corner to change into a dry T-shirt. Ståle took the opportunity to yawn without inhibition, pull out the top drawer and position his mobile so that he could see it easily. Then he looked up. Gazed at his patient's naked back. After Stavnes had started cycling to the sessions it had become a fixed routine that he would change his T-shirt in the office. Always with his back turned. The only change was that the window where Harry had been smoking was still open. The light fell in such a way that Ståle Aune could see Paul Stavnes's bare chest in the reflection.

Stavnes quickly pulled down his T-shirt and turned. "Your timing needs—"

"—tightening up," Ståle said. "I agree. It won't happen again."

Stavnes looked up. "Is there something the matter?"

"Not at all. Just got up a bit earlier than normal. Could you leave the window open so there's a bit of air in here?"

"There's a **lot** of air in here."

"As you wish."

Stavnes was about to close the window. Then held back. Stood staring at it. Turned slowly towards Ståle. A little smile appeared on his face.

"Finding it hard to breathe, Aune?"

Ståle Aune was aware of pains in his chest and arms. All of which were familiar symptoms of a heart attack. Except that this wasn't a heart attack. It was pure, unmitigated fear.

Ståle Aune forced himself to speak calmly, in a low key.

"Last time we talked again about you playing **Dark Side of the Moon.** Your father came into the room and switched off the amplifier and you watched the red light die as the girl you were thinking about also died."

"I said she went mute," Paul Stavnes said, annoyed. "I didn't say she died. That's different."

"Yes, it is," Ståle Aune said, reaching carefully for the phone in his drawer. "Did you wish she could speak?"

"I don't know. You're sweating. Are you unwell, Doctor?"

Again this jeering tone, this small, repugnant smile.

"I'm fine, thank you."

Ståle's fingers rested on the phone. He had to get the patient speaking so that he wouldn't hear him texting.

"We haven't talked about your marriage. What can you say about your wife?"

"Not much. Why do you want to talk about her?"

"A close relative. You seem to dislike people who are close. 'Despise' was the word you used."

"So you have been paying some attention after all?" Brief, sullen laugh. "I despise people because most of them are weak, stupid and down on their luck." More laughter. "Zero out of three. Tell me, did you sort out X?"

"What?"

"The policeman. The homo who tried to kiss another cop on the toilet. Did he recover?"

"Not really." Ståle Aune pressed the keys, cursing his fat sausage-fingers, which felt as if they had swollen even more with the tension.

"So if you think I'm like him, why do you reckon you can sort me out?"

"X was schizophrenic. He heard voices."

"And you think I'm in better shape?" The patient laughed bitterly as Ståle texted. Trying to write while the patient continued to talk, trying to camouflage the clicks by scraping his shoes against the floor. One letter. One more. Bastard fingers. There we are. He realised the patient had stopped talking. The patient, Paul Stavnes. Wherever he got that name from. You could always find a new name. Or get rid of the old one. It wasn't so easy with tattoos. Especially if they were big and covered your whole chest.

"I know why you're sweating, Aune," the patient said. "You happened to see the reflection in the window when I was changing, didn't you?"

Ståle Aune felt the pains in his chest increase, as though his heart couldn't make up its mind whether to beat faster or not at all, and he hoped the expression he put on looked as uncomprehending as he intended.

"What?" he said in a loud voice to drown the click as he pressed the Send button.

The patient pulled his T-shirt up to his throat.

A mute, screaming face stared at Aune from the man's chest.

The face of a demon.

"OK, shoot," Harry said, holding the phone to his ear as he drained the second cup of coffee.

"The jigsaw has got Valentin Gjertsen's fingerprints on," Bjørn Holm said. "And the cutting surface of the blade matches. It's the same blade that was used in Bergslia."

"So Valentin Gjertsen is the Saw Man," Harry said.

"Looks like it," Bjørn Holm said. "What surprises me is that Valentin Gjertsen would hide a murder weapon at home instead of dumping it."

"He was planning to use it again," Harry said.

Harry felt his phone vibrate. A text. He looked at

the display. The sender was S, so Ståle Aune. Harry read it. And read it again.

valentin is here sos

"Bjørn, send a patrol car to Ståle's office in Sporveisgata. Valentin's there."

"Hello? Harry? Hello?"

But Harry was already running.

31

"Being exposed is always an awkward business," the patient said. "But sometimes it's worse for the exposer."

"Exposing what?" Ståle said with a gulp. "It's a tattoo. So? It's not a crime. Lots of people have . . ." He nodded towards the demon face. ". . . tattoos like that."

"Do they?" the patient said, pulling his T-shirt down. "Was that why you looked as if you were going to drop dead when you saw it?"

"I don't understand what you mean," Ståle said in a tight voice. "Shall we talk about your father?"

The patient laughed out loud. "Do you know what, Aune? When I first came here I couldn't decide whether I was proud or disappointed you didn't recognise me."

"Recognise?"

"We've met before. I was charged with sex abuse, and it was your job to determine whether I was of sound mind or not. You must have had hundreds of cases like that. Well, it took you only forty-five minutes. Nevertheless, in a way, I wished I had made a greater impression on you."

Ståle stared at him. Had he done a psychological

evaluation of the man sitting in front of him? It was impossible to remember them all; however, he usually remembered at least their faces.

Ståle studied him. The two small scars under the chin. Of course. He had assumed his patient had had a facelift, but Beate had said that Valentin Gjertsen must have had major plastic surgery.

"But you made an impression on me, Aune. You **understood** me. You weren't put off by the details, you just continued drilling away. Asking about the right things. About the bad things. Like a good masseur knowing exactly where to find the knot. You found the pain, Aune. And that's why I came back. I hoped you could find it again, the damned boil, lance it, get the crap out. Can you do that? Or have you lost the passion, Aune?"

Ståle cleared his throat. "I can't do it if you lie to me, Paul."

"But I'm not lying, Aune. Just about the job and the wife. Everything else is true. Oh yes, and the name. Otherwise . . ."

"Pink Floyd. The girl?"

The man in front of him splayed his palms and smiled.

"And why are you telling me this now, Paul?"

"You don't need to call me that any more. You can say Valentin if you like."

"Val-what?"

The patient chuckled. "Sorry, but you're a lousy actor, Aune. You know who I am. You knew the minute you saw my tattoo reflected in the window."

"And what should I know?"

"That I'm Valentin Gjertsen. The one you're all looking for."

"All? Looking?"

"You forget I had to sit here listening to you talking to a cop about Valentin Gjertsen's doodles on a tram window. I complained and got a session free, do you remember?"

Ståle closed his eyes for a couple of seconds. Closed everything out. Told himself Harry would be there soon. He couldn't have been that far away.

"By the way, that's why I started cycling instead of catching the tram to our sessions," Valentin Gjertsen said. "I thought the tram would be under surveillance."

"But you still came."

Valentin shrugged and put a hand in his rucksack. "It's almost impossible to identify anyone when they're in a helmet and goggles, isn't it? And you didn't suspect a thing. You'd decided I was Paul Stavnes, **basta.** And I needed these sessions, Aune. I'm really sorry they have to stop . . ."

Aune stifled a gasp as he saw Valentin Gjertsen's hand emerge from the rucksack. The light flashed on the steel.

"Did you know this is called a survival knife?" Valentin said. "Bit of a misnomer in your case. But it's so versatile. This, for example . . ." He ran a fingertip along the jagged blade. ". . . is what mystifies most people. They just think it looks creepy. And do you know what?" Again he smiled the thin, ugly smile. "They're right. When you slide the knife across a throat, like this . . . it hooks onto the skin and tears. Then the next grooves tear what is inside. The thin membrane around a blood vessel, for example. And if it's a main artery under pressure . . . that's quite a sight, I can tell you. But don't be afraid. You won't notice, I promise."

Ståle's brain went into a whirl. He almost hoped it was a heart attack.

"So there's only one thing left, Ståle. Is it all right if I call you Ståle now the end is nigh? What's the diagnosis?"

"Dia . . . dia . . ."

"Dia . . . gnosis. Greek for 'through knowledge,' isn't it? What's wrong with me, Ståle?"

"I . . . I don't know. I—"

The movement that followed was so swift Ståle Aune wouldn't have been able to lift a finger even if he'd tried. Valentin had disappeared from view and when he heard his voice again, it was behind him, by his ear.

"Of course you know, Ståle. You've dealt with people like me all your professional life. Not exactly like me, that goes without saying, but similar. Damaged goods."

Ståle could no longer see the knife. He felt it. Against his quivering double chin as he breathed hard through his nose. It seemed contrary to nature that any human being could move so fast. He didn't want to die. He wanted to live. There was no space for any other thoughts.

"There's . . . there's nothing wrong with you, Paul."

"Valentin. Show some respect. I'm standing here ready to drain you of blood while my dick is gorged with blood. And you suggest there's nothing wrong with me?" He laughed in Aune's ear. "Come on. The diagnosis."

"Stark raving mad."

They both lifted their heads. Looked at the door, from where the voice had come.

"Time's up. Pay on your way out, Valentin."

The tall, broad-shouldered figure filling the doorway stepped inside. He was dragging something after him and it took Ståle a second to realise what it was. The barbell from above the sofa in the communal area.

"Stay out of this, cop," Valentin hissed, and Ståle felt the knife pressing against his skin.

"Patrol cars are on their way, Valentin. It's all over. Let the doc go now."

Valentin nodded towards the open window overlooking the street. "Can't hear any sirens. Go, or I'll kill the doctor right here."

"Don't think you will," Harry Hole said, lifting the bar. "Without him you've got no shield."

"In which case," Valentin said, and Ståle felt his arm being bent behind his back, forcing him to stand up, "I'll let the doctor go. With me."

"Take me instead," Harry Hole said.

"Why should I?"

"I'm a better hostage. There's a chance he'll panic and faint. And you won't need to worry about what tricks I might pull if you're holding on to me."

Silence. From the window they could hear a faint

sound. Perhaps a distant siren, perhaps not. The pressure from the blade slackened. Then—as Ståle was about to breathe again—he felt a pricking sensation and heard the snap of something being severed. It fell to the floor. The bow tie.

"One move from you and . . ." the voice hissed in his ear before turning to Harry. "As you wish, cop, but let go of the bar first. Then stand with your face to the wall, legs apart and—"

"I know the drill," Harry said, letting go of the bar, turning, placing his palms high up the wall and spreading his legs.

Ståle felt the grip on his arm loosen and the next moment he saw Valentin standing behind Harry, pushing his arm up his back and holding the knife against his throat.

"Let's go, handsome," Valentin said.

Then they were out of the door.

And Ståle could finally draw breath.

From the window the sirens rose and fell with the wind.

Harry saw the receptionist's terrified expression as he and Valentin walked towards her like a two-headed troll and passed her without a word. On the stairway Harry tried to walk more slowly, but soon felt a stinging pain in his side.

"This knife will go deeper into your kidney if you try anything."

Harry increased his speed. He couldn't feel the

blood yet as it was the same temperature as his skin, but he knew it was running down the inside of his shirt.

Then they were on the ground floor, and Valentin kicked open the door and pushed Harry through, but the knife never lost contact with him.

They stood in Sporveisgata. Harry heard the sirens. A man with sunglasses and a dog walked towards them. Passing by without so much as a glance, the white stick tapping on the pavement like a castanet.

"Stand here," Valentin said, pointing to a No Parking sign with a mountain bike locked to the post.

Harry stood by the post. His shirt had become sticky and the pain throbbed in his side with a pulse of its own. The knife pressed into his back. He heard keys and the rattle of a bike lock. The sirens were approaching. Then the knife was gone. But before Harry could react and jump away, his head was dragged backwards as something was clamped around his neck. Sparks appeared in his eyes as his head smacked against the post and he gasped for air. The keys rattled again. Then the pressure slackened and Harry instinctively raised his hand, inserted two fingers between his throat and whatever was holding him. Bloody hell.

Valentin swung out in front of him on his bike. Put the goggles on, saluted him with two fingers to his helmet and pushed down on the pedals.

Harry watched the black rucksack disappearing down the street. The sirens couldn't be more than two blocks away. A cyclist passed by. Helmet, black

rucksack. One more. No helmet, but a black rucksack. One more. Shit, shit, shit. The sirens sounded
as if they were in his head. Harry closed his eyes
and thought about the old Greek logic puzzle where
something is approaching, a kilometre away, half a
kilometre, a third of a kilometre, a quarter, a hundredth, and if it is true that a sequence of numbers is
infinite, it will never arrive.

32

"So you just stood there, fastened to a post with a bike lock around your neck?" Bjørn Holm asked, in disbelief.

"A sodding No Parking sign," Harry said, looking down at the empty coffee cup.

"Ironic," Katrine said.

"They had to send someone to get bolt cutters."

The Boiler Room door opened and Gunnar Hagen marched in. "I've just heard the news. What's going on?"

"Patrol cars are in the area looking for him," Katrine said. "Every single cyclist is being stopped and searched."

"Even though he must have got rid of his bike by now and is in a taxi or on public transport," Harry said. "Valentin is many things, but not stupid."

The Crime Squad boss threw himself onto a chair out of breath. "Did he leave any clues?"

Silence.

He looked in surprise at the wall of accusatory faces. "What's up?"

Harry coughed. "You're sitting on Beate's chair."

"Am I?" Hagen jumped up.

"He left his tracksuit top," Harry said. "Bjørn's handed it to Krimteknisk."

"Sweat, hair, the whole salami," Bjørn said. "Reckon we'll have it confirmed in a day or two that Paul Stavnes and Valentin Gjertsen are one and the same."

"Anything else in the top?" Hagen asked.

"No wallet, mobile, notebook or calendar showing plans for future murders," Harry said. "Just this."

Hagen automatically took it and looked at what Harry had passed him. An unopened little plastic bag containing three Q-tips.

"What was he going to do with these?"

"Kill someone?" Harry suggested laconically.

"They're for cleaning your ears," Bjørn Holm said. "But actually they're for scratching your ears, right? The skin gets irritated, we scratch even more, there's more wax and all of a sudden we **have** to have more Q-tips. Heroin for the ears."

"Or for make-up," Harry said.

"Oh?" Hagen said, studying the bag. "By which you mean . . . he wears make-up?"

"Well, it's a mask. He's already had plastic surgery. Ståle, you've seen him close up."

"I haven't thought about it, but you may be right."

"You don't need much mascara and eyeliner to achieve a difference," Katrine said.

"Great," Hagen said. "Have we got anything on the name Paul Stavnes?"

"Very little," Katrine said. "There's no Paul Stavnes on the national register with the date of birth he gave Aune. The only two people with the same name have been eliminated by police outside Oslo. And the elderly couple who live at the address he gave have never heard of any Paul Stavnes or Valentin Gjertsen."

"We're not in the habit of checking patients' contact details," Aune said. "And he settled up after every session."

"Hotel," Harry said. "Boarding house, hospice. They've all got their guests registered on databases now."

"I'll check." Katrine swivelled round on her chair and began to tap away on her keyboard.

"Is that kind of thing on the Internet?" Hagen asked in a sceptical tone.

"No," Harry said. "But Katrine uses a couple of search engines you'll wish didn't exist."

"Oh, why's that?"

"Because they have access to a level of codes that mean the best firewalls in the world are completely useless," Bjørn Holm said, peering over Katrine's shoulder, to a clicking landslide of keystrokes, like the feet of fleeing cockroaches on a glass table.

"How's that possible?" Hagen asked.

"Because they're the same codes the firewalls use," Bjørn said. "The search engines **are** the wall."

"Not looking good," Katrine said. "No Paul Stavnes anywhere."

"But he must live somewhere," Hagen said. "Is he renting a flat under the name Paul Stavnes? Can you check that?"

"Doubt he's your run-of-the-mill tenant," Katrine said. "Most landlords vet their tenants these days. Google them, check the tax lists anyway. And Valentin knows they would be suspicious if they couldn't find him anywhere."

"Hotel," said Harry, who had got up and was standing by the board where they had written what had seemed to Hagen at first sight like a chart of free associations with arrows and cues until he had recognised the names of the murder victims. One of them was referred to only as B.

"You've already said hotel, my love," Katrine said.

"Three Q-tips," Harry went on, leaning down to Hagen and retrieving the sealed plastic bag. "You can't buy a packet like this in a shop. You find it in a hotel bathroom with miniature bottles of shampoo and conditioner. Try again, Katrine. Judas Johansen this time."

The search was finished in less than fifteen seconds.

"Negative," Katrine said.

"Damn," Hagen said.

"We're not done yet," Harry said, studying the plastic bag. "There's no manufacturer's name on this, but usually Q-tips have a plastic stick and these are wooden. It should be possible to track down the suppliers and the Oslo hotels receiving the supplies."

"Hotel supplies," Katrine said, and the insect-like fingers were scampering again.

"I have to be off," Ståle said, getting up.

"I'll see you out," Harry said.

"You won't find him," Ståle said, outside Police HQ, looking down over Bots Park, which lay bathed in cold, sharp spring light.

"**We,** don't you mean?"

"Maybe," Ståle sighed. "I don't exactly feel I'm making much of a contribution."

"Contribution?" Harry said. "You got us Valentin all on your own."

"He escaped."

"His alias is out in the open. We're getting closer. Why don't you think we'll catch him?"

"You saw him yourself. What do you think?"

Harry nodded. "He said he went to you because you'd done a psychological assessment of him. At the time you concluded he was of sound mind in a legal sense, didn't you?"

"Yes, but, as you know, people with serious personality disorders can be convicted."

"What you were after was extreme schizophrenia, psychosis, at the time of the act and so on, wasn't it?"

"Yes."

"But he could have been a manic-depressive or a psychopath. Correction, bipolar II or a sociopath."

"The correct term now is dissocial." Ståle accepted the cigarette Harry passed him.

Harry lit them both. "It's good he goes to you even though he knows you work for the cops. But that he continues even after realising you're involved in the hunt for him?"

Ståle inhaled and shrugged. "I must be such a brilliant therapist he was willing to take the risk."

"Any other suggestions?"

"Well, maybe he's a thrill-seeker. Lots of serial killers have visited detectives under a variety of pre-texts to be in close contact with the hunt, to experience the triumph of fooling the police."

"Valentin took off his T-shirt even though he must have known you knew about the tattoo. A terrible risk if you're under investigation for murder."

"What do you mean?"

"Hm, yes, what do I mean?"

"You mean he has an unconscious desire to be caught. He wanted me to recognise him. And when I failed he unconsciously helped me by revealing his tattoo."

"And when he achieved his objective, he made a desperate attempt to flee?"

"The conscious took over. This could put the police murders in a new light, Harry. Valentin's murders are compulsive acts which, unconsciously, he wants to stop, he wants punishment, or exorcism, someone to stop the demon in him. So when we didn't manage to catch him for the original murders, he does what many serial killers do, he increases the risk factor. In his case, by targeting the police who couldn't catch him the first time round because he knows that for a crime against the police there is no limit to resources. And in the end he shows his tattoo to someone he knows is part of the investigation. I think you may well be right, Harry."

"Mm, don't know if I can take the credit for it. What about a simpler explanation? Valentin isn't as careful as we think he should be because he doesn't have as much to fear as we think he does."

"I don't understand."

Harry drew on his cigarette. Released the smoke as he inhaled it through his nose. It was a trick he'd been taught by a milky-white German didgeridoo player in Hong Kong: "Exhale and inhale at the same fucking time, mate, and you can smoke your cigarettes twice."

"Go home and have a rest," Harry said. "That was a tough deal."

"Thank you, but I'm the psychologist here, Harry."

"A murderer holding a knife to your throat? Sorry, Doc, but you're not going to be able to rationalise that away. The nightmares queue up—believe me, I've been there. So take it from a colleague. And that's an order."

"An order?" A twitch in Ståle's face suggested a smile. "Are you the boss now, Harry?"

"Were you ever in any doubt?" Harry groped in his pocket. Took out his phone. "Yes?"

He dropped the half-smoked cigarette on the ground. "Will you sort it for me? They've found something."

Ståle Aune watched Harry as he went through the door. Then he looked down at the smouldering cigarette on the tarmac. Gently placed his shoe on it. Increased the pressure. Turned his foot. Felt the cigarette being squashed under the thin leather sole. Felt the fury rising. Twisted it harder. Ground the filter, ash, paper and tobacco into the tarmac. Dropped his own cigarette. Repeated the movements. It felt good and bad at the same time. Felt like screaming, hitting, laughing, crying. He had tasted every nuance in the cigarette. He was alive. He was so bloody alive.

"Casbah Hotel in Gange-Rolvs gate," Katrine said before Harry had closed the door behind him. "It's mostly embassies who use the hotel for employees before getting them longer-term accommodation. Pretty reasonable rates, small rooms."

"Mm. Why this hotel in particular?"

"It's the only hotel which has these Q-tips delivered and is situated on the right side of town for the number 12 tram," Bjørn said. "I rang. They haven't got any Stavnes, Gjertsen or Johansen registered in the guest book, but I faxed Beate's drawing."

"And?"

"The receptionist said they've got someone like him, someone called Savitski who claimed he worked at the Belarusian embassy. He used to go to work wearing a suit, but now he's started wearing training gear. And riding a bike."

Harry already had the receiver in his hand. "Hagen? We need Delta. Right now."

33

"So that's what you want me to do?" Truls said, twirling the beer glass between his fingers. They were sitting in Kampen Bistro. Mikael had said it was a very good place to eat. East Oslo chic, popular among those who **count,** the ones with more cultural capital than money, the in-crowd who had salaries low enough to maintain their student lifestyle without it seeming pathetic.

Truls had lived in East Oslo all his life and had never heard of the place. "And why should I?"

"The suspension," Mikael said, pouring the rest of the mineral water into his glass. "I'll get it revoked."

"Oh?" Truls regarded Mikael with mistrust.

"Yes."

Truls took a swig from his glass. Ran the back of his hand across his mouth although the foam had settled long ago. Took his time. "If it's so easy, why didn't you do it before?"

Mikael closed his eyes, inhaled. "It's not so easy, but I want to do it."

"Because?"

"Because I'm screwed unless you help me."

Truls chuckled. "Strange how quickly the tables turn. Eh, Mikael?"

Mikael Bellman glanced in both directions. The room was full, but he had chosen it because it wasn't somewhere frequented by police officers, and he shouldn't be seen with Truls. And he had a feeling Truls knew. But so what?

"What's it going to be? I can ask someone else."

Truls guffawed. "Can you hell!"

Mikael scoured the room. He didn't want to tell Truls to keep his voice down, but . . . In times gone by Mikael had largely been able to predict how Truls would react, had been able to coax him into doing what he wanted. There had been a change in him; there was something sinister, something evil and unpredictable about his childhood friend now.

"I need an answer. It's urgent."

"Fine," Truls said, draining the glass. "The suspension's fine. But I need one more thing."

"What's that?"

"A pair of Ulla's panties—unwashed."

Mikael stared at Truls. Was he drunk? Or was the ferocity in his moist eyes a permanent feature now?

Truls laughed even louder and banged his glass down on the table. Some of those who count turned round.

"I . . ." Mikael started. "I'll see what—"

"I'm kidding, you dick!"

Mikael gave a short laugh. "Me too. Does that mean you will . . . ?"

"For Christ's sake, we've been pals since we were kids, haven't we?"

"Of course. You have no idea how grateful I am, Truls." Mikael struggled to smile.

Truls passed a hand across the table. Placed it heavily on Mikael's shoulder.

"Oh yes, I have."

Too heavily, Mikael thought.

There was no reconnaissance, no examining the floor plan for exits or possible escapes, no circle of police cars blocking the roads at the point where the Delta all-terrain vehicles drove in. There was a short briefing as they went, with Sivert Falkeid barking orders and the heavily armed men at the back staying quiet, which meant they understood.

It was a question of time, and even the world's best-laid plan would be useless if the bird had already flown.

Harry, sitting at the back of the nine-seater and listening, knew they didn't have the world's second- or even third-best-laid plan.

The first thing Falkeid had asked Harry was if he thought Valentin would be armed. Harry had answered that a gun had been used to murder René Kalsnes. And he thought Beate had been threatened with a gun.

He looked at the men in front of him. Police officers who had volunteered for armed operations. He knew what they were paid for the extra work, and it wasn't too much. And he also knew what taxpayers thought they could demand of Delta troops, and it was much too much. How many times had he heard people with the benefit of hindsight criticising the Delta officers for not exposing themselves to greater danger, for not having a sixth sense to tell them what was going on behind a closed door, in a hijacked plane, on a forest-clad beach and for not rushing in headlong? For a Delta officer with, on average, four missions a year, so approximately a hundred in a career of twenty-five years, such a policy would have meant being killed on active duty. But the main point was still this: being killed in the line of fire was the best way to ensure the failure of an operation and to expose other officers to danger.

"There's just one lift," Falkeid barked. "Two and Three, you take it. Four, Five and Six, you take the main stairs. Seven and Eight the fire escape. Hole, you and I'll cover the area outside if he exits via a window."

"I haven't got a gun," Harry said.

"Here," Falkeid said, passing him a Glock 17.

Harry held it, felt the solid weight, the balance.

He had never understood gun freaks, just as he had never understood car freaks or people who built houses to fit around their sound system. But he had never felt any real objection to holding a gun. Until last year. Harry thought back to the last time he had held a gun. To the Odessa in the cupboard. He dismissed the thought.

"We're here," Falkeid said. They parked in a quiet

street by the gate to a luxurious-looking, four-storey brick building, identical to all the other houses in the area. Harry knew that some of them were old money, some of the new ones wanted to look old, while others were embassies, ambassadors' residences, advertising bureaus, record companies and smaller shipping lines. A discreet brass sign on the gatepost confirmed that they had come to the right address.

Falkeid held up his watch. "Radio communication," he said.

The officers said their numbers—the same as the one painted in white on their helmets—in turn. Pulled down their balaclavas. Tightened the belts on their MP5 machine guns.

"On the count of one we'll go in. Five, four . . ."

Harry wasn't sure if it was his own adrenalin or adrenalin from the other men, but there was a distinct smell and taste, bitter, salty, like caps fired from a toy gun.

The doors opened and Harry saw a wall of black backs running through the gate and then the ten metres to the entrance, where they were swallowed up.

Harry stepped out after them, adjusting his bulletproof vest. The skin beneath was already soaked with sweat. Falkeid jumped down from the passenger seat after removing the keys from the ignition. Harry vaguely remembered an episode when the targets of a swoop had made their getaway in a police car with the keys left in. Harry passed the Glock to Falkeid.

"Haven't got an up-to-date certificate."

"Hereby issued on a provisional basis by me,"

Falkeid said. "Emergency. Police regulations paragraph such-and-such. Maybe."

Harry loaded the gun and strode up the gravel as a young man with a crooked turkey neck came running out. His Adam's apple was going up and down as if he'd just eaten. Harry observed that the name on the lapel of his black jacket tallied with the name of the receptionist he had spoken to on the phone.

The receptionist hadn't been able to say for certain if the guest was in his room or anywhere else in the hotel, but he had offered to check. Which Harry had ordered him in the strictest terms not to do. He was to continue with his normal duties and act as if nothing had happened, then neither he nor anyone else would be hurt. The sight of seven men dressed in black and armed to the teeth had probably made it difficult to act as if nothing had happened.

"I gave them the master key," the receptionist said in a pronounced East European accent. "They told me to get out and—"

"Stand behind our vehicle," Falkeid whispered, jerking his thumb behind him. Harry left them, walking with gun in hand around the building to the back, where a shadowy garden of apple trees extended down to the fence of the neighbouring property. An elderly man was sitting on the terrace, reading the **Daily Telegraph.** He lowered his newspaper and peered over his glasses. Harry pointed to the yellow letters spelling POLITI on his bulletproof vest, put a finger to his lips, acknowledged a brief nod and concentrated on the third-floor windows. The receptionist had told them where the alleged Belarusian's room was. It was at the end of the corridor and the window looked out onto the back.

Harry adjusted the earpiece and waited.

After a few seconds it came. The dull, confined explosion of a shock grenade followed by the tinkle of glass.

Harry knew that the air pressure itself wouldn't have much more effect than deafening those in the room. But the explosion combined with the blinding flash and the men's assault would paralyse even well-trained targets for the first three seconds. And those three seconds were all the Delta troops needed.

Harry waited. Then a subdued voice came through his earpiece. Just what he expected.

"Room 406 taken. No one here."

It was what came after that made Harry swear out loud.

"Looks like he's been here to pick up his stuff."

Harry was standing, arms crossed, in the corridor outside room 406 as Katrine and Bjørn arrived.

"Good shot. Hit the post?" Katrine asked.

"Missed an open goal," Harry said, shaking his head.

They followed him into the room.

"He came straight here, grabbed all his stuff and was gone."

"All?" Bjørn queried.

"All except for two used Q-tips and two tram tickets we found in the waste-paper basket. Plus the stub of this ticket to a football match I have a feeling we won."

"**We?**" Bjørn asked, looking around the bog-standard hotel room. "Do you mean Vålerenga?"

"Norway. Versus Slovenia, it says."

"We won," Bjørn said. "Riise scored in extra time."

"Sick. How can you men remember things like that?" Katrine said, shaking her head. "I can't even remember if Brann won the league or were demoted last year."

"I'm not like that," Bjørn objected. "I only remember it because it was heading for a draw and then I was called out, and Riise—"

"You remembered it anyway, Rain Man. You—"

"Hey." They turned to Harry, who was staring at the ticket. "Can you remember what it was for, Bjørn?"

"Eh?"

"The call-out?"

Bjørn Holm scratched one sideburn. "Let's see, it was early in the evening . . ."

"Never mind," Harry said. "It was the murder of Erlend Vennesla in Maridalen."

"Was it?"

"The same evening that Norway was playing at Ullevål Stadium. The date's here on the ticket. Seven o'clock."

"Aha," Katrine said.

Bjørn Holm's face showed a pained expression. "Don't say that, Harry. Please don't say Valentin Gjertsen was at the match. If he was there—"

"—he can't be the murderer," Katrine finished. "And we would very much like him to be, Harry. So please say something encouraging now."

"OK," Harry said. "Why wasn't this ticket in the basket with the Q-tips and the tram tickets? Why did he put it on the desk when he tidied everything else up? Placed it exactly where he knew we'd find it?"

"He's left his alibi," Katrine said.

"He left it for us so that we would stand here like we're doing now," Harry said. "Suddenly having doubts, unsure what to do. But this is only a stub. It doesn't prove he was there. On the contrary, it's pretty striking that not only was he at a football match, in a stadium where fans don't tend to remember each other, but also that, inexplicably, he has saved the ticket."

"The ticket's got a seat number," Katrine said. "Perhaps the people sitting next to him and behind him can remember who was there. Or if the seat was unoccupied. I can search for the seat number. Perhaps I'll find—"

"Do that," Harry said. "But we've been through this before with alleged alibis in the theatre or the cinema. Three or four days pass and people don't remember a thing about their neighbours."

"You're right," Katrine said, resigned.

"Internationals," Bjørn said.

"What about them?" Harry asked, heading for the bathroom, his flies already half undone.

"International matches are subject to FIFA rules and regulations," Bjørn said. "Hooliganism."

"Of course," Harry shouted from behind the bathroom door. "Well done, Bjørn!" Then the door slammed.

"What?" Katrine shouted. "What are you on about?"

"CCTV," Bjørn said. "FIFA requires match organisers to film the spectators in case there are any disturbances. The ruling came in during the wave of hooliganism in the 1990s to help the police find the troublemakers and charge them. They film the stands throughout the match with high-definition cameras so that they can zoom in and identify every single face. And we've got the seating area, row and seat number of where Valentin sat."

"**Didn't** sit!" Katrine shouted. "He's not allowed to be on any bloody footage, all right? Or we'll be back to square one."

"They may of course have deleted the images," Bjørn said. "There wasn't any trouble during the match, and I'm sure the data-archiving directive states how long they're allowed to keep—"

"The data-archiving directive . . ."

"If the images are stored electronically then all they have to do is press Delete for the files to disappear."

"Trying to remove files permanently is like trying to remove dog shit from your trainers. Difficult. How do you think we find child porn on computers pervs have handed in voluntarily, thinking they've got rid of the lot? Believe me, I'll find Valentin Gjertsen if he was at the stadium that evening. What was the assumed time of death for Erlend Vennesla?"

They heard the toilet flush.

"Between seven and half eight," Bjørn said. "In other words, right at the start of the game, after Henriksen equalised. Vennesla must have heard the cheering up in Maridalen. It's not far from Ullevål, is it?"

The bathroom door opened. "Which means he could have made it to the match after the murder in Maridalen," Harry said, doing up the last button. "Once he was in the stadium he could have done something that people around him would remember. Alibi."

"Valentin was **not** at the match," Katrine said. "But if he was I'll watch the sodding video from start to finish and time him if he so much as lifts his bum off the seat. Alibi, my arse."

There was a silence hanging over the large detached houses.

The silence before the storm of Volvos and Audis returning home after working for Norway Ltd, Truls Berntsen thought.

He rang the bell and looked around.

Nicely established garden. Well looked after. You probably had time to do that if you were a retired Chief of Police.

The door opened. He looked older. The same sharp blue eyes, but the skin around his neck was a little looser, his back not quite as straight. He was simply not as impressive as Truls remembered him. Perhaps it was just the faded casual clothes; perhaps that's how it is when your job doesn't keep you on your toes any more.

"Berentzen, Orgkrim." Truls held up his ID in the certain knowledge that if the old boy really read Berntsen he would think that was what he heard as well. Lies with backup. But the Chief nodded without looking. "I think I've seen you before. How can I help you, Berentzen?"

He gave no indication that he was going to invite Truls in. Which was fine by Truls. No one could see them and there was minimal background noise.

"It's about your son, Sondre."

"What about him?"

"We're running an operation to catch Albanian pimps, and for that purpose we've been keeping an eye on movements in Kvadraturen and taking pictures. We've identified a number of cars seen picking up prostitutes and we're intending to bring the owners in for questioning. We'll offer them reduced sentences if we can act on information they give us about the pimps. And one of the cars we've photographed belongs to your son."

The Chief of Police raised his bushy eyebrows. "What's that? Sondre? Impossible."

"I thought so too. But I wanted to confer with you. If you think this must be some misunderstanding, that the woman he picks up is not even a prostitute, we'll shred the photo."

"Sondre is happily married. I brought him up. He knows the difference between right and wrong, believe me."

"Of course, I just wanted to be sure that this is how you see the matter as well."

"My God, why would he buy . . ." The man in front of Truls was grimacing as if he had been chewing a rotten grape. ". . . sex in the street? The danger of infection. The children. No, no, no."

"Sounds like we agree there's no point following this up. Even though we have reason to suspect that the woman is a prostitute, your son may have lent his car to someone else. We don't have a photo of the driver."

"So you don't even have any proof. No, you'd better just forget this one."

"Thank you. We'll do as you say."

The Chief of Police nodded slowly while carefully studying Truls. "Berentzen at Orgkrim, did you say?"

"Correct."

"Thank you, Berentzen. You officers are doing a good job."

Truls beamed. "We do the best we can. Have a good day."

"What was that you said again?" Katrine said, staring at the black screen in front of her. In the world outside the Boiler Room, where the air was thick with evaporating human being, it was afternoon.

"I said there was a good chance the images of the crowds had been deleted because of the data-archiving directive," Bjørn said. "And as you can see, I was right."

"And what did **I** say?"

"You said that files are like dog shit on trainers," Harry said. "Impossible to remove."

"I didn't say **impossible,**" Katrine said.

The four members of the team sat around Katrine's computer. When Harry had rung Ståle and asked him to join them, Ståle had sounded relieved more than anything else.

"I said it was difficult," Katrine said. "But as a rule there's a mirror image of them somewhere. Which a clever computer man will be able to find."

"Or woman?" Ståle suggested.

"Nope," Katrine said. "Women can't park, they don't remember football results and they can't be bothered to learn the fiddly bits on computers. For that you need weird men with band T-shirts and minimal sex lives, and it's been like this ever since the Stone Age."

"So you can't—"

"I keep trying to explain that I'm not a computer specialist, Ståle. My search engines searched the files of the Norwegian Football Association, but all the recordings had been deleted. And I'm afraid that from here on in I'm no use."

"We could have saved ourselves a bit of time if you'd listened to me," Bjørn said. "So what do we do now?"

"I don't mean I'm no use for anything," Katrine said, still addressing Ståle. "You see, I'm equipped with a few relative virtues. Such as feminine charm, unfeminine get-up-and-go and no shame. Which can give you an edge in nerd land. The guy who showed me these search engines also got me in with an Indian IT man, known as Side Cut. And an hour ago I rang Hyderabad and put him on the case."

"And . . . ?"

"And here's the footage," Katrine said, pressing the return button.

The screen lit up.

They stared.

"That's him," Ståle said. "He looks lonely."

Valentin Gjertsen, alias Paul Stavnes, was sitting in front of them with his arms crossed. He was watching the match without any visible interest.

"Goddamn!" Bjørn cursed under his breath.

Harry asked Katrine to fast-forward.

She pressed a button and the crowd around Valentin Gjertsen began to move jerkily as the clock and the counter in the bottom right-hand corner raced forward. Only Valentin Gjersten sat still, like a lifeless statue amid a swarm of life.

"Faster," Harry said.

Katrine clicked again and the same people became even more active, leaning forward and back, getting up, throwing their arms in the air, leaving, returning with a hot dog or a coffee. Then lots of empty blue seats shone back at them.

"One–one, and halftime," Bjørn said.

The stadium filled up again. Even more movement in the crowd. The clock in the corner was running. Heads shaking and obvious frustration. All of a sudden: arms in the air. For a couple of seconds the image seemed to be frozen. Then people jumped up from their seats at once, cheering, bouncing up and down, embracing each other. All except for one.

"Riise penalty in extra time," Bjørn said.

It was over.

People vacated their seats. Valentin sat, unmoving, until everyone had left. Then he got up and was gone.

"Suppose he doesn't like queueing," Bjørn said.

The screen was black once more.

"So," Harry said. "What have we seen?"

"We've seen my patient watching a football match," Ståle said. "I imagine I have to say my ex-patient, providing he doesn't turn up for the next therapy session. Nevertheless, it was apparently an entertaining match for everyone apart from him. As I know his body language, I may say with some certainty that this did not interest him. Which of course prompts the question: why go to a football match then?"

"And he didn't eat, go to the toilet or get up from his seat during the whole game," Katrine said. "Just sat there like a bloody pillar of salt. How spooky's that? As though he knew we would check this recording and didn't want us to miss ten seconds of his damn alibi."

"If only he'd made a call on his mobile," Bjørn said. "Then we could have blown up the picture and perhaps seen the number he dialled. Or clocked the split second he rang and checked it against outgoing calls at the base stations covering Ullevål Stadium and—"

"He didn't ring," Harry said.

"But if—"

"He didn't ring, Bjørn. And whatever Valentin Gjertsen's motive for watching the match at Ullevål, it's a fact that he was sitting there when Erlend Vennesla was murdered in Maridalen. And the other fact is . . ." Harry gazed above their heads, at the bare white-brick wall. ". . . we're back to square one."

34

Aurora sat on the swing looking at the sun filtering through the leaves of the pear trees. At least, Dad stubbornly maintained they were pear trees, but no one had ever seen any pears on them. Aurora was twelve years old and a bit too big for a swing and a bit too big to believe everything her dad told her.

She had come home from school, done her homework and gone into the garden while Mum went to the shop. Dad wouldn't be home for dinner; he'd started working long days again. Even though he'd promised her and Mum that now he would come home like other dads, he wouldn't do police work in the evenings, just do his psychotherapy in his consulting room and then come home. But now he was working for the police after all. Neither Mum nor Dad had wanted to tell her exactly what it was he was doing.

She found the song she was looking for on her iPod, Rihanna singing that if he wanted her he should come and take a walk with her. Aurora stretched out her long legs to get more speed. The legs that had become so long she had to fold them underneath her or hold them up high so they wouldn't drag along the ground under the swing. She would soon be as tall as her mother. She leaned her head back, felt the weight of her long, thick hair hanging from her scalp. So nice. Closed her eyes to the sun above the trees and the swing ropes, heard Rihanna singing, heard the low creak of the branch whenever the swing was at the lowest point. Heard another sound as well, the gate opening and footsteps on the gravel path.

"Mummy," she called, not wanting to open her eyes, not wanting to move her face away from the sun which was so wonderfully hot. But she didn't receive an answer and remembered she hadn't heard a car pull up, hadn't heard the hectic growl of her mother's little blue dog kennel.

She dragged her heels along the ground, slowing the swing down until it was stationary, her eyes still closed, not wanting to abandon the wonderful bubble of music, sun and daydreams.

She felt a shadow fall across her and at once it was cold, like when a cloud passes in front of the sun on a chilly day. She opened her eyes and saw a figure standing over her, no more than a silhouette against the sky, with a halo round the head where the sun had been. And for a moment she blinked, confused by the thought that had struck her.

That Jesus was back. That he was standing here, now. And it meant that Mum and Dad were wrong. God really did exist, and there was forgiveness for all our sins.

"Hello, little girl," the voice said. "What's your name?"

Jesus could speak Norwegian if push came to shove.

"Aurora," she said, squeezing one eye shut to see his face better. No beard or long hair, anyway.

"Is your father at home?"

"He's at work."

"I see. So you're on your own, are you, Aurora?"

Aurora was about to answer. But something stopped her; quite what, she didn't know.

"Who are you?" she said instead.

"Someone who needs to talk to your father. But you and I can talk. Since we're alone, I mean. Can't we?"

Aurora didn't answer.

"What kind of music are you listening to?" the man asked, pointing to her iPod.

"Rihanna," Aurora said, pushing the swing back. Not just to get out of the man's shadow but to see him better.

"Oh yes," the man said. "I've got lots of her CDs at home. Would you like to borrow some?"

"I listen to the songs I haven't got on Spotify," Aurora said, establishing that the man looked quite normal, at least there wasn't anything particularly Jesus-like about him.

"Oh yes, Spotify," the man said, crouching down, not just to be at her height but lower. It felt better. "You can listen to all the music you like then."

"Almost," Aurora said. "But I've got the free Spotify, and there are lots of ads between the songs."

"And you don't like that?"

"I don't like the talking. It messes up the atmosphere."

"Did you know there are records where they talk and they're the best songs?"

"No," Aurora said, tilting her head, wondering why the man spoke so softly, it didn't sound like it was his usual voice. It was the same voice that Emilie, her friend, used when she was asking Aurora for a favour, such as to borrow her favourite clothes, but Aurora didn't like lending them because it was such a messy arrangement. You never knew where your clothes were.

"You should listen to Pink Floyd."

"Who's that?"

The man looked round. "We can go inside to the computer and I'll show you. While we're waiting for your dad."

"You can spell it for me. I'll remember."

"Best to show you. Then I can have a glass of water at the same time."

Aurora looked at him. Now that he was sitting below her she had the sun in her face again, but it didn't warm her any more. Strange. She leaned back on the swing. The man smiled. She saw something glint between his teeth. As if the tip of his tongue was there and gone again.

"Come on," he said, standing up. He held one of the ropes, at head height.

Aurora slipped off the swing and darted under his arm. Started walking towards the house. She heard his footsteps behind her. The voice.

"You'll like it, Aurora. I promise."

Gentle, like a priest administering confirmation.

That was Dad's expression. Perhaps he was Jesus after all? But Jesus or not, she didn't want him in the house. Still, she kept walking. What would she say to Dad? That she had stopped someone he knew coming in for a glass of water? No, she couldn't do that. She walked more slowly to give herself time to think, to find an excuse for not letting him in. But she couldn't find one. And because she slowed down he came closer, and she could hear his breathing. Heavy, as though the few steps he had walked from the swing had made him breathless. And there was a weird smell coming from his mouth that reminded her of nail varnish remover.

Five paces to the doorsteps. An excuse. Two paces. The doorsteps. Come on. No. They were at the door.

Aurora swallowed. "I think it's locked," she said. "We'll have to wait outside."

"Oh?" the man said, gazing round from the top step, as though searching for Dad somewhere behind the hedges. Or neighbours. She felt the heat from his arm as it stretched across her shoulder, grabbed the door handle and pushed it down. It opened.

"Well, hello," he said, and he was breathing faster now. And there was a light quiver to his voice. "We were lucky there."

Aurora faced the doorway. Stared into the darkened hall. Just a glass of water. And this music with the talking that didn't have any interest for her. In the distance there was the sound of a lawnmower. Angry, aggressive, insistent. She stepped inside.

"I have to . . ." she began, came to an abrupt halt, and at that moment felt his hand on her shoulder, as though he had crossed a line. Felt the heat of his hand where her shirt stopped and her skin started. Felt her little heart pounding. Heard another lawnmower. Which wasn't a lawnmower but an excitedly purring little engine.

"Mummy!" Aurora shouted and squirmed out of the man's grip, dived past him, jumped down all four steps, landed in the gravel and raced off. Shouting over her shoulder:

"I have to help with the shopping."

She ran to the gate, listened for footsteps coming after her, but the crunch of her trainers on the gravel was almost deafening. Then she was at the gate, tearing it open and watching her mother get out of the little blue car in front of the garage.

"Hi, sweetheart," Mum said, looking at her with a quizzical smile. "That was quite a turn of speed."

"There's someone here asking for Dad," Aurora said, realising the gravel path was longer than she thought, she was out of breath anyway. "He's on the steps."

"Oh?" Mum said, passing her one of the bags from the rear seat, slamming the door and walking with her daughter through the gate.

No one was on the steps, but the front door was still open.

"Has he gone inside?" Mum asked.

"Don't know," Aurora said.

They went into the house, but Aurora stayed in

the hallway, close to the open door while her mother continued past the living room towards the kitchen.

"Hello?" she heard her mother call. "Hello?"

Then she was back in the hall, without the shopping bags.

"There's no one here, Aurora."

"But he was here. I promise you!"

Mum looked at her in surprise and laughed. "Of course he was, sweetheart. Why wouldn't I believe you?"

Aurora didn't answer. Didn't know what to say. How could she explain that it might have been Jesus? Or the Holy Spirit. At any rate, someone not everyone could see.

"He'll turn up again if it was important," Mum said, going back to the kitchen.

Aurora stood in the hallway. That sweet, stale smell, it was still there.

35

"Tell me, have you got a life?"

Arnold Folkestad looked up from his papers. Catching sight of the tall guy leaning against the door frame, he smiled.

"No, I haven't either, Harry."

"It's after nine and you're still here."

Arnold chuckled and stacked his papers together. "I'm on my way home anyway. You've just come and how long are you going to stay?"

"Not long." Harry took one long stride to the spindle-back chair and sat down. "And I've got a woman I can be with at weekends."

"Oh yes? I've got an ex-wife I can **avoid** at weekends."

"Have you? I didn't know that."

"Ex-cohabitant anyway."

"Coffee? What happened?"

"Run out of coffee. One of us had the terrible idea of thinking a marriage proposal was the next step. Things went downhill from there. I called it off after all the invitations had been sent out, and so she left. Couldn't live with it, she said. Best thing that's ever happened to me, Harry."

"Mm." Harry used his thumb and middle finger to clear his eyes.

Arnold stood up and took his jacket from the hook on the wall. "Slow going in the Boiler Room?"

"Well, we had a setback today. Valentin Gjertsen . . ."

"Yes?"

"We think he's the Saw Man. But he's not the one who's been murdering all the officers."

"Are you sure?"

"At least, not on his own."

"Could there be several?"

"Katrine's suggestion. But the fact is that in ninety-eight point six per cent of sexually motivated murders there's only one perpetrator."

"So . . ."

"She wouldn't give in. Pointed out that in all likelihood there were two men involved in the murder of the girl at Tryvann."

"Is that where the body was found scattered over several kilometres?"

"Yep. She thought Valentin might have been working with someone. To confuse the police."

"Taking turns to kill and thereby securing an alibi?"

"Yes. And in fact that's been done before. Two ex-cons, violent criminals, in Michigan, got together sometime in the sixties. They made it look like classic serial killings by setting a pattern they followed every time. The murders were copies. Like crimes both of them had committed before. They each had their own sick predilections and ended up attracting the attention of the FBI. But when first one and then the other had watertight alibis for several of the murders they were, naturally enough, eliminated from inquiries."

"Smart. So why don't you think something similar happened here?"

"Ninety-eight—"

"—point six per cent. Isn't that thinking a bit rigid?"

"It was thanks to your percentage of key witnesses dying of unnatural causes that I found out Asayev didn't die of natural ones."

"But you still haven't done anything about that case?"

"No. But drop that one now, Arnold. This one's more urgent." Harry rested his head against the wall behind him. Closed his eyes. "We think along the same lines, you and I, and I'm bloody knackered. So I came straight here to ask you to help me to think."

"Me?"

"We're back to square one, Arnold. And your brain's got a couple of neurons mine obviously hasn't."

Folkestad took off his jacket again, hung it neatly across the back of the chair and sat down.

"Harry?"

"Yes?"

"You have no idea how good this feels."

Harry pulled a wry smile. "Good. Motive."

"Motive. Yes, that's square one."

"That's where we are. What could this murderer's motive be?"

"I'll go and see if I can rustle up some coffee after all, Harry."

Harry talked his way through the first cup and was well down the second before Arnold spoke up.

"I think the murder of René Kalsnes is important because it's an exception, because it doesn't fit in. That is to say, it does and it doesn't. It doesn't fit in with the original murders, the sex, sadism and use of knives. It fits in with the police murders because of the violence to the head and face with a blunt object."

"Go on," Harry said, putting down the cup.

"I remember the Kalsnes murder well," Arnold said. "I was in San Francisco on a course when it happened, staying at a hotel where everyone had the **Gayzette** delivered to the door."

"The gay newspaper?"

"They ran the story of this murder in little Norway on the front page, calling it yet another hate crime against a homosexual man. The interesting bit was that none of the Norwegian papers I read later carried any suggestion of a hate crime. I wondered how this American paper could draw such a categorical and premature conclusion, so I read the whole article. The journalist wrote that the murder had all the classic features: the homosexual who exhibits his leanings so provocatively is picked up, driven to some out-of-the-way place where he is subjected to ritual, frenzied violence. The murderer has a gun, but it's not enough to shoot Kalsnes straight away, his face has to be obliterated first. He has to give vent to his homophobia by smashing the far too attractive, effeminate face, doesn't he? It's premeditated, it's planned and it's a homo murder—that was the journalist's conclusion. And do you know what, Harry? I don't think it's an unreasonable conclusion."

"Mm. If it's a 'homo murder,' as you call it, it definitely doesn't fit in. There's nothing to suggest that any of the other murder victims were gay, neither the original ones nor the officers."

"Maybe not. But there is something interesting here. You said the Kalsnes case was the only one that linked all the murdered policemen, didn't you?"

"With such a small circle of detectives it's often the same people, Arnold, so that doesn't make it much of a coincidence."

"Nevertheless, I have a hunch it's important."

"You've got your head in the clouds now, Arnold."

The red-bearded man sat up with an injured expression. "Did I say something wrong?"

" 'I have a hunch'? I'll tell you when you've reached the point when your hunches are an argument."

"Because not many of us reach that point?"

"Exactly. Go on, but keep your feet on the ground, OK?"

"OK. But might I perhaps be allowed to say that I have a hunch you agree with me?"

"Maybe."

"Then I'll take a punt and suggest you employ all of your resources to find out who killed the homosexual officer. The worst that can happen is that you solve one case. The best is that you solve all the police murders as well."

"Mm." Harry finished his coffee and got up. "Thank you, Arnold."

"Thank **you.** Unlicensed policemen like me are happy just to be listened to, you know. Speaking of which, I met Silje Gravseng in reception earlier today. She was handing in her pass. She was . . . something."

"Student rep."

"Yes. Whatever, she asked after you. I didn't say anything. Then she said you were a fake. Your boss had told her it wasn't true that you had a hundred per cent clear-up rate. Gusto Hanssen, she said. Is that true?"

"Mm. Sort of."

"Sort of? What does that mean?"

"I investigated the case and never arrested anyone. How did she seem?"

Arnold Folkestad pinched one eye shut and looked at Harry as if he were aiming a weapon at him, searching his face.

"Who knows. She's an odd girl, Silje Gravseng. She invited me to do some shooting practice in Økern. Just like that, out of the blue."

"Mm. And what did you answer?"

"I blamed my poor eyesight and the shakes. I said, and it's true, I would have to have the target half a metre in front of me to be sure of hitting anything. She accepted that, but afterwards I wondered why she would go to a firing range when she no longer needed to pass the police firearms test."

"Well," Harry said, "sometimes people just like shooting for shooting's sake."

"It's up to them," Arnold said, getting up. "But she looked good, it has to be said."

Harry watched his colleague hobble out of the door. Mused, then found the number for the Police Chief in Nedre Eiker. Afterwards he sat chewing over what she'd said. It was true that Bertil Nilsen had not been part of the investigation into René Kalsnes's death in the neighbouring municipality of Drammen. On the other hand, he had been on duty when they had received the call telling them there was a car in the river near Eikersaga and had turned out when it was unclear whose jurisdiction it was. She also told him the Drammen police and Kripos had read them the riot act because Nilsen had churned up the soft ground where they might otherwise have found good tyre tracks. "So you might say he had an indirect effect on the investigation."

It was almost ten o'clock, and the sun had long gone down behind the green hill to the west when Ståle Aune parked his car in the garage and walked up the gravel path to his house. He noticed there was no light on in the kitchen or the living room. Nothing unusual about that. She often went to bed early.

He could feel the weight of his body on his knee joints. Goodness, how tired he was. It had been a long day, but he had hoped she would still be up.

Then they could have had a chat. And he would have calmed down. He had done as Harry had said and contacted a colleague. Talked about the knife attack. About how he had been sure he would die. He had done all that, now it was time to sleep. To be **allowed** to sleep.

He unlocked the door. Saw Aurora's jacket hanging on the peg. Another new one. Heavens, how that child was growing. He kicked off his shoes. Straightened up and listened to the silence in the house. He couldn't quite put his finger on what it was, but it seemed to him the house was quieter than usual. There was a sound missing, one which he obviously wasn't aware of when it was there.

He went upstairs. Every step was a little slower, like an overloaded scooter going uphill. He would have to start getting fit, take off ten kilos, or thereabouts. It was good for your sleep, good for your well-being, good for long days at work, for your life expectancy, for your sex life, for your self-esteem, in a word, good. But he was damned if he was going to do it.

He trudged past Aurora's bedroom.

Stopped, hesitated. Went back. Opened the door.

Just wanted to see her asleep, as he always used to. Soon it wouldn't be so natural to do that any more, he could already feel she was more aware of certain things, private things. It wasn't that she minded being naked when he was around, but she didn't strut about quite so nonchalantly. And when he noticed it had stopped being natural for her, it also stopped being natural for him. But he still wanted to do this on the QT, watch his daughter sleeping peacefully, safe, protected from all the things he had experienced out there today.

But he didn't. He would see her tomorrow at breakfast anyway.

He sighed, closed the door and went into the bathroom. Undressed and took his clothes into their bedroom, hung them over a chair and was about to crawl into bed when he was struck by it again. The silence. What was it that was missing? The hum of a fridge? The whisper of a ventilation hatch, which they usually left open?

He couldn't be bothered to give it any further thought and snuggled down under the duvet. Saw Ingrid's hair sticking up. He wanted to touch her, just stroke her hair, down her back, feel that she was **there.** But she was such a light sleeper and hated being woken up, he knew that. He was about to close his eyes, then changed his mind.

"Ingrid?"

No answer.

"Ingrid?"

Silence.

It could wait. He closed his eyes again.

"Yes?" He noticed that she had turned over.

"Nothing," he mumbled. "Just . . . this case . . ."

"Say you don't want it."

"Someone has to do it." It sounded like the cliché it was.

"They won't find anyone better than you."

Ståle opened his eyes. Looked at her, caressed her hot, round cheek. Now and then—no, more than now and then—nothing in existence was better than her.

Ståle Aune closed his eyes. And now it came. Sleep. The loss of consciousness. The **real** nightmares.

36

The morning sun glinted off the rooftops still wet after the short, intense burst of rain.

Mikael Bellman pressed the doorbell and looked around.

Well-tended garden. That was probably how you made time pass when you were old.

The door opened.

"Mikael! How nice."

He looked older. The same sharp, blue eyes, but, well, older.

"Come in."

Mikael wiped his wet shoes on the doormat and stepped inside. There was a smell in the house he could remember from his childhood, but which he was unable to isolate and identify.

They sat down in the living room.

"You're alone," Mikael said.

"Wife's with the eldest. They needed a hand from Grandma and she's a soft touch." He beamed. "Actually, I thought I should get in contact with you. Now, the council hasn't reached a final decision, but we both know what they want, so it's probably wise to talk about how we do this. The division of labour and so on, I mean."

"Yes," Mikael said. "Perhaps you could brew up some coffee?"

"Sorry?" The bushy eyebrows were raised high up on the old man's forehead.

"If we're going to be sitting here for a while, a cup would be nice?"

The man studied Mikael. "Yes, yes, of course. Come on, we can sit in the kitchen."

Mikael followed him. Passed a forest of family photographs on the table and cabinet. They reminded him of the barricades on the D-Day beaches, a futile bulwark against external attacks.

The kitchen was a half-hearted nod to modernity, resembling a compromise between a daughter-in-law's insistence on the minimum you can demand of a kitchen and the owners' basic desire to change nothing more than a broken fridge.

While the old man took a packet of coffee from a high-up cabinet with a frosted-glass door, pulled off the elastic and measured it with a yellow spoon, Mikael Bellman sat down, put his recording device on the table and pressed play. Truls's voice sounded metallic and thin: "Even though we have reason to suspect that the woman is a prostitute, your son may have lent his car to someone else. We don't have a photo of the driver."

The ex-Chief of Police's voice sounded more distant, but there was no background noise, so the words were easy to hear: "So you don't even have any proof. No, you'd better just forget this one."

Mikael saw the coffee spill from the spoon as the old man recoiled and froze, as though someone had thrust a gun barrel in his back.

Truls's voice: "Thank you. We'll do as you say."

"Berentzen at Orgkrim, did you say?"

"Correct."

"Thank you, Berentzen. You officers are doing a good job."

Mikael pressed stop.

The ex-Chief turned slowly. His face was pale. Ashen, Mikael Bellman thought. An appropriate colour for someone declared dead. The man's mouth twitched a few times.

"What you're trying to say," Mikael Bellman said, "is 'What's this?' And the answer is this is the ex-Chief of Police putting pressure on a public servant to prevent his son being subjected to the same investigation and legal action as any other citizen of this country."

The old man's voice sounded like a desert wind. "He wasn't even there. I spoke to Sondre. His car has been in the garage since January because of a fire in the engine. He **can't** have been there."

"Does that sting a little?" Mikael said. "You didn't even need to save your son, and now the press and the council are going to hear how you tried to corrupt a policeman."

"There is no photo of the car and this prostitute, is there?"

"Not now, anyway. You ordered it to be shredded. And who knows, perhaps it was taken before January?" Mikael smiled. He didn't want to, but he couldn't help himself.

The colour returned to the man's cheeks along with the bass tone in his voice. "You don't surely imagine you're going to get away with this, do you, Bellman?"

"I don't know. I only know that the council won't want to have a demonstrably corrupt man as their Chief of Police."

"What do you want, Bellman?"

"You'd be better off asking yourself what **you** want. To live a life of peace and quiet with a reputation as a good, honest policeman? Yes? Then you'll see we're not very different, because that's exactly what I want. I want to perform my job as Chief of Police in peace and quiet, I want to solve the police murders without the bloody Councillor for Social Affairs interfering, and afterwards I want to enjoy a reputation as a good policeman. So how do we both achieve this?"

Bellman waited until he was sure the old man had collected himself sufficiently to be able to follow all the details.

"I want you to tell the council that you've immersed yourself in the case and you're so impressed by the professional manner in which it's being handled that you can't see any point in stepping in and taking over. Quite the contrary, you think it would reduce the chances of a swift resolution. Also you have to question the Social Affairs Councillor's assessment of this case. She should know that police work has to be methodical and avoid the pitfalls of short-term thinking, and it appears she has reacted in a knee-jerk fashion. We have all been under pressure as a result of this case, but it is a requirement of all political and professional leaders that they don't lose their heads in situations where they most need them. You therefore insist that the incumbent Chief of Police continue his work without any interference, as that strategy, from your perspective, has the greatest chance of success and accordingly you withdraw your candidacy."

Bellman took an envelope from his inside pocket and pushed it across the table.

"That in brief is what is written in this personal letter to the chair of the City Council. All you have to do is sign it and send it. As you can see, it even has a stamp. By the way, you can have this recording for keeps when I've received a satisfactory response from the council regarding their decision." Bellman nodded to the kettle. "How's it doing? Any chance of that coffee?"

Harry took a swig of coffee and surveyed his town.

The Police HQ canteen was on the top floor and had a view of Ekeberg, the fjord and the new part of town that was emerging in Bjørvika. First, though, he looked for the old landmarks. How often had he sat here in his lunch break trying to see cases from other angles, with other eyes, with new and different perspectives, while the urge for a cigarette and alcohol tore at him and he told himself he wasn't allowed to go onto the terrace for a cigarette until he had at least one new testable hypothesis?

He had yearned for that, he thought.

A hypothesis. One which wasn't just a figment of the imagination but anchored in something that could be tested, responded to.

He raised his coffee cup. Put it down again. No more swigs until his brain had found something. A motive. They had been banging their heads against the wall for so long that perhaps it was time to start somewhere else. Somewhere where there was light.

A chair scraped. Harry looked up. Bjørn Holm. He put his coffee down on the table without spilling it, removed his Rasta hat and rumpled his red hair. Harry watched him absent-mindedly. Did he do this to air his scalp? Or to avoid the familiar hair-plastered-to-scalp look his generation feared, but which Oleg appeared to like? Fringe stuck to a sweaty forehead above a pair of horn-rimmed glasses. The well-read nerd, the webwanker, the self-conscious urbanite who embraced the loser image, the fake outsider role. Was that what he looked like, the man they were after? Or was he a red-cheeked country boy in the big city with light blue jeans, practical shoes, a haircut from the most convenient hairdresser's, the type who cleaned the stairs when it was his turn, was polite and helpful and no one had a bad word to say about him? Non-testable hypotheses. No swig of coffee.

"Well?" Bjørn said, treating himself to a huge swig.

"Well . . ." Harry said. He had never asked Bjørn why a country boy would walk around wearing a reggae hat and not a Stetson. "I think we should take a closer look at René Kalsnes. And forget the motive, just look at the forensic facts. We have the bullet that he was killed with. Nine mil. The world's most common calibre. Who would use it?"

"Everyone. Absolutely everyone. Even we would."

"Mm. Did you know that in peacetime policemen are responsible for four per cent of all murders worldwide? In the Third World the figure is nine per cent. And that makes us the world's most lethal occupational group."

"Wow," Bjørn said.

"He's kidding," Katrine said. She pulled up a chair and placed a large cup of steaming tea on the table in front of her. "When people use statistics, in seventy-two per cent of cases, they've made them up on the spur of the moment."

Harry laughed.

"Is that funny?" Bjørn asked.

"It's a joke," Harry said.

"How?" Bjørn said.

"Ask her."

Bjørn looked at Katrine. She smiled as she stirred her tea.

"I don't get it!" Bjørn said, glaring at Harry.

"It proves the point. She made the seventy-two per cent up herself, didn't she?"

Bjørn shook his head, bemused.

"Like a paradox," Harry said. "Like the Greek who says all Greeks lie."

"But it doesn't mean it isn't true," Katrine said.

"The seventy-two per cent, that is. So you think the murderer is a policeman, do you, Harry?"

"I didn't say that," Harry smiled, folding his hands behind his head. "I just said—"

He stopped. Felt his hair standing on end. The good old hairs on the back of the neck. The hypothesis. He gazed down into his cup. He really felt like a swig now.

"Police," he repeated, looked up and saw the other two staring at him. "René Kalsnes was killed by a policeman."

"What?" Katrine said.

"There's our hypothesis. The bullet was a nine mil, used in Heckler & Koch service pistols. A police baton was found not far from the crime scene. It's also the only one of the original murders that has a common link with each of the police murders. Their faces were smashed in. Most of the original murders were sexually motivated, but this is a hate crime. Why do people hate?"

"Now you're back to motive, Harry," Bjørn protested.

"Quickly, why?"

"Jealousy," Katrine said. "Revenge for being humiliated, rejected, jilted, ridiculed, having your wife, child, brother, sister, future prospects, pride taken from you—"

"Stop right there," Harry said. "Our hypothesis is that the murderer has some connection with the police. And with that as the basis we have to dig up the Kalsnes case again and find out who killed him."

"Fine," Katrine said. "But even if there are a couple of clues in it, it's still unclear to me why it's suddenly so obvious we're looking for a policeman."

"If no one can give me a better hypothesis, five, four . . ." Harry sent both of them a questioning stare.

Bjørn groaned. "Let's not go there, Harry."

"What?"

"If the rest of the force hears we're conducting an investigation into our own—"

"We'll have to put up with it," Harry said. "Right now we're at rock bottom and we have to start somewhere. At worst we solve a cold case. At best we find—"

Katrine finished the sentence for him: "—the person who killed Beate."

Bjørn chewed his lower lip. Then he shrugged and nodded to say he was in.

"Good," Harry said. "Katrine, you check the registers of guns that have been reported missing or stolen and check if René had contact with anyone in the police. Bjørn, you go through the forensic evidence in the light of our hypothesis, see if it turns up anything new."

Bjørn and Katrine got to their feet.

Harry watched them walk through the canteen to the door, saw a table of officers working for the larger investigative unit and the looks they exchanged. Someone said something and they burst out laughing.

Harry closed his eyes and listened to his senses. Searching. What could it be, what was it that had happened? He asked himself the same question

Katrine had asked: why was it so obvious that it was a policeman they were after? Because there was something. He concentrated, blocked everything out, knowing it was like a dream, he had to hurry before it went. Slowly he sank inside himself, sank like a deep-sea diver without a torch, groping in the darkness of his subconscious. Caught something, could feel it. Something to do with Katrine's meta-joke. Meta. Commenting on itself. Proving a point. Was the murderer proving a point? It slipped through his fingers, and at that moment he was lifted up by his own buoyancy, back to the light. He opened his eyes and sound returned. The clatter of plates, chatting, laughing. Shit, shit, shit. He had almost had it, but now it was too late. He only knew the joke was telling him something, had a catalytic effect on something deep inside him. Which he wasn't able to grasp now, but which he just hoped would float to the surface of its own accord. Nevertheless, the reaction had given them something, a direction, a starting point. A testable hypothesis. Harry took a deep swig of coffee, got up and walked towards the terrace to have a cigarette.

Bjørn Holm was handed two plastic boxes across the Evidence Room counter and signed the enclosed inventory.

He took the boxes with him to Krimteknisk in Bryn, and started on the box from the original murder.

The first thing that made him wonder was the bullet found in René's head. It was fairly misshapen after passing through flesh, cartilage and bone, which after all are fairly soft materials. The second was that the bullet hadn't gone green after years in this box. Age didn't leave particularly noticeable marks on lead, but he thought this bullet looked conspicuously new.

He flicked through the crime-scene photos of the dead man. Stopped at a close-up showing the side of his face with the entry wound, where a broken cheekbone protruded. There was a black stain on the shiny white bone. He took out his magnifying glass. It looked like a cavity, like you get in a tooth, but you don't get black holes in cheekbones. An oil stain from the smashed car? A bit of rotten leaf or caked mud from the river? He took out the autopsy report.

Searched until he found it.

A small amount of black paint stuck to the maxillaris. Origin unknown.

Paint on the cheek. Pathologists usually wrote no more than they could account for, preferably a little less.

Bjørn flicked through the photos until he found the car. Red. So not car varnish.

Bjørn shouted from where he was sitting. "Kim Erik!"

Six seconds later a head appeared in the doorway. "Did you call?"

"Yes. You were in the forensics team for the Mittet murder in Drammen, weren't you? Did you find any black paint?"

"Paint?"

"Something that might come off a blunt instrument if you hit out like this . . ." Bjørn demonstrated by beating his fist up and down as if playing rock-paper-scissors. "The skin tears, the cheekbone cracks and sticks out, but you keep hitting the jagged end of the bone with the blunt instrument, removing paint from whatever it is you're holding."

"No."

"OK. Thank you."

Bjørn Holm took the lid off the second box, the one with the Mittet case material, but noticed the young forensics officer was still standing in the doorway.

"Yes?" Bjørn said without looking up.

"It was navy blue."

"What was?"

"The paint. And it wasn't the cheekbone. It was the jawbone, the fracture. We analysed it. It's pretty standard paint, used on iron tools. Sticks well and prevents rust."

"Any suggestions for what kind of tool it might have been?"

Bjørn could see Kim Erik veritably swelling in the doorway. He had personally trained him, and now the master was asking the apprentice if he had "any suggestions."

"Impossible to say. It can be used on anything."

"OK, that's all."

"But I've got a suggestion."

Bjørn could see his colleague was bursting to tell him. He was going to go a long way.

"Out with it."

"Carjack. All cars are supplied with a jack, but there wasn't a jack in the boot."

Bjørn nodded. Hardly had the heart to say it. "The car was a VW Sharan, 2010 model, Kim Erik. If you check it out you'll find it's one of the few cars that doesn't come with a jack."

"Oh." The young man's face crumpled like a punctured beach ball.

"Thanks for your help, though, Kim Erik."

He would go a long way all right. But in a few years of course.

Bjørn systematically went through the Mittet box.

There was another thing that set his mind whirring.

He put the lid back on and walked to the office at the end of the corridor. Knocked at the open door. Blinked first, a little confused, at the polished head, before realising who it was sitting there: Roar Midtstuen, the oldest and most experienced forensics officer of them all. Once upon a time Midtstuen had struggled with the idea of working for a boss who was not only younger but also a woman. But the situation had eased as he'd seen that Beate Lønn was one of the best things that had ever happened to their department.

He had just returned to work after being off sick for some months, ever since his daughter had been killed in a collision. She was returning from top-rope climbing a mountain face to the east of Oslo. Her bike had been found in a ditch. The driver still hadn't been found.

"How do, Midtstuen."

"How do, Holm." Midtstuen spun round in the swivel chair, shrugged, smiled and tried to exude energy, but it wasn't there. Bjørn had barely recognised the bloated face when he'd reappeared for work. Apparently it was a normal side effect of antidepressants.

"Have police batons always been black?"

As forensics officers, they were used to somewhat bizarre questions about detail, so Midtstuen didn't even raise an eyebrow.

"They've definitely been dark." Midtstuen had grown up in Østre Toten, like Holm, but it was only when the two of them spoke that their childhood dialect resurfaced. "But there was a period in the nineties when they were blue, I seem to remember. Bloody irritating that is."

"What is?"

"That we're always changing the colour, that we can't stick to one. First of all, patrol cars are black and white, then they're white with red-and-blue stripes, and now they're going to be white with black-and-yellow stripes. This fiddling about just weakens the brand. Like the Drammen cordon tape."

"What cordon tape?"

"Kim Erik was at the Mittet crime scene and found bits of police tape and thought it had to be from the old murder. He . . . we were both on the case of course, but I always forget the name of that homo . . ."

"René Kalsnes."

"But young folk like Kim Erik don't remember that

police tape at that time was light blue and white," Midtstuen hastened to add as though afraid he'd put his foot in it: "But Kim Erik is going to be good."

"I reckon so, too."

"Good." Midtstuen's jaw muscles churned as he chewed. "Then we agree."

Bjørn rang Katrine as soon as he was back in his office, asked her to drop by the police station, on the first floor, scrape a bit of paint off one of their batons and send it to Bryn with a message.

Afterwards he sat thinking that he had automatically gone to the office at the end of the corridor, where he had always gone for advice. He had been so absorbed in his work that he had simply forgotten she wasn't there any longer. That the office had been taken over by Roar Midtstuen. And for a brief instant he thought he could understand Midtstuen, how the loss of another person could suck the marrow out of you and make it impossible to get anything done, make it meaningless even to get out of bed. He dismissed the thought. Dismissed the sight of Midtstuen's round, bloated face. Because they had something here, he could feel it.

Harry, Katrine and Bjørn sat on the roof of the Opera House looking across to the islands of Hovedøya and Gresholmen.

It had been Harry's suggestion. He thought they needed fresh air. It was a warm, cloudy evening, the tourists had decamped ages ago, and they had the whole of the marble roof to themselves, even where it sloped down into Oslo Fjord, which glittered with lights from Ekeberg Ridge, Havnelageret and the Denmark ferry docked at Vippetangen.

"I've gone through all the police murders again," Bjørn said. "And tiny bits of paint were found on Vennesla and Nilsen as well as on Mittet. It's standard paint used everywhere, also on police batons."

"Well done, Bjørn," Harry said.

"And then there were the remains of the cordon tape they found at the Mittet crime scene. It couldn't have been from the investigation of the Kalsnes murder. They didn't use that kind of tape then."

"It was tape from the day before," Harry said. "The murderer rang Mittet, told him to come to what Mittet thinks is a police murder committed at the old crime scene. So when Mittet gets there and sees the police tape he doesn't smell a rat. Perhaps the murderer is even wearing his uniform."

"Shit," Katrine said. "I've spent the whole day cross-checking Kalsnes with police employees and didn't find a thing. But I can see we're on to something here."

Excited, she looked at Harry, who was lighting a cigarette.

"So what do we do now?" Bjørn asked.

"Now," Harry said, "we call in service pistols to see if they match our bullet."

"Which ones?"

"All of them."

They eyed Harry in silence.

"What do you mean by 'all'?" Katrine asked.

"All the service pistols in the police force. First in Oslo, then in Østland and, if necessary, in the whole country."

Another silence as a gull screamed shrilly in the darkness above them.

"You're kidding?" Bjørn tested.

The cigarette bobbed up and down between Harry's lips as he answered. "Nope."

"It ain't feasible. Forget it," Bjørn said. "People think it takes five minutes to run a ballistics test because it looks like that on **CSI.** Even officers think that. The fact is that to check one gun is almost a day's work. All of them? In Oslo alone that's . . . how many officers are there?"

"One thousand eight hundred and seventy-two," Katrine said.

They gawped at her.

She shrugged. "Read it in the annual report for Oslo Police District."

They were still gawping at her.

"The TV doesn't work, and I couldn't sleep, OK?"

"Anyway," Bjørn said, "we haven't got the resources. It can't be done."

"The crucial thing is what you said just now about even officers thinking it takes five minutes," Harry said, blowing cigarette smoke into the night sky.

"Oh?"

"It's important they think an operation like this

can be done. What happens when the murderer finds out his gun has to be checked?"

"You crafty devil," Katrine said.

"Eh?" Bjørn said.

"He'll report his gun missing or stolen as quick as a flash," Katrine said.

"And that's where we start looking," Harry said. "But maybe he's one step ahead, so we'll start by making a list of all the service pistols that have been reported missing since the murder of Kalsnes."

"One problem," Katrine said.

"Yup," Harry answered. "Will the Chief of Police agree to put out an order which in practice points a finger of suspicion at all his officers? He'll imagine the papers having a field day." Harry drew a rectangle in the air with his thumb and forefinger: "POLICE CHIEF SUSPECTS OWN OFFICERS. POLICE TOP BRASS LOSING IT."

"Doesn't sound very likely," Katrine said.

"Well," Harry said, "say what you like about Bellman, but he's not stupid and he knows which side his bread is buttered. If we can make a case for the murderer being a policeman and sooner or later we catch him, whether Bellman's with us or not, he knows it will look really bad if the Chief of Police is seen to have delayed the whole investigation out of sheer cowardice. So what we have to explain to him is that investigating his own officers shows the world that the police will leave no stone unturned in their efforts, whatever corruption it reveals. It shows courage, leadership, mental agility, all good things."

"And you reckon **you** can persuade him with that?" Katrine snorted. "If my memory serves me correctly, Harry Hole is pretty high up his hate list."

Harry shook his head. "I've put Gunnar Hagen on the case."

"And when will it happen?" Bjørn asked.

"It's happening as we speak," Harry said, looking at the cigarette. It was almost down to the filter already. He felt an urge to throw it away, watch the sparks arcing into the darkness as it bounced down the shimmering marble slope. Until it landed in the black water and was immediately extinguished. What was stopping him? The thought that he was polluting the town or witnesses' disapproval of his polluting the town? The act itself or the punishment? The Russian he had killed in Come As You Are was a simple matter; it had been self-defence: the Russian or him. But the so-called unsolved murder of Gusto Hanssen, that had been a choice. And yet, among all the ghosts that regularly haunted him, he had never seen the young man with the girlish good looks and the vampire teeth. An unsolved case, bollocks.

Harry flicked the cigarette. Glowing tobacco swept into the darkness and was gone.

37

The morning light filtered through the blinds over the surprisingly small windows in Oslo City Hall where the chairman coughed the cough that meant the meeting had started.

Around the table sat the nine councillors each with their own responsibility, as well as the ex-Chief of Police, who had been summoned to give a brief account of how he would tackle the case of the murdered police officers or "the cop killer" case as the press was consistently referring to it. The formalities were dealt with in seconds, with brief minutes and nods of agreement, which the secretary acknowledged and noted.

The chairman then moved on to the business of the day.

The former Chief of Police looked up, caught an enthusiastic, encouraging nod from Isabelle Skøyen and began.

"Thank you, Mr. Chairman. I won't take up much of the council's time today."

He glanced over at Skøyen, who appeared to be less enthusiastic about this unpromising opening.

"I've gone through the case as requested. I have

examined the police's ongoing work and their progress, the leadership, the strategies that have been
applied and their execution. Or to use Councillor
Skøyen's words, the strategies that may have been
applied, but have definitely not been executed."

Isabelle Skøyen's laughter was rich and self-
indulgent, but somewhat curtailed, perhaps because
she discovered she was the only person laughing.

"I have employed all my skills accumulated over
many years as a police officer and reached an unam-
biguous conclusion about what has to be done."

He saw Skøyen nod—the glint in her eye reminded
him of an animal, though which, he couldn't say.

"Now the solving of a single crime doesn't necessarily mean that the police are well managed. Just as
an unsolved crime is not necessarily down to poor
management. And having seen what the present
incumbents, and Mikael Bellman in particular, have
done I can't see what I would have done differently.
Or to make the point even clearer, I don't think I
could have done it as well."

He noted that Skøyen's jaw had dropped, and, feeling
to his surprise a certain sadistic pleasure, he continued.

"The craft of criminal investigation is evolving, as
is everything else in society, and from what I can see,
Bellman and his staff are cognisant with and adept
at utilising new methods and technological advances
in a way which I and my peers would probably not
have managed. He enjoys the full confidence of
his officers, he is an excellent motivator and he has
organised his work in a manner which colleagues

in other Scandinavian countries say is exemplary. I don't know if Councillor Skøyen is aware, but Mikael Bellman has just been asked to give a lecture at the Interpol conference in Lyons about criminal investigation and management with reference to this particular case. Skøyen suggested that Bellman was not up to the job, and it does have to be said that he is young to be a Chief of Police. But he is not only a man for the future. He is a man for the present. He is, in sum, exactly the man you need in this situation, Mr. Chairman. Which makes me surplus to requirements. This is my unequivocal conclusion."

The former Chief of Police straightened his back, shuffled the two sheets of notes he had been holding and did up the top button of his jacket, a carefully selected capacious tweed jacket favoured by pensioners. Pushed back his chair with a scrape, as though he needed space to be able to stand up. Saw that Skøyen's jaw had reached the nadir of its descent and that she was staring at him in disbelief.

He waited until he heard the chairman draw breath to say something so that he could proceed to the final act. The finale. The **coup de grâce.**

"And if I may add, since this is also about the council's competence and management of serious cases such as the police murders, Mr. Chairman . . ."

The chair's bushy eyebrows, which usually arched high above smiling eyes, were now low and protruded like greyish-white awnings over an angry glare. The ex-Chief waited for the chairman to nod.

". . . I appreciate that on this matter the council has

been subject to immense personal pressure—after all it is their area of responsibility, and the case has attracted huge media coverage. But when a city council cedes to pressure and acts in panic by attempting to cut off the head of its Chief of Police, the question is perhaps more: is the council up to its job? We, of course, understand that this may be an excessively demanding issue for a newly elected city council. It's unfortunate that a situation requiring experience and routine procedure should come so early in the council's period of office."

He saw the chairman recoil as he recognised the phrasing.

"It would have been better if this had landed on the desk of the previous City Council, given its long years of experience and its many achievements."

He could see from Skøyen's suddenly pale face that she too recognised her own words about Bellman at the previous meeting. And he had to confess that it was indeed a long time since he'd had such fun.

"I'm sure," he concluded, "that is what everyone in this room would have wished for, including the current council."

"Thank you for being so clear and candid," the chairman said. "I assume this means you do not have any alternative plan of action."

The old man nodded. "I don't. But there's a man outside whom I have taken the liberty of summoning in my place. He'll give you what you've asked for."

He stood up, gave a brief nod and walked towards the door. He thought he could feel Isabelle Skøyen's glare burning holes in his tweed jacket somewhere between his shoulder blades. But it didn't matter; he had no plans she could thwart. And he knew that tonight what he would revel in most, over a glass of wine, would be the two small words he had woven into the text. They contained all the subtext the council needed. One was "attempting," as in "attempting to cut off the head of its Chief of Police." The other was "current," as in "the current council."

Mikael Bellman got up from his chair as the door opened.

"Your turn," said the man in the tweed jacket, proceeding past him to the lift without gracing him with a glance.

Bellman assumed he must have been mistaken when he thought he detected a tiny smile on the man's lips.

Then he swallowed, took a deep breath and entered the same room where not so long ago he had been butchered into little pieces.

The long table was encircled by nine faces. Eight of them oddly expectant, a bit like an audience at the start of the second act after a successful first. One was oddly pale. So pale that for a moment he hardly recognised her. The butcher.

Fourteen minutes later he had finished. He had presented the plan to them. Had explained that the police's patience had paid dividends, their systematic work had led to a breakthrough in the investigation.

The breakthrough was both pleasing and painful because there was a chance that the guilty party might be someone from their own ranks. But they couldn't turn their backs on that. They had to show the public they were willing to look under every stone, whatever they might find there. Show that they were not cowards. He was prepared for a storm, but in such situations it was all about showing courage, genuine leadership and mental agility. Not just at Police HQ, but also at City Hall. He was ready to stand proudly at the helm, but he needed the council's confidence to take up arms.

He had noticed that his language had become a little pompous at the end, more pompous than it had seemed when Gunnar Hagen had used it in his living room at home last night. But he knew that he definitely had a few of them on board, a couple of the women had even coloured up, especially when he hammered home the final point. Which was that when all the service pistols in the whole country were checked against this bullet, like a prince with a shoe searching for his Cinderella, he would be the first to hand in his gun for ballistic examination.

However, what counted now was not his way with women but what the chairman thought. And he was rather more poker-faced.

Truls Berntsen put the phone in his pocket and nodded to the Thai woman to bring him another cup of coffee.

She smiled and was gone.

Obliging, these Thais. Unlike the few Norwegians left serving at tables. They were lazy and moody and looked aggrieved at having to do an honest day's work. Not like the Thai family running this little restaurant in Torshov, who jumped into action if he so much as raised an eyebrow. And when he paid for a lousy spring roll or a coffee, they beamed from ear to ear and bowed holding their palms together as though he were the great white God who had descended from the skies. He had vaguely considered going to Thailand. But it wouldn't happen. He wanted to work again.

Mikael had just rung and told him their ploy had worked. His suspension would soon be lifted. He hadn't wanted to specify exactly what he meant by soon, he had just repeated it, "soon."

The coffee came, and Truls took a sip. It wasn't particularly good, but he had reached the conclusion that he didn't really like what other people called good coffee. This was how it should taste, percolated in a well-used percolator. The coffee should have a hint of paper filters, plastic and ancient toasted coffee-bean grease. But probably that was why he was the only customer here. People drank their coffee elsewhere and came here later in the day to have a cheap meal or to buy a takeaway.

The Thai woman went to sit at the corner table where the rest of her family looked over what he presumed was the bill. He listened to the buzz of their strange language. Didn't understand a word, but he liked it. Liked sitting near them. Nodding back graciously when they sent him a smile. Feeling he was part of this community. Was that why he came here? Truls rejected the idea. Concentrated on the problem in hand again.

The rest of what Mikael had said.

They had to hand in their service pistols.

He had said they were going to be checked in connection with the police murders, and he himself— to show the summons applied to everyone, high and low—had handed in his gun for ballistic examination this morning. Truls would have to do the same as quickly as possible, he said, even though he was suspended.

It had to be the bullet in René Kalsnes. They had worked out it had to be from a police gun.

He wasn't too worried himself. Not only had he swapped the bullet, he had also reported the gun he had used missing, stolen. Of course he had waited for a while—a whole year in fact—to be sure no one would link the weapon with Kalsnes's murder. Then he had wrenched open the door to his flat with a crowbar to make it look convincing and reported a burglary. He had listed loads of things that had been taken and got forty thousand off the insurance company. Plus a new service pistol.

It wasn't that that was the problem.

The problem was the bullet in the evidence box. It had—how did it go?—it had seemed like a good idea at the time. But now all of a sudden he needed Mikael Bellman. If he was suspended, he wouldn't be able to lift Truls's suspension. Anyway, too late to do anything about that now.

Suspended.

Truls grinned at the notion and raised his coffee cup to toast himself in the reflection from the sunglasses he had put on the table in front of him. Then realised he must have laughed out loud, because the Thais were sending him strange looks.

"I don't know if I can pick you up from the airport," Harry said, walking past the place where there should have been a park, but the council in a collective aberration had erected a prison-like sports stadium for an international event being arranged for this year, but otherwise not too much happened.

He had to press the phone to his ear to hear her above the noise of rush-hour traffic.

"I forbid you to pick me up," Rakel said. "You have more important things to do now. In fact, I was wondering whether I should stay here this weekend, and give you a bit of space."

"Space for what?"

"Space to be Inspector Hole. It's sweet of you to pretend I wouldn't get under your feet, but we both know the state you get in when you're on a case."

"I want you to be here. But if you don't want—"

"I want to be with you **all** the time, Harry. I want to sit on you so that you can't go anywhere, that's what I want. But I don't think the Harry I want to spend my life with is at home right now."

"I like you sitting on me. And I'm not going anywhere."

"That's exactly the point. We're not going anywhere. We've got all the time in the world. OK?"

"OK."

"Fine."

"Sure? Because if it would make you happier if I nagged you a bit more, I would gladly do it."

Her laughter. Just that.

"And Oleg?"

She told him. He smiled a couple of times. Laughed at least once.

"I have to go now," Harry said, standing in front of the door to Schrøder's.

"OK. What sort of meeting is it, by the way?"

"Rakel . . ."

"Yes, I know I shouldn't ask. It's just so boring here. Harry?"

"Yes?"

"Do you love me?"

"I love you."

"I can hear traffic, so does that mean you're in a public place and you've said you love me out loud?"

"Yes."

"Did people turn their heads?"

"I wasn't looking."

"Would it be childish of me to ask you to do it again?"

"Yes."

More laughter. Christ, he would do anything to hear it.

"So?"

"I love you, Rakel Fauke."

"And I love you, Harry Hole. I'll call you tomorrow."

"Say hello to Oleg."

They rang off. Harry opened the door and went in.

Silje Gravseng was sitting alone at a table by the window, Harry's old table. The red skirt and the red blouse stood out like fresh blood against the big old paintings of Oslo on the wall behind her. Only her mouth was redder.

Harry sat down opposite her.

"Hi," he said.

"Hi," she said.

38

"Thanks for coming at such short notice," Harry said.

"I arrived half an hour ago," Silje said, nodding towards the empty glass in front of her.

"Am I . . . ?" Harry started, looking at his watch.

"Not at all. I just couldn't wait."

"Harry?"

He looked up. "Hi, Rita. Nothing today."

The waitress left.

"Busy?" Silje asked. She was sitting very straight in her chair, in a red dress with her arms crossed beneath her bosom and a face that kept changing from pretty and doll-like to something else, something nigh on ugly. The only thing that was constant was the intensity of her gaze. Harry had a feeling that you ought to be able to see every little swing of mood or emotion in that gaze. He must have been blind. Because all he could see was the intensity, nothing else. The desire for God knows what. Because it was not just about what she wanted, one night, one hour, a ten-minute rape-simulated fuck, it wasn't that simple.

"I wanted to talk to you because you were on duty at the Rikshospital."

"I've already spoken to the police about it."

"About what?"

"About Anton Mittet telling me something before he was killed. About arguing with someone or being in a relationship with someone at the hospital. But I told them this wasn't some isolated murder with a jealous husband, this was the cop killer. It all added up, didn't it? I've read a lot about serial killings, as you probably noticed during the lectures."

"There aren't any lectures about serial killings, Silje. I was wondering if you saw anyone coming or going while you sat there, someone or something that didn't tally with the routines, that made you sit up, in brief anything that—"

"—shouldn't have been there?" She smiled. Young, white teeth. Two of them crooked. "That's from your lecture." Back arched more than necessary.

"Well?" Harry said.

"You think the patient was killed and that Mittet was in on it, don't you?" She had angled her head, boosted her cleavage, and Harry wondered if she was acting, or she was really so sure of herself. Or if she was just a deeply disturbed person trying to imitate what she considered normal behaviour, but kept getting it slightly wrong. "Yes, you do," she said. "And so you think Mittet was killed afterwards because he knew too much. And that the murderer disguised it as one of the police murders?"

"No," Harry said. "If he'd been killed by people like that his body would have been dumped in the sea with weights in the pockets. Please think carefully, Silje. Concentrate."

She took a deep breath, and Harry avoided looking at her heaving chest. She tried to catch his eye, but he lowered his head and scratched his neck. Waiting.

"No, there was no one," she said at length. "Same routine all the time. A new anaesthetic nurse came, but he stopped after one or two visits."

"OK," Harry said, putting his hand in his jacket pocket. "What about him on the left?"

He placed a printout on the table in front of her. He had found the picture online, Google Images. It showed a young Truls Berntsen on the left of Mikael Bellman by Stovner Police Station.

Silje studied the picture. "No, I never saw him at the hospital, but the one on the right—"

"You saw him there?" Harry interrupted.

"No, no, I was just wondering if it was—"

"Yes, it is, it's the Chief of Police," Harry said, wanting to take the picture back, but Silje placed her hand on his.

"Harry?"

He could feel the heat from her soft palm on his hand. Waiting.

"I've seen them before. Together. What's the other man's name?"

"Truls Berntsen. Where?"

"They were together on the firing range in Økern not so long ago."

"Thank you," Harry said, pulling his hand away with the picture. "Then I don't want to take up any more of your time."

"As far as time goes, you've made sure I've got more than enough, Harry."

He didn't answer.

She sniggered. Leaned forward. "You didn't ask me to come here just for that, did you?" The light from the little table lamp danced in her eyes. "Do you know what wild idea struck me, Harry? You had me kicked out of the college so that you could be with me without getting into any trouble with management. So why don't you tell me what you **really** want?"

"What I really want, Silje—"

"Shame your colleague turned up last time we met, right when we—"

"—is to ask you about the hospital—"

"I live in Josefines gate, but you've probably already googled that—"

"—The last time was very wrong of me, I messed up, I—"

"It takes eleven minutes and twenty-three seconds to walk. Exactly. I timed myself on the way here."

"—can't. I don't want to. I—"

"Let's—" She made as if to get up.

"—I'm getting married this summer."

She slumped back down on the chair. Staring at him. "You're . . . getting married?" Her voice was barely audible in the noisy room.

"Yes," Harry said.

Her pupils contracted. Like a starfish someone had poked with a stick, Harry thought.

"To her?" she whispered. "To Rakel Fauke?"

"That's her name, yes. But married or not, student or not, something happening between us is out of the question. So I apologise for . . . the situation that arose."

"Getting married . . ." She repeated it in a somnambulistic voice, staring right through him.

Harry nodded. And felt something vibrate against his chest. For an instant he thought it was his heart, then realised it was the phone in his jacket pocket.

He took it out. "Harry."

Listened to the voice. Then he held the phone in front of him, looking at it as if there was something wrong with it.

"Repeat," he said, putting the phone to his ear.

"I said I've found the gun," Bjørn Holm said. "And, yes, it's his."

"How many people know?"

"No one."

"See how long you can keep it quiet."

Harry broke the connection and dialled another number. "I've got to go," he said to Silje and shoved a banknote under her glass. Saw her painted mouth open, but stood up and left before she could say anything.

By the time he was at the door Katrine was on the phone. He repeated what Bjørn had told him.

"You're joking," she said.

"So why aren't you laughing?"

"But . . . but this is just unbelievable."

"Probably why we don't believe it," Harry said. "Find it. Find the mistake."

And over the phone he could hear the ten-legged insect already scrabbling across the keyboard.

Aurora trudged to the bus stop with Emilie. It was getting dark, and it was the kind of weather where you think it's going to rain the whole time and then it doesn't after all. And it kind of puts you in a bad mood, she thought.

She said so to Emilie. Who said "Mm," but Aurora noticed that she didn't understand.

"If it would only start then it'd be finished, wouldn't it?" Aurora said. "It's actually better if it rains because then you don't dread it."

"I like rain," Emilie said.

"Me too. At least, a little. But . . ." She gave up.

"What happened at training?"

"What do you mean what happened?"

"Arne shouted at you because you didn't cover the wing."

"I was a bit late, that's all."

"No. You stood stock-still staring up at the stand. Arne says defence is the key in handball. And cover is the key in defence. And that means cover is the key in handball."

Arne says a load of rubbish, Aurora thought. Though she didn't say it aloud. Knowing Emilie wouldn't understand that either.

Aurora had lost her concentration because she was sure she had seen him in the stand. He wasn't so difficult to spot, because the only other people there were the boys' team, who were waiting impatiently for the hall to be cleared after the girls. But it had been him, she was almost certain. The man who had been in their garden. Who had asked for Dad. Who had wanted her to listen to a band whose name she had already forgotten. Who wanted a glass of water.

Then she must have stood still, the others had scored and their coach, Arne, had stopped the game and shouted at her. And as usual she was sorry. She had tried to fight it; she hated it when she got upset about such stupid things, but it was no use. Her eyes just filled with tears, which she wiped away with the sweatband around her wrist, wiped her forehead at the same time so that it would seem as if she was only drying sweat. And when Arne had finished, and she had looked up again at the stand, he was gone. Exactly like before. Except that this time it had happened so quickly she wondered if she had really seen him or it was just something she had imagined.

"Oh no," Emilie said, reading the bus timetable. "The 149 won't be here for at least another twenty minutes. Mum's made pizza for us this evening. It'll be **freezing** cold now."

"What a shame," Aurora said, reading down further. She didn't particularly like pizza or sleepovers. But it was what everyone did now. Everyone had sleepovers with everyone; it was like a circle dance you had to join. That or you were off the map. And Aurora didn't want to be off the map. Not entirely at any rate.

"Emilie," she said, looking at her watch, "it says here

the 131 will be along in a minute, and I've remembered I've left my toothbrush at home. The 131 goes past our house, so if I catch that one I can cycle over afterwards."

She could see Emilie didn't like the idea. Didn't like the idea of standing here in the darkness, in the almost-rain that would never be rain, to catch the bus home alone. And she probably already suspected that Aurora would find some excuse for not sleeping over after all.

"Hm," Emilie grunted, fiddling with her sports bag. "We won't wait for you with the pizza though."

Aurora saw the bus coming round the bend at the bottom of the hill. The 131.

"And we can share a toothbrush," Emilie said. "After all, we're friends."

We are **not** friends, Aurora thought. **You** are Emilie, friends with all the girls in the class, Emilie who always wears the right clothes, Emilie, Norway's most popular name, who never falls out with anyone because you're so great and never criticise anyone, at least not when they're within earshot. Whereas I'm Aurora, who does what she has to do—but nothing more—to be with you all because she doesn't have the courage to be alone. Who all of you consider strange, but smart enough and confident enough for you not to pick on her.

"I'll be at your place before you," Aurora said. "I promise."

• • •

Harry was sitting in the modest stand, head supported on his hands, looking at the track.

There was rain in the air, it could pour down at any moment and there was no roof on Valle Hovin.

He had the whole ugly little stadium to himself. Knew he would have, concerts here were few and far between now, and it was even longer to the ice-skating season when anyone who wanted could come and train. This was where he had sat watching Oleg taking his first tentative steps and slowly but surely developing into a promising skater in his age category. He hoped he would soon see Oleg here again. So that he could time his circuits without him realising. Note his progress and plateaus. Encourage him when things were sluggish, lie about the conditions and the state of his skates, and maintain a neutral tone when things were going well, not letting his internal jubilation come across. Be a kind of compressor to even out the peaks and troughs. Oleg needed that, otherwise his emotions would have free rein. Harry didn't know much about skates, but he did know a lot about this. Affective control, Ståle called it. How to console yourself. It was one of the most important features of a child's development, but not everyone developed it to the same degree. Ståle thought, for example, that Harry needed more affective control. He lacked the average person's ability to flee from what hurt, to forget, to focus his mind on nicer, lighter topics. He had used alcohol to cope with his job. Oleg's father was also an alcoholic, who drank his family fortune and life away in Moscow, Rakel had told him. Perhaps that was one of the reasons Harry felt such tenderness for the boy. They shared this lack of affective control.

Harry heard footsteps on the concrete. Someone was coming through the darkness from the other side of the track. Harry took a full drag of the cigarette so that the glow would show him where he was sitting.

The man swung a leg over the fence and walked with light, agile strides up the stand's concrete steps.

"Harry Hole," the man said, stopping two steps below.

"Mikael Bellman," Harry said. In the night the white patches on Bellman's face seemed to light up.

"Two things, Harry. This had better be important. My wife and I had planned a cosy evening together."

"And the second?"

"Stub that out. Cigarette smoke damages your health."

"Thank you for your concern."

"I was thinking about me, not you. Please put it out."

Harry rubbed the end on the concrete and dropped it back into the packet while Bellman took a seat beside him.

"Unusual place to meet, Hole."

"Only hangout I have, besides Schrøder's. And less populated."

"Too unpopulated, in my opinion. I wondered for a moment if you were the cop killer trying to lure me here. We still believe it's a policeman, do we?"

"Absolutely," Harry said, already craving the cigarette. "We've matched the gun."

"Already? That was damn quick. I didn't even know you'd started calling in all—"

"We don't need to. The first gun matched."

"What?"

"Your gun, Bellman. It was fired and the result matched the bullet in the Kalsnes case."

Bellman burst out laughing. The echo carried between the stands. "Is this some kind of joke, Harry?"

"I'm afraid you'll have to tell me, Mikael."

"To you I'm the Chief of Police or herr Bellman, Harry. And I don't **have** to tell you anything. What's going on?"

"That's what you'll have to—sorry—is **should** better? . . . you should tell me, Police Chief Bellman. Otherwise we'll have to—and I do mean **have to** here—summon you to an official interview. And I'm sure everyone would prefer to avoid that. Are we agreed?"

"Get to the point, Harry. How could this have happened?"

"I can see two possible explanations," Harry said. "The first and more obvious one is that you shot René Kalsnes, Police Chief Bellman."

"I . . . I . . ."

Harry watched Mikael Bellman's mouth moving as the light seemed to pulsate in the white patches, as though he were some kind of exotic deep-sea creature.

"You've got an alibi," Harry completed for him.

"Have I?"

"When we got the result I put Katrine Bratt on the case. You were in Paris the night René Kalsnes was shot."

"Was I?"

"Your name was on the Air France passenger list from Oslo to Paris and in the guest book at the Golden Oriole Hotel the same night. Anyone you met who can confirm you were there?"

Mikael Bellman blinked hard as if to see better. The northern lights in his skin went out. He nodded slowly. "The Kalsnes case, yes. That was the day I went for a job interview with Interpol. I could definitely find a few witnesses from that trip. We even went out to a restaurant in the evening."

"So there's just the question of where your gun was on that date."

"At home," Mikael Bellman said with total certainty. "Locked up. The key was on the key ring I had with me."

"Can you prove that?"

"Doubt it. You said there were two possible explanations here. Let me guess. The second is that the ballistics boys—"

"Most of them are girls now."

"—have made a mistake, have mixed up the fatal bullet with one of mine, or something like that."

"No. The lead bullet in the box in the Evidence Room comes from your gun, Bellman."

"What do you mean?"

"By what?"

"By saying 'the bullet in the box in the Evidence Room' and not 'the bullet found in Kalsnes's skull.'"

Harry nodded. "Now we're getting warm, Bellman."

"Getting warm how?"

"The other possibility, the way I see it, is that someone swapped the bullet in the Evidence Room with one from your gun. There is one thing about the bullet that doesn't add up. It's crushed in a way that suggests it hit something much harder than flesh and bone."

"Right. What do you think it hit then?"

"The steel sheet behind the paper target on the firing range in Økern."

"What on earth would make you believe that?"

"It's not so much what I believe as what I know, Bellman. I got the ballistics girls to go up there and run a test with your gun. And guess what? The test bullet looked identical to the one in the evidence box."

"And what made you think of the firing range precisely?"

"Isn't it obvious? That's where police officers fire most of the shots that are not meant to hit people."

Mikael Bellman slowly shook his head. "There's more. What is it?"

"Well," Harry said, taking out his packet of Camels, holding it out to Bellman, who shook his head, "I thought about how many burners I know in the police. And do you know what? I could only think of one." Harry took the half-smoked cigarette, lit it and took a long, rasping drag. "Truls Berntsen. And as chance would have it I've spoken to a witness who recently saw you practising together on the range. The bullets drop into a container after they've hit the steel plate. It would be simple for someone to take a used bullet after you'd gone."

"Do you suspect that our mutual colleague Truls Berntsen planted false evidence to incriminate me, Harry?"

"Don't you?"

Bellman looked as if he was about to say something, but changed his mind. He shrugged. "I don't know what Berntsen's up to, Hole. And, to be honest, I don't think you do, either."

"Well, I don't know how honest you are, but I do know the odd fact about Berntsen. And Berntsen knows the odd fact about you too. Isn't that true?"

"I have an inkling you're insinuating something, but I have no idea what, Hole."

"Oh yes, you do. But not much that can be proved, I would assume, so let's give it a miss. What I'd like to know is what Berntsen is after."

"Your job, Hole, is to investigate the police murders, not to take advantage of the situation to conduct a personal witch-hunt against me or Truls Berntsen."

"Is that what I'm doing?"

"It's no secret that you and I have had our differences, Harry. I suppose you see this as a chance to get your own back."

"What about you and Berntsen? Any differences there? You're the one who suspended him on suspicion of corruption."

"No, that was the Appointments Board. And that misunderstanding is about to be rectified."

"Oh?"

"In fact, it was my mistake. The money that went into his account came from me."

"From you?"

"He built the terrace on our house, and I paid him in cash, which he put into his account. But I wanted the money back because of faults in the construction. That was why he didn't declare the sum to the tax authorities. He didn't want to pay tax on money that wasn't his. I sent the information to the Fraud Squad yesterday."

"Faults in the construction?"

"The concrete base is damp and smells. When the Fraud Squad picked up on the mysterious sum of money, Truls was labouring under the misapprehension that it would put me in a tricky position if he said where he got the money from. Anyway, it's all sorted now."

Bellman rolled up his jacket sleeve and the dial of his TAG Heuer watch shone in the darkness. "If there are no further questions about the bullet from my gun I have other things to do, Harry. And I suppose you do too. Lectures have to be prepared, for example."

"Well, I'm spending all my time on this now."

"You **used** to spend all your time on this."

"Meaning?"

"We have to make savings where we can, so I'm going to order, with immediate effect, that Hagen's alternative little group stops using consultants."

"Ståle Aune and me. That's half the group."

"Fifty per cent of staffing costs. I'm congratulating myself on the decision already. But as the group is barking up the wrong tree I think I'll cancel the whole project."

"Have you got that much to fear, Bellman?"

"You don't have to fear anything when you're the biggest animal in the jungle, Harry. And I am, after all—"

"—the Chief of Police. You certainly are. The Chief."

Bellman got up. "I'm glad that's sunk in. And I know that when you begin to pull in trusted colleagues like Berntsen, this is not an impartial investigation but a personal vendetta stage-managed by a bitter, alcoholic former policeman. And as Chief of Police it is my duty to protect the reputation of the force. So you know what I'll answer when I'm asked why we shelved the case of the Russian who got a corkscrew inserted around his carotid artery at Come As You Are, don't you? I'll answer that we have to prioritise investigations, and that the case is nowhere near shelved, it's just not a priority at this moment. And even if everyone with a toe in the police force knows the rumours about who was responsible for it, I will pretend I haven't heard them. Because I'm the Chief of Police."

"Is that supposed to be a threat, Bellman?"

"Do I need to threaten a PHS lecturer? Have a good evening, Harry."

Harry watched Bellman sidle along the row down to the fence, buttoning up his jacket as he went. He knew he should keep his mouth shut. This was a card he had decided to hold back in case it was needed. But now he had been told to pack everything in, there was nothing left to lose. All or nothing. He waited until Bellman had one leg over the fence.

"Did you ever meet René Kalsnes, Bellman?"

Bellman froze mid-stretch. Katrine had run a cross-check on Bellman and Kalsnes without coming up with a single hit. And if they had so much as shared a restaurant bill, bought a cinema ticket online, had seats near each other on a plane or a train she would have found it. But, well, he froze. Stood with one leg on either side of the fence.

"Why such a stupid question, Harry?"

Harry took a drag on his cigarette. "It was fairly well known that René Kalsnes sold sex to men whenever the opportunity arose. And you've watched gay porn online."

Bellman hadn't moved; he had evidently committed himself. Harry couldn't see the expression on his face in the darkness, only the white patches shining in the same way his watch dial had.

"Kalsnes was known as a greedy cynic without a moral bone in his body," Harry said, studying the cigarette glow. "Imagine a married man, with significant social standing, being blackmailed by someone like René. Perhaps he had some photos of them having sex. That would sound like a motive for murder, wouldn't it? But René might have talked about the married man and afterwards someone might come forward and reveal that there was a motive. So the married man gets someone to commit the murder. Someone he knows very well, someone he already has a hold over, someone he trusts. The murder is committed while the married man has a perfect alibi, a meal in Paris, for example. But afterwards the two childhood friends fall out. The hit man is suspended from his job and the married man refuses to tidy up for him even though, as the boss, he is actually in a position to do this. So the hit man takes a used bullet from the married man's gun and puts it in the evidence box. Either out of sheer revenge or to pressurise the married man into giving him his job back. You see, it's not so easy for someone unfamiliar with the art of burning to have this bullet removed again. Did you know, by the way, that Truls Berntsen reported his service pistol missing a year after Kalsnes was shot? I found his name on a list I was given by Katrine Bratt a couple of hours ago." Harry inhaled. Closed his eyes so that the glow would not affect his night vision. "What do you say to that, Chief of Police?"

"I say: thank you, Harry. Thank you for concluding my deliberations on closing down the alternative group. It will be done first thing in the morning."

"Does that mean you're claiming you never met René Kalsnes?"

"Don't try those questioning techniques on me,

Harry. I brought them to Norway from Interpol. Anyone can stumble across gay pictures online, they're everywhere. And we have no need for groups of detectives who use that sort of thing as valid evidence in a serious investigation."

"You didn't stumble across it, Bellman. You paid for films with your credit card and downloaded them."

"You're not listening! Aren't you curious about taboos? When you download pictures of a murder that doesn't mean you're a murderer. If a woman is fascinated by the thought of rape, it doesn't mean she wants to be raped!" Bellman had his other leg over. He was standing on the other side now. Off the hook. He adjusted his jacket.

"Just a final word of advice, Harry. Don't come after me. If you know what's good for you. For you and your woman."

Harry watched Bellman's back recede into the darkness, and heard only the heavy footsteps sending a dull echo around the stands. He dropped the cigarette end and stamped on it. Hard. Trying to force it through the concrete.

39

Harry found Øystein Eikeland's battered Mercedes in the taxi rank to the north of Oslo Central Station. The taxis were parked in a circle and looked like a wagon train forming a defensive ring against Apaches, tax authorities, competitors and anyone else who came to take what they considered legally theirs.

Harry took a seat in the front. "Busy night?"

"Haven't taken my foot off the gas for a second," Øystein said, carefully pinching his lips around a microscopic roll-up and blowing smoke at the mirror, where he could see the queue behind him growing.

"How often in the course of a night do you actually have a paying passenger in the car?" Harry asked, taking out his packet of cigarettes.

"So few that I'm thinking about switching on the taxi meter now. Hey, can't you read?" Øystein pointed to the No Smoking sign on the glove compartment.

"I need some advice, Øystein."

"I say no. Don't get married. Nice woman, Rakel, but marriage is more trouble than fun. Listen to someone who's been around the block a few times."

"You've never been married, Øystein."

"That's exactly the point." His childhood pal bared

yellow teeth in his lean face and tossed his head, lashing the headrest with his ultra-thin ponytail.

Harry lit a cigarette. "And to think that I asked you to be my best man . . ."

"The best man has to have his wits about him, Harry, and a wedding without getting smashed is as meaningless as tonic without gin."

"OK, but I'm not asking you for marriage guidance."

"Spit it out then. Eikeland's listening."

The smoke stung Harry's throat. The mucous membranes were no longer used to two packs of cigarettes a day. He knew all too well that Øystein couldn't give him any advice on the case, either. Not good advice anyway. His homespun logic and principles had formed a lifestyle so dysfunctional that it could only tempt those with very specific interests. The pillars of the Eikelandian house were alcohol, bachelorhood, women from the lowest rung, an interesting intellectuality—which was unfortunately in decline—a certain pride and a survival instinct which despite everything resulted in more taxi driving than drinking and an ability to laugh in the face of life and the devil, which even Harry had to admire.

Harry breathed in. "I suspect an officer is behind all these police murders."

"Then bang him up," Øystein said, taking a flake of tobacco off the tip of his tongue. Then stopped suddenly. "Did you say police murders? As in **police murders**?"

"Yup. The problem is that if I arrest this man he'll drag me down with him."

"How come?"

"He can prove it was me who killed the Russian in Come As You Are."

Øystein stared wide-eyed into the mirror. "Did you snuff a Russian?"

"So what do I do? Do I arrest the man and go down with him? In which case Rakel has no husband and Oleg no father?"

"Quite agree."

"Quite agree with what?"

"Quite agree that you should use them as a front. Very smart to have that kind of philanthropic pretext up your sleeve. You sleep a lot better then. I've always gone in for that. Do you remember when we were apple scrumping and I legged it and left Tresko to face the music? Of course he couldn't run that fast with all the weight and the clogs. I told myself that Tresko needed a thrashing more than me, to stiffen his spine, morally speaking, to point him in the right direction. Because that was where he really wanted to go, privet-hedge country, wasn't it? While I wanted to be a bandit, didn't I? What good was a flogging to me for a few lousy apples?"

"I'm not going to let other people take the rap here, Øystein."

"But what if this guy snuffs a few more cops and you know you could have stopped him?"

"That's the point," Harry said, blowing smoke at the No Smoking sign.

Øystein stared at his pal. "Don't do it, Harry . . ."

"Don't do what?"

"Don't . . ." Øystein lowered the window on his side and flicked out what was left of the roll-up, two centimetres of spit-stained Rizla paper. "I don't want to hear about it. Just don't do it."

"Well, the most cowardly option is to do nothing. To tell myself I have no absolute proof, which is true by the way. To turn a blind eye. But can a man live with that, Øystein?"

"Certainly bloody can. But you're a bit of a weirdo in that regard, Harry. Can **you** live with it?"

"Not normally. But, as I said, I have other considerations now."

"Can't other officers arrest him?"

"He's going to use everything he knows about everyone in the force to negotiate himself a reduced punishment. He's worked as a burner and a detective and he knows all the tricks in the book. On top of that, he'll be rescued by the Chief of Police. The two of them know too much about each other."

Øystein took Harry's packet of cigarettes. "Do you know what, Harry? Sounds to me like you've come here to get my blessing for murder. Does anyone else know what you're up to?"

Harry shook his head. "Not even my team of detectives."

Øystein took out a cigarette and lit it with his lighter.

"Harry."

"Yes."

"You're the fucking lonesomest guy I know."

Harry looked at his watch, midnight soon, peered

through the windscreen. "Loneliest, I think the word is."

"No. Lonesomest. It's your choice. And you're weird."

"Anyway," Harry said, opening the door, "thanks for your advice."

"What advice?"

The door slammed.

"What fucking advice?" Øystein shouted to the door and the hunched figure heading into the Oslo murk. "And what about a taxi home, you stingy bastard?"

The house was dark and still.

Harry sat on the sofa staring at the cupboard.

He hadn't said anything about his suspicions regarding Truls Berntsen.

He had rung Bjørn and Katrine and said he'd had a brief conversation with Mikael Bellman. And that as the Police Chief had an alibi for the night of the murder, there had to be a mistake or the evidence had been planted, so they would keep quiet about the bullet in the evidence box matching Bellman's gun. Not a word about what they had discussed.

Not a word about Truls Berntsen.

Not a word about what had to be done.

This was how it had to be; it was the kind of case where you had to be alone.

The key was hidden on the CD shelf.

Harry closed his eyes. Tried to give himself a break,

tried not to listen to the dialogue churning round and round in his head. But it was no good; the voices began to scream as soon as he relaxed. Truls Berntsen was crazy, they said. This was not an assumption, it was a fact. No sane person would embark on a killing spree targeting their own colleagues.

It was not without parallels; you just had to look at all the incidents in America, where someone who had been fired or humiliated in some other way returned to their place of work and shot their colleagues. Omar Thornton killed eight of them at a distribution warehouse after being let go for stealing beer; Wesley Neal Higdon killed five after being told off by his boss; Jennifer San Marco fired six fatal shots into the heads of colleagues at the post office after she had been dismissed for—what else?—being insane.

The difference here was the degree of planning involved and the ability to execute the plans. So how crazy was Truls Berntsen? Was he crazy enough for the police to reject his claims that Harry Hole had killed someone in a bar?

No.

Not if he had proof. Proof couldn't be declared insane.

Truls Berntsen.

Harry let his mind run.

Everything fitted. But did the essential ingredient fit? The motive. What was it Mikael Bellman had said? If a woman fantasises about rape, it doesn't mean she wants to be raped. If a man fantasises about violence it doesn't mean . . .

For Christ's sake. Stop it!

But it wouldn't stop. It wouldn't give him any peace until he had solved the problem. And there were only two ways it could be solved. There was the old way. The one that every fibre of his body was screaming for now. A drink. The drink that multiplied, expunged, veiled, numbed. That was the provisional way. The bad way. The other was the final way. The necessary way. The one that eradicated the problem. The devil's alternative.

Harry jumped to his feet. There was no alcohol in the house, there hadn't been since he moved in. He started pacing the floor. Then stopped. Eyed the old corner cupboard. It reminded him of something. A drinks cabinet he had once stood and stared at in just this way. What was holding him back? How many times before had he sold his soul for less reward than this? Perhaps that was precisely the point. That the other times it had been for small change, justified by moral indignation. While this time it was . . . unclean. He wanted to save his own neck while he was at it.

But he could hear it inside him now, whispering to him. **Take me out, use me. Use me in the way I should be used. And this time I'll finish the job off. I won't let a bulletproof vest fool me.**

It would take him half an hour to drive from here to Truls Berntsen's flat in Manglerud. With the arsenal in his bedroom that Harry had seen with his own eyes. Weapons, handcuffs, gas mask. Baton. So why was he putting it off? He knew what had to be done.

But was he right? Did Truls Berntsen really kill René Kalsnes on Mikael Bellman's orders? There was no doubt Truls was off his trolley, but was Mikael Bellman as well?

Or was it just a construct his brain had assembled with the pieces he had at his disposal, forcing them to fit because it wanted, needed, **demanded** a picture, any picture which would give if not meaning then an answer, a feeling that the dots were joined up?

Harry took the phone from his pocket and selected A.

Ten seconds went by before he heard a grunt. "Yeah?"

"Hi, Arnold, it's me."

"Harry?"

"Yes. Are you at work?"

"It's one in the morning, Harry. Like most normal people I'm in bed."

"Sorry. Do you want to go back to sleep?"

"Since you ask, yes."

"OK, but now you're awake . . ." He heard a groan at the other end. "I'm wondering about Mikael Bellman. You used to work at Kripos when he was there. Did you ever notice anything to suggest he might be sexually attracted to men?"

There followed a long silence in which Harry listened to Arnold's regular breathing and a train rattling by. From the acoustics Harry deduced that Arnold had a window open, you could hear more outside the bedroom than inside. He must have got used to the noise, and it didn't interfere with his sleep. And it suddenly struck him, not like a revelation, more like a stray thought, that this was perhaps how it was with the case. Perhaps it was the noises, the familiar noises they didn't hear and which therefore didn't wake them, they should be listening to?

"Have you fallen asleep, Arnold?"

"Not at all. The idea is so new to me that I have to let it sink in first. So. In retrospect, putting everything in a different light . . . And even then I can't make . . . but it's obvious . . ."

"What's obvious?"

"Well, it was Bellman and that dog of his with the boundless loyalty."

"Truls Berntsen."

"Exactly. The two of . . ." Another pause. Another train. "Well, Harry, I can't see them as a couple, if you know what I mean."

"I see. Sorry to have woken you. Goodnight."

"Goodnight. By the way . . . just a mo . . ."

"Mm?"

"There was a guy at Kripos. I'd forgotten all about it, but I went to the toilet once, and he and Bellman were over by the basins, both with very red faces. As though something had happened. Know what I mean? I remember the thought crossing my mind, but didn't take too much notice of it. But the guy left Kripos soon afterwards."

"What was his name?"

"No idea. I can find out, but not now."

"Thanks, Arnold. And sleep well."

"Thanks. What's happening?"

"Not a lot, Arnold," Harry said, rang off and slipped the phone into his pocket.

Opened his other hand.

Stared at the CD shelf. The key was under W.

"Not a lot," he repeated.

He took off his T-shirt on the way to the bathroom. He knew the bedlinen was white, clean and cold. And the silence outside the open window would be total and the night air suitably crisp. And he wouldn't be able to sleep for a second.

In bed, he lay listening to the wind. It was whistling. Whistling through the keyhole of a very old, black corner cupboard.

The duty officer on the switchboard received the message about a fire at 4:06 a.m. When she heard the fireman's agitated voice she automatically assumed it had to be a major incident, one that might require the traffic to be redirected, personal possessions to be safeguarded or casualties and fatalities to be dealt with. She was therefore a little surprised when the fireman said that smoke had triggered an alarm in a bar in Oslo, which had been closed for the night, and that the fire had burnt itself out before they arrived. And even more surprised when the fireman told her to get some officers there right away. She could hear that what she had at first taken for agitation in the man's voice was horror. The voice trembled, like the voice of someone who had probably seen a lot in his career but nothing that could have prepared him for what he was trying to communicate.

"There's a young girl. She must have been doused in something. There are empty bottles of spirits on the bar."

"Where are you?"

"She's . . . she's completely charred. And she's been tied to a pipe."

"Where are you?"

"Round the neck. Looks like a bike lock. You've got to come, I'm telling you."

"Yes, but where—?"

"Kvadraturen. The place is called Come As You Are. Jesus Christ, she's only a young girl . . ."

40

Ståle Aune was woken at 6:28 by a ringing sound. For some reason, he thought at first it was the phone, before realising it was his alarm clock. Must have been something in his dream. But since he didn't believe in interpreting dreams any more than he believed in psychotherapy he made no attempt to trace his train of thought back. He brought his hand down hard on the clock and closed his eyes to enjoy the two minutes before a second alarm clock went off. As a rule, this was when he heard Aurora's bare feet hit the floor and make a sprint for the bathroom to get in first.

Silence.

"Where's Aurora?"

"She's got a sleepover at Emilie's," Ingrid mumbled in a thick voice.

Ståle Aune got up. Showered, shaved, had breakfast with his wife in companionable silence while she read the newspaper. Ståle had become pretty good at reading upside down. He skipped the police murders, no news there, only new speculation.

"Isn't she coming home before she goes to school?" Ståle asked.

"She had her school things with her."

"Oh, right. Is it OK to have a sleepover when you have school the next day?"

"No, it's bad for her. You should do something about it." She turned a page.

"Do you know what lack of sleep does to the brain, Ingrid?"

"The Norwegian state funded six years of research for you to find out, Ståle, so I would regard it as a waste of my taxes if I also knew."

Ståle had always felt a mixture of annoyance and admiration for Ingrid's ability to be, cognitively, so alert at such an early hour. She wiped the floor with him before ten. He didn't get a verbal jab in until closer to midday. Basically he didn't have a hope of winning a round until about six.

He was musing about this as he was reversing the car out of the garage and driving to his consulting room in Sporveisgata. He didn't know if he could stand living with a woman who didn't give him a daily trouncing. And if he hadn't known so much about genetics it would have been a mystery how the two of them could have produced such an endearing, sensitive child as Aurora. Then he forgot about her. The traffic was slow, but no slower than usual. The most important thing was the predictability of it, not the time it took. There was a meeting at the Boiler Room at twelve, and there were three patients before that.

He switched on the radio.

Listened to the news and heard his phone ring

at the same time, knowing instinctively there was a connection.

It was Harry. "We have to postpone the meeting. There's been another murder."

"The girl they're talking about on the radio?"

"Yes. At least we're pretty sure it's a girl."

"You don't know who it is?"

"No. No one's been reported missing."

"How old is she?"

"Impossible to say, but from the size and shape of the body I would guess somewhere between ten and fourteen."

"And you think this has something to do with our case?"

"Yes."

"Why?"

"Because she was found on the site of an unsolved murder. A bar called Come As You Are. And because . . ." Harry cleared his throat. ". . . she has a cycle lock around her neck, attaching her to a pipe."

"Sweet Jesus!"

He heard Harry cough again.

"Harry?"

"Yes?"

"Are you OK?"

"No."

"Is there . . . is there something wrong?"

"Yes."

"Apart from the cycle lock? I appreciate it's . . ."

"He doused her in alcohol before striking a match. The empty bottles are on the bar here. Three, all the same brand. Even though there are many other bottles he could have taken."

"It's . . ."

"Yes, Jim Beam."

". . . your brand."

Ståle heard Harry shout at someone not to touch anything. Then he was back. "Do you want to come and see the crime scene?"

"I've got some patients. Afterwards perhaps."

"OK, it's up to you. We'll be here for quite a while."

They rang off.

Ståle tried to concentrate on driving. He could feel his breathing was laboured, his nostrils were flaring and his chest was heaving. Today, he knew, he was going to be an even worse therapist than usual.

Harry went out of the door into the busy street where people, bicycles, cars and trams were hurrying past. Blinked into the light after all the darkness, watched the meaningless hustle and bustle of life which was unaware that a few metres behind him there was an equally meaningless death, sitting on a chair with a melted plastic seat, in the form of the blackened corpse of a girl. They had no idea who she was. Well, Harry had an **idea,** but he didn't dare think it through. He took several deep breaths and thought it through anyway. Then he rang Katrine, whom he had sent back to the Boiler Room to sit by her computer.

"Still no one reported missing?" he asked.

"No."

"OK. Check which detectives have daughters aged between eight and sixteen. Start with those on the Kalsnes case. If there is anyone, ring them and ask if they've seen their daughter today. Tread warily."

"Will do."

Harry broke the connection.

Bjørn came out and stood beside him. His voice was low, soft, as if they were in church.

"Harry?"

"Yes?"

"That's the worst thing I've ever seen."

Harry nodded. He was aware of some of the things Bjørn had seen, but knew this was true.

"The person who did this . . ." Bjørn raised his hands, took a quick breath, sighed in desperation and dropped his hands again. "He should be plugged with lead."

Harry clenched his fists in his jacket pockets. Knowing this was true as well. He should be shot. Using a bullet or three from an Odessa in a cupboard in Holmenkollveien. Not now, he should have been shot last night. When a very cowardly ex-cop went to bed because he couldn't be the executioner as long as he didn't have his own motives clear. Was he doing it for the potential victims' sakes, for Rakel and Oleg's sakes or just for his own? Well. The girl inside wouldn't be asking him about his motive. For her and for her parents it was too late. Shit, shit, shit!

He looked at his watch.

Truls Berntsen knew Harry was after him now and he would be ready. He had invited him, tempted him by committing the murder on this former crime scene, humiliated him by using the drunk's regular poison, Jim Beam, and the lock half the force had heard about. The great Harry Hole had been attached to a No Parking sign in Sporveisgata like a dog on a lead.

Harry inhaled. He could throw in his cards, tell all, about Gusto, Oleg and the dead Russian and afterwards raid Truls Berntsen's flat with Delta, and if Berntsen escaped he could spread a net from Interpol to every rural police station in the country. Or . . .

Harry went to pull out the creased packet of Camels. Pushed it back down. He was sick of smoking.

. . . or he could do precisely what the bastard wanted.

It wasn't until the break after the second patient that Ståle completed his train of thought.

Or trains—there were two of them.

The first was that no one had reported the girl's disappearance. A girl aged from ten to fourteen years old. The parents should have missed her when she didn't turn up in the evening. Should have reported her.

The second was what connection the victim could possibly have to the police murders. So far the murderer had only targeted detectives and now perhaps the typical tendency of serial killers to step up their violence had reared its head: what more could you do to someone than kill them? Simple, kill their offspring. The child. So in that case the question was:

whose turn was next? Obviously not Harry's. He didn't have any children.

And that was when cold sweat without warning or restraint broke from all the pores of Ståle Aune's voluminous body. He grabbed the phone in the open drawer, found Aurora's name and called.

It rang eight times before he went through to her voicemail.

She didn't answer of course, she was at school and, quite sensibly, they were not allowed to have their phones on.

What's was Emilie's surname? He had heard it often enough, but this was Ingrid's domain. He considered ringing, but decided not to worry her unnecessarily and instead looked for "school camp" in his inbox. Sure enough, he found lots of emails from last year with the addresses of all the parents in Aurora's class. He scanned through them hoping to find it and erupt with an "Aha!" He didn't have to wait long. Torunn Einersen. Emilie Einersen—it was even easy to remember. And, best of all, the parents' telephone numbers were listed underneath. He noticed his fingers were trembling, it was hard to hit the right keys, he must have been drinking or he hadn't had enough coffee.

"Torunn Einersen."

"Oh, hello, this is Ståle Aune, Aurora's father. I . . . er, just wanted to know if everything was OK last night."

Pause. Too long.

"With the sleepover," he added. And to be absolutely sure: "With Emilie."

"Oh, I see. I'm afraid Aurora didn't come for a sleepover. I know they were chatting about it, but—"

"I must have misremembered," Ståle said, and could hear his voice was taut.

"Yes, it's not easy to keep track of who's having a sleepover with whom these days," Torunn Einersen laughed, but her voice was uneasy on his behalf, for the father who didn't know where his daughter had spent the night.

Ståle rang off. His shirt was already well on the way to becoming wet.

He called Ingrid. Got her voicemail. Left a message for her to ring. Then got up and dashed out of the door. The last patient, a middle-aged woman in therapy for reasons unfathomable to Ståle, looked up.

"I'm afraid I have to cancel today's session . . ." He intended to say her name, but couldn't remember it until he was downstairs, out of the door and running down Sporveisgata to his car.

Harry sensed he was squeezing the paper cup of coffee too hard as the covered stretcher was carried past them into the waiting ambulance. He scowled at the flock of rubbernecks thronging nearby.

Katrine had phoned. Still no one had been reported missing, and no one in the investigation team on the Kalsnes case had a daughter between eight and sixteen. So Harry had asked her to extend her search to the rest of the force.

Bjørn came out of the bar. He pulled off the latex gloves and the hood of the white overall.

"Still no news from the DNA team?" Harry asked.

"No."

The first thing Harry did when he arrived at the crime scene was to have a tissue sample taken and sent urgently to Forensics. A full DNA test took time, but getting the initial profile could happen quite quickly. And that was as much as they needed. All the murder investigators, plainclothes and forensics officers, had registered their DNA profiles in case they contaminated a crime site. Over the last year they had also registered officers who arrived first at the scene or who guarded crime scenes, even civilians who it was thought might conceivably be there. It was a simple probability calculation. With only the first three or four digits out of eleven they would already have eliminated the most relevant police officers. With five or six, all of them. That is, if he was correct, minus one.

Harry looked at his watch. He didn't know why, didn't know what they were trying to do, only knew they didn't have a lot of time. **He** didn't have a lot of time.

Ståle Aune parked his car in front of the school gates and switched on the hazard lights. He heard the echo of his running feet resound between the buildings around the playground. The lonely sound of childhood. The sound of arriving late for lessons. Or the sound of summer holidays when everyone had left town, of being abandoned. He tore open the heavy door, sprinted down the corridor, no echo now, just his own panting. That was the door to her classroom. Wasn't it? Group or class? He knew so little about her everyday life. He hadn't seen much of her over the last six months. There was so much he wanted to know. He would spend so much time with her from now on. So long as, so long as . . .

Harry looked around the bar.

"The lock on the back door was picked," the officer behind him said.

Harry nodded. He had seen the scratch marks around the lock.

Lock picking. Police handiwork. That was why the alarm hadn't gone off.

Harry hadn't seen any signs of resistance. No objects had been knocked over, nothing on the floor, no chairs or tables kicked out of a position it would be natural to leave them in overnight. The owner was being questioned. Harry had said he didn't need to meet him. He hadn't said he didn't **want** to meet him. He hadn't given any reason. Such as not wanting to risk being recognised.

Harry sat on a bar stool, reconstructing how he had sat there that night with an untouched glass of Jim Beam in front of him. The Russian had attacked from behind; he had tried to press the blade of the Siberian knife into his carotid artery. Harry's titanium prosthesis had been in the way. The owner had stood behind the bar, paralysed with fear, as Harry had scrabbled for the corkscrew. The blood that had discoloured the floor beneath them, as if a full bottle of red wine had been knocked over.

"Nothing in the way of clues so far," Bjørn said.

Harry nodded again. Of course not. Berntsen had had the place to himself, he was able to take his time. Clear up after him before he wet her, doused her . . . The word came to him without his wanting it to. Marinated her.

Then he had flicked the lighter.

Gram Parsons' "She" sounded and Bjørn lifted his phone to his ear.

"Yes? . . . A match? Hang on . . ."

He took out a pencil and his ever-present Moleskine notebook. Harry suspected Bjørn liked the patina of the cover so much he erased the notes when the book was full and used it again.

"No record, no, but he's worked on murder investigations . . . Yes, I'm afraid we had a suspicion . . . And his name is?"

Bjørn had put his notebook down on the bar counter, ready to write. But the pencil tip stopped. "What did you say the father's name was?"

Harry could hear from his colleague's voice that something was wrong. Terribly wrong.

• • •

As Ståle Aune tore open the classroom door the following thoughts whirled through his head: he had been a bad father; he wasn't sure if Aurora's class had their own room; and if they did, if it was still this room.

It was two years since he had been here, during a school open day when all the classes had exhibited drawings, matchstick models, clay figures and other nonsense that had left him unimpressed. A better father would have been impressed of course.

The voices went quiet, and the class turned in his direction.

And in the silence he scoured the young, soft-skinned faces. The unscarred, undefiled faces that had not lived as long as they would, faces that were yet to be formed, yet to assume character and over the years stiffen into the mask which would become who they were inside. Which he had become. His girl.

His sweeping gaze found faces he had seen in class photos, at birthday parties, all too few handball games, last days of term. Some he could identify by name, most he couldn't. Continued searching for the one face, as her name was formed, grew like a sob in his throat: Aurora. Aurora. Aurora.

Bjørn slipped the phone into his pocket. Stood by the counter with his back to Harry, motionless. Slowly shaking his head. Then he turned. His face looked as if it had been bled. Pale, bloodless.

"It's someone you know well," Harry said.

Bjørn nodded slowly, like a sleepwalker. Swallowed. "It just can't be possible . . ."

"Aurora."

The wall of faces gawped up at Ståle Aune. Her name had crossed his lips like a sob. Like a prayer.

"Aurora," he repeated.

At the margins of his field of vision he saw the teacher move towards him.

"What isn't possible?" Harry asked.

"His daughter," Bjørn said. "It . . . just can't be possible."

Ståle's eyes were swimming with tears. He felt a hand on his shoulder. Then a figure rose, came towards him, the contours blurred like in a fairground mirror. Yet he thought the figure resembled her. Resembled Aurora. As a psychologist he of course knew that this was the brain's escape, our way of tackling the intolerable, of lying. Of seeing what we want to see. Nevertheless he whispered her name.

"Aurora."

And he could even swear the voice was hers.

"Is something the matter . . . ?"

He also heard the last word at the end of the sentence, but wasn't sure if it was her or his brain that had added it.

"... Dad?"

"Why isn't it possible?"

"Because . . ." Bjørn said, staring at Harry as though he wasn't there.

"Yes?"

"Because she's already dead."

41

It was a quiet morning in Vestre Cemetery. All that could be heard was the distant hum of traffic in Sørkedalsveien and the clatter of the trams conveying people to the city centre.

"Roar Midtstuen, yes," Harry said, striding between the gravestones. "How many years has he actually been with you?"

"No one knows," Bjørn said, struggling to keep up. "Since the dawn of time."

"And his daughter died in a car accident?"

"Last summer. It's sick. It just can't be right. They've only got the first part of the DNA code. There's still a ten, fifteen per cent chance it's someone else's DNA, perhaps someone—" He almost walked into Harry, who had come to a sudden halt.

"Well," Harry said, sinking to his knees and sticking his fingers into the earth by the gravestone bearing Fia Midtstuen's name, "that chance just plummeted to zero." He raised his hand and sprinkled freshly dug soil between his fingers. "He dug up the body, transported it to Come As You Are. And set fire to it."

"F . . ."

Harry heard the tears in his colleague's voice. Avoided looking at him. Left him in peace. Waited. Closed his eyes, listened. A bird sang a—to human ears—meaningless song. The carefree, whistling wind nudged the clouds along. A metro train rattled westwards. Time went, but did it have anywhere to go any more? Harry opened his eyes again. Coughed.

"We'd better ask them to dig up the coffin and have this confirmed before we contact the father."

"I'll do that."

"Bjørn," Harry said, "this is better. This wasn't a young girl burned alive. OK?"

"Sorry, I'm just exhausted. And Roar was in a bad enough state before, so I . . ." He threw up his arms in desperation.

"That's fine," Harry said, getting up.

"Where are you going?"

Harry looked to the north, to the road and the metro. The clouds were drifting towards him. A northerly. And there it was again. The sensation that he knew something he didn't know yet, something down there in the murky depths inside him, but it would not float to the surface.

"I have to take care of something."

"Where?"

"Just something I've put off for too long."

"Right. By the way, there was something I was wondering about."

Harry glanced at his watch and nodded.

"When you spoke to Bellman yesterday what did he think could have happened to the bullet?"

"He had no idea."

"What about you? You usually have at least one hypothesis."

"Mm. I've got to be off."

"Harry?"

"Yes?"

"Don't . . ." Bjørn gave a sheepish smile. "Don't do anything stupid."

Katrine Bratt leaned back in her chair and looked at the screen. Bjørn Holm had just rung to say they had found the father, a Midtstuen who had investigated the murder of Kalsnes, but the reason they hadn't found him among the police officers with young daughters was that his daughter was already dead. And as that meant Katrine was temporarily unemployed she had looked at her search history from the day before. They hadn't had any hits for Mikael Bellman and René Kalsnes. When she had looked for a list of the people most frequently connected with Mikael Bellman, three names stood out. First was Ulla Bellman. Then came Truls Berntsen. And in third place, Isabelle Skøyen. It was no surprise that his wife came first, nor was it strange that the Councillor for Social Affairs, his superior, should come third.

But she was taken aback by Truls Berntsen.

For the simple reason that there was an internal note directed from Fraud Squad to the Police Chief, written right there in Police HQ. There was a cash sum that Truls Berntsen refused to account for, and they had asked for permission to start an investigation into possible corruption.

She couldn't find an answer, so she supposed that Bellman must have given a verbal response.

What she found strange was that the Chief of Police and an apparently corrupt policeman had rung and exchanged texts so often, used credit cards at the same places and at the same times, travelled at the same time by plane and train, checked into the same hotel on the same date and had been in the same firing range. When Harry had told her to run a thorough check on Bellman, she discovered that Bellman had been watching gay porn online. Could Truls Berntsen be his lover?

Katrine sat looking at the screen.

So what? It didn't have to mean anything.

She knew Harry had met Bellman the previous night, in Valle Hovin. And confronted him with the discovery of his bullet. And before leaving Harry had mumbled something about a feeling he knew who had switched the bullet in the Evidence Room. To her enquiry, Harry had only answered "The Shadow."

Katrine widened her search to include more of the past.

She read through the results.

Bellman and Berntsen were inseparable throughout their careers. Which had clearly started at Stovner Police Station after they had left Police College.

She got up a list of other employees during that period.

Her eyes ran down the screen. Stopped at one name. Dialled a number starting with 55.

"And high time too, frøken Bratt," the voice sang, and she felt so liberated to hear genuine Bergen dialect again. "You were supposed to have been here for a physical examination some time ago!"

"Hans—"

"Dr. Hans, thank you very much. Please be so kind as to remove your top, Bratt."

"Pack it in," she warned him, with a smile on her lips.

"May I ask you not to confuse medical expertise with unwanted sexual attentions in the workplace, Bratt?"

"Someone told me you were back on the beat."

"Yep. And where are you at this minute?"

"In Oslo. By the way, I can see from a list here that you worked at Stovner Police Station at the same time as Mikael Bellman and Truls Berntsen."

"That was straight after Police College, and only because of a woman, Bratt. The nightmare with the knockers—have I told you about her?"

"Probably."

"But when it was all over with her, it was over with Oslo as well." He burst into song. **"Vestland, Vestland über alles—"**

"Hans! When you worked with—"

"No one worked **with** those two boys, Katrine. You either worked for them or you worked against them."

"Truls Berntsen has been suspended."

"And high time too. He's beaten someone up again, I assume?"

"Beaten up? Did he beat up prisoners?"

"Worse than that. He beat up police officers."

Katrine felt the hairs on her arms stand on end. "Oh? Who did he beat up?"

"Everyone who tried it on with Bellman's wife. Beavis Berntsen was head over heels in love with them both."

"What did he use?"

"What do you mean?"

"When he beat them up."

"How should I know? Something hard, I suppose. At least it looked like that when that young Nordlander was stupid enough to dance too close to fru Bellman at the Christmas dinner."

"Which Nordlander?"

"His name was . . . let me see . . . something with R. Yes, Runar. It was Runar. Runar . . . let me see now . . . Runar . . ."

Come on, Katrine thought, as her fingers automatically scampered across the keyboard.

"Sorry, Katrine, it's a long time ago. Perhaps if you take off your top?"

"Tempting," Katrine said. "But I've found it without your help. There was only one Runar at Stovner at that time. Bye, Hans—"

"Wait! A little mammogram doesn't have to—"

"Have to run, sicko."

She rang off. Pressed Enter. Let the search engine

work while she stared at the surname. There was something familiar about it. Where had she heard it? She closed her eyes, mumbling the name to herself. It was so unusual it couldn't be chance. She opened her eyes. The result was in. There was a lot. Enough. Medical records. Admission to hospital for drug addiction. The correspondence between the head of a detox clinic in Oslo and the Police Chief. Pure, innocent, blue eyes looking at her. She suddenly knew where she had seen them before.

Harry let himself into the house, and strode over to the CD shelf without removing his shoes. Stuck his fingers between Waits's **Bad As Me** and **A Pagan Place** which he had placed first in the line of the Waterboys CDs, though not without some agonising, as strictly speaking it was a remastered version from 2002. It was the safest place in the house. Neither Rakel nor Oleg had ever voluntarily selected a CD featuring Tom Waits or Mike Scott.

He coaxed out the key. Brass, small and hollow, weighing almost nothing. And yet it felt so heavy that his hand seemed to be drawn towards the floor as he went over to the corner cupboard. He inserted it in the keyhole and turned. Waited. Knowing there was no way back after he had opened it. The promise would be broken.

He had to use his strength to pull open the swollen cupboard door. He knew it was only old wood being released by the frame but it sounded as though a deep sigh came from inside the darkness. As though it realised it was free at last. Free to inflict hell on earth.

It smelt of metal and oil.

He inhaled. Felt as if he was sticking his hand into a den of snakes. His fingers groped before finding the cold, scaly skin of steel. He grabbed the reptile's head and lifted it out.

It was an ugly weapon. Fascinatingly ugly. Soviet Russian engineering at its most brutally effective, it could take as much of a beating as a Kalashnikov.

Harry weighed the gun in his hand.

He knew it was heavy, and yet it felt light. Light now that the decision had been taken. He breathed out. The demon was free.

"Hi," Ståle said, closing the Boiler Room door behind him. "Are you alone?"

"Yeah," Bjørn said from his chair, staring at the phone.

Ståle sat down on a chair. "Where . . . ?"

"Harry had to sort something out. Katrine was gone when I arrived."

"You look as if you've had a tough day."

Bjørn smiled wanly. "You, too, Dr. Aune."

Ståle ran a hand across his pate. "Well, I've just entered a classroom, embraced my daughter and sobbed with the whole class watching. Aurora claims it was an experience that will mark her for life. I tried to explain to her that fortunately most children are born with enough strength to bear the burden that is their parents' love and that from a Darwinian point of view she should therefore be able to survive this as well. All because she had a sleepover with Emilie and there are two Emilies in the class. I rang the mother of the wrong Emilie."

"Did you get the message that we've postponed the meeting for today? A body has been found. Of a girl."

"Yes, I know. It was grim by all accounts."

Bjørn nodded slowly. Pointed to the phone. "I have to ring the father now."

"You're dreading it of course."

"Of course."

"You're wondering why the father has to be punished in this way? Why he has to lose her twice? Why once isn't enough?"

"That sort of thing."

"The answer is because the murderer sees himself as the divine avenger, Bjørn."

"Oh yeah?" Bjørn said, sending the psychologist a vacant look.

"Do you know your Bible? 'God is jealous, and the Lord revengeth; the Lord revengeth, and is furious; the Lord will take vengeance on his adversaries, and he reserveth wrath for his enemies.' You get the gist anyway, don't you?"

"I'm a simple boy from Østre Toten who scraped through confirmation and—"

"That's why I'm here now." Ståle leaned forward in his chair. "The murderer is an avenger, and Harry's right, he kills out of love, not out of hatred, profit or sadistic enjoyment. Someone has taken something from him that he loved, and now he's taking from the victims what they loved most. It could be their lives. Or something they value more: their children."

Bjørn nodded. "Roar Midtstuen would have happily given his life to save his daughter."

"So what we have to look for is someone who's lost something they loved. An avenger out of love. Because that . . ." Ståle Aune clenched his right hand. ". . . because that's the only motive that's strong enough here, Bjørn. Do you understand?"

Bjørn nodded. "I think so. But I reckon I'll have to call Midtstuen now."

"I'll leave you in peace then."

Bjørn waited until Ståle had gone, then he dialled the number he had been looking at for so long it felt as if it had been stamped on his retina. He took deep breaths as he counted the rings. Wondering how many times he should let it ring before putting the receiver down. Then all of a sudden he heard his colleague's voice.

"Bjørn, is that you?"

"Yes. You've got my number saved then?"

"Yes, of course."

"I see. Right. I'm afraid there's something I have to tell you."

Pause.

Bjørn swallowed. "It's about your daughter. She—"

"Bjørn, before you go any further, I don't know what this is about, but I can hear from your tone that it's serious. And I can't take any more phone calls about Fia. This is just like it was then. No one could look me in the eye. Everyone rang. Seemed to be easier. Please would you come here? Look me in the eye when you say whatever it is. Bjørn?"

"Of course," Bjørn Holm said, taken aback. He had never heard Roar Midtstuen talk so openly and honestly about his frailty before. "Where are you?"

"It's exactly nine months today, so as it happens I'm on my way to the place where she was killed. To lay a few flowers, think—"

"Just tell me exactly where it is and I'll be there right away."

Katrine Bratt gave up looking for somewhere to park. It had been easier finding the telephone number and address online. But after ringing four times and getting neither an answer nor an answerphone, she had requisitioned a car and driven to Industrigata in Majorstuen, a one-way street with a greengrocer's, a couple of galleries, at least one restaurant, a picture-framing workshop, but, well, no free parking spaces.

Katrine made a decision, drove up onto the pavement, killed the engine, put a note on the windscreen saying she was a police officer, which she knew meant sod all to traffic wardens, who, according to Harry, were all that stood between civilisation and total chaos.

She walked back the way she had come, towards Bogstadsveien's stylish shopping hysteria. Stopped outside a block of flats in Josefines gate where once or twice during her studies at Police College she had ended up for a late-night coffee. So-called late-night coffee. Alleged late-night coffee. Not that she'd minded. Oslo Police District had owned the block and rented out rooms to students at the college. Katrine found the name she was searching for on the panel of doorbells, pressed and waited while contemplating the simple four-storey facade. Pressed again. Waited.

"No one at home?"

She turned. Automatic smile. Guessed the man was in his forties, perhaps a well-kept fifty-year-old. Tall, still with hair, flannel shirt, Levi's 501s.

"I'm the caretaker."

"And I'm Detective Katrine Bratt, Crime Squad. I'm looking for Silje Gravseng."

He studied the ID card she held out and shamelessly examined her from top to toe.

"Silje Gravseng, yes," the caretaker said. "Apparently she's left PHS, so she won't be here for much longer."

"But she's still here?"

"Yes, she is. Room 412. Can I pass on a message?"

"Please. Ask her to ring this number. I want to talk to her about Runar Gravseng, her brother."

"Has he done something wrong?"

"Hardly. He's sectioned and always sits in the middle of the room because he thinks the walls are people who want to beat him to death."

"Oh dear."

Katrine took out her notebook and wrote her name and number. "You can tell her it's about the police murders."

"Yes, she seems to be obsessed by them."

Katrine stopped writing. "What do you mean?"

"She uses them like wallpaper. Newspaper cuttings about dead policemen, I mean. Not that it's any of my business. Students can put up what they like, but that's a bit . . . creepy, isn't it?"

Katrine looked at him. "What did you say your name was?"

"Leif Rødbekk."

"Listen, Leif. Do you think I could have a peek at her room? I'd like to see the cuttings."

"Why's that?"

"Can I?"

"No problem. Just show me the search warrant."

"I'm afraid I don't—"

"I was kidding," he grinned. "Come with me."

A minute later they were in the lift on their way to the third floor.

"The rental agreement says I can go into the rooms as long as I've given advance warning. Right now we're checking all the electric radiators for accumulated dust. One of them caught fire last week. And we tried to give her advance warning before we entered, but Silje didn't answer the intercom. Sound all right to you, Detective Bratt?" Another grin. Wolfish grin, Katrine thought. Not without charm. If he'd taken the liberty of using her Christian name at the end of the sentence, it would of course have been over, but he did have a certain lilt. Her gaze sought his ring finger. The smooth gold was matt. The lift doors opened and she followed him down the narrow corridor until he stopped in front of one of the blue doors.

He knocked and waited. Knocked again. Waited.

"Let's go in," he said, turning the key in the lock.

"You've been very helpful, Rødbekk."

"Leif. And it's a pleasure to be able to help. It's not every day I run into such a . . ." He opened the door for her but stood in such a way that if she wanted to go in she would have to squeeze past him. She sent him an admonitory glance. ". . . serious case," he said with laughter dancing in his eyes and stepped to the side.

Katrine went in. The rooms hadn't changed a lot. There was still a kitchenette and the bathroom door at one end and a curtain at the other, behind which Katrine remembered there was a bed. But the first thing that struck her was that she had entered a girl's room and it couldn't be a very mature girl living here. Silje Gravseng must long for something in the past. The sofa in the corner was covered with a motley collection of teddy bears, dolls and various cuddly toys. Her clothes, strewn across the table and chairs, were brightly coloured, predominantly pink. On the walls there were pictures, a human menagerie of fashion victims; Katrine guessed they were from boy bands or the Disney Channel.

The second thing to strike her was the black-and-white newspaper cuttings between the lurid glamour shots. She walked round the room, but was drawn to the wall above the iMac on the desk.

Katrine went closer although she had already recognised most of the cuttings. They had the same ones on the wall of the Boiler Room.

The cuttings were fastened with drawing pins and bore no notes other than the date written in pen.

She rejected her first thought and instead tested a second: that it was not so strange for a PHS student to be fascinated by such a high-profile ongoing murder case.

Beside the keyboard lay the newspapers the cuttings had been taken from. And between the papers a postcard with a picture of a north Norwegian mountain peak she recognised: Svolværgeita in Lofoten. She picked up the card and turned it over, but there wasn't a stamp, or an address or signature. She had already put the card down when her brain told her what her eyes had registered where they had automatically searched for a signature. A word in block capitals where the writing had finished. POLITI. She picked up the card again, holding it by the edges this time and read it from the start.

They think the officers have been killed because someone hates them. They still haven't understood that it's the other way round, that they were killed by someone who loves the police and the police's sacred duty: catching and punishing anarchists, nihilists, atheists, the faithless and the creedless, all the destructive forces. They don't know that what they're hunting is an apostle of righteousness, someone who has to punish not only vandals but also those who betray their responsibilities, those who out of laziness and indifference do not live up to the standard, those who do not deserve to be called POLITI.

"Do you know what, Leif?" Katrine said, without moving her eyes from the microscopic, neat, almost childish letters written in blue ink. "I really wish I had a search warrant."

"Oh?"

"I'll get one, but you know how it is with these things. They can take time. And by then what I'm curious about may have disappeared."

Katrine looked up at him. Leif Rødbekk returned her gaze. Not flirtatiously, but as if to find confirmation. That this was important.

"And do you know what, Bratt?" he said. "I've just remembered that I have to nip down to the basement. The electricians are changing cupboards there. Can you manage on your own for a while?"

She smiled at him. And when he returned her smile too, she wasn't sure what kind of smile it was.

"I'll do my best," she said.

Katrine pressed the space bar on the iMac the second she heard the door close behind Rødbekk. The screen lit up. She put the cursor on Finder and typed in Mittet. No hits. She tried a couple of other names from the investigation, crime scenes and "police murders," but no hits.

So Silje Gravseng hadn't used the computer. Smart girl.

Katrine pulled at the desk drawers. Locked. Strange. What girl of twenty-something would lock the drawers in her own room?

She got up, went over to the curtain and drew it aside.

It was as she remembered, an alcove.

With two large photographs on the wall above the narrow bed.

She had seen Silje Gravseng only twice, the first time at PHS when Katrine had visited Harry. But the family likeness between the blonde Silje and the person in the photo was so striking she was sure.

There was no doubt about the man in the other photo.

Silje must have found a high-res photo online and enlarged it. Every scar, every line, every pore in the skin of the ravaged face stood out. But it was as though they were invisible, as though they faded in the gleam of the blue eyes and the furious expression as he spotted the photographer and told him there would be no cameras on his crime scene. Harry Hole. This was the photo the girls in the row in front of her in the auditorium had been talking about.

Katrine divided the room into squares and started with the top left, then scanned the floor, looked up again to start the next row, the way she had been taught by Harry. And recalled his thesis: "Don't search for **something,** just search. If you search for something the other things won't speak to you. Make sure everything speaks to you."

After going through the room, she sat down at the iMac again, his voice still buzzing in her head: "And when you've finished and think you haven't found anything, think inversely, a mirror image, and let the other things speak to you. The things that **weren't** there, but should have been. The bread knife. The car keys. The jacket from a suit."

It was the last item that had helped her to conclude what Silje Gravseng was doing now. She had flicked through all the clothes in the wardrobe, in the linen basket in the little bathroom and on the hooks beside the door, but she hadn't found the tracksuit Silje had been wearing the last time Katrine had seen her, with Harry in the basement flat where Valentin had lived. Dressed in black from top to toe. Katrine remembered she had reminded her of a marine on night manoeuvres.

Silje was out running. Training. As she had done to pass the entry requirements for PHS. To get in and do whatever she could do. Harry had said the motive for the murders was love, not hatred. Love for a brother, for instance.

It was the name that had brought a reaction. Runar Gravseng. And after further investigation a lot had come to light. Among other things, the names of Bellman and Berntsen. Runar Gravseng had in conversation with the head of the detox clinic claimed that he had been beaten up by a masked man while working at Stovner Police Station. That had been the reason for the doctor's certificate, his resignation and his increased drug consumption. Gravseng maintained the perp was one Truls Berntsen and the motive for the violence was a slightly too cosy dance with Mikael Bellman's wife at the police station's Christmas dinner. The Chief of Police had refused to take the wild accusations of an out-and-out drug addict any further, and the head of the detox clinic had supported this. He had only wanted to pass on information, he'd said.

Katrine heard the lift go in the corridor as her gaze fell on something protruding from under the desk, which she'd missed. She bent down. A black baton.

The door opened.

"Electricians doing their job?"

"Yes," said Leif Rødbekk. "You look as if you intend to use that."

Katrine smacked the baton against her palm. "Interesting object to have lying around in your room, don't you think?"

"Yes. I said the same when I was changing the washer on the bathroom tap last week. She said it was for training, for an exam. And in case the cop killer turned up." Leif Rødbekk closed the door behind him. "Find anything?"

"This. Ever seen her take it out?"

"A couple of times, yes."

"Really?" Katrine pushed herself backwards on the chair. "What time of day?"

"At night of course. Dolled up, high heels, blow-dried hair and the baton." He chuckled.

"Why on—?"

"She said it was protection against rapists."

"She'd lug a baton into town for that?" Katrine weighed the baton in her hand. (It reminded her of the top of an IKEA hat stand.) "It would have been easier to avoid the parks."

"Not her. She went straight to the parks."

"What?"

"She went to Vaterlandsparken. She wanted to practise hand-to-hand combat."

"She wanted perverts to try it on and then . . ."

"And then beat them black and blue, yes." Leif Rødbekk put on his wolfish grin again, sending Katrine such a direct look that she wasn't sure who he meant when he said: "Quite a girl."

"Yes," Katrine said, getting up. "And now I have to find her."

"Busy?"

If Katrine felt any unease at this question, it didn't reach her consciousness until she was past him and out of the door. But on the stairs, going down, she thought, no, she wasn't that desperate. Even if the slow-coach she was waiting for never got his act together.

Harry drove through Svartdalstunnel. The lights shone across the bonnet and windscreen. He didn't go any faster than was necessary, no need to arrive any sooner than he had to. The gun was on the seat next to him. It was loaded and had twelve Makarov 9x18mm bullets in the magazine. More than enough to do what he was going to do. It was just a question of having the stomach for it.

He had the heart for it.

He had never shot anyone in cold blood before. But this was a job that had to be done. Simple as that.

He shifted his grip on the steering wheel. Changed down as he came out of the tunnel, into the fading light, into the hills towards the Ryen intersection. Felt his mobile ring and pulled it out with one hand. Glanced at the display. It was Rakel. It was an unusual time for her to ring. They had an unspoken agreement that their phone time was after ten in the evening. He couldn't talk to her now. He was too nervous. She would notice and ask. And he didn't want to lie. Didn't want to lie any more.

He let the phone finish ringing, then he switched it off and put it beside the gun. For there was nothing to think about any more, the thinking was over, letting his doubts surface would mean starting again, only to take the same long route and end up exactly where he was already. The decision was taken, that he wanted to back out was understandable, but it was out of the question. Shit! He smacked his hand against the wheel. Thought about Oleg. About Rakel. It helped.

He went round the roundabout and took the turning to Manglerud. To the block of flats where Truls Berntsen lived. Felt the calm descending. At last. It always did when he knew he had crossed the threshold, where it was too late, where he was in the wonderful free fall, where conscious thought stopped and everything was automatic, targeted action and well-oiled routine. But it had been so long ago, and he felt that now. He had been unsure whether he still had it in him. Well. He had it in him.

He drove slowly down the streets. Leaned forward and looked up at the blue-grey clouds streaming in, like an unannounced armada with unknown objectives. Sat back in the seat. Saw the high-rise buildings above the lower rooftops.

Didn't need to look down at the gun to know it was there.

Didn't need to think through the order of events to be sure he would remember.

Didn't need to count his heartbeats to know his pulse was at rest.

And for a moment he closed his eyes and visualised what would happen. And then it came, the feeling he'd had a couple of times earlier in his life as a policeman. The fear. The same fear he could sometimes sense in those he was chasing. The murderer's fear of his own reflection.

42

Truls Berntsen raised his hips and forced his head back against the pillow. He closed his eyes, emitted low grunts, and came. Felt the spasms shake his body. Afterwards he lay still, drifting in and out of dreamland. In the distance—he assumed it must have been from the big car park—an alarm had started to wail. Otherwise a resounding silence reigned outside. Odd, really, that in a peaceful place where so many mammals lived above one another it was quieter than in even the most dangerous forests where the slightest sound could mean you had become the prey. He raised his head and met Megan Fox's eyes.

"Was it good for you too?" he whispered.

She didn't answer. But her eyes didn't flinch, her smile didn't wither, the invitation of her body language was the same. Megan Fox, the only person in his life who was constant, loyal and reliable.

He leaned over to the bedside table and grabbed the toilet roll. Cleaned himself up and found the remote control for the DVD player. Pointed it at Megan, who quivered in the freeze-frame on the fifty-inch flat-screen TV, a Pioneer in the series they had to stop making because it was too expensive, too good for the price they commanded. Truls had got the last one, bought with money he had earned by burning evidence against a pilot who had been smuggling heroin for Asayev. Taking the rest of the money to the bank and putting it straight into his account had been idiocy of course. Asayev had been dangerous for Truls. And when Truls had heard Asayev was dead his first thought was that now he was free. The slate had been wiped clean, no one could get him.

Megan Fox's green eyes glinted at him. Emerald green.

It had been on his mind for a while that he should buy emeralds for her. Ulla dressed in green. Like the green sweater she took off when she was on the sofa reading. He had even dropped by a jeweller's. The owner had quickly sized Truls up, estimated the carat and value and then explained to him that emeralds of the finest water were even more expensive than diamonds, perhaps he ought to consider something else, what about an elegant opal if it absolutely had to be green? Or perhaps a stone with chrome in, it was the chrome that lent the emerald the green colour, that was all there was to the mystery.

That was all there was to the mystery.

Truls had left the shop with a promise to himself. The next time he was contacted by anyone for a burn scam he would suggest they break into this particular jewellery shop first. And they should burn it. Quite literally. Burn it the same way the young girl at Come As You Are had burned. He had heard it on the police radio while driving around town and had considered going over to see if he could help. After all, his suspension had been lifted. Mikael had said there were only a few formalities to clear up before he could go back to work. His plans to terrorise Mikael were on ice now, they would be able to re-establish their friendship, no problem, and everything would be as before. Yes, at last he would be allowed to join in, have a go, contribute. Get the psycho cop killer. If Truls got the chance he would personally . . . well. He glanced at the cabinet beside his bed. Inside, he had enough weapons to expedite fifty psychos.

The doorbell rang.

Truls sighed.

Someone wanted something off him. Experience told him it could be one of four possibilities. 1) He should become a Jehovah's Witness and dramatically increase his chances of ending up in Paradise. 2) He should donate money to some collection or other for an African president who based his wealth on collection campaigns. 3) He should open the door to a gang of youths who said they'd forgotten the key but only wanted to break into the storage rooms in the cellar. Or 4) Some of the housing co-op sticklers wanted him to go down and do some chore he had forgotten to do. None of them was reason enough to get out of bed.

The bell rang for the third time.

Even Jehovah's Witnesses gave up after two.

Of course it might be Mikael, wanting to talk about things that were best avoided on the phone. To make sure they were singing from the same hymn sheet if there were any more interviews about the money in his account.

Truls deliberated for a few minutes.

Then he swung his legs out of bed.

"This is Aronsen from C block. You own a silver-grey Suzuki Vitara, right?"

"Yes," Truls said into the intercom. It should have been an Audi Q5 2.0 6-speed manual. It should have been the reward for the last job for Asayev. The last instalment after serving them up that irritating detective, Harry Hole. Instead he had a Japanese car people made jokes about. Suzuki Viagra.

"Can you hear the alarm?"

Truls heard it more clearly now through the intercom.

"Oh, shit," he said. "I'll see if I can switch it off with the remote."

"If I were you I'd get down here right away. They'd smashed a side window and were taking out the radio and CD player when I arrived. I reckon they're hanging around to see what will happen."

"Oh, shit!" Truls repeated.

"Not at all, pleasure to be able to help," Aronsen said.

Truls put on his trainers, checked he had his car keys and then a thought struck him. He went back to the bedroom, opened the cabinet door and took out one of the guns, a Jericho 941, shoved it into the waistband of his trousers. Stopped. He knew the plasma TV was prone to screen burn if it was paused for too long. But he'd be back shortly. Then he hurried into the corridor. Just as quiet here.

The lift was on his floor, so he stepped in straight away, pressed the button for the ground floor, realised he hadn't locked his front door, but didn't stop the lift. It would only take a few minutes.

Half a minute later he jogged into the clear, chilly evening towards the car park. It was surrounded by flats, but the cars were still frequently broken into. They should put up more lamp posts, the black tarmac swallowed all the light there was; it was too easy to sneak around between the cars after dark. He'd had problems sleeping after the suspension, that's how it goes when you have the whole day to sleep, wank, sleep, wank, eat and wank. And on some nights he had sat on the balcony with night-vision goggles and the Märklin rifle in the hope of catching some of them in the car park. Sadly, no one had turned up. Or happily. No, not happily. But for Christ's sake, he wasn't a murderer.

Of course there was the biker from Los Lobos he had drilled a hole in, but that had been a complete accident. And now he was part of the terrace up in Høyenhall.

Then there was the trip he'd taken to Ila Prison when he'd spread the rumour that Valentin Gjertsen was behind the killings in Maridalen and Tryvann. Not that they were a hundred per cent sure he'd done it, but if he hadn't there were enough other reasons for the bastard to get as long a sentence as possible.

But he couldn't know the nutters would kill the guy. If it was him they'd killed, that is. The communication on the police radio at the moment suggested not.

The closest Truls had been to murder was of course the lady boy with the make-up in Drammen. But that was something that had to be done, he'd been asking for it. He really fucking had. Mikael had come to Truls and told him about the call he'd received. Some guy claimed he knew that Mikael and a colleague had beaten up the homo working at Kripos. And he had proof. And now he wanted money to stop him taking it further. A hundred thousand kroner. He wanted the money delivered to a deserted area outside Drammen. Mikael told Truls to sort it out, Truls was the one who had gone too far this time, who had caused the problem. And when Truls got in his car to go and meet the guy he knew he was on his own. Completely on his own. And he always had been.

He had followed the signs up some deserted forest roads outside Drammen and stopped at a turnaround by a cliff plummeting down towards the river. Waited for five minutes. Then the car had arrived. It pulled up, with the engine running. And Truls had done as agreed, taken the brown envelope to the car. The side window slid down. The guy was wearing a woollen hat and had a silk scarf tied around the lower half of his face. Truls wondered if the guy was a retard; it was unlikely the car had been stolen, and the plates were fully visible. In addition, Mikael had already traced the conversation to a club in Drammen. There couldn't be many employees so it wouldn't be hard to track him down.

The guy had opened the envelope and counted the money. Obviously he had lost count. He started again, frowned and looked up with annoyance. "This isn't a hund—"

The blow had hit him in the mouth, and Truls had felt the baton sink in as his teeth cracked. The second blow had smashed his nose. Easy. Cartilage and thin bones. The third made a soft crunch as it hit the forehead.

Then Truls had walked round and got into the passenger seat. Waited until the guy regained consciousness. And when he did, a short conversation followed.

"Who . . . ?"

"One of them. What proof have you got?"

"I . . . I . . ."

"This is a Heckler & Koch and it's dying to speak. So which of you is going to do it first?"

"Don't—"

"Come on then."

"The one you two beat up. He told me. Please, I only needed—"

"Did he name us?"

"What? No."

"So how do you know who we are?"

"He only told me the story. Then I checked out the descriptions with someone at Kripos. And it had to be you two." When the guy saw his face in the mirror it had sounded like the whine a Hoover makes after you switch it off. "My God! You've destroyed my face!"

"Shut up and sit still. Does the man you say we beat up know you're blackmailing us?"

"Him? No, no, he'd never—"

"Are you his lover?"

"No! He might think so, but—"

"Anyone else know?"

"No! I promise! Just let me go. I promise not to—"

"So no one else knows you're here now."

Truls enjoyed the sight of the guy's gawping expression as the implication of what Truls had said laboriously trickled through to his brain. "Yes, yes, they do! Lots of people do—"

"You're not that bad at lying," Truls said, putting the barrel to the man's forehead. The gun had felt surprisingly light. "But not that good, either."

Then Truls had pulled the trigger. It hadn't been a difficult decision. Because there had been no choice. It was just something that had to be done. Sheer survival instinct. The guy had something on them, which sooner or later he would find a way to use. That was the way hyenas like him ticked. Cowardly and subservient face to face, but greedy and patient. They would allow themselves to be humiliated, to be cowed, and wait, but attack as soon as you turned your back.

Afterwards he had wiped the seat and wherever he had left fingerprints, wrapped a scarf around his hand as he released the handbrake and put the car into neutral. Rolled it over the cliff. Listened to the eerie silence as the vehicle fell. Followed by a dull report and the sound of metal buckling. Looked down at the car lying in the river beneath him.

He had got rid of the baton as quickly and efficiently as possible. Quite a way down the forest road he had opened the window and slung it through the trees. It was unlikely to be found, but if it was, there still wouldn't be any fingerprints or DNA to link it to the murder or him.

The gun was a different matter; the bullet could be linked to the gun and so to him.

Thus he had waited until he drove over Drammen Bridge. He had driven slowly and watched the gun fly over the railing and down to where the river meets the fjord. A place where it would never be found, under ten or twenty metres of water. Brackish water. Dubious water. Neither completely salt water nor completely fresh water. Neither completely wrong nor completely right. Death in marginal areas. But he had read somewhere that there were species which specialised in surviving in these hybrid waters. Species that were so perverted they couldn't cope with the water normal life forms had to have.

Truls pressed the remote before he reached the car park, and the alarm was silenced right away. There was no one to be seen outside or on the balconies surrounding him, but Truls thought he could detect a collective sigh from the blocks: about bloody time too, pay more attention to your car, you could have set the length of the alarm, you muppet.

A side window was smashed in, that was true. Truls stuck his head in. He couldn't see any sign of anyone having tampered with the radio. What had Aronsen meant by . . . and who was Aronsen? C block, could be anyone. Anyone at all . . .

Truls's brain had come to a conclusion a fragment of a second before he felt the steel on his neck. He instinctively knew it was steel. The steel of a gun barrel. He knew there was no Aronsen. No gang of youths breaking in.

The voice whispered by his ear:

"Don't turn, Berntsen. And when I put my hand in your trousers, don't move. Well, well, feel that. Nice tight abs . . ."

Truls knew he was in danger, he just didn't understand what kind. There was something familiar about Aronsen's voice.

"Oooh, bit sweaty, eh, Berntsen? Or do you like it? But this is what I was after. Jericho? What were you going to do with this? Shoot someone in the face? Like you did to René?"

And now Truls Berntsen knew what kind of danger. Mortal danger.

43

Rakel stood by the kitchen window squeezing the phone and staring into the dusk again. She may have been imagining things, but she thought she'd seen a movement between the spruces on the other side of the drive.

But she was always seeing movements in the darkness.

That was how deep the wound was. Don't think about it. Be frightened, but don't think about it. Let your body play its stupid games, but ignore them the way you ignore an unreasonable child.

She was bathed in the light from the kitchen, so if there was really someone outside they would be able to study her at their leisure. But she didn't move. She had to practise, mustn't let fear determine what she did, where she stood, this was her house, her home, for goodness' sake!

Music was coming from the first floor. He was playing one of Harry's old CDs. One of them she liked as well. Talking Heads. **Little Creatures.**

She looked down at the phone again, urging it to ring. Twice she had rung Harry, but still there was no answer. They had planned it as a nice surprise.

The news had come from the clinic the day before. It was earlier than the date they'd set, but they had decided he was ready. Oleg had been so excited and it had been his idea not to say anything before they arrived. Just go home and then when Harry came home, jump out and say boo.

That was the word he had used: "boo."

Rakel had had her doubts. Harry didn't like surprises. But Oleg had insisted. Harry would bloody well have to put up with suddenly being happy. And so she had gone along with it.

But now she regretted having done so.

She went from the window, put the phone down on the worktop beside his coffee cup. Usually he was painfully scrupulous about clearing everything away before leaving the house. He must have been stressed by these police murders. He hadn't mentioned Beate Lønn in their nightly conversations recently, a sure sign that he was thinking about her.

Rakel spun round. It wasn't her imagination this time, she **had** heard something. Shoes crunching on the gravel. She went back to the window. Stared into the darkness, which seemed to her to be deepening by the second.

Froze.

Someone was there. A figure had just moved from the tree it had been standing by. And it was coming this way. A person dressed in black. How long had it been there?

"Oleg!" Rakel shouted, her heart racing. "Oleg!"

The music upstairs was turned down. "Yes?"

"Come down here! Now!"

"Is he coming?"

Yes, she thought. He's coming.

The figure that approached was smaller than she'd thought at first. It was moving towards the front door, and as it came closer in the light from the outside lamps, she saw to her surprise and relief that it was a woman. No, a girl. In a tracksuit, it appeared. Three seconds later, the bell rang.

Rakel hesitated. Glanced at Oleg, who had stopped halfway down the stairs and was looking at her with a quizzical expression.

"It's not Harry," Rakel said with a quick smile. "I'll get it. Just go back up, Oleg."

The girl standing on the step calmed Rakel's heart rate even further. She looked frightened.

"You're Rakel," she said. "Harry's girlfriend."

It struck Rakel that this introduction ought to have unsettled her. A beautiful young girl with a trembling voice addressing her with a reference to her husband-to-be. Probably she ought to check the tight-fitting tracksuit top for an incipient stomach bulge.

But she wasn't unsettled, and she didn't check. Just nodded by way of a response.

"That's me."

"And I'm Silje Gravseng."

The girl looked at Rakel expectantly, as though waiting for a reaction, thinking the name should mean something to her. Rakel noticed the girl had her hands behind her back. A psychologist had once told her people who hid their hands had something to hide. Yes, she'd thought. Their hands.

Rakel smiled. "So how can I help you, Silje?"

"Harry is . . . **was** my lecturer."

"Oh yes?"

"There's something I have to tell you about him. And about me."

Rakel frowned. "Really?"

"May I come in?"

Rakel hesitated. She didn't want anyone else in the house. She wanted only Oleg, herself and Harry, when he came. The three of them. No one else. And definitely not someone who had to tell her something about Harry. And about herself. And then it happened anyway. Her eyes involuntarily scanned the young girl's stomach.

"It won't take long, fru Fauke."

Fru. What had Harry told her? She considered the situation. Heard Oleg had turned his music up again. Then she opened the door.

The girl stepped inside, bent down and started untying her trainers.

"Don't bother with that," Rakel said. "We'll wrap this up quickly, OK. I'm a bit busy."

"Right," the girl said. It was only now, in the brighter light in the hall, that Rakel saw the glistening layer of sweat on the girl's face. She followed Rakel into the kitchen. "The music," she said. "Is Harry at home?"

Rakel sensed it now. The anxiety. The girl had automatically connected the music with Harry. Was that because she knew this was the kind of music Harry listened to? And the thought came too fast for Rakel to reject: music that he and this girl had listened to together?

The girl sat down at the big table. Laid her palms on the surface and stroked the wood. Rakel eyed her movements. She stroked it as if she already knew how the rough, untreated wood felt against her skin, pleasant, alive. Her gaze was fixed on Harry's coffee cup. Had she . . . ?

"What did you want to tell me, Silje?"

The girl smiled a sad, almost painful smile, without taking her eyes off the cup.

"Has he really not said anything about me, fru Fauke?"

Rakel closed her eyes for an instant. This wasn't happening. She trusted him. She opened her eyes again.

"Say what you want to say as if he hasn't, Silje."

"As you wish, fru Fauke." The girl looked up from the cup and at her. It was an almost unnaturally blue-eyed gaze, as innocent and unknowing as a child's. And, Rakel thought, as cruel as a child's.

"I want to talk to you about rape," Silje said.

Rakel suddenly noticed she had difficulty breathing, as though someone had sucked the air from the room, like vacuum-packing.

"What rape?" she managed to ask.

• • •

Darkness was beginning to descend when Bjørn Holm finally found the car.

He had turned off by Klemetsrud and continued eastwards on the B155, but had obviously passed the sign for Fjell. It was on his way back, after he'd realised he'd gone too far and had had to turn, that he'd seen it. The side road was even less busy than the B-road, and now, in the darkness, it seemed like total wasteland. The dense forest on both sides seemed to be creeping closer when he saw the rear lights of the car beside the road.

He slowed down and glanced in his mirror. Only darkness behind him, only a couple of solitary red lights in front of him. Bjørn pulled in behind the car. Got out. A bird hooted from somewhere in the forest, a hollow, melancholy sound. Roar Midtstuen was crouching in the ditch in the light from the headlamps.

"You came," Roar said.

Bjørn grabbed his belt and hitched up his trousers. This was something he'd started doing—he had no idea where he'd got it from. Oh, yes, in fact, he did. His father had always hitched up his trousers by way of an introduction, a preface to something weighty that had to be said or done. He'd started behaving like his father. Except that he seldom had anything weighty to say.

"So this is where it happened?" Bjørn said.

Roar nodded. Then looked down at the bouquet of flowers he had laid on the tarmac. "She'd been climbing here with friends. On her way home she stopped to have a pee in the woods. Told the others to go on ahead. They think it must have happened when she ran back out and jumped on her bike. Keen to catch up with the others, right? She was that kind of girl, enthusiastic, you see . . ." He was already fighting to keep his voice under control. "And then she probably veered into the road, her bike was still wobbling, and so . . ." Roar lifted his head to show where the car had come from. ". . . and there were no skid marks. No one remembered what the car looked like, even though it must have passed Fia's friends straight afterwards. But they were busy talking about the climbs they'd tried and they said lots of cars must have passed them. They were well on their way to Klemetsrud before it struck them that Fia should have caught them up long ago and that something must have happened."

Bjørn nodded. Cleared his throat. Wanted to get it over and done with. But Roar wouldn't let him get a word in.

"I wasn't allowed to investigate, Bjørn. Because I was the father, they said. Instead they put novices on the case. And when at last they realised this case wasn't going to be child's play, that the driver wouldn't turn himself in or give any clues, it was too late to trundle in the big guns. The trail was cold and people's memories were blank."

"Roar . . ."

"Bad police work, Bjørn. Nothing less. We spend our whole lives working for the force, we give it everything we've got and then—when we lose the dearest thing we have—what have we got left? Nothing. It's a dreadful betrayal, Bjørn." Bjørn watched his colleague's jaws moving in a regular ellipse as he tightened and slackened, tightened and slackened the muscles. Must be giving the chewing gum a right hammering, he thought. "Makes me ashamed to be a police officer," Midtstuen said. "Just like with the Kalsnes case. Terrible workmanship from start to finish. We let the murderer slip through our fingers and afterwards no one is held to account. And no one holds **anyone** to account. Foxes in the henhouse, Bjørn."

"The girl who was found burned in Come As You Are this morning—"

"Anarchy. That's what it is. Someone has to be held to account. Someone—"

"It was Fia."

In the ensuing silence Bjørn heard the bird hoot again, but from somewhere else this time. It must have moved. A thought struck him. That it was another bird. There could be two of them. Two of the same species. Which hooted to each other in the forest.

"Harry's rape of me." Silje looked at Rakel as calmly as if she had just told her the weather forecast.

"Harry raped you?"

Silje smiled. A fleeting smile, no more than a muscle twitch, an expression that had no time to reach her eyes before it was gone. Along with everything else, steadfastness, indifference. And her eyes, instead of lighting up with a smile, filled with tears.

My God, Rakel thought, she isn't lying. She opened her mouth for oxygen and knew with a hundred per cent certainty: the girl might be off her rocker, but she wasn't lying.

"I was so in love with him, fru Fauke. I thought we were meant for each other. So I went to his office. I had put on make-up. And he misunderstood."

Rakel watched as the first tear detached itself from her eyelashes and fell, then it was caught by the soft, young cheek. It rolled down. Moistening the skin. Making it pink. She knew there was a roll of paper towels on the worktop behind her, but she didn't get it. No way.

"Harry doesn't do misunderstandings," Rakel said, surprised by the composure in her voice. "Nor rape." The composure and the conviction. She wondered how long it would last.

"You're wrong," Silje said, smiling through the tears.

"Am I?" Rakel felt like smacking a fist into her smug, spoiled face.

"Yes, fru Fauke. Now you're the one who misunderstands."

"Say what you have to say and get out."

"Harry . . ."

Rakel hated the sound of his name from her mouth with such intensity that she instinctively looked around for something to silence it. A frying pan, a blunt bread knife, gaffer tape, whatever came to hand.

". . . he thought I went to ask him about course-work. But he misunderstood. I went to seduce him."

"Do you know what, my girl? I already knew that's what you did. And now you're claiming you got what you wanted, but it was still rape? So, what happened? Did you gasp your hot little pseudo-chaste no, no, no's until it became one no which afterwards you reckoned you meant, and he should have known what you really meant before you did?"

Rakel could hear how her rhetoric suddenly sounded like the defence counsel's refrain she had heard so often during rape trials, the refrain Rakel hated with a passion but which lawyers understood and accepted had to be recited. But it wasn't just rhetoric, it was what she felt, the way it had to be, it **couldn't** be any different.

"No," Silje said. "What I want to tell you is that he **didn't** rape me."

Rakel blinked. Had to rewind a couple of seconds to be sure she had heard correctly. **Didn't** rape.

"I threatened to report him for rape because . . ." The girl used the knuckle of her first finger to take the tears from her eyes that had filled up again. ". . . because he wanted to report me to the board of governors for behaving inappropriately towards him. Which he had every right to do. But I was desperate. I tried to thwart him by accusing him of rape. I've been wanting to tell him I've had a change of heart and I regret what I've done. Tell him it . . . yes, what I did was a crime. Wrongful accusation. Paragraph 168 of the Penal Code. Recommended sentence: eight years."

"Correct," Rakel said.

"Ah, yes." Silje smiled through the tears. "I forgot you were a lawyer."

"How do you know?"

"Oh," Silje said with a sniffle, "I know a lot about Harry's life. I've studied him, you might say. He was my idol, and I was just a stupid girl. I even investigated the police murders for him, thought I could give him a helping hand. Me, a student who knows nothing. I started with a short lecture to explain to him how it all fitted. I wanted to tell Harry Hole how to catch the cop killer." Silje produced another forced smile while shaking her head.

Rakel grabbed the paper towel roll behind her and passed it to Silje. "And you came here to tell him this?"

Silje nodded slowly. "I knew he wouldn't answer a call from me. So I came out here on my run to see if he was at home. I saw the car was gone and was about to continue on my way when I saw you in the kitchen window. And decided it would be even better to say it straight to your face. It would be the best proof that I meant it, that I had no ulterior motives for coming here."

"I saw you standing outside," Rakel said.

"Yes. I had to think it through. Then man up."

Rakel could feel how her anger for the confused,

lovelorn girl with the much too open eyes had shifted to Harry. He hadn't said a word! Why not?

"It was good that you came, Silje. But now perhaps you should go."

Silje nodded. Got up. "There's some schizophrenia in our family," she said.

"Oh?" Rakel said.

"Yes. I may not be completely normal." And added in a grown-up tone: "But that's fine too."

Rakel accompanied her to the door.

"You won't see me again," the girl said, standing on the doorstep.

"Good luck, Silje."

Rakel stood on the steps with her arms crossed, watching her run across the drive. Had Harry omitted to say something because he thought she wouldn't believe him? That there would always be a shadow of doubt?

The next thought came in its wake. Would there be a shadow of doubt? How well did they know each other? How well **could** one person know another?

The black-clad figure with the blonde, bouncing ponytail was gone long before the sound of trainers crunching on gravel.

"He'd dug her up," Bjørn Holm said.

Roar Midtstuen sat with bowed head. Scratching his neck where the short bristles stuck up like a brush. The night stole in, without a sound, as they sat there in the beams of Midtstuen's car headlamps. When

Midtstuen did finally say something Bjørn had to lean forward to hear what it was.

"My only child." Then a short nod. "I suppose he was only doing what he had to do."

At first Bjørn thought he had heard wrong. Then he thought Midtstuen must have **said** it wrong. He didn't say what he meant, a word had been moved, omitted or put in the wrong place in the sentence. And yet the sentence was so correct and clear it sounded natural. It sounded like the truth. The cop killer was only doing what he had to do.

"I'll get the rest of the flowers," Midtstuen said, rising to his feet.

"OK," Bjørn said, staring at the small bouquet lying there as the other man went round the car into the darkness. He heard the boot lid being opened while he mused about what Midtstuen had said. My only child. It reminded him of his confirmation and what Aune had said about the killer being God. An avenging God. But God had also made a sacrifice. He had sacrificed his only son. Hung him on a cross. Displayed him for all to see. To see and imagine the suffering. The son's and the father's.

Bjørn visualised Fia Midtstuen on the chair. My only child. The two of them. Or the three of them. There had been three of them. What was it the priest had called it again?

Bjørn heard a clink coming from the boot and thought the box of flowers must be under something metallic.

The trinity. That was it. The third had been the

Holy Spirit. The ghost. The demon. The one they never saw, who popped up here and there in the Bible and was gone again. Fia Midtstuen's head had been attached to the pipe in such a way that she wouldn't collapse, that the body would be displayed. Like the crucifixion.

Bjørn Holm heard footsteps behind him.

Who was sacrificed, crucified by his own father. Because that was how the story had to be. What were the words he used?

"He was only doing what he had to do."

Harry stared at Megan Fox. Her beautiful contours were trembling, but her gaze was constant. The smile didn't fade. The invitation her body offered stood. He lifted the remote control and switched off the television. Megan Fox both disappeared and stayed. The silhouette of the film star was burned into the plasma screen.

Both gone and still here.

Harry looked around Truls Berntsen's bedroom. Then he went to the cabinet where he knew Berntsen kept his goodies. In theory a person could fit in there. Harry held the Odessa ready. Tiptoed over to the cabinet, hugged the wall and opened the door with his left hand. Saw the light inside come on automatically.

Otherwise nothing happened.

Harry poked his head forward and withdrew it as quickly. But he had seen what he wanted. No one there. So he stood in the doorway.

Truls had replaced what Harry had taken the last time he was here, the bulletproof vest, the gas mask, the MP5, the riot gun. He still had the same guns as far as he could see. Apart from in the middle of the board where an outline of a gun had been drawn around one of the hooks.

Had Truls Berntsen found out Harry was on his way, taken a gun and fled from his flat? Without bothering to lock the door or switch off the television? If so, why hadn't he just set an ambush for him inside?

Harry had searched the whole flat now and knew there wasn't a living soul around. He sat down on the leather sofa with the Odessa's safety catch off, ready, with a view of the bedroom door but out of sight of the keyhole.

If Truls was in there, the first person to make an appearance would be the loser. The stage was set for a duel. So he waited. Unmoving, breathing calmly, deeply, inaudibly, with the patience of a leopard.

After forty minutes had passed and nothing had happened he went into the bedroom.

Harry sat down on the bed. Should he ring Berntsen? It would warn him, but, as it was, he already seemed to be aware that Harry was after him.

Harry took out his phone and switched it on. Waited until it was connected and keyed in the number he had memorised before leaving Holmenkollen almost two hours ago.

After it had rung three times and no one had answered he gave up.

Then he called his contact at the telephone company. And got an answer in two seconds.

"What do you want, Hole?"

"I need you to track down a phone signal. For one Truls Berntsen. He's got a police line, so he must be one of your customers."

"We can't keep meeting like this."

"This is official police business."

"Follow the procedures then. Contact the police lawyer, send the case to the Crime Squad boss and call us back when you've got permission."

"This is urgent."

"Listen, I can't keep giving you—"

"This is about the police murders."

"It should only take a few seconds to get permission from the boss, Harry."

Harry cursed under his breath.

"Sorry, Harry, but it's more than my job's worth. If anyone finds out that I check police movements without authorisation . . . What's the problem with getting permission?"

"See you." Harry rang off. He had two unanswered calls and three text messages. They must have come through while he had the phone off. He opened the texts in turn. The first was from Rakel.

Tried calling. I'm home. Make you something nice if you tell me when you're coming. Got a surprise. Someone to beat you at Tetris.

Harry read the message again. Rakel had come home. With Oleg. His first instinct was to jump in the car straight away. Drop this mission. He had made a mistake; he shouldn't be here now. While knowing that was exactly what it was: a first instinct. An attempt to flee from the inevitable. The second message was from a number he didn't recognise.

Have to talk to you. Are you at home? Silje G

He deleted the message. However, he recognised the number of the third message at once.

Think you're looking for me. I've got a solution for our problem. Meet me at the G crime scene asap. Truls

44

When Harry crossed the car park he noticed a car with a smashed side window. The light from the street lamp glinted on the glass splinters on the tarmac. It was a Suzuki Vitara. Berntsen had been driving round in one like it. Harry rang the police switchboard.

"Harry Hole here. I'd like a car checked for the owner."

"Everyone can do that online now, Hole."

"You can do it for me then, can't you?"

He received a grunt in response and read out the registration number. The answer came in three seconds.

"Truls Berntsen. Address—"

"That's fine."

"Any report to make?"

"What?"

"Has it been involved in anything? Does it look as if it's been stolen or broken into, for example?"

Pause.

"Hello?"

"No, it looks fine. Just a misunderstanding."

"A mis—"

Harry rang off. Why hadn't Truls Berntsen driven

away in his car? No one on a police salary took taxis in Oslo any more. Harry tried to visualise the metro network in Oslo. There was a line only a hundred metres away. Ryen Station. He hadn't heard any trains. They must go through a tunnel. Harry blinked into the darkness. He had just heard something else.

The crackle as the hair on his neck stood on end.

He knew it was impossible to hear, yet it was all he could hear. He took out his phone again. Pressed K.

"Finally," Katrine answered.

"Finally?"

"Can't you see I've been trying to ring you?"

"Oh yes? You sound out of breath."

"I've been running, Harry. Silje Gravseng."

"What about her?"

"She's got newspaper cuttings of the police murders all over her room. She keeps a baton for beating up rapists, according to the caretaker. And she's got a brother in the funny farm after being beaten up by two policemen. And she's nuts, Harry. Off her trolley."

"Where are you?"

"In Vaterlandsparken. She's not here. I think we should put out an alert for her."

"No."

"No?"

"She's not the person we're after."

"What do you mean? Motive, opportunity, state of mind. It's all there, Harry."

"Forget Silje Gravseng. I want you to check a statistic for me."

"A statistic!" She shouted so loud the membrane crackled. "I'm standing here with half the criminal records from the Vice Squad dribbling their filth all over me, looking for a possible police murderer, and now you want me to check a **statistic**! Sod you, Harry Hole!"

"Check the FBI's statistics for witnesses who have died in the period between their initial summons and the start of the trial."

"What's that got to do with anything?"

"Just give me the figures, OK?"

"Not OK!"

"Well, regard it as an order then, Katrine Bratt."

"OK, but . . . hey, just a minute! Who's the boss here?"

"If you have to ask, I doubt it's you."

Harry heard more Bergensian swearing before he broke the connection.

Mikael Bellman was sitting on the sofa with the TV on. The news had finished, the sport was starting, so Mikael's gaze wandered from the TV to the window. To the town lying in the black cauldron far beneath them. The item about the City Hall chairman had lasted ten seconds. He had said that reshuffles at City Hall were standard practice, and that this time it was because of an unusually large burden on this particular post, so it was reasonable to pass the baton on to someone else. Isabelle Skøyen would return to her post as secretary to the committee for Social Affairs, which would allow the council to benefit from her skills there. Skøyen herself was unavailable for comment, it was said.

It glittered like a jewel, his town.

He heard the door to one of the children's rooms close gently and immediately afterwards she snuggled up to him on the sofa.

"Are they sleeping?"

"Like logs," she said, and he felt her breath on his neck. "Feel like watching TV?" She bit his earlobe. "Or . . . ?"

He smiled, but didn't budge. Enjoying the moment, feeling how perfect it was. Being here right now. At the top of the pile. The alpha male with women at his feet. One hanging on his arm. The other neutralised and rendered innocuous. The same was true of the men. Asayev was dead, Truls reinstated as his henchman, the former Police Chief an accomplice in their shared wrongdoing in such a way that he would obey if Mikael needed him again. And Mikael knew that now he had the council's confidence even if it took time to find the cop killer.

It was a long time since he had felt so good, so relaxed. He felt her hands on him. Knew what they would do before she knew herself. She could turn him on. Though not set him alight the way other people could. Like her, the one he had cut down to size. Like him, the one who had died in Hausmanns gate. But she could arouse him enough to know he would be fucking her soon. That was marriage. And it was good. It was more than enough, and there were more important things in life.

He pulled her to him and put his hand up her green sweater. Bare skin, like placing your hand on a stove ring on low heat. She sighed softly. Leaned over to him. He didn't actually like using his tongue when kissing her. Maybe he had once, but not any more. He had never told her that. Why should he as long as it was something she wanted and he hated? Marriage. Nevertheless it felt like a tiny relief when the cordless phone began to warble on the little table by the sofa.

He took it. "Yes?"

"Hi, Mikael."

The voice said his Christian name in such an intimate way that at first he was convinced he knew it, he just needed a couple of seconds to place the person in question.

"Hi," he answered accordingly and got off the sofa. Walked towards the terrace. Away from the sound of the TV. Away from Ulla. It was an automatic movement, perfected over the years. Half out of consideration for her. Half out of consideration for his secrets.

The voice at the other end chuckled. "You don't know me, Mikael. Relax."

"Thank you. I am relaxed," Mikael said. "I'm at home. And for that reason it would be nice if you could get to the point."

"I'm a nurse at the Rikshospital."

That was a thought that hadn't struck Mikael before, at least not that he could remember. However, it was as if he knew what was coming off by heart. He opened the door to the terrace and stepped onto the cold flagstones without taking his phone from his ear.

"I was Rudolf Asayev's nurse. You remember him, Mikael. Yes, of course you do. You and he did business together. He opened his heart to me when he came out of the coma. About what you two were doing."

It had clouded over, the temperature had plummeted and the flagstones were so cold that they were hurting his feet through his socks. Nevertheless, Mikael Bellman's sweat glands were working flat out.

"Talking about business," the voice said. "Perhaps we have something to discuss as well."

"What do you want?"

"I want some of your money to keep mum, let me put it like that."

It had to be him, the nurse from Enebakk. The one Isabelle had hired to get rid of Asayev. She had claimed he would gladly take his payment in sex, but obviously that hadn't been enough.

"How much?" Bellman asked, attempting to be businesslike, but noticed he failed to sound as cold-blooded as he would have liked.

"Not much. I'm a man of simple tastes. Ten thousand."

"Too little."

"Too little?"

"It sounds like a first instalment."

"We could say a hundred thousand."

"So why don't you?"

"Because I need money tonight, now, the banks are closed and you can't get more than ten thousand from an ATM."

Desperate. That was good news. Or was it? Mikael walked to the edge of the terrace, looked down over his town and tried to concentrate. This was one of those situations where he was usually at his best, where everything was at stake and one false move could prove fatal.

"What's your name?"

"Well, you can call me Dan. As in Danuvius."

"Great, Dan. You realise, do you, that although I'm negotiating with you, it doesn't mean I admit anything? I could be trying to entice you into a trap and then arrest you for blackmail."

"The only reason you're saying that is that you're scared I'm a journalist who's heard a rumour and is trying to trick you into giving yourself away."

Damn.

"Where?"

"I'm at work, so you'll have to come here. But somewhere discreet. Meet me in the locked ward. There's no one there now. In three-quarters of an hour in Asayev's room."

Three-quarters of an hour. He was in a rush. It could of course be a precaution. He didn't want to give Mikael time to set a trap. But Mikael believed in simple explanations. Like being faced with a junkie anaesthetic nurse who had suddenly run out of supplies. And, if so, that would make things easier. He might even be able to keep that particular cat in the bag for good.

"Fine," Mikael said, and rang off. Breathed in the strange, almost suffocating smell coming from the terrace. Then he went into the living room and shut the door behind him.

"I have to go out," he said.

"Now?" Ulla said, staring at him with the wounded expression that would normally annoy him enough to snap at her.

"Now." He thought of the gun he had locked in the boot of his car. A Glock 22, a present from an American colleague. Unused. Unregistered.

"When will you be back?"

"I don't know. Don't wait up."

He walked towards the hall, feeling her eyes on his back. He didn't stop. Not until he reached the doorway.

"No, I'm not meeting **her.** OK?"

Ulla didn't answer. Just turned to the TV and pretended to be interested in the weather report.

Katrine swore, dripping with sweat in the Boiler Room's clammy heat, but she kept typing.

Where the hell was it hiding, the FBI's statistic about dead witnesses? And what the hell did Harry want with it?

She looked at her watch. Sighed and rang his number.

He didn't pick up. Of course not.

She left a message saying she needed more time.

She was deep in the FBI's website, but this statistic had to be either very bloody secret or he'd misunderstood. Chucked the phone onto the desk. She felt like calling Leif Rødbekk. No, not him. Some other idiot who could be bothered to fuck her tonight. The first person to pop into her head produced a frown. Where did **he** come from? Sweet, but . . . but what? Had she been unconsciously nurturing this thought for a while?

She dismissed the notion and concentrated on the screen again.

Perhaps it wasn't the FBI, perhaps it was the CIA?

She tried new search terms. Central Intelligence Agency, witness, trial and death. Return. The computer whirred. The first hits came in.

The door behind her opened, and she felt the draught from the culvert outside.

"Bjørn?" she said, without looking up from the screen.

Harry parked his car outside Jakob Church in Hausmanns gate and walked up to number 92.

He stopped outside and looked up at the facade.

There was a dim light on the second floor, and he noticed there were bars on the windows now. The new owner was probably sick of the burglaries via the rear fire escape.

Harry had imagined he would feel more. After all, this was where Gusto had been killed. Where he had almost had to pay with his own life.

He felt the door. It was just like before. He opened up, went straight in. At the bottom of the stairs he took out the Odessa, released the safety catch, peered up the steps and listened as he breathed in the smell of urine- and vomit-marinated woodwork. Total silence.

He started up the stairs. Moving as noiselessly as he could over wet newspaper, milk cartons and used syringes. On the second floor he stopped by the door. This was new as well. A metal door. Multiple locks. Only extremely motivated burglars would bother with this.

Harry saw no reason to knock. No reason to surrender any possible element of surprise. So when he pressed the handle, felt the door react with taut springs, but found it unlocked, he gripped the Odessa with both hands and kicked the heavy door with his right foot.

He dashed inside and to the left, so as not to stand like a silhouette in the doorway. The springs slammed the door shut behind him.

Then all was still, there was only a low ticking sound.

Harry blinked in astonishment.

Apart from a small portable TV on standby, with white digits showing the wrong time, nothing had changed. It was the same cluttered junkie pit with mattresses and rubbish all over the floor. And one item of rubbish was sitting on a chair staring at him.

It was Truls Berntsen.

At least he thought it was Truls Berntsen.

Had been Truls Berntsen.

45

The chair had been placed in the centre of the room, beneath the only light, a torn ricepaper lampshade hanging from the ceiling.

Harry thought that the light, the chair and the TV with the stuttering ticking sound of a dying electrical appliance had to be from the seventies, but he wasn't sure.

The same was true of the body on the chair.

Because it wasn't easy to say if it was Truls Berntsen, born sometime in the seventies, dead this year, who was taped to the chair. The man had no face. What had once been there was a mush of relatively fresh red blood, black dried blood and white bone fragments. This mush would have run if it hadn't been held in place by a transparent membrane of plastic wrapped tightly round the head. One of the bones stuck through the plastic. Cling film, Harry thought. Freshly packed mincemeat the way you see it in shops.

Harry forced himself to look away and tried holding his breath to hear better as he hugged the wall. With his gun half raised, he scanned the room from left to right.

Stared at the corner leading to the kitchen, saw the side of the old fridge and the work surface, but someone could have been there in the semi-darkness.

Not a sound. Not a movement.

Harry waited. Reasoned. If this was a trap someone had set for him, he should already be dead.

He drew a deep breath. He had the advantage of having been here before, so he knew there was nowhere else to hide other than in the kitchen and the toilet. The disadvantage was that he would have to turn his back on one to check the other.

He took a decision, strode towards the kitchen, poked his head round the corner, pulled it back fast and waited for his brain to process the information it had received. Stove, piles of pizza boxes and the fridge. No one there.

He went towards the toilet. He stood in the doorway and pressed the light switch. Counted to seven. Thrust his head out. Back in. Empty.

Slid down to the floor with his back to the wall. Only now feeling how hard his heart had been pounding against his ribs.

He sat like that for some seconds. Recovering.

Then he walked over to the body on the chair. Crouched down and examined the red mass behind the plastic film. No face, but a prominent forehead, underbite and the cheap haircut left Harry in no doubt: it was Truls Berntsen.

Harry's brain had already started processing the fact that he had been wrong. Truls Berntsen was not the cop killer.

The next thought came hard on its heels. It was definitely not alone.

Could that be what he was witnessing here: the murder of an accessory, a murderer covering his tracks? Could Truls "Beavis" Berntsen have been working with someone as sick as himself, who committed this atrocity? Could Valentin have been deliberately sitting in front of the CCTV at Ullevål Stadium while Berntsen performed the murder in Maridalen? And, if so, how had they divvied the murders between them? Which murders did Berntsen have alibis for?

Harry straightened up and cast his eyes around. And why had he been summoned here? They would have found the body soon enough. And there were several things that didn't tally. Truls Berntsen had never been involved in the investigation into Gusto Hanssen's murder. It had been a small investigative unit consisting of Beate and a couple of other forensics officers who hadn't had much to do because Oleg had been arrested as the presumed perpetrator minutes after they'd arrived and the evidence had supported the presumption. The only . . .

In the silence Harry could still hear the low ticking. Regular, unchanging, like clockwork. He completed his thought.

The only other person bothered enough to investigate this trivial, sordid drug murder was here in the room. Himself.

He had been—like the other policemen—summoned to die at the crime scene for the unsolved murder.

The next second he was by the door pressing down the handle. And it was as he feared: it gave easily, no resistance, without opening. It was like a hotel-room door. Except that he didn't have a key card.

Harry scanned the room again.

The thick windows with the steel bars on the inside. The iron door that had slammed shut by itself. He had walked straight into the trap like the crazed idiot he had always been, caught up in the thrill of the chase.

The ticking hadn't got louder; it just seemed like it.

Harry stared at the portable TV. At the seconds ticking away. It wasn't the wrong time. It wasn't telling the time; clocks don't go backwards.

It had been 00:06:10 when he came in, now it was 00:03:51.

It was a countdown.

Harry walked over, grabbed the TV and tried to lift it. In vain. It must have been screwed to the floor. He aimed a hard kick at the top of the TV, and the plastic casing cracked with a bang. He looked inside. Metal pipes, glass tubes, leads. Harry was definitely no expert, but he had seen the innards of enough TVs to know there was too much in this one. And enough pictures of improvised explosives to recognise a pipe bomb.

He assessed the leads and dismissed the idea at once. One of the bomb blokes in Delta had explained to him that cutting the blue or red wires and being home and dry was the good old days; now it was digital hell, with Bluetooth signals, codes and safeguards that sent the counter to zero if you fiddled with anything.

Harry took a run-up and threw himself against the door. The door frame may have had frailties of its own.

It didn't.

Nor the bars on the windows.

His shoulders and ribs ached as he got to his feet again. He screamed at the window.

No sounds came in, no sounds went out.

Harry took out his mobile phone. Ops Room. Delta. They could use explosives. He looked at the clock on the TV. 00:03:04. They would hardly have time to transmit the address. 00:02:59. He stared at the contact list. R.

Rakel.

Ring her. Say farewell. To her and Oleg. Tell them he loved them. That they had to go on living. Living better than he had done. Be with them for the last two minutes. So as not to die alone. Have company, share a last traumatic experience with them, let them have a taste of death, give them a final nightmare to accompany them on their way.

"Fuck, fuck, fuck!"

Harry slipped the phone back in his pocket. Looked around. The doors had been removed. So that there was nowhere to hide.

00:02:40.

Harry strode into the kitchen, which constituted the short part of the L-shaped room. It wasn't long enough. A pipe bomb would smash everything in here as well.

He eyed the fridge. Opened it. A milk carton, two bottles of beer and a packet of liver paste. For a brief second he weighed up the alternatives, beer or panic, before plumping for panic and pulling out the shelves, sheets of glass and plastic boxes. They clattered to the ground behind him. He curled up and forced himself inside. Groaned. He couldn't bend his neck enough to get his head inside. Tried again. Cursing his long limbs as he organised them in the most ergonomic way.

Bloody impossible!

He looked at the clock on the TV. 00:02:06.

Harry shoved his head in, pulled up his knees, but now his back wasn't flexible enough. Shit! He laughed out loud. The offer of free yoga he had rejected when he was in Hong Kong, was that going to be his downfall?

Houdini. He remembered something about breathing in and out and relaxing.

He breathed out, tried to clear his mind, concentrate on relaxing. Ignore the seconds. Just feel how his muscles and joints were becoming more flexible, more supple. Feel how he was gradually compressing himself.

Possible.

Hallelujah, it really was possible! He was inside the fridge. A fridge with enough metal and insulation to save him. Perhaps. If it wasn't the pipe bomb from hell.

He held the edge of the door, cast a final glance at the TV before trying to close it. 00:01:47.

Wanted to close it but his hand wouldn't obey. It wouldn't obey because his brain refused to reject what his eyes had seen, but the rationally controlled section of his brain tried to ignore. To ignore because it had no relevance for the only thing that was important now, surviving, saving itself. To ignore because he couldn't afford to do otherwise, didn't have the time, didn't have the empathy.

The mincemeat on the chair.

It had acquired two white spots.

White as in the whites of the eyes.

Staring straight at him through the cling film.

The bugger was alive.

Harry let out a yell and squeezed out of the fridge. Ran to the chair with the TV screen at the margin of his vision. Ripped the cling film off the face. The eyes in the mince blinked and he heard a shallow breath. He must have got some air through the hole where the bone had punctured the film.

"Who did this?" Harry asked.

Got no more than breath by way of an answer. The mincemeat mask began to trickle down like melting candle wax.

"Who is he? Who's the cop killer?"

Still only breath.

Harry looked at the clock. 00:01:26. It would take time to squeeze back in.

"Come on, Truls! I can catch him."

A bubble of blood began to grow where Harry

guessed the mouth had to be. As it burst there was an almost inaudible whisper.

"He wore a mask. Didn't speak."

"What kind of mask?"

"Green. All green."

"Green?"

"Sur . . . geon . . ."

"Surgeon's mask?"

A small nod, then the eyes closed again.

00:01:05.

No more to be gleaned. He ran back to the kitchen. He was faster this time. He closed the door and the light went out.

Shivering in the darkness, he counted the seconds. Forty-nine.

The bastard would have died anyway.

Forty-eight.

Better that someone else did the job.

Forty-seven.

Green mask. Truls Berntsen had given Harry what he knew without asking for anything in return. So there was a bit of policeman left in him.

Forty-six.

No point thinking about it. There wasn't any more room for him in here anyway.

Forty-five.

Besides, there was no time to release him from the chair.

Forty-four.

Even if he'd wanted to, there was no time left now.

Forty-three.

All over now.
Forty-two.
Shit.
Forty-one.
Shit, shit, shit!
Forty.
Harry kicked open the fridge door with one foot and squeezed himself out with the other. Pulled open the drawer under the worktop, grabbed what had to be a bread knife, ran to the chair and cut off the tape on the arms of the chair.

Avoided glancing at the TV, but heard the ticking.
"Fuck you, Berntsen!"
He walked round the chair and cut the tape on the back and around the chair legs.

Put his arms round his chest and heaved.

Needless to say, the bugger was extremely heavy.

Harry pulled and cursed, dragged and cursed, no longer hearing the words coming from his mouth, hoping only they offended heaven and hell enough so that at least one of them would intervene in this idiotic but inevitable course of events.

He aimed at the open fridge, manoeuvred Truls Berntsen through the opening. The bloodstained body slumped and slipped out again.

Harry tried to stuff him in again, but it was no use. He pulled Berntsen out of the fridge, leaving trails of blood along the linoleum, let go, dragged the fridge from the wall, heard the plug come out, pushed the fridge over onto its back between the worktop and the stove. Grabbed Berntsen and thrust him up and in. Crawled in after him. Used both legs to push him as close to the back of the fridge as possible, to where the heavy refrigeration motor was housed. Lay on top of Berntsen, inhaling the smell of sweat, blood and piss that comes from sitting in a chair knowing your death is imminent.

Harry had hoped there would be room for them both, as it had been the height and width of the fridge that had been the problem, not the depth.

But now it was the depth.

He couldn't close the bloody door behind them.

Harry tried to force it, but it wouldn't close. There was less than twenty centimetres to go, but unless the fridge was hermetically sealed they didn't have a hope. The shock waves would burst the liver and the spleen, the heat would burn out the eyeballs, every unattached object in the room would turn into a bullet, a machine gun spraying salvos and lacerating everything to pieces.

He didn't even need to make a decision, it was too late.

Which also meant there was nothing to lose.

Harry kicked the door open, jumped out, got behind the fridge and pushed it upright again. Saw from over the edge that Truls Berntsen had slid out onto the floor. Couldn't help looking past him at the TV screen. The clock showed 00:00:12. Twelve seconds.

"Sorry, Berntsen," Harry said.

Then he seized Berntsen around the chest, dragged him to his feet and backed into the upright fridge.

Put his hand out past Truls, pulled the door half to. And began to rock. The heavy motor was so high up that the cabinet had a high centre of gravity, and that, he hoped, would help him.

The fridge tipped backwards. They were teetering on the cusp. Truls flopped against Harry.

They mustn't fall that way!

Harry resisted, tried to push Truls back, against the door.

Then the fridge made up its mind, fell into place and tipped the other way.

Harry caught a final glimpse of the TV screen as the fridge toppled and fell forwards.

The breath was knocked out of him as they crashed to the floor, and he panicked as he couldn't get any oxygen. But it was dark. Pitch black. The weight of the motor and the fridge had done what he hoped, closed the door against the floor.

Then the bomb went off.

Harry's brain imploded, shut down.

Harry blinked into the darkness.

He must have been out for a few seconds.

His ears were howling and his face felt as if some-one had thrown acid into it. But he was alive.

So far.

He needed air. Harry squeezed his hands between him and Truls, pressed his back against the back of the fridge and shoved as hard as he could. The fridge swung round on its hinges and fell on its side.

Harry rolled out. Stood up.

The room looked like some kind of dystopian wasteland, a grey dust-and-smoke hell, without a single identifiable object; even what once had been a fridge looked like something else. The metal door in the hall had been blown off its frame.

Harry left Berntsen where he was. Hoping only that the bastard was dead. Staggered down the steps, into the street.

Stood gazing down Hausmanns gate. Saw the sirens on the police cars, but heard only the whistling in his ears, like a printer without paper, an alarm that someone would have to switch off soon.

And while he stood there gazing at the silent police cars he had the same thought as when he had been listening for the metro in Manglerud. That he couldn't hear. He couldn't hear what he should have heard. Because he hadn't been thinking. Until he had been in Manglerud and had considered where the Oslo metro network ran. And then he finally realised what it was, what had been submerged in the darkness and hadn't wanted to surface. The forest. There was no metro in the forest.

46

Mikael Bellman stopped.

Listened and stared down the empty corridor.

Like a desert, he thought. Nothing to catch your eye, only a quivering white light that erased all contours.

And this sound, the vibrating hum of neon tubes, the desert heat, like a prelude to something that nonetheless never happens. Only an empty hospital corridor with nothing at the end. Perhaps it is all a Fata Morgana: Isabelle Skøyen's solution to the Asayev problem, the phone call an hour ago, the thousand-krone notes that had just spewed out of an ATM in the city centre, this deserted corridor in an empty wing of the hospital.

Let it be a mirage, a dream, Mikael thought and started walking. But checked in his coat pocket that the safety catch on the Glock 22 was off. In the other pocket he had the wad of notes. If the situation demanded, he would have to pay up. If there were several of them, for example. But he didn't think there would be. The amount was too small to be shared. The secret too great.

He passed a coffee machine, rounded a corner and

saw the corridor continue with this same flat white-
ness. But he also saw the chair. The chair that Asayev's
guard had sat on. It hadn't been removed.

He turned to be sure that no one was behind him
before he went on.

Took long paces and placed his soles softly, almost
soundlessly, on the floor. Felt the doors as he passed.
They were all locked.

Then he was there, in front of the door, by the
chair. A sudden intuition made him put his left hand
on the chair seat. Cold.

He took a deep breath in and his gun out. Looked
at his hand. It wasn't trembling, was it?

Best at decisive moments.

He put the gun back in his pocket, pressed the
handle of the door, and it opened.

No reason to surrender whatever surprise element
there was, Mikael Bellman thought, pushing open
the door and stepping in.

The room was bathed in light but was empty and
bare, apart from the bed where Asayev had been. It
had been pushed into the centre of the room and there
was a lamp over it. Beside it, sharp, polished instruments gleamed on a metal trolley. Perhaps they had
converted the room into a basic operating theatre.

Mikael caught a movement behind the one window and his hand squeezed his gun as he squinted.
Did he need glasses?

By the time he had focused, realised it was a reflection and the movement was **behind** him, it was much
too late.

He felt a hand on his shoulder and reacted at once, but it was as if the stab of pain in his neck instantly severed the connection to his gun hand. And before the darkness descended he saw the man's face close to his own in the black reflection from the window. It wore a green cap and a green mask over its mouth. Like a surgeon. A surgeon about to operate.

Katrine was too busy with the computer to react to the fact that she hadn't received an answer from the person who had walked in behind her. But she repeated the question when the door closed, locking out the noises from the culvert.

"Where have you been, Bjørn?"

She felt a hand on her shoulder and neck. And her first thought was that it was not at all unpleasant to feel a hot hand on the bare skin of her neck, a man's friendly hand.

"I've been to the crime scene to lay some flowers," the voice behind her said.

Katrine frowned in surprise.

No files found, the screen said. Really? No files anywhere showing the statistics for dead key witnesses? She pressed Harry's name on the phone. The hand had started massaging her neck muscles. Katrine groaned, mostly to show she liked it, closed her eyes and leaned her head forward. Heard it ring at the other end.

"Down a bit. Which crime scene?"

"A country road. A girl. Hit-and-run. Never solved."

Harry didn't answer. Katrine took the phone from her ear and tapped in a message. **No files found for statistic.** Pressed Send.

"That took a long time," Katrine. "What did you do afterwards?"

"Helped the other person there," the voice said. "He broke down, you might say."

Katrine had finished doing what she had to do, and it was as though the other things in the room finally had access to her senses. The voice, the hand, the aroma. She swivelled slowly in her chair. Looked up.

"Who are you?" she asked.

"Who am I?"

"Yes, you're not Bjørn Holm."

"No?"

"No. Bjørn Holm is prints, ballistics and blood. He doesn't do massages that leave you with your mouth tasting of sugar. So, what is it you want?"

She saw the blush shoot up the pale, round face. The cod-eyes bulged even more than usual, and Bjørn drew back his hand and started frenetically scratching one mutton chop.

"Er, well, sorry, I didn't mean . . . I just . . . I . . ."

The redness of his cheeks and the stuttering became more intense until finally he just dropped his hand and looked at her with a desperate expression of capitulation. "Goddamn, Katrine, this is pathetic."

Katrine looked at him. Started laughing. The prat looked so sweet when he was like that.

"Did you drive here?" she asked.

• • •

Truls Berntsen woke up.

Staring ahead of him, around him, everything was white and well lit. And he no longer felt any pain. On the contrary, it felt wonderful. White and wonderful. He had to be dead. Of course he was dead. Strange. Or even stranger that he had been sent to the wrong place. To the good place.

He felt his body turn. Perhaps he was a bit premature about the good place, he was still on the way there. And now he could hear sounds as well. The distant lament of a foghorn rising and falling. The ferryman's foghorn.

Something appeared in front of him, something that shielded him from the light.

A face.

Another face appeared. "He can have more morphine if he starts screaming."

And then Truls felt it return. The pain. His whole body ached, his head felt like it was about to explode.

They turned again. Ambulance. He was in an ambulance with its sirens wailing.

"I'm Ulsrud from Kripos," the face above him said. "Your ID card says you're Officer Truls Berntsen."

"What happened?" Truls whispered.

"A bomb went off. It smashed all the windowpanes in the neighbourhood. We found you in the fridge inside the flat. What happened?"

Truls closed his eyes and heard the question

repeated. Heard the other man, presumably a medic, telling the policeman not to push the patient. Who after all was on morphine, so could make up anything he liked.

"Where's Hole?" Truls whispered.

He noticed the bright light was blocked again. "What did you say, Berntsen?"

Truls tried to moisten his lips, feeling he had no lips to moisten.

"The other guy. Was he in the fridge too?"

"There was only you in the fridge, Berntsen."

"But he was there. He . . . he saved my life."

"If there was anyone else in the flat I'm afraid whoever it was is now new wallpaper and paint. Everything inside was blown to smithereens. Even the fridge you were in was pretty smashed up, so you're lucky to be alive. If you can tell me who was behind the bomb we could start looking for him."

Truls shook his head. Imagined he was shaking his head at least. He hadn't seen him, he had been behind him when he led him from his own car to another where he had sat at the back with the gun trained on Truls's head while Truls drove. Drove them to Hausmanns gate 92. An address so tainted with narcotic criminality he had almost forgotten it was a crime scene. Gusto. Of course. And it was then that he knew what until then he had managed to repress. That he was going to die. That it was the cop killer behind him as they went up the steps, in through the metal door, who taped him to the chair, staring at him from behind the green mask. Truls had watched him walk around the portable TV and insert a screwdriver, noticed that the counter, which had started working on the screen when the door closed behind them, had stopped and was then turned back to six minutes. A bomb. Then the man in green had taken out a baton, identical to the one he himself had used, and had started hitting Truls in the face. With concentration, without any visible enjoyment or emotional involvement. Light blows, not enough to break bones, but enough to burst veins and arteries, swelling the face with the blood pouring out and lying beneath the skin. Then he had started to hit him harder. Truls had lost all feeling in his skin, he could only feel that it burst, could feel the blood running down his neck and chest, the dull pain in his head, in his brain— no, even deeper than his brain—whenever the baton landed. And he saw the man in green, a dedicated church bell-ringer convinced of the importance of his work, swinging the hammer at the inside of the bronze bell, as little jets of blood spattered Rorschach blots on the green smock. Heard the crunch of nasal bone and cartilage being crushed, felt his teeth crack and fill his mouth, felt his jaw loosen and hang from its own nerve fibres . . . and then—finally— everything went black.

Until he woke again, to the pains of hell, and he saw him without the surgeon outfit. Harry Hole standing in front of a fridge.

At first he was confused.

Then it seemed logical. Hole would want to dispatch someone who knew his litany of sins in such detail and he would disguise it as one of the police murders.

But Hole was taller than the other man. His expression was different. And Hole was clambering into a damn fridge. Fighting his way in. They were in the same boat. They were just two officers at the same crime scene. Who would die together. The two of them, what irony! If he hadn't been in such pain he would have laughed.

Then Hole got out of the fridge, cut the tape and lifted him into the fridge. Which is more or less when he lost consciousness again.

"Can I have some more morphine?" Truls whispered, hoping he would be heard over the bloody sirens, waiting impatiently for the wave of well-being he knew would wash through his body, washing away the unnerving pain. And thought it had to be the drug that was making him think what he was thinking. Because actually it suited him down to the ground. Nevertheless he thought it anyway.

How irritating that Harry Hole should die like this.

Like a bloody hero.

Giving his place to, sacrificing himself for, an enemy.

And the enemy would have to cope with the fact that he was alive because a better man had chosen to die for him.

Truls felt it coming from the small of his back, the chill the pain was pushing ahead of it. To die for something, anything, just something different from the wretchedness which was yourself. Perhaps that was what this was about ultimately. In which case, fuck you, Hole.

He looked for the medic, saw the window was wet, it must have started to rain.

"More morphine, for Christ's sake!"

47

The policeman with the phonetic tripwire of a name—Karsten Kaspersen—was sitting in the duty office at PHS staring at the rain. It was falling like stair rods in the black of the night, drumming on the gleaming black tarmac, dripping from the gate.

He had switched off the light so that no one could see the office was manned so late. By "no one" he meant the types who steal batons and other equipment. Some of the old cordon tape they used in training was gone too. And as there were no signs of a break-in it had to be someone with a pass. And as it was someone with a pass this was not just a matter of a few lousy batons or cordon tape but the fact that they had thieves in their midst. Thieves who might be walking around as police officers in the not-too-distant future. And they weren't damn well having any of that, not in his police force.

Now he could see someone approaching in the rain. The figure had emerged from the darkness down by Slemdalsveien, passed under the lights by Chateau Neuf and was heading for the gate. Not a walk he recognised, exactly. More like a stagger. And the guy was listing, as though there was a gale on the port side.

But he swiped a card in the machine and next minute he was inside the college. Kaspersen—who knew the walks of everyone who belonged to this section of the building—jumped up and stepped out. For this was not something that could be explained away. Either you had access or you didn't, there was no middle ground.

"Hello there!" Kaspersen shouted, leaving the office, having already puffed himself up, something from the animal kingdom making itself look as big as possible; he didn't really know why it worked, only that it did. "Who the hell are you? What are you doing here? How did you get hold of that card?"

The stooped, drenched individual in front of him turned, tried to straighten up. The face was hidden in the shadow from the hoodie, but a pair of eyes sparkled inside, and it struck Kaspersen that he could feel the heat, so intense was the gaze. He instinctively gasped for breath, and for the first time he remembered he wasn't armed. How on earth had he not thought about that? He should have brought something to deter thieves.

The individual pushed the hood back.

Forget **deter,** Kaspersen thought. I need something to defend myself with.

The individual in front of him was not from this world. His coat was torn with great gaping holes, and the same applied to his face.

Kaspersen backed into his office, wondering if the key was on the inside of the door.

"Kaspersen."

The voice.

"It's me, Kaspersen."

Kaspersen stopped. Angled his head. Could that really be . . . ?

"Jesus, Harry. What happened to you?"

"Only an explosion. It looks worse than it is."

"Worse? You look like a Christmas orange studded with cloves."

"It's just—"

"I mean a Christmas blood orange, Harry. You're bleeding. Hang on a sec, I'll get the first-aid box."

"Can you come up to Arnold's office? I've got to sort something urgently."

"Arnold isn't there now."

"I know."

Karsten Kaspersen dashed towards the medicine cabinet in the office. And while he was removing plasters, gauze bandages and scissors it was as if his subconscious was re-examining the conversation and stopping at the final sentence. The way Harry had said it. The emphasis. **I know.** As though he hadn't said it to him, Karsten Kaspersen, but to himself, Harry Hole.

Mikael Bellman woke up and opened his eyes.

And pinched them shut again as the light broke into the membranes and lenses of his eyes, but still it felt as though the light was burning a bare nerve.

He was unable to move. He twisted his head and tried to look around him. He was still in the same room. He looked down. Saw the white tape used to bind him to the bed. To bind his arms to his sides and his legs together. He was a mummy.

Already.

He heard the clink of metal behind him and twisted his head the other way. The person standing by his side fiddling with the instruments was dressed in green and wore a mask over his mouth.

"Oh dear," said the man in green. "Has the anaesthetic worn off already? Yes, well, I'm not exactly an anaesthetics expert, am I? To tell the truth, I'm not a specialist in anything at all in the hospital."

Mikael engaged his mind, tried to hack his way out of the confusion. What the hell was going on?

"By the way, I found the money you brought with you. Nice of you, but I don't need it. And it's impossible to compensate for what you did, Mikael."

If he wasn't the anaesthetic nurse, how did he know about the connection between Mikael and Asayev?

The man in green held up an instrument to the light.

Mikael could hear the fear pounding. He didn't feel it yet; the drug was still floating through his brain like wisps of fog, but when the veil of anaesthetics had lifted completely what was behind would be revealed: pain and fear. And death.

Because Mikael had understood now. It was so obvious that he should have known before he left home. This was the scene of an unsolved murder.

"You and Truls Berntsen."

Truls? Did he believe that Truls had anything to do with the murder of Asayev?

"But he's already received his punishment. What do you think it's best to use when you cut off a face? A handle number three with a blade number ten is for skin and muscles. Or this one: a handle number seven with a blade number fifteen?" The man in green held up two seemingly identical scalpels. The light was reflected in one of the blades, casting a thin stripe of light over the man's face, including one eye. And in that eye he saw something he vaguely recognised.

"The supplier didn't write which one was best for this particular operation, you see."

There was something familiar about his voice as well, wasn't there?

"Yes, well, we'll have to manage with what we've got. I'm going to have to tape your face down, Mikael."

Now the fog had lifted completely and he saw it. The fear.

And it saw him and rose in his throat.

Mikael gasped as he felt his head being forced down onto the mattress and the tape stretched across his forehead. Then the man's face was directly above his. The mask had slipped. But Mikael's brain was slowly rotating his vision, upside down became downside up. And he recognised him. And knew why.

"Do you remember me, Mikael?" he asked.

It was him. The homo. The one who had tried to kiss him when he was working at Kripos. In the toilet.

Someone had come in. Truls had beaten him black and blue in the boiler room, and he had never returned to work. He had known what would be awaiting him. As Mikael did now.

"Mercy." Mikael felt his eyes filling with tears. "I stopped Truls. He would have killed you if I hadn't—"

"—hadn't stopped him so that you could save your career and become Chief of Police."

"Listen, I'm ready to pay whatever—"

"Oh, you'll pay all right, Mikael. You'll pay in full for what you took from me."

"Took . . . What did we take from you?"

"You took revenge from me, Mikael. Punishment for the person who killed René Kalsnes. You all let the murderer off the hook."

"Not all cases can be solved. You yourself know that—"

Laughter. Cold, brief, with the brakes suddenly applied. "I know you didn't try, that's what I know, Mikael. You didn't give a damn for two reasons. First of all, you found a baton close to the scene of the crime, so you were afraid that if you searched too hard you would find out it was one of your own who had killed this creep, this revolting homo. And what was the second reason, Mikael? René wasn't as hetero as the police force likes us officers to be. Or what, Mikael? But I loved René. Loved him. Do you hear that, Mikael? I'm saying out loud that I—a man— loved the boy, wanted to kiss him, stroke his hair, whisper sweet nothings into his ear. Do you think that's revolting? Deep down, though, you know, don't you? That it's a gift to be able to love another man. It's something you should have told yourself before, Mikael, because now it's too late for you, you're never going to experience it, what I offered you when we were working at Kripos. You were so frightened of your other self that you lost your temper. You had to beat him out. Beat **me** out."

He had gradually raised his voice, but now he lowered it to a whisper.

"But that was just stupid fear, Mikael. I've felt it myself, and I would never have punished you this hard for that alone. What you and all the other so-called police officers on the René Kalsnes case received the death sentence for is that you sullied the only person I have ever loved. Demeaned his human value. Said the victim wasn't even worth the work you're paid to do. Wasn't worth the oath you swore to serve the public and to uphold justice. Which means you fail us all, you desecrate the flock, Mikael, the flock which is all that is sacred. That and love. And so you have to be removed. The way you removed the apple of my eye. But enough chit-chat—I have to concentrate if we're going to get this right. Fortunately for you and me there are very instructive videos online. What do you think about this?"

He held up a picture in front of Mikael.

"Should be simple surgery, don't you think? But shush, Mikael! No one can hear you, but if you yell like that I'll have to tape up your mouth as well."

• • •

Harry fell into Arnold Folkestad's chair. It emitted a long, hydraulic wheeze and sank under his weight as Harry switched on the computer and the screen lit up the darkness. And while it started up, with creaks and groans, activated programs and prepared itself for use, Harry read Katrine's text message yet again.

No files found for statistic.

Arnold had told him the FBI had statistics to the effect that in ninety-four per cent of all the serious cases when the prosecution's witnesses died, the deaths were suspicious. That was what had made Harry examine Asayev's death more closely. But the statistic didn't exist. It was like Katrine's joke, the one that had been nagging away at Harry's cortex, the one he remembered and couldn't understand why:

"When people use statistics, in seventy-two per cent of cases, they've made them up on the spur of the moment."

Harry must have been ruminating on it for a long time. Must have had a suspicion. That this statistic was one Arnold had made up on the spur of the moment.

Why?

The answer was simple. To persuade Harry to have a closer look at Asayev's death. Because Arnold knew something, but couldn't say straight out what it was or how he had acquired the information. Because it would blow his cover. But, being the zealous policeman he was, morbidly keen to solve a murder, he had still been willing to take the risk by putting Harry onto the case.

Because Arnold Folkestad knew that the trail could not only lead Harry to the fact that Asayev had been murdered and to his potential murderer, it could also lead to himself, Arnold Folkestad, and another murder. Because the only person who could know and might also have a particular need to say what actually happened up there at the hospital was Anton Mittet. The sedated, remorse-ridden guard. And there was only one reason Arnold Folkestad and Anton Mittet—total strangers to each other—should have been in contact.

Harry shivered.

Murder.

The computer was ready to search.

48

Harry stared at the computer screen. He rang Katrine's number again. Was about to end the call when he heard her voice.

"Yes?"

She was out of breath, as if she'd been running. But the acoustics suggested she was indoors. And it struck him that he should have heard that the time he'd rung Arnold Folkestad late at night. The acoustics. He'd been outside, not inside.

"Are you in the gym or what?"

"Gym?" She queried the word as though unfamiliar with the concept.

"I was wondering if that was why you didn't answer my calls."

"No, I'm at home. What's up?"

"OK, get your pulse down now. I'm at PHS. I've just seen someone's search history. And I can't get any further."

"What do you mean?"

"Arnold Folkestad has been on medical supply websites. I want to know why."

"Arnold Folkestad? What's this got to do with him?"

"I think he's our man."

"Arnold Folkestad is the cop killer?"

As Katrine spoke he heard a sound which he immediately identified as Bjørn Holm's smoker's cough. And what might have been the creaking of a mattress.

"Are you and Bjørn in the Boiler Room?"

"No, I told you . . . we . . . yes, we're in the Boiler Room."

Harry mused. And concluded that in all his years as a policeman he had never heard worse lying.

"If you're near a computer, try to find out if Arnold has been buying medical equipment. And if his name turns up in connection with any old crime scenes or murder investigations. And then ring me back. And now give me Bjørn."

He heard her hand over the phone, say something and then Bjørn's somewhat thick voice.

"Yuh?"

"Get your threads on and hotfoot it to the Boiler Room. Find a police lawyer and get a warrant to tap Arnold Folkestad's mobile phone. And then check who rang Truls Berntsen this evening, OK? In the meantime, I'll tell Bellman to deploy Delta. OK?"

"Yes. I . . . we . . . well, you know . . ."

"Is this important, Bjørn?"

"No."

"Right."

Harry rang off, and at that moment Karsten Kaspersen came in through the door.

"I found some iodine and cotton. And tweezers as well. So we can pull out the splinters."

"Thanks, Kaspersen, but the splinters are more or

less holding me together, so just leave the stuff on the table."

"But, heck, you—"

Harry waved the protesting Kaspersen out while calling Bellman. Was put through to his voicemail. Swore. Searched for Ulla Bellman, found a landline number in Høyenhall. And then heard a gentle, melodic voice articulate the surname.

"Harry Hole here. Is your husband there?"

"No, he just went out."

"This is pretty important. Where is he?"

"He didn't say."

"When—?"

"He didn't say."

"If—"

"—he turns up I'll tell him to call you, Harry Hole."

"Thank you."

He hung up.

Forced himself to wait. Wait while sitting with his elbows on the table and his head in his hands, listening to blood dripping onto unmarked tests. Counted the drips as if they were ticking seconds.

The forest. The forest. There's no metro in the forest. And the acoustics. He had sounded as if he was outside, not inside.

When Harry had called Arnold that night Arnold had claimed he was at home.

Yet Harry had heard the metro in the background.

There could of course have been relatively innocent reasons for Arnold Folkestad lying about where he was. A female acquaintance he wanted to keep quiet, for example. And it could have been a coincidence that when Harry rang, the young girl was being dug up in Vestre Cemetery. Close to where the metro passes by. Coincidences. But enough to cause other things to surface. The statistic.

Harry glanced at his watch again.

Thought about Rakel and Oleg. They were at home.

Home. Where he would have been. Where he **should** have been. Where he would never be. Not completely, not fully, not the way he wanted to be. Because it was true, he didn't have it in him. Instead he had this otherness in him, like a flesh-eating bacterium, which consumed everything else in his life, which not even alcohol could keep down and which he still, after all these years, didn't completely understand. Only that in some way or other it had to be similar to what Arnold Folkestad had. An imperative so strong and all-encompassing that it could almost justify all it destroyed. Then—at long last—she rang.

"He ordered quite a few surgical instruments and items of clothing some weeks ago. You don't need any kind of special authorisation to do that."

"Anything else?"

"No, he doesn't seem to have been online much. Seems to have been quite cautious in fact."

"Anything else?"

"I checked whether he'd had any physical injuries or anything like that. And some hospital records came up. From several years ago."

"Oh?"

"Yes. He was admitted with what the doctor said in his report was a beating, but the patient claimed he fell down the stairs. The doctor rejected this as a cause and referred to the widespread injuries all over his body. He wrote that the patient was a police officer and would have to judge for himself what should be reported. He also wrote that his knee would never completely recover."

"So he was beaten up. What about the crime scenes and the cop killer?"

"I didn't find any links there, though it looks as if he worked on some of the original murder cases when he was at Kripos. And I did find a link with one of the victims."

"Oh?"

"René Kalsnes. At first he just cropped up by chance, but then I refined the search. These two had quite a lot to do with each other. Flights abroad with Folkestad paying for both of them, double rooms and suites registered in both their names in a variety of European cities. Jewellery I doubt Folkestad would have worn, but he bought it in Barcelona and Rome. In short, looks like the two of them—"

"—were lovers," Harry said.

"I'd say more like secret lovers," Katrine said. "When they travelled from Norway they sat in different rows, sometimes even on different flights. And when they stayed at hotels in Norway it was always in single rooms."

"Arnold was a policeman," Harry said. "He thought it was safest to stay in the closet."

"But he wasn't the only person wooing this René with weekends away and endless gifts."

"I'm sure he wasn't. And what is equally sure is that the previous investigation teams should have seen this."

"Now you're being harsh, Harry. They didn't have my search engines."

Harry ran a hand carefully over his face. "Maybe not. Maybe you're right. Maybe I'm being unfair when I think the murder of a promiscuous gay man didn't arouse in the detectives involved an urge to graft for a result."

"Yes, you are."

"Fine. Anything else?"

"Not for the moment."

"OK."

He slipped the phone into his pocket. Glanced at his watch.

A sentence uttered by Arnold Folkestad ran through his mind.

Anyone who doesn't dare to stand up for justice should have a guilty conscience.

Was that what Folkestad was doing with these revenge murders? Standing up for justice?

And what had he said when they spoke about Silje Gravseng's mental state? "I have some experience of OCD." Meaning he knew what it was like to stop at nothing.

The man had been sitting opposite Harry and spelling it out for him.

Bjørn rang after seven minutes.

"They've checked Truls Berntsen's line and no one has rung tonight."

"Mm. So Folkestad went straight to Berntsen's place and picked him up. What about Folkestad's phone?"

"It's switched on and can be located in the area round Slemdalsveien, Chateau Neuf and—"

"Shit," Harry said. "Hang up and ring his number."

Harry waited for a few seconds. Then he heard a vibration somewhere. It came from one of the desk drawers. Harry pulled at them. Locked. Apart from the bottom one, the deepest. A display shone up at him. Harry took the phone and accepted the call.

"Found it," he said.

"Hello?"

"Harry, Bjørn. Folkestad's smart. He left the phone registered in his name here. I'd guess it was here when all the murders were committed."

"So that no one at the phone company would be able to go back and reconstruct his movements."

"And as evidence that he's been working here as usual if he should need an alibi. Since it isn't even locked up, my guess is we won't find anything revealing on the phone."

"You mean he's got another one?"

"Pay as you go, bought with cash, perhaps in someone else's name. That's how he calls the victims."

"And as the phone's there tonight . . ."

"He's been out and about, yes."

"But if he needs to use the phone as an alibi, it's strange he hasn't taken it. Taken it home. If the signals show it's been at PHS all night—"

"It won't work as a plausible alibi. There is another possibility."

"What's that?"

"He hasn't finished tonight's work yet."

"Oh Christ. Do you think—?"

"I don't think anything. I can't get hold of Bellman. Could you ring Hagen, explain the situation and ask if he would authorise the mobil-isation of Delta? To raid Folkestad's home address."

"You think he's at home?"

"No. But we—"

"—start searching where there is light," Bjørn completed.

Harry hung up again. Closed his eyes. The whistling in his ears had almost gone. Instead there was another noise. Ticking. The seconds being counted down. Shit! He pressed his knuckles against his eyes.

Could anyone else have received an anonymous call today? Who? And where from? From a pay-as-you-go phone. Or a payphone. Or a large switchboard where the number didn't come up.

Harry sat still for a few seconds.

Then he took his hands away.

Looked at the big black telephone on the desk. Hesitated. Then he lifted the receiver. Got the switchboard's dialling tone. Hit the redial key and with small, excited beeps the phone started ringing the last number that had been dialled. He heard the number ringing. The call being answered.

The same gentle, melodic voice.

"Bellman."

"Sorry, wrong number," Harry said, cradling the receiver. Closed his eyes. Shit, shit, shit!

49

Not how or why.

Harry tried to purge his brain of all the redundant information. To concentrate on the only issue that was important now. Where.

Where the hell could Arnold Folkestad be?

At a crime scene.

With surgical equipment.

When Harry understood, there was one thing and one thing alone that surprised him: that he hadn't clicked before. It was so obvious that even a first-year student with a mediocre imagination would have managed to crunch the data and follow the perpetrator's train of thought. Crime scene. A scene where a man dressed and masked like a surgeon would not attract much attention.

It was two minutes by car from PHS to the Rikshospital.

He could do it. Delta couldn't.

It took Harry twenty-five seconds to get out of the building.

Thirty to reach his car, start it and turn into Slemdalsveien, which would take him almost straight to where he was heading.

One minute and forty-five seconds after that he pulled up in front of the entrance to the Rikshospital.

Ten seconds after that he had pushed through the swing door and passed reception. He heard a "Hey, you there!" but steamed ahead. His footsteps resounded against the walls and ceiling of the corridor. As he ran he fumbled behind his back. Got hold of the Odessa he had stuffed inside his belt. Felt his pulse counting down, faster and faster.

He passed the coffee machine. Slowed down so as not to make too much noise. Stopped by the chair outside the door that led to the crime scene. Many people knew a dope baron had died in there, but not many knew he had been murdered. And that the crime was unsolved. However, Arnold Folkestad did.

Harry stepped up to the door. Listened.

Checked the safety catch was off.

His pulse had counted down and was calm.

Along the corridor he heard running footsteps. They were on their way to stop him. And before Harry Hole silently opened the door and stepped inside, he had time for one more thought: this was a very bad dream where everything recurred, time after time, and it had to stop here. He had to wake up. To blink into the sun one morning, wrapped in a cold, white duvet, with her arms holding him tight. Refusing to let go, refusing to let him be anywhere except with her.

Harry closed the door quietly behind him. Stared at a man in green bent over a bed containing a man he knew. Mikael Bellman.

Harry raised his gun. Cocked the trigger. Already imagining the salvo ripping up the green material, severing the nerves, smashing the marrow, the back arching and falling forward. But Harry didn't want that. He didn't want to shoot this man in the back and kill him. He wanted to shoot him in the face and kill him.

"Arnold," Harry said in a husky voice, "turn around."

There was a clatter on the metal table as the man in green dropped something shiny, a scalpel. He turned slowly. Pulled down the green mask. Looked at Harry.

Harry stared back. His finger tightened around the trigger.

The footsteps outside were getting closer. There were a lot of them. He would have to hurry if he was going to do this without witnesses. He felt the resistance on the trigger ceding; he had reached the trigger's eye of the storm, where all is still. The silence before the explosion. Now. Not now. He had let his finger slip back a tiny fraction. It wasn't him. It wasn't Arnold Folkestad. Had he been mistaken? Had he been mistaken again? The face before him was smooth, the mouth open, the black eyes unfamiliar. Was this the cop killer? He looked so . . . uncomprehending. The green figure took a step to the side, and it was only now that Harry saw the person the green outfit covered was a woman.

At that moment the door burst open behind him,

and he was pushed to the side by two other people in green operating attire.

"What's the score?" asked one of the new arrivals in a high-pitched authoritative voice.

"Unconscious," the woman answered. "Low pulse."

"Blood loss?"

"There's not much blood on the floor, but it could have run into the stomach."

"Determine the blood type and order three bags."

Harry lowered his gun.

"Police," he said. "What's happened here?"

"Get out. We're trying to save a life here," the authoritative voice said.

"Same here," Harry said, raising his gun again. The man stared at him. "I'm trying to stop a murderer, Mr. Surgeon. And we don't know if he's finished his handiwork for the day, OK?"

The man turned away from Harry. "If it's only this wound and no damage to the inner organs then there won't have been much blood lost. Is he in shock? Karen, help this officer."

The woman spoke through her mask without moving away from the bed. "Someone in reception saw a man in bloodstained scrubs and a mask come from the empty wing and walk straight out. This was so unusual she sent someone in to check. The patient was on the way to dying when he was found."

"Anyone know where the man could have gone?" Harry asked.

"They say he just disappeared."

"When will the patient come round again?"

"We don't know if he'll survive. You look as if you need medical help yourself by the way."

"Not much else we can do beyond covering it with a patch," the authoritative voice said.

No more information to be gleaned. Yet Harry stayed where he was. Took two steps forward. Stopped. Stared at Mikael Bellman's white face. Was he conscious? It was hard to say.

One eye stared straight up at him.

The other wasn't there.

Just a black cavity with blood-streaked shreds of sinew and white threads hanging out.

Harry turned and left. Took out his phone as he strode down the corridor in search of fresh air.

"Yes?"

"Ståle?"

"You sound upset, Harry."

"The cop killer got Bellman."

"Got?"

"He performed an operation on him."

"What do you mean?"

"He removed one of his eyes. And left him to bleed to death. And it was the cop killer who was behind the explosion this evening, which I'm sure you heard about on the news. He tried to kill two policemen, one of whom was me. I need to know what he's thinking because I've got no bloody idea any more."

Silence. Harry waited. Heard Ståle Aune's heavy breathing. And then at last his voice again.

"I really don't know . . ."

"That's not what I want to hear, Ståle. **Pretend** you know, all right?"

"OK, OK. What I can say is that he's out of control, Harry. The emotional pressure has escalated, he's boiling over now, so he's stopped following patterns. He could do anything from now on."

"So what you're saying is you have no idea what his next move will be?"

Another silence.

"Thanks," Harry said and hung up. The phone rang at once. Bjørn.

"Yes?"

"Delta's on the way to Folkestad's address."

"Good! Tell them that he could be heading there now. And that we'll give them an hour before we sound a general alert so he doesn't get a tip-off from police radio or something. Call Katrine and tell her to come to the Boiler Room. I'm going there now."

Harry arrived at reception, saw people stare at him and recoil. A woman screamed, and someone ducked behind a counter. Harry discovered the reason in the mirror behind the counter.

Almost two metres of bomb-ravaged man with the world's ugliest automatic still in his hand.

"Sorry, folks," Harry mumbled, and left through the swing doors.

"What's going on?" Bjørn asked.

"Not much," Harry said, raising his face to the rain to cool the fire for a second. "Bjørn, I'm five minutes away from home, so I'll drive there for a shower, some bandages and some more substantial clothes first."

They rang off, and Harry saw the parking warden standing beside his car with his notepad out.

"Thinking of fining me?" Harry asked.

"You're blocking the entrance to a hospital, so you can bet your life I am," said the warden without looking up.

"Perhaps better if you move and then we can get the car out of the way," Harry said.

"I don't think you should talk to me like—" the warden started, looked up and froze when he saw Harry and the Odessa. And was still frozen to the spot when Harry got into his car, stuffed the gun back in the belt, twisted the key, let go of the clutch and shot off down the road.

Harry turned into Slemdalsveien, accelerated and passed an oncoming tram. Said a silent prayer that Arnold Folkestad would be on his way home just like him.

He swung into Holmenkollveien. Hoping Rakel wouldn't freak out when she saw him. Hoping Oleg . . .

God, how he was looking forward to seeing them. Even now, in the state he was in. Especially now.

He slowed before turning into the drive up to the house.

Then he jammed on the brakes.

Put the car into reverse.

Backed up slowly.

He looked at the parked cars he had just passed, lining the pavement. Stopped. Breathed through his nostrils.

Arnold Folkestad had been on his way home, true enough. Just like him.

For parked between two cars which were more typical of Holmenkollen—an Audi and a Mercedes—was a Fiat of indeterminate vintage.

50

Harry stood under the spruce trees for a few seconds studying the house.

From there he couldn't see any signs of a break-in, neither through the door with the three locks nor through the bars on the windows.

Of course it was by no means certain that it was Folkestad's Fiat on the road. Lots of people had a Fiat. Harry had placed his hand on the hood. It was still warm. He had left his own car in the middle of the road.

Harry ran through the trees until he was at the back of the house.

Waited, listened. Nothing.

He crept over to the wall. Stretched, peered in through the windows, but saw nothing, only darkened rooms.

He continued round the house until he came to the illuminated windows of the kitchen and the living room.

Stood up on his tiptoes and looked in. Ducked down again. Leaned back against the rough timber and concentrated on breathing. Because he had to breathe now. Had to ensure his brain had enough oxygen to think at speed.

A fortress. And what bloody good had that been?
He had them.

They were there.

Arnold Folkestad. Rakel. And Oleg.

Harry concentrated on memorising what he had seen.

They were sitting in the entrance hall by the front door.

Oleg on a spindle-back chair placed in the middle of the room, with Rakel right behind him. Oleg had a white gag in his mouth, and Rakel was tying him to the chair.

And a few metres behind them, ensconced in an armchair, was Arnold Folkestad with a gun in his hand, evidently giving Rakel orders.

The details. Folkestad's gun was a Heckler & Koch, standard police issue. Reliable, wouldn't jam. Rakel's mobile phone was on the living-room table. Neither of them looked hurt for the moment. For the moment.

Why . . . ?

Harry stopped thinking. There wasn't room, there wasn't time for any whys, just how he could stop Folkestad.

Harry had already seen that it was an impossible shot. He wouldn't be able to hit Arnold Folkestad without endangering Oleg and Rakel.

Harry raised his head above the windowsill and ducked down again.

Rakel would soon have finished her job.

Folkestad would soon start his.

He had seen the baton. It was leaning against the

bookcase beside the armchair. Soon Folkestad would smash Oleg's face the way he had with the others. A young boy who wasn't even a policeman. And Folkestad had to be under the illusion that Harry was already dead, so the revenge was pointless. Why . . . ? Stop. No whys.

He had to ring Bjørn. Get Delta sent here. They were in the forest on the wrong side of town. It could easily take forty-five minutes. Fuck! He would have to do this on his own!

Harry told himself he had time.

He had several seconds, maybe a minute.

But he couldn't hope for the element of surprise if he tried to burst in, not with three locks to open. Folkestad would hear him long before he was inside. Holding a gun to either Rakel's or Oleg's head.

Quickly, quickly! Something, anything, Harry.

He took out his mobile phone. Wanting to text Bjørn. But his fingers wouldn't obey, they had frozen, they were numb, as though the blood supply had been cut off.

Not now, Harry, don't freeze. This is a standard number. It's not them, they are . . . victims. Faceless victims. They are . . . the woman you were going to marry, and the boy who called you Dad when he was small and was so tired he forgot himself. The boy you never wanted to disappoint, but whose birthday you still forgot and that—that on its own—could make you cry and you became so desperate you had to trick him. You always had to trick him.

Harry blinked into the darkness.

You old trickster.

The mobile phone on the table. Should he ring Rakel's phone, see if it would make Folkestad stand up and move away from Rakel and Oleg? Shoot him as he picked it up?

And what if he didn't? If he stayed where he was?

Harry took another peek. Ducked down, hoping Folkestad hadn't seen the movement. Folkestad had got up with the baton in his hand and pushed Rakel to one side. And even if he got a clear shot in there was very little chance that at a distance of almost ten metres he would be lucky enough to stop Folkestad in his tracks. A better precision weapon was required than a Russian Odessa and a more suitable calibre than a Makarov 9x18mm. He had to get closer, preferably within two metres.

He heard Rakel's voice through the window.

"Take me! Please."

Harry pressed his head against the wall, squeezing his eyes shut. Act, act. But how? Most merciful God, how? Give a terrible sinner of a trickster a hint and he'll pay you back with . . . whatever you want. Harry inhaled, whispering a promise.

Rakel stared at the man with the red beard. He was standing directly behind Oleg's chair with the end of the baton resting on his shoulder. In the other hand he was holding a gun pointed at her.

"I'm really sorry, Rakel, but I can't spare the boy. He's the real target, you see."

"But why?" Rakel wasn't aware of the crying, only the hot tears running down her cheeks, like a physical reaction disengaged from what she felt. Or didn't feel. The numbness. "Why are you doing this, Arnold? It's just . . . it's just . . ."

"Sick?" Arnold Folkestad smiled, apologetically—or so it seemed. "That's probably what all of you'd like to believe. That we can all enjoy our grandiose revenge fantasies, but none of us is willing, or even capable, of carrying them out."

"But why?"

"Because I can love, I can hate. Well, now I can't love any more. So I've replaced it with . . ." He raised the baton aloft. ". . . this. I'm honouring my beloved. René, you see, wasn't just any lover. He was . . ." He put the baton down on the floor, rested it against the back of the chair and groped in his pocket, but without lowering the gun by so much as a millimetre. ". . . the apple of my eye. Who was taken from me. And nothing was done about it."

Rakel stared at what he was holding. Knowing she should be shocked, unnerved, frightened. But she felt nothing; her heart was already frozen.

"He had such nice eyes, Mikael Bellman did. So I took from him what he took from me. The best he had."

"An eye. But why Oleg?"

"Do you really not understand, Rakel? He's a seed. Harry told me he was going to be a policeman. And he's already failed in his duty, and that makes him one of them."

"Duty? What sort of duty?"

"The duty to catch murderers and pass judgement on them. He knows who killed Gusto Hanssen. You look surprised. I've had a look at the case. And it's obvious that if Oleg didn't kill him himself, he knows who the guilty party is. Anything else is a logical impossibility. Hasn't Harry told you? Oleg was there, present, when Gusto was killed, Rakel. And do you know what I thought when I saw Gusto in the crime-scene photos? How beautiful he was. He and René were beautiful young men with their whole lives before them."

"My boy has his whole life too! Please, Arnold, you don't need to do this."

As she took a step towards him he raised the gun. Pointing it, not at her but at Oleg.

"Don't worry, Rakel. You'll have to die as well. You're not a target as such, but you're a witness, and I'll have to dispose of you."

"Harry will find you. And he'll kill you."

"I'm sorry to have to bring you so much pain, Rakel. I really do like you. But I think it's only right that you should know. You see, Harry won't find anything. He's already dead, I'm afraid."

Rakel stared at him in disbelief. He **was** really sorry. Suddenly the phone on the table lit up and emitted a simple whistling tone. She glanced at it.

"Looks like you're wrong," she said.

Arnold Folkestad frowned. "Give me the phone."

Rakel picked it up and passed it to him. He

pressed the gun against Oleg's neck while grabbing the phone. Read the message quickly. Sent Rakel a sharp glare.

" 'Don't let Oleg see the present.' What's that supposed to mean?"

Rakel shrugged. "It means he's alive anyway."

"Impossible. They said on the radio my bomb had gone off."

"Can't you just get out right now, Arnold? Before it's too late."

Folkestad blinked pensively while staring at her. Or through her.

"I see. Someone beat Harry to it. Went into the flat. Ka-boom. Of course." He chuckled. "Harry's on his way here now, isn't he? He doesn't suspect a thing. I can shoot you first and then wait for him to come through that door."

He seemed to run through his reasoning one more time and nodded as if he had come to the same conclusion. And pointed the gun at Rakel.

Oleg began to wriggle on the chair, tried to jump, and groaned desperately through the gag. Rakel stared into the muzzle of the gun. Felt her heart stop beating. As though her brain had accepted the inevitable and was starting to close down. She was no longer afraid. She wanted to die. To die for Oleg. Perhaps Harry would get here before . . . perhaps he would save Oleg. For she knew something now. She closed her eyes. Waited for something she didn't know. A blow, a stab, pain. Darkness. She had no gods she wanted to pray to.

A lock on the front door rattled.

She opened her eyes.

Arnold had lowered his gun and was staring at the door.

A small pause. Then it began to rattle again.

Arnold stepped back, seized the blanket from the armchair and slung it over Oleg so that it covered both him and the chair.

"Act as if nothing's happened," he whispered. "If you say one word I'll put a bullet through the back of your son's head."

There was a third rattle. Rakel saw Arnold position himself behind Oleg and the chair so that the gun couldn't be seen from the front door.

Then the door opened.

And there he was. A towering figure, beaming smile, open jacket and ravaged face.

"Arnold!" he exclaimed with delight. "What a pleasure!"

Arnold laughed back. "You're quite a sight, Harry! What happened?"

"Cop killer. A bomb."

"Really?"

"Nothing of any consequence. What brings you here?"

"I was passing. And remembered I had to discuss a couple of things about the timetable. Would you mind coming over here for a second?"

"Not until I've given her a good hug," he said and opened his arms to Rakel, who flew into his embrace. "How was the trip, darling?"

Arnold cleared his throat. "You can let him go now, Rakel. I've got a few things to do tonight."

"Now you're being a bit stern, Arnold," Harry laughed and let go of Rakel, pushing her away and taking off his coat.

"Come over here then," Arnold said.

"There's better light here, Arnold."

"My knee hurts. Come over here."

Harry bent down and pulled at his shoelaces. "I've been in one helluva an explosion today, so you'll have to excuse me if I remove my shoes first. You'll have to use your knee on the way out anyway, so bring the timetable over here if you're in such a hurry."

Harry stared down at his shoes. The distance from Arnold and the chair covered with the blanket was six or seven metres. Too far for someone who had admitted that his vision and the shakes meant he couldn't hit a target more than half a metre away. And now, the target had suddenly crouched down and made itself much smaller by lowering its head and leaning forward so that it was protected by its shoulders.

He pulled at the laces, pretending they were knotted.

Tempting Arnold. He had to tempt him over.

For there was only one way. And perhaps that was what had made him so calm and relaxed. All or nothing. The bet was already made. The rest was in the lap of the gods.

And perhaps it was this calmness that Arnold sensed.

"As you wish, Harry."

Harry heard Arnold walking across the floor. Still

concentrating on his laces. Knew Arnold had passed Oleg on the chair, Oleg who was perfectly still, as though he knew what was going on.

Then Arnold passed Rakel.

The moment had arrived.

Harry looked up. Stared into the gun muzzle, the black eye staring at him from twenty, thirty centimetres.

He had known from the moment he entered the house that the slightest sudden move would set Arnold off. Shooting the closest person first. Oleg. Had Arnold known that Harry was armed? Had he known that he would take a gun with him to the meeting with Truls Berntsen?

Maybe. Maybe not.

It didn't make any difference. Harry would never have time to draw a weapon now, however accessible it was.

"Arnold, why—?"

"Farewell, my friend."

Harry watched Arnold Folkestad's finger tighten around the trigger.

And he knew it wouldn't be coming, the clarification, the one we think we will glimpse at our journey's end. Neither the big revelation, why we are born and die, and what the point is of both, plus the bit in between. Nor the small one, what makes a person like Folkestad willing to sacrifice his life to destroy the lives of others. Instead, there would be this syncope, this swift cessation of life, this trivial but logically placed pause in the middle of a word. The where for.

The powder burned with—literally—explosive speed, and the pressure created dispatched the bullet from the brass cartridge at a speed of approximately three hundred and sixty metres per second. The soft lead was shaped by the grooves in the barrel, making the bullet rotate so that it would be more stable through the air. But in this case that wasn't necessary. Because after only a few centimetres of air the chunk of lead penetrated the skin and was slowed in its encounter with the skull. And when the bullet reached the brain its speed was down to three hundred kilometres an hour. The projectile passed through and destroyed first the motor cortex, paralysing all movement, then it pierced the parietal lobe, smashed the functions in the right and front lobes, sliced the optical nerve and hit the inside of the cranium on the opposite side. The angle and reduced speed meant that the bullet, instead of continuing and exiting, ricocheted, hit other parts of the skull at slower and slower rates and finally came to a halt. By then it had already done so much damage the heart had stopped beating.

51

Katrine shivered and snuggled up under Bjørn's arm. It was cold in the large church. Cold inside, cold outside, and she should have put on more clothes.

They were waiting. Everyone in Oppsal Church was waiting. Coughing. Why was it that people started coughing as soon as they entered a church? Was it the room itself that provoked tight throats and pharynxes? Even in a modern church made of glass and concrete like this? Was it their anxiety not to make a sound which they knew would be amplified by the acoustics that created this compulsive action? Or was it just a human way of releasing pent-up emotion, coughing it out instead of bursting into tears or laughter?

Katrine craned her head. There was a small turnout, only those closest. Few enough people to have only an initial in Harry's contacts list. She saw Ståle Aune. Wearing a tie for once. His wife. Gunnar Hagen, also with wife.

She sighed. She should have worn more. Even if Bjørn didn't seem to be cold. Dark suit. She hadn't known he would look so good in a dark suit. She brushed his lapel. Not that there was anything on it, it was just what you did. An intimate act of love. Monkeys picking lice from the coat of another monkey.

The case was solved.

For a while they had been afraid they'd lost him, that Arnold Folkestad—now also known as the Cop Killer—had managed to escape abroad or find a hidey-hole in Norway. It would have had to be a deep, dark hole, for during the twenty-four hours after the initial alert, his description and personal information had been broadcast on every media outlet in such detail that every person of sound mind in the country had grasped who Arnold Folkestad was and what he looked like. And Katrine had at that point come to her own conclusions about how close they had been earlier in the case when Harry had asked her to check the connections between René Kalsnes and other police officers. If she had only widened her search to include **former** officers they would have found Arnold Folkestad's ties to the young man.

She stopped brushing Bjørn's lapel and he flashed her a smile of gratitude. A quick, forced smile. A little tremble around the chin. He was going to cry. She saw it now, for the first time she was going to see Bjørn Holm cry today. She coughed.

Mikael Bellman slipped into the end of the row. Glanced at his watch.

He had another interview in three-quarters of an hour. **Stern.** A million readers. Another foreign journalist wanting the story of how the young Chief of

Police had worked indefatigably week after week, month after month, to catch this murderer, and how in the end he had himself almost become the Cop Killer's victim. And Mikael would once again pause briefly before saying that the eye he had sacrificed was a cheap price for what he had achieved: preventing an insane murderer from taking even more of his officers' lives.

Mikael Bellman pulled the sleeve over his watch. They should have started by now. What were they waiting for? He had given some thought to his choice of dress today. Black, to match the moment and the eyepatch? The patch was a real hit; it told his story in such a dramatic and effective way that according to **Aftenposten** he was the most photographed Norwegian in the international press this year. Or should he choose something dark but more neutral, which would be acceptable and not so conspicuous for the interview afterwards? He would have to go straight from the interview to a meeting with the City Council chairman, so Ulla had opted for dark, neutral colours.

If they didn't start soon he would be late.

He mused. Did he feel anything? No. What should he feel? After all, it was only Harry Hole, not exactly a close friend, nor one of his officers in Oslo Police District. But there was a certain possibility that the press were waiting outside, and of course it was good PR to show your face in church. It was indeed impossible to get around the fact that Harry Hole had been the first to point the finger of guilt at Arnold Folkestad, and with the dimensions this case had taken on that linked Mikael and Harry. And PR was going to be even more important than ever. He already knew what the meeting with the City Council chairman was going to be about. The party had lost a strong personality with Isabelle Skøyen and was on the lookout for someone new. A popular, respected person they would like to have on the team, to lead Oslo forward. When the chairman had rung he had opened by singing the praises of the warm, contemplative impression Bellman had made in the **Magasinet** interview. And then wondered if their party political programme chimed with Mikael Bellman's own political standpoints.

Chimed.

Lead Oslo forward.

Mikael Bellman's town.

So get that organ cranked up!

Bjørn Holm could feel Katrine trembling under his arm, felt the cold sweat under his suit trousers and reflected that it was going to be a long day. A long day before he and Katrine could take off their clothes and crawl into bed. Together. Let life carry on. The way life carried on for those of them who were left, whether they wanted it to or not. And as his gaze swept across the rows of pews he thought of all those who were **not** here. Of Beate Lønn. Of Erlend Vennesla. Anton Mittet. Roar Midtstuen's daughter, Fia. And of Rakel Fauke and Oleg Fauke, who weren't here either. Who had paid the price for attaching themselves to the man who was being positioned in front of them by the altar. Harry Hole.

And in a strange way it was as though the man at the front was continuing to be what he had always been: a black pit sucking in everything that was good around him, consuming all the love he was offered and also the love he wasn't.

Katrine had said yesterday after they had gone to bed that she had also been in love with Harry Hole. Not because he deserved it, but because he had been impossible not to love. As impossible as he was to catch, keep or live with. Yes, of course she had loved him. But it had passed, the desire had cooled, or at least she had tried to cool it. But the delicate little scar after the short heartbreak she shared with several women would always be there. He had been someone they'd had on loan for a while. And now it was over. Bjørn had asked her to drop the subject there.

The organ piped up. Bjørn had always had a weakness for organs. His mother's organ in the sitting room in Skreia, Gregg Allman's B3 organ, creaking pump organs squeezing out an old hymn, to Bjørn it was all the same, like sitting in a bathtub of warm notes and hoping the tears didn't get you.

They had never caught Arnold Folkestad; he had caught himself.

Folkestad had probably come to the conclusion that his mission had ended. And with it, his life. So he had done the only logical thing. It took them three days to find him. Three days of desperate searching.

Bjørn had had the feeling the whole country had been on the march. And perhaps that was why it felt like a bit of an anticlimax when the news came that he'd been found in the forest in Maridalen, only a few hundred metres from where Erlend Vennesla had been spotted. With a small, almost discreet, hole in his head and a gun in his hand. It was his car that had put them on the track; it had been seen in a car park close to where the trail paths started: an old Fiat that had also featured in the nationwide alert.

Bjørn himself had led the forensics team. Arnold Folkestad had looked so innocent lying on his back in the heath, like a leprechaun with his red beard. He lay beneath a patch of open sky unprotected by the trees clumped together around him. In his pockets they had found the keys for the Fiat and the door that was blown up in Hausmanns gate 92, a standard Heckler & Koch gun as well as the one he held in his hand, together with a wallet containing a dog-eared photo of a man Bjørn immediately recognised as René Kalsnes.

As it had rained non-stop for at least twenty-four hours and the body had been out in the open for three days there hadn't been much evidence to examine. But it didn't matter; they had what they needed. The skin around the entry wound in his right temple had scorch marks from the flame discharge of the weapon and the residue of burnt powder, and the ballistic results showed the bullet in his head came from the gun in his hand.

For that reason it was not there they concentrated

their efforts. The investigation began when they broke into his house, where they found most of what they needed to clear up all the police murders. Batons covered with blood and hair from the victims, a bayonet saw with Beate Lønn's DNA on it, a spade smeared with soil and clay that matched the ground in Vestre Cemetery, plastic ties, police cordon tape of the same kind that had been found outside Drammen, boots that tallied with the footprint at Tryvann. They had everything. And afterwards, as Harry had so often said, but which only Bjørn Holm had experienced, the void.

Because there was suddenly nothing else.

It wasn't like crossing a finish line, drifting into a harbour or pulling into a station.

It was more like the tarmac, the bridge, the rails had disappeared. It was the end of the road, and that was where the dive into nothingness began.

Finished. He hated the word.

So, almost in desperation, he had delved even deeper into the investigation of the original murders. And had found what he had been searching for, a link between the murder of the girl at Tryvann, Judas Johansen and Valentin Gjertsen. A quarter of a fingerprint didn't give a match, but thirty per cent probability wasn't to be sneered at. No, it wasn't finished. It was never finished.

"They're starting now."

It was Katrine. Her lips were almost touching his ear. The organ notes soared, grew into music, music he knew. Bjørn swallowed hard.

• • •

Gunnar Hagen closed his eyes for a second and listened only to the music, not wanting to think. But thoughts came. The case was over. Everything was over. They had buried what had to be buried now. Yet there was this one matter, one he could not bury, never managed to get underground. And which he still hadn't mentioned to anyone. He hadn't mentioned it because it could no longer be of any use. The Swedish words Asayev had whispered in his hoarse voice the seconds he had spent with him that day at the hospital. "What can you offer me if I agree to testify against Isabelle Skøyen?" and "I don't know who, but I know she worked with someone high up in the police force."

The words were dead echoes of a dead man. Unprovable claims that would be damaging rather than beneficial now that Skøyen was off the scene.

So he had kept this to himself.

Like Anton Mittet with the bloody baton.

The decision had been taken, but it still kept him awake at night.

"I know she worked with someone high up in the police force."

Gunnar Hagen opened his eyes again.

Slowly, he ran his eyes across the assembled congregation.

• • •

Truls Berntsen sat with the window of the Suzuki Vitara rolled down so that he could hear the organ music from the small church. The sun shone from a cloudless sky. Warm and awful. He had never liked Oppsal. Just hooligans. He had given a lot of beatings. Taken a lot of beatings. Not as bad as in Hausmanns gate of course. Luckily it had looked worse than it was. And in hospital Mikael had said it didn't matter with people as ugly as he was and how serious could concussion be for someone who didn't have a brain?

It was meant to be a joke, and Truls had tried with his grunted laughter to show he appreciated it, but the broken jawbone and the smashed nose had hurt too much.

He was still taking strong painkillers, he still wore big bandages around his head, and of course he was not allowed to drive, but what could he do? He couldn't sit at home waiting for the dizziness to go and the wounds to heal. Even Megan Fox had begun to bore him and he didn't actually have the doctor's permission to watch TV either. So he might just as well sit here. In a car outside a church to . . . well, to do what? To show his respect for a man he had never had any respect for? An empty gesture for a sodding idiot who didn't know what was good for him, who saved the life of the one man whose death he had everything to gain by? Truls Berntsen couldn't bloody fathom it. He only knew he wanted to be back working as soon as he was well enough. And the town to be his again.

• • •

Rakel breathed in and out. Her fingers round the bouquet felt clammy. Stared at the door. Thought about the people sitting inside. Friends, family, acquaintances. The priest. Not that there were so many, but they were waiting. Couldn't start without her.

"You promise you won't cry?" Oleg said.

"No," she said, smiled fleetingly and stroked his cheek. He had grown so tall. He was so good-looking. Towered above her. She'd had to buy a dark suit for him, and it was only when they were standing in the shop and measuring up that she realised her son was close to Harry's one metre ninety-two. She sighed.

"We'd better go in," she said, threading her arm through his.

Oleg opened the door, was given a nod by the verger inside and they began to walk up the aisle. And when Rakel saw all the faces turned to her, she felt her nervousness vanish. This had not been her idea, she had been against it, but in the end Oleg had persuaded her. He thought it was only right that it should all finish like this. That was precisely the word he had used: finish. But wasn't it above all else a beginning? The start of a new chapter in their lives? At least that was how it felt. And suddenly this did feel right. Being here, now.

And a smile spread across her face. She smiled at all the other smiling faces. For a moment she thought that if their smiles or her own got any broader there could be a serious accident. And the notion of this, the sound of tearing faces, which ought to have made her shudder, caused bubbles of laughter in her stomach. Don't laugh, she told herself. Not now. She noticed that Oleg, who so far had been concentrating on walking in time with the organ, sensed her mood, and she glanced at him. Met his surprised, admonitory expression. But then he had to look away; he had seen. That his mother was having a fit of the giggles. Here, now. And he found that so inappropriate that he started laughing as well.

To focus her mind on something else, on what was about to happen, on the solemnity, she fixed her gaze on the man who was waiting by the altar. Harry. In black.

He stood facing them with an idiotic grin plastered across his handsome, pug-ugly face. As tall and proud as a peacock. When he and Oleg had stood back-to-back at Gunnar Øye's, the outfitter's, the assistant with the tape measure had announced that only three centimetres separated them, in Harry's favour. And the two overgrown schoolboys had high-fived as though both were satisfied with the outcome of some competition.

But now, at this moment, Harry looked very adult. The rays from the June sun falling through the stained-glass windows enveloped him in a kind of celestial light and he seemed taller than ever. And as relaxed as he had been throughout. At first she didn't understand how he could be so relaxed after all that had happened. But gradually it had rubbed off, this calm, this unshakeable belief that everything had sorted itself out. She hadn't been able to sleep for the first few weeks after Arnold Folkestad had come to their home, even though Harry had snuggled up close and whispered in her ear that it was over. That it had gone well. That they were out of danger. He had repeated the same words night after night like a soporific mantra, which still hadn't been enough. But then, gradually, she had begun to believe it. And after a few more weeks to know it. Everything **had** sorted itself out. And she had begun to sleep. Deep sleep without any dreams she could remember, until she was woken by him slipping out of bed in the morning light, thinking as usual she didn't notice, and as usual she pretended she didn't notice because she knew how proud and happy he would be if he thought she had only woken up when he coughed and stood there with a breakfast tray in his hands.

Oleg had given up trying to keep in rhythm with Mendelssohn and the organist now, and it made no difference to Rakel, she had to take two steps for his one anyway. They had decided that Oleg would perform a double function. It had felt completely natural as soon as she'd thought about it. Oleg should accompany her to the altar, give her away to Harry and also be best man.

Harry didn't have a best man. He had the witness he had first chosen, though. The chair on his side by the altar was empty, but a photo of Beate Lønn had been placed on the seat.

They were there now. Harry hadn't let her out of his sight for an instant.

She had never understood how a man with such a low resting pulse, who could go for days in his own world, almost without speaking and without any need for outside stimulation, could press a switch and was suddenly conscious of everything, every ticking second, every quivering tenth and hundredth of a second. With a calm, husky voice that in very few words could express more emotions, information, astonishment, foolishness and wisdom than all the windbags she had ever met could manage over a seven-course meal.

And then there were the eyes. Which in their own good-natured, almost bashful, way had this ability to hold your attention, to force you to **be** there.

Rakel Fauke was going to marry the man she loved.

Harry looked at her as she stood there. She was so beautiful he had tears in his eyes. He simply hadn't expected this. Not that she wouldn't be beautiful. It was obvious that Rakel Fauke would look amazing in a white bridal gown. He hadn't expected that he would react in this way. His uppermost thoughts had been that he hoped it wouldn't take too long and the priest wouldn't get too spiritual or inspired. And he had imagined that as usual on occasions which called for great emotions, he would become immune, numb, a cold and slightly disappointed observer of other people's floods of feelings and his own drought. But he had determined that at any rate he would play the role as best he could. After all, he was the one who had insisted on a church wedding. And now here he was, with tears, genuine, big, fat, salty drops, in the corners of his eyes. Harry blinked, and Rakel watched him. Met his gaze. Not with that now-I'm-looking-at-you-and-all-the-guests-can-see-I'm-looking-at-you-and-I'm-trying-to-look-as-happy-as-I-can look.

It was the look of a teammate.

Of someone saying we can nail this, you and I. Let's do it.

Then she smiled. And Harry discovered that he was smiling too, without knowing which of them had started it. She had started shaking. She was laughing inside and filling up so fast it was only a question of time before the laughter exploded out of her. Solemnity generally had that effect on her. And on him. So, in order not to laugh, she looked over at Oleg. But she got no help there, for the boy looked as if he was going to burst into laughter as well. He just managed to restrain himself by lowering his head and firmly shutting his eyes.

What a team, Harry thought proudly and focused on the priest.

The team that had caught the Cop Killer.

Rakel had understood the text message. **Don't let Oleg see the present.** Reasonable enough for Arnold Folkestad not to become suspicious. Clear enough for Rakel to understand what he wanted. The old birthday trick.

So, when he entered the house she had embraced him, grabbed what he had stuffed down his belt at the back and then backed away with her hands in front of her so that Arnold couldn't see that she was holding something. She was holding a loaded Odessa with the safety catch off.

What was more worrying was that even Oleg had understood. He had stayed quiet, knowing he mustn't ruin what was looming. Which could only mean that he had never fallen for the birthday trick, and he had never let on. What a team.

What a team, coaxing Arnold Folkestad into moving towards Harry and leaving Rakel behind him, so that she could step forward and, at close quarters, fire a shot through Folkestad's temple as he was about to dispatch Harry.

An unbeatable team of champions, that's what it was.

Harry sniffed quickly and wondered if the damned mega-tears would have the sense to stay where they were or if he would simply have to wipe them away before they slid down his cheeks.

He took a risk with the latter.

She had asked him why he'd insisted that they get married in a church. To the best of her knowledge he was about as Christian as a chemical formula. And she was the same, despite her Catholic upbringing. But Harry answered that, outside their house, he had made a promise to a fictional God that if this went well, in recompense he would succumb to this one stupid ritual act: getting married in the sight of this alleged God. And then Rakel had burst out laughing, said that this didn't show much faith in God, it was an advanced version of bloody knuckles, boys' stuff, that she loved him and of course they would get married in a church.

After they had freed Oleg, they had embraced one another in a kind of group hug. For one long, silent minute they had just stood there, hugging one another, stroking one another, to make sure they really were unhurt. It was as if the sound and the smell of the shot still hung in the walls, and they had to wait until it was gone before they could do anything. Afterwards Harry had told them to sit round the kitchen table, and he'd poured them a cup of coffee from the machine that was still on. And involuntarily he'd wondered: if Arnold Folkestad had succeeded in killing them all, would he have switched off the machine before he left the house?

He had sat down, taken a swig from his cup, cast a glance at the body lying on the floor in the room a few metres from them, and when he had turned back he had met the questioning look in Rakel's eyes: why hadn't he already rung the police?

Harry had taken another swig from his cup, nodded at the Odessa lying on the table and looked at her. She was an intelligent woman. So it was just a question of giving her a bit of time. She would reason her way through to the same conclusion. That if he picked up the phone he would be sending Oleg to prison.

And then Rakel had nodded slowly. She had understood. When the forensics people examined the gun to check if it matched the bullet that the pathologists would extract from Folkestad's head, they would immediately link it to the murder of Gusto Hanssen, where the murder weapon was never found. After all, it wasn't every day—or every year—that someone was killed with a 9x18mm Makarov bullet. And if they discovered it matched a weapon they could link to Oleg, he would be rearrested. And this time charged and sentenced on the basis of what to everyone in court would seem like irrefutable, damning evidence.

"You two will have to do what you have to do," Oleg had said. He had long grasped the gravity of the situation.

Harry had nodded, but hadn't taken his eyes off Rakel. There had to be total unanimity. It had to be their joint decision. As now.

The priest finished reading from the Bible, the congregation sat down again and the priest cleared his throat. Harry had asked him to keep the sermon short. He saw the priest's lips moving, saw the composure on his face and remembered the same composure on Rakel's that night. The composure after first shutting her eyes tight and then opening them. As though wanting to make sure this was not a nightmare you could wake up from. Then she had sighed.

"What can we do?" she'd asked.

"Burn," Harry had answered.

"Burn?"

Harry had nodded. Burn. What Truls Berntsen did. The difference was that burners like Berntsen did it for money. That was all.

And so they had sprung into action.

He had done what had to be done. **They** had done

what had to be done. Oleg had driven Harry's car from the road up to the garage while Rakel packed and tied up the body in bin bags, and Harry had made a makeshift stretcher out of a tarpaulin, rope and two aluminium pipes. After putting the body in the boot Harry had gone down to the road with the keys for the Fiat, and Harry and Oleg each drove a car to Maridalen while Rakel set about cleaning up and removing all the traces.

As they had predicted, there was no one around the Grefsenkollen mountain in the rain and darkness. Nevertheless they had taken one of the narrow paths to be sure they didn't meet anyone.

The rain had made carrying the body a wearing, slippery business; on the other hand, Harry knew the rain would wash away their tracks and they hoped any telltale signs. They didn't want anything to suggest that the body had been transported there.

It had taken them more than an hour to find a suitable spot, a place where people wouldn't stumble across the body straight away, yet where their elkhounds would find the scent before too long. Long enough for the forensic evidence to have been destroyed or at least rendered hard to identify. But too short a time for society to have wasted a great deal of resources on a manhunt. Harry almost had to laugh at himself when he realised the latter was indeed a factor. In the end he was a product of his upbringing as well, a brainwashed, herd-following, bloody Social Democrat who suffered physical pain at the thought of leaving a light on all night or discarding plastic in the countryside.

The priest finished his sermon and a girl—a friend of Oleg's—sang from the gallery. Dylan's "Boots of Spanish Leather." Harry's wish, Rakel's blessing. The sermon had been more about the importance of working together in a marriage and less about being in God's sight. And Harry had thought about how they had taken the bin bags off Arnold, placed him in a position that would seem logical for a man who had chosen the forest to fire a bullet through his temple. And Harry knew he would never ask Rakel about it, about why she had held the muzzle close to Arnold Folkestad's right temple before firing instead of doing what nine out of ten people would have done, quickly shot him in the back of the head or the back.

It might of course have been because she had been scared the bullet would go through Folkestad and hit Harry.

But it could also have been because her lightning-fast, almost frighteningly practical brain had managed to think one stage further, about what would have to happen afterwards. There would have to be some camouflage to save them all. A circumlocution of the truth. A suicide. The woman at Harry's side **might** have worked out that suicide victims don't shoot themselves through the back of the head from a range of half a metre. But—given that Arnold Folkestad was right-handed—through the right temple.

What a woman. All the things he knew about her. All the things he didn't know about her. That was the question he had been obliged to ask himself even after seeing her in action. After spending months with Arnold Folkestad. And more than forty years with himself. How well **can** you know someone?

The hymn was over and the priest had started on the marriage vows—Will you love and honour her . . . ?—but he and Rakel ignored the ceremony and still faced each other, and Harry knew he would never let her go, however much he had to lie, however impossible it was to promise you would love a person until their dying day. He hoped the priest would soon shut up so that he could say the yes that was already bubbling joyfully in his chest.

Ståle Aune took the handkerchief from his breast pocket and passed it to his wife.

Harry had just said yes and the echo of his voice still hung beneath the church's vaulted roof.

"What?" Ingrid whispered.

"You're crying, love," he whispered.

"No, **you're** the one who's crying."

"Am I?"

Ståle Aune checked. He was indeed crying. Not much, but enough for him to detect wet patches on his handkerchief. He didn't cry proper tears, Aurora would say. It was just thin, invisible water that, without any kind of prior warning, could run down both sides of his nose, although no one around him had considered the situation, film or conversation especially moving. It was just a gasket that blew inside and then the water flowed. He would have liked to have Aurora along with them, but she was taking part in a two-day handball tournament at Nadderud Sports Hall, and had just texted him to say they had won the first match.

Ingrid straightened Ståle's tie and placed a hand on his shoulder. He put his on hers and knew she was thinking the same thoughts as he was, about their own wedding.

The case was over and he had written a psychological report. In it he had speculated that the weapon Arnold Folkestad had shot himself with was the same one that had been used to murder Gusto Hanssen. And that there were several similarities between Gusto Hanssen and René Kalsnes. Both were very attractive young men who had no scruples about selling sexual favours to men of all ages, and it may have been that Folkestad had a propensity to fall in love with such types. Nor was it improbable that someone with Folkestad's paranoid schizophrenic symptoms might have murdered Gusto out of jealousy or for a whole string of other reasons based on delusions as a result of a profound psychosis, though this might not necessarily have been noticeable to the outside world. Here Ståle had attached notes from the time Arnold Folkestad had worked in Kripos and come to him complaining about hearing voices. Even though psychologists had long concurred that hearing voices was not always synonymous with schizophrenia, Aune had tended to the view that in Folkestad's case it was and started preparing a diagnosis that would have finished Folkestad's career as a detective. But it had never become necessary to send the report as

Folkestad decided to resign after telling Aune about his approach towards an unnamed colleague. He had also terminated the treatment and thus disappeared off Aune's radar. However, it was clear that there had been a couple of events that might have triggered his deterioration. One was the head injuries he had received which had necessitated a longish stay in hospital. There was significant research showing that even light blows to the brain could cause behavioural changes, such as increased aggression and decreased impulse control. The blows, incidentally, bore a likeness to those he dealt to his victims. And the second event was the loss of René Kalsnes, with whom, witnesses' testimonies suggested, he had been wildly, almost manically, in love. It was no surprise that Folkestad had concluded what he obviously regarded as his mission by taking his own life. The only caveat had to be that he hadn't left anything in writing or said anything to justify what he had done. It was normal for megalomaniacs to feel a need to be remembered, understood, declared a genius, admired and to find a well-deserved place in history.

The psychological report had been well received. It was the final piece in the puzzle, Mikael Bellman had said.

But Ståle Aune had a suspicion that it was another aspect which had been of paramount importance for the police. With this diagnosis he put an end to what otherwise could have become a bitter and problematic issue: how could one of the force's own men be behind the massacre? Folkestad was only an ex-policeman, it was true, but nevertheless, what did this say about the profession and what did it say about the culture inside the police force?

Now they could shelve the debate because a psychologist had concluded that Arnold Folkestad had been insane. Insanity has no cause. Insanity just is, a kind of natural disaster that strikes out of the blue, the kind of thing that can happen. And afterwards you have to get on with your life because what else can you do?

That was how Bellman and the others reasoned.

That was not how Ståle Aune reasoned.

But it would have to rest for now. Ståle was back in his consulting room full-time, but Gunnar Hagen had said he would like to have the Boiler Room gang as a unit permanently on call, a bit like Delta. Katrine had already been offered a job as a detective in Crime Squad and had accepted it. She claimed she had several compelling reasons to move from her wonderful, beautiful Bergen to the wretched capital.

The organist started up, Ståle could hear the creak of the pedals, and then came the notes. And then the bride and groom. Now the newlyweds. They didn't need to nod left and right, there were so few people in the church you could encapsulate them all in one glance.

The party afterwards was to be at Schrøder's. Harry's watering hole was of course not quite what you associated with a wedding celebration, but according to Harry it had been Rakel's decision, not his.

The guests turned and followed Rakel and Harry,

who continued past the empty rows of pews at the back towards the door. Towards the June sun, Ståle thought. Towards the rest of the day. Towards the future. The three of them, Oleg, Rakel and Harry.

"Oh, Ståle," Ingrid said, tugging the handkerchief from his breast pocket and handing it to him.

Aurora sat on the bench and could hear from the cheering that her teammates had scored again.

It was the second match today they were on their way to winning, and she reminded herself that she had to text Dad. Actually for herself she didn't much care whether they won or lost, and Mummy definitely didn't care. But Dad always reacted as if she was the new world champion whenever she reported another victory in the girls' under-13s league.

As Emilie and Aurora had played almost all the first match, they were on the bench for most of this one. Aurora had started counting the spectators in the stands on the other side of the court, and there were only two rows left. Most of them were parents of course and players from other teams who were taking part in the tournament, but she thought she had seen a familiar face up there.

Emilie nudged her. "Aren't you following the match?"

"Yes, I am. I just . . . Can you see the man up there in the third row? He's sitting apart from the others. Have you seen him before?"

"Don't know. Too far away. Don't you wish you'd gone to the wedding?"

"No, it's grown-up stuff. I need a pee. Are you coming?"

"In the middle of the match? What if they want us to go on."

"It's Charlotte's or Katinka's turn. Come on."

Emilie looked at her. And Aurora knew what she was thinking. That Aurora didn't usually ask anyone to go with her to the toilet. Didn't usually ask for company anywhere.

Emilie hesitated. Turned back to the court. Glanced at the coach standing with his arms crossed on the sideline. Shook her head.

Aurora wondered whether she could wait until the game was over, and the others were streaming towards the changing rooms and the toilets.

"I'll be back in a mo," she whispered, getting up and jogging over to the stairs. Turned in the doorway and looked up at the stands. Searched for the face she thought she recognised, but couldn't see it. Then she ran down the stairs.

Mona Gamlem stood alone in the cemetery by Bragernes Church. She had driven from Oslo to Drammen and it had taken her some time to find the place. And she'd had to ask her way to the gravestone. The sunlight glistened on the crystals in the stone around his name. Anton Mittet. It glistened now more than when he was alive, she thought. But he had loved her. He had, of that she was sure. She popped a piece of mint chewing gum into her mouth.

Thinking about what he had said when he had driven her home after the shift at the Rikshospital and they had kissed: he liked the minty taste of her tongue. And the third time, when they were parked in front of her house and she had leaned over to him, un-buttoned his fly and—before she began—discreetly removed the gum from her mouth and stuck it under his seat. And straight afterwards she had started chewing a fresh piece of gum before they kissed again. Because she had to taste of mint; that was the taste he wanted. She missed him. Without having any right to miss him, and that made it even worse. Mona Gamlem heard footsteps crunching up the path behind her. Perhaps it was her. The other woman. Laura. Mona Gamlem started to walk ahead without turn-ing, trying to blink the tears from her eyes, trying to stay on the gravel path.

The church door opened, but Truls couldn't see any-one coming out yet.

He glanced at the magazine on the passenger seat. **Magasinet.** An interview with Mikael. The happy family man pictured with his wife and three children. The astute, humble Chief of Police who said that the Cop Killer case would not have been solved without his wife Ulla's support at home. Without all his excel-lent colleagues at Police HQ. And that the unmask-ing of Folkestad meant another case had been cleared up. The ballistics report showed that the Odessa gun

Arnold Folkestad had shot himself with was the same one that Gusto Hanssen had been killed with.

Truls had grinned at the thought. No fucking chance. Harry Hole had had a finger in the pie and had been up to his usual tricks. Truls had no idea how or why, but at any rate it meant that Oleg Fauke was off the hook and could stop looking over his shoulder. Hole would get the boy into PHS now as well, you see.

Fair enough. Truls wouldn't stand in his way. Great burner job. Respect. Anyway, he hadn't saved the magazine because of Harry, Oleg or Mikael.

It was the photo of Ulla he'd been after.

A temporary setback, that was all, he would get rid of the magazine afterwards. Get rid of her.

He thought about the woman he had met in the cafe the day before. Internet dating. Of course she couldn't hold a candle to Ulla or Megan Fox. Bit too old, arse a bit too fat and talked a bit too much. But apart from that he'd liked her. If a woman failed in the age, face and arse categories **and** was totally unable to keep her mouth shut—could she be any good at all?

He wasn't sure. He only knew that he'd liked her.

Or, to be more precise, he liked the fact that she had apparently liked **him.**

Perhaps it had been his ravaged face and she'd felt sorry for him. Or perhaps Mikael had been right: his face had been so unattractive in the first place that a slight rearrangement wouldn't make any difference.

Or in some way or other things had changed inside him. What or how he didn't know exactly, but some days he woke up and felt new. He thought in a different way. Could even talk to people around him in a new way. And it was as though they noticed. As though they treated him in a new way as well. A better way. And that had given him the courage to take another tiny step in this new direction, although he had no idea where it would lead. Not that he had found redemption or anything. The change was minimal. And on some days he didn't feel new at all.

Anyway, he thought he would ring her again.

The police radio crackled. He could hear from the voice rather than the words that it was something important, different from the boring traffic jams, basement break-ins, domestics and rabid drunks. A body.

"Does it look like murder?" the unit leader asked.

"I would imagine it is." The answer was an attempt to deliver the laconic, cool tone that especially the younger guard aspired to. Not that they didn't have their own models in the older guard. Even though Hole was no longer among them his sayings were still alive and well. "Her tongue . . . I think it's her tongue. It's been cut off and stuffed up . . ." The young officer couldn't take the heat; his voice cracked.

Truls could feel the exhilaration coming. The life-giving beats as his heart pumped a little faster.

This sounded nasty. June. She'd had lovely eyes. And he guessed pretty big tits beneath all the clothes. Yes, it was going to be a great summer.

"Got an address?"

"Alexander Kiellands plass, number 22. Shit, loads of sharks here."

"Sharks?"

"Yes, on those little surfboards. Place is full of them."

Truls put the Suzuki into gear. Straightened his sunglasses, pressed the accelerator and let go of the clutch. Some days were new. Others weren't.

The girls' toilet was at the end of the corridor. As the door closed behind Aurora it struck her at first how quiet it was. The noise of all the people upstairs was gone, and there was just her.

She quickly locked herself in one of the cubicles, pulled down her shorts, knickers and sat on the cold plastic seat.

Thought about the wedding. Actually she would have preferred to be there. She had never seen anyone get married before, not properly. She wondered if she would get married one day. Tried to imagine it, standing outside a church, laughing and ducking under the shower of confetti, a white dress, a house and a job she liked. A boy she would have children with. She tried to imagine the boy.

The door opened and someone came into the room.

Aurora was sitting on a swing in the garden with the sun straight in her eyes and couldn't see the boy. She hoped he was great. A boy who thought a bit like her. Bit like Dad, but not so scatty. No, as a matter of fact, **just** as scatty.

The footsteps were too heavy for a woman.

Aurora stretched out for some toilet paper, but held back. She had tried to take a breath, but there was nothing there. No air. She felt her throat tighten.

Too heavy to be a woman's footsteps.

They had stopped now.

She looked down. In the big gap between the door and floor she saw a shadow. And the tips of a pair of long, pointed shoes. Like cowboy boots.

Aurora didn't know if the ringing in her head was the wedding bells or the beating of her heart.

Harry came out onto the steps. Squinted into the bright June sun. Stood with his eyes closed for a moment listening to the church bells pealing out over Oppsal. Feeling that everything was right with the world, at rest, in harmony. Knowing this was how things should end, like this.

A NOTE ABOUT THE AUTHOR AND THE TRANSLATOR

Jo Nesbø is a musician, songwriter, economist and author. He has won the Glass Key Award for best Nordic crime novel. His other Harry Hole novels include **The Redbreast, Nemesis, The Devil's Star, The Snowman, The Leopard** and **Phantom.** He lives in Oslo.

Don Bartlett lives in Norfolk, England, and works as a freelance translator of Scandinavian literature. He has translated, or cotranslated, Norwegian novels by Lars Saabye Christensen, Roy Jacobsen, Ingvar Ambjørnsen, Kjell Ola Dahl, Gunnar Staalesen and Pernille Rygg.

If you enjoyed this large print edition of
POLICE,
here are a few of Jo Nesbo's latest
bestsellers also available in large print.

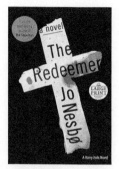

The Redeemer
(paperback)
978-0-8041-2108-8
($26.00)

Phantom
(paperback)
978-0-307-99081-5
($26.00)

The Leopard
(paperback)
978-0-307-99066-2
($27.00)

The Snowman
(paperback)
978-0-7393-7819-9
($26.00)

Large print books are available wherever books
are sold and at many local libraries.

All prices are subject to change. Check with your
local retailer for current pricing and availability.
For more information on these and other large print titles,
visit www.randomhouse.com/largeprint.